Messin Man

Charles V. Kirk

Pentland Press, Inc.
ENGLAND·USA·SCOTLAND

PUBLISHED BY PENTLAND PRESS, INC.
5122 Bur Oak Circle, Raleigh, North Carolina 27612
United States of America
(919) 782-0281

ISBN:1-57197-098-3
Library of Congress Catalog Card Number 97-075790
Copyright 1997 Charles V. Kirk

This is a work of fiction. Names, places, incidents, and characters either are used fictitiously or are products of the author's imagination. Any resemblance to actual events or places or persons, living or dead, is entirely coincidental.

All rights reserved, which includes the right to reproduce this book or portions thereof in any form whatsoever except as provided by the U.S. Copyright Law.
         Printed in the United States of America

Tribal Library
Saginaw Chippewa Indian Tribe
7070 E. Broadway
Mt. Pleasant MI 48858

WITHDRAWN

Messin Man

Dedication

To my beloved wife, Eleanor, whose love, devotion, patience, understanding, and strength was truly the wind beneath my wings.

To Mel Brooks, my idol of spoof.

Table of Contents

Introduction ix

Chapter One 1

Chapter Two 13

Chapter Three 29

Chapter Four 49

Chapter Five 71

Chapter Six 91

Chapter Seven 107

Chapter Eight 129

Chapter Nine 147

Chapter Ten 165

Chapter Eleven 185

Chapter Twelve 203

Chapter Thirteen 219

Chapter Fourteen 237

Epilogue 251

Introduction

Those with tongue-in-cheek seldom bite off more than they can chew.

The red man and the white man shared belief in a Supreme Being. Whether known to them as the Great Spirit, the Everywhere Spirit, Wakan-Manitou, or God, each believed that any challenge to His authority could have dire consequences— and they were so right! The senseless destruction of a pristine territory and its inhabitants in His name by the newly arrived white man offended God. His method of correction highlighted three heretofore unknown facts about God: He has a great sense of humor, He loves to play a board game called Destiny, and He has a pet, a bull named Dilemma.

Proof of His humor was demonstrated by His choice of players on His game board of Destiny: a small band of Indians whose sole attribute of renown was passing wind, a Medicine Man prone to dilemma, and, as a final touch, a horny Scotsman.

Their objective in the game: to prevent the white man from entering the Indian lands west of the Mississippi River to continue the white man's destructive ways. It has been said that God moves in strange ways; the following pages bear this out.

If your reaction to the above is to scoff, be forewarned; even God's sense of humor has its limit. Then He tends to become a bit testy—as the aforementioned group discovered.

Vision is like a teacher. The latitude of each is determined by pupils.

Three Hands, as visualized by:

Bea Ware A bull in heat, snorting and pawing the ground, wild eyes searching for a lascivious heifer.

Fireanda Brimstone A knight astride a war horse with lance fully extended and eager to impale his opponent in combat.

Lynn Gweeney An emotion-rousing parade, led by a flag bearer. The only part of the scene in focus is the two hands and the flagpole.

Lotta Lasagna A summer sausage–a delicious treat to be consumed slowly, but completely.

Different visions, but each would agree that he was one super messin man!

Chapter One

A trail has no beginning until one takes the first step.

To a casual observer standing at a high-up pass through the Kie Ro Practic Mountain Range in the summer of 1830, the panoramic view presented an image of perfect beauty. The towering Ucumfastus trees covering the plateau, the roaring waterfall cascading four hundred feet down the rock face to the right, the steep path to the left descending to the prairie below, and the sea of waving buffalo grass stretching to the western horizon formed an eye-pleasing picture. A word of caution: this was the land of the Hiup and illusion was commonplace.

At this very moment, unseen, and moving with a singleness of purpose at a speed surpassing that of a Chinook wind, Fate was heading straight for these lands of the Hiup. It had chosen Three Hands, messin man of the Hiup, as its priority for this day, and the impact of its mission would spell disaster for every Indian tribe of North America!

The subject of Fate's mission, now in his sixty-fourth summer and already a legend among his peers, was totally unaware of Fate's intent. He was seated on his favorite perch, a small ledge jutting out from the rock-face to the right of the pass. Perhaps it was a touch of irony that, after a large helping of chico bean soup, his sole priority for this day appeared to be focusing on the trail below while passing time and wind.

Messin Man

To some, the latter action would seem crass; to the Hiup, it was a way of life.

Upon reaching the crest of the pass, the inexperienced eye of a neophyte settler-to-be heading out from St. Lou E to inherit the west never would have seen Three Hands. However, a true frontiersman whose senses had been honed to survival edge, whose ears could detect the sound of a falling leaf, whose nostrils started to quiver at the faintest scent of man or beast two hundred yards upwind, whose eyes could pick out the slightest distortion of a natural setting, and whose reflexes were disciplined to react instantly and without question, may have seen him. Even if the eyes had failed to detect Three Hands' presence, the traveler's nostrils certainly would have ignited a reaction of alarm by their desperate effort to close. Chico bean exhaust had the same effect as a whiff of chlorine gas!

In any event, neither neophyte settler nor true frontiersman would have failed to see the two structures at either side of the trail. One was a series of connected sheds, each with a door and a half-moon opening above it. The other was a large sign emblazoned, "PAY UP PASS." Carved into it were the charges for travel in the lands of the Hiup:

Party of 1-3	5 cents each
Party of 4-6	20 cents
Over 6	25 cents
Horse or ox	10 cents
Wagon	10 cents

EXACT CHANGE ONLY

The charge for litter left on the trail will vary

This pass was located about ten days travel by wagon directly west of St. Lou E, a large settlement on the eastern bank of the Mississippi River. It was the central of only three passes through the Kie Ro Practic mountain range. One pass was located five hundred miles to the south and the other two hundred miles to the north.

The terrain rose gradually from the Mississippi River to the base of the Kie Ro Practics, whose near-vertical rock face rose majestically to separate the woodlands of the east from the plains of the west. Only a slender thread of the gradual incline continued on through each pass.

This unique range had been created by cataclysmic internal pressure striving for release during the birthing period of the Earth. The surface crust had been heaved upward to great heights in a line running from north to south by this natural relief valve. Erosion by wind and water over eons of time had created a flat plateau at the central pass. Towering peaks continued to the north. To the south, the peaks decreased in height as they neared the waters of the gulf. A snow and spring-fed stream ran through this area, creating a magnificent waterfall as it fell to the valley below. After a brief run along the base, its waters disappeared into subterranean caverns. To the west flowed a vast sea of buffalo grass, the surface broken only by buffalo traces.

For centuries, the stream had proven to be a favorite watering hole for migrating buffalo. As they fed on the grass and drank the cool water, their chips (droppings) created a fertile area. These dried chips were used as fuel by Indians. A brave who stopped at the stream to fish could get his fish and chips at the same location. Records indicate that the first white man to visit this area was a Scottish distiller by the name of Angus "Jock" MacDaniels. He was drawn here after hearing rumors of a place where there was an abundance of fish and chips—free!

Such a prized area was the domain of peaceful Indians known as the Hiup, who lived on the plateau just north of the pass. Deer and buffalo abounded and water was plentiful, as were wood and chips for their campfires. Fish thrived in the stream, and the topography formed a natural barrier to the fierce tribes to the west.

That the Hiup were peace-loving was not due solely to this protective barrier. If a foe persisted, the barrier could be overrun. It was their diet that provided an impervious protective barrier. This diet also eliminated any possibility of their gaining a reputation as warriors, like the Apache or Sioux.

The three basic requirements for achieving warrior status were: an ambitious leader, a ferocious nature, and stealth. The Hiup lacked all three. The leader of the Hiup was content with the status quo, a gentle nature was inbred, and stealth was made impossible by their diet. No meal would be complete without an ample portion of their beloved chico bean soup, which made its presence known as it exited after meandering through the digestive system. Its propensity to change into a gaseous state created an intense internal pressure. The body, in a natural endeavor to relieve itself, ejected the gas through the renowned sphincter of Oddi. Its passage through this diminutive opening produced such an explosive sound that any enemy would be alerted to the Hiup's position from a great distance.

Sound was not the only byproduct of the gas. Those close enough to the "ejector" would experience an instantaneous closing of the nostrils, which greatly impeded on one's ability to breathe, and the eyes would water profusely to cleanse an intense burning sensation that stifled vision. No enemy in his right mind would hold a Hiup captive!

Mother Earth, the first to experience the gratuity of the chico bean, exhibited her generosity by giving the Hiup immunity from their own folly. Explosions went unnoticed as natural phenomena among the Hiup unless an individual wished to gain attention by exhibiting exceptional sphincter muscle control. The resulting exhibitions ranged from a long, drawn-out wail like a banshee to an earsplitting roar. In any case, these exhibitions of superb holding power were politely acknowledged by those within hearing range with a nod or a smile. The prevailing west wind acted as an odor-dispersing fan.

The topographic and geographic location of Hiup lands did, however, place some constraints on social activities and interaction among tribal members, resulting in unique customs. The isolation and abundance of natural resources could have led to a stifling of social interaction or individual creativity, but this was not the case among the Hiup.

To other tribes, bravery in battle, a personal victory under adverse conditions, or conquest of a savage animal during a hunt would win unanimous approval from the men of the tribe. Since the Hiup never had to do battle with anyone and adverse conditions were practically nonexistent, one might think that this would put a crimp on achieving acknowledgment within the tribe. Not so. It was customary to reward an individual for any outstanding performance exerted on behalf of the tribe.

As with all Indians, respect for nature was inherent in every custom and social order of the Hiup. To live in harmony with Mother Earth was a law that was never abused. Full use was made of all things needed for survival and respect shown to them. For the Hiup, it was a matter of letting the chips fall where they may, so to speak.

The Hiup loved to party. Any signal in nature's order, such as the Autumn Gathering, the Spring Awakening, New Moon, or even the monthly tribal business meeting, was an excuse to celebrate. Participation in the meeting of the council at each new moon was limited to males only. Many times the agenda was so brief that other items were injected to enhance the occasion. After the passing of the pipe, braves would recall past deeds and the Rem A Nisser (He Who Remembers) would weave spellbinding tales of Hiup exploits of the past. The enraptured young males sat at the perimeter of the circle. They listened intently to the words of their elders and envisioned the day when they would gain recognition and join the inner circle.

Squaws used this time at their own circle. Here tales were also passed along as hands produced intricate patterns on moccasins, loincloths, and other articles of clothing. Nothing was missed by the young females seated at the perimeter. Gossip seems to be innate in females.

The biggest and most looked-forward-to event (second only to the Spring Awakening) was celebrated on the first night of the half moon. During this event, every member of the tribe participated in a night of singing and dancing. The highlight of the celebration was the time set aside for individual interpretation of a dance or song, which, if accepted, became custom. In this way, customs were not only expanded but constantly refined.

Such vehicles allowed for recognition of individual achievement and skills other than those of battle or hunting. Two cases in point were He Who Stares and He Who Walks Funny. He Who Stares probably would have gone unnoticed in the mainstream of tribal life, as he seemed to be, more often than not, in a world of his own. For long periods of time, he sat and meditated while staring into space, hearing no one and seeing no one. Many tried to sit before him and outstare him, but failed. To his close friends, he was known simply as A Stare.

A Stare was anything but passive whenever the drummers started their practice sessions for Dance Night. The sound seemed to act as an adrenaline that set his blood surging. His body started to gyrate and his feet would propel him into unbelievable dance patterns. The customary steps no longer presented a challenge to A Stare. His innovative mind, which otherwise appeared to be devoid of any ability beyond sitting and staring, was a source of dance patterns that enthralled his audience. Thirty-two of his creative routines had been adopted as custom dances. His contributions won him recognition and resulted in his role as instructor at A Stare's School of the Dance.

It was recorded in tribal legend that A Stare had given his most memorable performance on the ninth moon of his twenty-first summer. For that performance he had sewn thin, flat rocks onto the heel and toe of each moccasin. He performed his dance routine on a section of the ground that had been trampled to rocklike hardness by countless years of dancing feet. The tribe was captivated by the sound the rocks on his moccasins made on the hard earth; a rhythmic sound like a woodpecker tapping on a hollow tree.

He Who Walks Funny made another significant contribution to the tribe with his performance on Dance Night, but in a manner that drew questionable response from the males. The customary heel and toe-stomping dance patterns were replaced. His style was dancing on his toes, spinning and pirouetting, and then leaping into the air like a graceful deer. The females adored his style! When not by the waterfall watching the men bathe, he could be found conducting classes for the females (and an occasional male) at his school. He held a respected position in the tribe.

The Hiup did observe status levels within the tribe. At the top level was chief, followed by either messin man or council member (depending on certain conditions), brave, male artisans, squaws, and finally, the children (cubs).

Messin Man

The tribe numbered about 250 and was led by Chief Ten, whose only claim to fame was being a classy dresser. Still, he could manage everyday decisions. It was his messin man's son who would rise above the level of chief to become the legendary leader of all Indians; a status chosen by the Great Spirit, Wakan-Manitou.

The Hiup messin man's given name was He Who Messes With Herbs and Spices, Interprets Dreams, Treats Common Ailments of the Body, Predicts Weather, Advises, and Sees the Future.

His tribal name was shortened to "Messin," for obvious reasons. His position in the tribe was determined by his percentage of accuracy. Messin men of some tribes were so successful that they held a position second only to chief.

Messin had but one child (not much success in that category), a son named Little Brave. As with most fathers, he wished his son to achieve status greater than his own. The passive nature of the Hiup offered dim hope of a messin man attaining rank second to chief. His position, like his prescriptions, was subject to hit or miss. His son could become the bravest of braves, or perhaps even an assistant chief; anything but messin man. It became an obsession to guide his son to a higher station in life.

Hiup spoiled their children and exerted no pressure on them to embark on serious training for adulthood until their tenth summer. Little Brave's time had arrived; it was time for Tracking 101.

On the morning of initiation, Messin drew his son aside. Carefully choosing words to inspire and highlight the necessity for doing well, he began, "Son, you have had a pretty easygoing life to this point. Now it is time to get serious. You will be a man soon and you don't get there by fooling around. Well, maybe some fooling around, but you have to start training to learn the essential aptitudes of a position, set goals, then strive to attain those goals."

"Father," Little Brave replied, "I know that you are trying to tell me something in your own way, but you've lost me. Is this the 'Birds and Bees' lecture?"

"You've missed the point altogether, Son. That lecture won't come for three summers. Don't get smart and jump the bow," Messin growled.

Shaking his head, he continued, "There comes a time in one's life when he must decide what he wants out of life and what his responsibility to the tribe is. Now the highest position is chief. Unfortunately, a tribe has only one chief. Since our chief has a son, it's pretty certain that he will train him to fill his position when he leaves to join his ancestors. Council member is next highest, but only elders are selected. That leaves the position of brave. There are quite a few openings, due to the fatality rate, yet still one to consider. Then we have my position, which is next to that of squaw at the present time, and nothing to aspire to."

"How about He Who Walks Funny? He's not in one of the groups you mentioned," said Little Brave. "He's twenty-four summers and about all he does is dance or sit next to the waterfall watching the men bathe."

"He couldn't pass the test for manhood on three attempts, that's why," replied Messin. "'Three times and you're out' is the law of the tribe, therefore he cannot aspire to a leadership position. I said that this was serious business; let's not waste time. I've got a spell to cast before the sun is gone. The position of chief is out; there may be a slight chance of assistant chief if something happens to Chief Ten and his son, Has It Made. It's something to keep in mind."

"What's wrong with messin, Father? You seem to enjoy your work and you could teach me all that you know. I am your son, so how about it?"

Little Brave had uttered the words all fathers yearn to hear—except Messin. He hurried on to rationalize his stance. "Son, my position looks easy only because I work hard to make every spell, every weather forecast, and every prediction of the future a success. Many a night I have lain awake mentally trying new methods, new techniques, and improving my flair for the mystic while everyone else was snoring their heads off. I want something better for you. I want you to become someone the tribe respects."

"What's so great about being a brave?" questioned Little Brave.

"Well, Son, you know who our greatest brave is—One Eye. When he went in close to that grizzly bear and got his eye torn out and scars from his scalp to his knees, he gained respect. There's Short Arm, who jammed his arm down the mountain lion's throat to avoid being bitten. He lost most of his arm, yet gained respect. Those are but two of many examples of a brave. Now let us begin your training. We may sidetrack later and include some assistant chief training, just in case."

Little Brave, unbeknownst to his father, had set his extraordinary mental processes to work ingesting the information and arguments put forth by his father. The examples and rewards for attaining the position of brave did have an influence on his thinking; just not quite the way his father had hoped. In a steadfast dedication to logic, he decided to incorporate every innovative action necessary to avert attaining the position of brave and its potential for body part losses! His plan was to act and sound plausible while aiming toward acceptance as a messin man. "Let's go, Father, I'm yours to command," set the stage and brought a sigh of relief from Messin.

Tracking 101 presented the opportunity for Little Brave to put his plan into action. He and his father entered the forest and formal training began. The first object of attention was a tree with hair entwined in its bark.

Messin began, "Now, Son, the signs of Mother Earth are most important to read accurately when one is on the trail. To do so may mean the difference between success or failure on the hunt; perhaps between life or death. Can you tell me how these hairs got here?"

"A squaw used the bark to clean her comb," came the reply.

"You're not even close," said Messin. "That's the hair from a young bear who used the tree to scratch his back!"

Little Brave grinned, "I was going to say an old squaw relieving a groin itch, but I didn't want to appear flippant."

"Very amusing. Let's go on."

Coming to the bank of a stream, Messin pointed to some tracks and declared, "Now, here's an easy one. What animal made this track, which way was it going, and how long ago did it pass? The signs are here for us to read."

Looking very studious and deep in thought, Little Brave examined the signs. He walked back and forth, stooped to feel the ground, and emitted a "hmmm" periodically. He finally presented his conclusions: "I would say that these are the tracks of that same young bear going upstream to fish; it passed here one sun ago." He then stood up and faced his father with what appeared to be a look of expectation for praise.

Messin shook his head in disbelief. "Your eyes and your brain appear to have failed to leave the tipi with you. Any simpleton would know a hoof from a paw print! These are the tracks of a large buck leaping across the stream, and with water still oozing into them, I'd say that it had just passed." Messin shook his head in disbelief.

The rest of the day followed the same pattern, with Messin's patience pushed to inhuman limits by the replies of his son when reading simple trail signs. As the sunlight faded, the two headed for their tipi, one with a leaden step and the other with a light and bouncy one.

Many days of training followed. Instruction in arrow making, skinning game, bow stringing, and all other areas of legendary competency had the same result—frustration and failure.

The last straw was reached when the two were tracking a deer. While Little Brave crept forward for the kill, Messin dropped back about twenty paces, savoring the possibility that his string of instructional failures was about to be broken. As he moved forward, Little Brave's mind was deep in concentration, but not on the kill. This would be his chance if his scheme worked. At precisely the right moment, he rose silently to a shooting position, notched his arrow with his right hand, pushed the bowstring forward with his left, and fired. The arrow sped true, not toward the deer, but over his right shoulder. It struck a tree just inches from Messin's right ear.

When the full impact of this action dawned on Messin, he lost his final remnant of patience and of his dream. "Foolish One! Foolish One!" were the only words he could utter to describe his son's action. "I've told you over and over, the bow is held in your left hand. The arrow faces the target and the rawhide is pulled with your right hand!"

Messin promptly decided that his son could not be trusted with weapons for his own safety, as well as that of anyone within range. So ended another father's dream and any chance for a higher station in life for his son. Formal training as his apprentice in messin was the only option remaining.

The disappointments Messin had experienced in "brave" training were quickly replaced by feelings of amazement, awe, and pride as the training progressed. Little Brave's inherent deep pool of curiosity found release to flow unchecked like a roaring, cascading waterfall. A strong bond between father and son was forged through unlimited opportunities for exploration. The result of improved health for their people was a shared joy.

Little Brave was eager to learn every mix, every spell, and how to read every sign necessary for predicting the future. He was a source of never-ending questions, but not the busy and pointless questions asked by most young people as part of their grand design to keep parents off guard about their real motives. His questions implied a mind that sorted, organized, and placed things in a logical structure that demanded conclusion. Each new experience was mentally ingested, catalogued, sorted, ejected, or stored as an essential item in his mental library for instant recall when needed.

Messin was so impressed by his son's progress and natural intuitiveness that he found himself asking questions and advice regarding the possibilities of certain approaches for remedies and cures. He discovered a gratifying sense of mutual respect; a singleness of purpose constantly reinforced their relationship. He was pleased! No father could have been more proud of his son.

Part of the training was "on the job"; Little Brave was taken on "tipi calls" to witness the relationship of proper diagnosis and prescription as it affected the general health of their people. The success of this relationship also influenced Messin's position within the tribe; the greater his success, the greater his status.

Messin began to include his son in actual diagnosing and shared the resulting success (and the occasional failure) with Little Brave. Finally, Little Brave was given some clients of his own. They were mostly the aged ones, since failures could be attributed to the Everywhere Spirit's decision to invite them to join their ancestors in the spirit world.

Little Brave quickly grasped the significance of the personal and social involvement between his father and client as a key to success. Successful involvement could be broken down into 10 percent knowledge, 60 percent showmanship, and 30 percent luck. He discovered that success was enhanced by combining showmanship and luck as one element, which left the impression with his patients that it was 90 percent knowledge and 10 percent luck. This illusion seems to persist (in reverse order) in the medical profession today.

Training continued until Little Brave's fourteenth spring, when it was time to take the test for manhood and receive his adult name. This test was an annual ritual for the tribe as a salute to the awakening of puberty. Male and female alike took part in the ceremony to prove that they were ready to move from adolescence to adulthood.

For their time, the Hiup were quite progressive and logical in their thinking. If, for example, a son was named Small Beaver, but at puberty had attained 6'2" and 210 pounds, a name change might possibly avoid ridicule and ill feelings. A name change to Thundering Buffalo would be in order. Females were accorded the same prerogative. Quiet One might aptly be changed to Running Mouth.

Messin had hopes that only a slight change would be needed for his son. Great Messin, Messin Two, or even Herb Seeker would have suited him fine. But it would be Chief Ten, not Messin, who would give Little Brave his adult name.

Mother Earth had smiled favorably on Messin's son. Perhaps at times she liked to remind man that she, too, had a sense of humor. To Little Brave, she had endowed a wry sense of humor and the mental sharpness of an opportunist, yet her greatest endowment was just that— a great endowment. A collector of church or school bells would acknowledge that he had a tremendous clapper!

The Awakening Ritual was a relatively simple procedure. Messin was in charge, so he directed every male in the tribe not taking part in the test to line up in a line stretching from north to south. Every non-testing female was directed to form a parallel line facing the males, with ten paces separating them. Messin then drew a line in the earth connecting the noncontestant lines at the center. This line was humorously called the "line of the rising son." A male "testee" would start from the east opening and move toward the drawn line. At the same time, his female counterpart would start from the west opening and move toward the same line.

The objective of the female was to use any seductive movement or gesture available to arouse the awakening sexual urges and instincts of the male. If she was successful, it would be obvious when observing the position of the male's loincloth. If the male was ready to cross the line of puberty, it would be readily evident before he reached the drawn line. If there was no reaction, both would fail the test. They would have to wait until the next year to try again. The test had great significance, since a squaw's ability to arouse the male, and the male's ability to be aroused, were both a necessity for the perpetuation of the tribe.

Messin was fidgety. Little Brave's actions, or inactions, were about to be tested. If this was anything like the test results from "brave training," his son might forever carry the name Never Do Well. His hope was that his son's success as a neophyte messin man would carry over to this test.

Little Brave was determined to succeed. Swift Feet was at the other end of the course, just as determined to succeed. She had failed the test the previous spring on her first try, but a year of planning and practice found her prepared with a few innovative tricks to ensure success.

Both started slowly toward the center. Swift Feet waved her arms suggestively, beckoning Little Brave to come on. No reaction. She ran her hands up and down her thighs and over her ample breasts. Still no reaction. The loincloth hung limp, as did the object of concern.

The line was getting closer! Finally, she drew up her buckskin skirt and started a bucking motion with her buttocks while slowly stroking her pubic area. Little Brave's loincloth was flung to one side as his "clapper" rose to the occasion to get a better and unrestricted view! Such a magnificent sight brought sounds of wonderment from the females and yelling, catcalls, stomping of feet, and side-holding by the males.

Little Brave moved quickly to the line. Swift Feet took one look at the monster she had called forth and quickly turned to live up to her name—in the opposite direction. She had passed the test, but thought it prudent not to press her good fortune any further.

When the object of his awakening turned and left the scene, Little Brave became aware of his condition. This triggered a valiant effort to cover his compromising position. His first reaction was normal. He tried to cover it with his hands, but came up short of total success. This sight only increased the reaction of the crowd.

Chief Ten strode forward and saved further stress on the newest addition to the tribe's manhood circle. "I see that our new man has tried to get the situation in hand, but obviously needs more help. I will provide assistance by giving him a most appropriate manhood name. From this time on, he will be called Three Hands."

The very memory of that momentous day in his life and the irony associated with it brought a faint smile to the face of Three Hands as he sat on the ledge this day many years later. Reminiscing could be a pleasant pastime, but he was there for a more serious purpose. The survival of his people depended on the arrival of the last component of his master plan. But, wait! Although the long-awaited objects had not appeared on the trail below, his peripheral vision did pick up motion — the sudden appearance of three short puffs of black smoke from the right side of the valley.

Memories were forgotten, as was the reason for his vigil. Now the once stonelike figure became a blur of motion. He leaped from his perch and dashed down the slope to the valley below, where Fate stood, waiting to greet him with open arms!

Chapter Two

The trail to understanding is short, for the answers sought are as close as one's mental tipi.

Judgment is the domain of the Everywhere Spirit alone. To man, He gave the potential for duplicating these traits of humor, organizational skills, optimism, patience, purpose, and compassion, along with the intelligence to project them. Man's lazy habit of assuming, rather than rationalizing to logical conclusions, has triggered the Terrible Swift Tomahawk quite frequently.

That this day on the trail is one of joy and fulfillment does not insure that tomorrow nor tomorrow's tomorrow will be likewise. For tomorrow to be so calls for logical planning, which includes options in case unforeseeable hazards arise to bar the trail. Options must be the means to circumvent these hazards, in line with His laws, to prevent the triggering of His tomahawk. Fate is the messenger sent with the message that judgment had been made only after repeated warnings had been ignored!

Visualize the hunter, who has meticulously planned the hunt, stalked the quarry according to plan, and arrived at the point where only the release of his missile of death is needed. At this precise moment, a "hunter" mosquito lands on the hunter's ear after stalking him as he planned, and releases his missile of destruction. For one split second, the release of the human hunter's arrow is withheld as the death of this insolent insect intruder becomes the priority. The movement and accompanying sound needed to accomplish this goal catch the eyes and ears of his original quarry, which promptly bounds out of danger.

The hunter berates himself for succumbing to such a slight distraction instead of totally concentrating on the hunt according to plan. If only he could relive that brief moment of distraction, he certainly would not allow anything to deter him from carrying out his plan, and the quarry would be his. Fortunately, his action was not fatal, and he would have opportunities in the future to remember this error and not repeat it.

Three Hands, usually the master of logical, purposeful planning with multioption inclusion, let a slight distraction alter his master plan. His "mosquito" had intruded in the form of a smoke signal. If Fate had chosen some way to share the consequence of Three Hands' exclusion of options in his plan for this day, the messin man certainly would have remained on his perch and ignored the "smoke mosquito." His doom, as well as that of his people, had been sealed by his impromptu change in plans!

His plan for this day was to await the arrival from the west of the two persons upon whom the success of his master plan depended. While focusing his eyes on the trail on the plains below, he would stay perched on his ledge and reminisce about events and experiences that had impacted himself and his people. This practice of reminiscing was the vehicle he used to refine and double-check his priorities. It was also his catalyst for actions necessary to reach his life-goal according to his master plan. Three Hands was a goal-oriented person, and his planning and organizational skills had been honed to lancepoint sharpness by this, his sixty-fourth summer.

The feeling that his final goal soon would be realized may have led to his break in concentration. Only the final bead needed stitching on his Wampum Belt of Life, and it was to arrive today. Unfortunately, that final bead was lost in the trail of dust created by his rapid descent in response to the distracting smoke message.

Lost also would be the strong memories of his father, whose patience had been so sorely tested in his efforts to elevate his position in the tribe. The memories of Chief Ten, Has It Made, and others of his tribe whose efforts had guided him to this point in time, where he was within a hair's width of success, would also be lost. Those losses would be remembered and recorded on the Wampum Belt of Life of every red man!

Also lost, and regrettably so, would be the memories of how he, as messin man of the Hiup, had patiently and meticulously carried out his responsibilities to his red brothers. The knowledge and skills that his father had imparted to him before joining his ancestors in Three Hands' twentieth summer had served as the foundation for his development as the greatest messin man of all time!

Three Hands was an innovator, not an imitator. His innovative practices had earned him not only respect within the tribe but a reputation carried afar by impressed traveling tradesmen from many tribes. His advice had been solicited by messin men from as far away as the banks of the mighty waters of salt in the west. His medicinal successes were phenomenal, his predictions of the future were highly accurate, and his techniques for sparking up council meetings were without peer.

Being without a squaw, one might assume that he lived a simple life. Wrong! Where each family had one tipi, Three Hands had four to accommodate his lifestyle. One, organized as a storehouse, contained shelving of saplings bound together by sinew. On the shelves were deerskin pouches of ready-made prescriptions grouped according to ailment. He could make a diagnosis and instantly present the remedy in most cases, which certainly appealed to those in pain. Everything from wart dissolver to body ointments was at his fingertips.

A second tipi was arranged as a consultation lodge where those who could walk would come for private consultation or examination. The females liked this arrangement of privacy; the braves found it to be a quiet place where their personal problems, especially in the area of sex, could be discussed in the strictest of confidence.

A brave's "sensitive condition" was common. Usually, in a short time after a complaint, his squaw would be in seeking a cure for a long-standing ailment of male "droopsy." The messin man would give her the same prescription for "rebound" that he had given her brave. Each would be given a half dose, since he knew that both halves would end up in the brave.

He was also aware that his prescriptions were more psychological than medicinal. The pouch that held the remedy for droopsy contained equal portions of deer antler, the tooth of a wild boar, the testicle of a bull buffalo and a finger length (middle) of a Ucumfastus tree root. The ingredients were ground to a fine powder, and one chico bean added as a catalyst. Once combined with spring water, things really moved!

The number of requests for droopsy prescriptions usually increased after a brave had reached his fortieth summer. Three hands had sought a combination of herbs and spices that would effect a physical cure to replace the psychological one. He felt that his reputation would be further enhanced if he found a surefire cure to share with other tribes. Success had eluded him, yet he felt that it was only a matter of time.

His third tipi was set up as a laboratory where the mixing of herbs, minerals, animal parts, and other ingredients took place. Each concoction was then placed into appropriately catalogued pouches for storage in his medicinal tipi. He used a system of dyes to classify the pouches. This made identification easier and more accurate. Here too, he practiced incantations which, after long hours of practice, paid off. Special sounds were incorporated into his spells, predictions of the future, and "attention getters" at council meetings.

One of his favorite "attention getters" was to set up a tightly drawn sinew of deer hide between two saplings at the edge of the forest near the council meeting area. This sinew was so thin and tight that it was invisible to those seated in the meeting circle. He had discovered through experimentation that a particular yellow, crystal-like rock, when rubbed along the sinew, produced a high-pitched sound that made the spine tingle.

Through practice of varying hand pressure and the distance moved along the sinew, he could produce voicelike sounds. Coupled with specially created incantations, he appeared and sounded like he was communicating with the spirits. Of course, he led his audience to believe that only he could interpret the responses of these spirits!

Whenever he performed this exercise, there was always a dead silence from his audience, for each member wanted to catch every word from the spirits in case their name was mentioned. Three Hands had found that name-dropping in his translation of spirit messages made for good rapport with his people, especially when favors were needed. One mention of a certain brave's courage would insure him of a pair of bull's balls for his potions after the next hunt.

His fourth tipi, used as living quarters, was the smallest and the least used. Eating and sleeping took a lower priority than his insatiable passion for "M and M," or Messin and Manipulation. Clothing was no problem, as squaws kept him in the finest of beaded loincloths and moccasins in exchange for his messin skills.

Three Hands had all of the ingredients for success in any endeavor, including an intense desire to learn, curiosity, keen wit, the ability to listen, vision, natural talent for understanding the machinations of social relationships, self-assurance, and a sense of humor. He was not easily discouraged by failure and never repeated a mistake. A master opportunist, he thoroughly enjoyed impromptu situations that arose to challenge his ability to instantly appraise, evaluate, and manipulate these situations to his own advantage. He observed (or created, if called for) and used important signs that others failed to notice, whether in a natural setting or in human interaction. Though not recorded in the legends of the Hiup, two corroborating situations did occur. The first occurred when Three Hands was running short of bull's balls for his aphrodisiac potion. Having declined to learn the rudiments of hunting, he had to maneuver others into a position that would fulfill his needs.

The next meeting of the council, when he could easily resolve the problem through name-dropping, was many suns away. He needed "b-balls" now! No problem. He sought out Bald Eagle, the tribe's best buffalo hunter. "Bald Eagle," he said, "I have seen a crispy moth with a torn left wing resting on your lodgepole for two suns. I have also noticed the shadow of the blue jay twice crossed the entrance to your tipi while flying to hide his acorns. Have you taken action to prevent this illness?"

"Three Hands has the eyes of our brother the hawk," came the reply. "I have noticed none of the signs of which you speak. I am now preparing for the hunt, two suns hence. What is the meaning of these signs?"

"Forgive me, oh greatest of hunters, for mentioning what is probably an insignificant warning. The signs indicate only a temporary disablement and are easily missed when one's mind is on the hunt. The moth sign means that your left arm will develop a severe pain. The blue jay sign says that the pain will come in two suns and you will not be able to leave your tipi until the pain is gone."

"I know that your eyes do not read signs falsely," said an apprehensive Bald Eagle. "I am pleased that you have shared these signs with me. What should I do?"

"When I saw these signs," replied Three Hands, "I prepared an ointment for you, in case you had not done so on your own. I also asked the Spirit of Pain to heed my prayer, for your strength and courage is needed to feed our people."

"I thank you for your good words and thoughts on my behalf. Tell me of this ointment and what I must do to appease the Spirit of Pain."

"Apply this ointment to your left arm now and each of the next two suns. If you see that the crispy moth has gone when you return to your tipi, it is the proper messin. The blue jay should not cross the entrance of your tipi and the pain will not develop. If this is so, send a prayer to the Spirit of Pain and thank him for sparing you pain," directed the messin man while maintaining (with great effort) a straight face.

"I heed your words and will follow them," said Bald Eagle as he applied the ointment to his left arm.

Four suns later, Bald Eagle appeared at Three Hands' consultation tipi with a deerskin pouch in his hand.

"I come to show my gratitude for your good messin, Three Hands. I did as you said and never had a bit of pain in my arm. For you, I have brought a share of the hunt, the sacs of two bull buffalo. You have indicated in the past that they could be used in your messin."

"The words that you have shared with me of a successful hunt and of your freedom from pain make my heart full. I welcome your generous gift and will use it to appease the Spirit of Pain for our people." A psychological suggestion, a touch of bear grease and a bit of "bull" gave Three Hands all of the real bull he needed for a moon's supply of the major ingredient of "hormone powder."

A second demonstration of his skill in quickly sizing up a situation and turning it to his own advantage began by his being in the right place at the right time. He wasted no time in applying this opportunity to elevate his position in his tribe, and beyond, to unimaginable heights!

He was on one of his extended expeditions to replenish his prescription stock. His travel took him eastward for three suns. Root and bark samples were coded and placed in collection pouches. He moved at a leisurely pace, making certain that all aspects of an area were observed and its potential mentally recorded before moving on to another.

While preparing his camp for the night, an unexpected visitor arrived. As he straightened up from gathering an armload of pine boughs, his eyes caught an almost indiscernible movement at the edge of the clearing. His movements continued uninterrupted until he had deposited the boughs where his bed was to be. Then and only then did he speak, even though his back was to the newcomer.

"My brother, who moves as silently as the shadow of night and whose manners are those of a friend, welcome to my camp. What I have is yours to share." Having uttered these words of praise and welcome, he turned to face his visitor and raised his right hand in greeting. "I am Three Hands, messin man of the Hiup."

The stranger stepped forward into the clearing and raised his hand in greeting. "Thank you, Three Hands of the Hiup, for your welcome. I have heard of your greatness from those I have met on the trail. I am He Who Walks On, of the Seneca. Long have I been on the trail this sun and am grateful for your offer."

"I have just the thing to refresh you from the rigors of your trail," said Three Hands. "A gourd of freshly brewed ginseng tea and the breast of brother Rabbit should renew your strength. Sit, while I make the fire to prepare these refreshments."

The two consumed their meal, then talked far into the night. Three Hands learned that He Who Walks On was a trader and new to the trail. His guest proved to be a natural storyteller who enjoyed spicing his tales with humor, a trait dear to the heart of the messin man. He could not suppress eruptions of laughter as his guest shared anecdotes of the trail.

In the course of conversation, Three Hands learned that his guest came from the lands near the Great Waters to the east and had been his tribe's best lancepoint maker. Men called The Hairy Ones, because of the long hair on their faces, had come over the Great Waters in large, winged canoes, and in such numbers that they soon forced his tribe to move westward. After several moves, He Who Walks On decided that taking his lancepoints on the trading trail would be better than waiting for the next eviction. He enjoyed traveling, making new friends, seeing new sights, and especially the bartering process. He was as much an opportunist as Three Hands.

Three Hands told of his background and his people; he proved to be just as adept at storytelling as his guest. When he told some of his "bedside" stories, including the one about Bald Eagle, his guest held his sides in a valiant effort to control his laughter. Their shared skill in highlighting humor acted as an adhesive. A strong bond of comradeship began to develop and their exchanges lasted until the first light of the sun, when sleep finally overcame laughter.

After a refreshing sleep and meal, He Who Walks On joined Three Hands as he went about collecting herbs; Three Hands explained which were used for certain cures, which ones to avoid, and how to proportion for best results. Some, known by his guest, were in turn shared with him, which enlarged his scope of cures.

The evening of the third sun, He Who Walks On told his host that he would return to his trail at the next sun. Three Hands shared his regret with understanding. They agreed to keep in touch via others traveling on the same trail. Both were moved at the thought of parting. It was then that Three Hands decided to invoke the highest level of esteem one could offer—to become blood brothers.

The solemn pause for reflection and prayer following the ritual had ended when He Who Walks On decided to share a secret with his new blood brother, a secret that would have tremendous impact on Three Hands and his future.

"My brother," asked He Who Walks On, "would you like to meet my other brothers who travel with me as silently as the shadow of the wolf?"

Three Hands was momentarily perplexed, but decided that this was an introduction to another tale. He was right to some degree. "I would be honored," he replied.

He Who Walks On picked up a burning stick from the fire and held it high in front of him. "Oh, Brother of Fire, give greetings to our new brother, Three Hands."

From the burning stick came a voice in reply, "Greetings to our brother of the Hiup. Would you like to put me in your blanket? I could warm you up faster than a young squaw!"

The look of bewilderment on the face of Three Hands brought a wide grin to the face of his blood brother. Before he could regain his composure, a different voice came from the pine tree behind him. "I don't wish to needle you, but the boughs that you took from me were for the birds!" The voice went silent after several peals of laughter.

By this time, He Who Walks On was rolling on the ground, doubled over with laughter. Three Hands stood as if rooted, a dazed look on his face.

His blood brother finally exhausted his laughter and stood up. "Well, how do you like my other brothers? I have many more waiting in the forest."

Three Hands finally regained his composure, but remained silent. He was at a loss for words, but his mind was churning and analyzing the events he had witnessed. He was certain that the Everywhere Spirit was playing some sort of a game with him to test his reaction. Surely, no other man had heard fire and trees actually speak. Signs, yes, but voices, never!

He Who Walks On decided that his trick had run its course and the time for confession was here. "Those voices were really mine," he said.

Three Hands sat frozen in disbelief.

His visitor smiled, then continued, "I have never revealed this secret to any living man until now because I have never met anyone I felt worthy of sharing it with. No one has thought me worthy of being a blood brother since I left my people, except you. You, my brother, have readily shared your greatest secrets with me and asked nothing in return. Now I will share mine with you, knowing that you will use it wisely."

The messin man sat, eyes growing larger, as He Who Walks On unfolded a most astonishing story. "In my twentieth summer, I left the camp of my people and went to the nearby camp of the Hairy Ones. I wanted to learn how he lived, his language, and his customs. They had set up their lodges only a short time before and I thought it would be friendly to exchange language and customs with them.

"In the entrance to one lodge, I saw a man sitting with a doll on his lap. Dolls, I said to myself, are for female cubs, but perhaps the customs of the Hairy Ones also allowed men to play with them. Since I was there to learn, I went closer. The man was speaking to the doll and to my amazement, the doll answered him! I could not understand the language. Even so, I could see great magic was at the command of this man who was able to communicate with wooden dolls.

"My thoughts were to casually turn and make a speedy return to our camp before he turned me into a doll. The Hairy One beckoned me to come closer. My feet managed, under great protest from the rest of my body, to move me toward him.

"When I got close enough, the man reached out and took my hand, placing my fingers lightly on his throat. I could feel the muscles of his throat move, but his mouth remained almost closed. Each time his throat muscles moved, the doll spoke. After several repeats, I understood that, although no movement of his lips was evident, he was speaking through the lips of the doll, which did move.

"I nodded my understanding and he began to smile. It was not magic after all. It was a trick, and a masterful one, I might add. It was a trick that I wanted to master. Through sign language, I indicated my desire to learn the trick, and offered some lancepoints in exchange. He declined my offer. However, through sand drawings, he indicated that a deer would be acceptable, and I agreed.

"Returning to my camp, I immediately prepared for the hunt, for I was anxious to begin my lessons. Killing a deer was no problem. I informed my father that I would be away for some time, went on the hunt, killed a deer, and returned with it to the lodge of the Hairy One.

"I remained with him for one moon and learned the basics of the trick, along with much of his language. We parted as friends. I found some of the Hairy Ones to be good, like my friend, but many are bad messin. Do not trust them until they prove themselves worthy, for they tend to speak with forked tongue so often."

Three Hands sat fascinated until the tale ended. He was not long in seeking answers to the intense itch of curiosity that was consuming him. "I sit before you, my brother, just as you must have faced the Hairy One at your first meeting. I know the amazement you must have experienced."

Although his blood was coursing through his body at vein-breaking speed, good manners kept him from asking the one question needed to send his hopes soaring. Fortunately, his brother anticipated his question.

"My brother, we have shared a good camp. Since I left my people, I have made many new friends, but not one has filled my heart with joy as you have done. In you, I see myself. We think as one, view the meaning of life as one, have the same curiosity to learn all things, and are aware of the importance of humor in viewing all things clearly and with a cool head.

"When I accepted your offer to become brothers of blood, I also made the decision to share my secret with you if you wished to learn it. Timing is vital to success, so I waited to catch you in a receptive mood. Would you care to learn the 'brother' trick?"

The release of breath that Three Hands had been holding, while hoping for this question to be asked, came not a moment too soon. Another breathless instant would surely have resulted in a dead faint.

Postponing his departure, He Who Walks On spent seven suns instructing Three Hands in the basics of voice throwing. His pupil was an attentive one, as proven by his quickness in mastering these rudiments.

At the setting of the seventh sun, He Who Walks On shared the last campfire with his student brother. "You have been an excellent student," he said. "You now have another brother and the knowledge to create many more. The more that you have at your command, the greater the impression you can create. At the rising of the next sun, I will take the trail west. It is my wish that our trails cross again, and I will plan my trail so that my moccasins point this way again. May the wishes of the spirits be as mine in this matter."

"You have shared much with me, my brother," replied Three Hands. "It is my wish also that our trails cross again. I will think of you each time the voice of a 'brother' is used. I pray that your trail will be a good one. My heart is heavy at our parting, but my spirit is high that our trails have crossed."

Three Hands awoke the next morning to find himself alone in camp. He prepared to move on to continue his gathering. He did so with a light step and high spirits. By the time he returned to his people, he was in total command of three new "brothers." Unknown to him at the time, this new skill would be the key to the survival of his people.

Like a young cub with his first bow and arrows, he was eager to try out his new skills on his people. Still, he was not one to rush into a situation without adequate planning, preparation, and purpose. He remembered the importance of timing; the fastest way to spread the word was via a female.

Being on the trail for many suns made natural needs more noticeable, especially in the form of a warm glow in the area of his groin. Whenever he passed a young squaw, his lodgepole raised his loincloth to such a height that it seemed to be waving a greeting to the sun god passing overhead. His condition hardly went unnoticed. The young squaws blushed and, in many cases, felt parts of their body grow warmer as he passed. Some of the older squaws were stirred to such warmth that they summoned their mates into their tipis and insisted that they "bury their tomahawks," figuratively speaking. Some squaws, however, remembered why he was so named, and the vision of a young sapling being split asunder by a bolt of lightning was reason enough for them to turn and look another way. Some of the more seasoned squaws, who were willing to accept such a challenge if offered, failed to get a rise out of him.

There were some squaws among the tribe who either had an overwhelming desire to satisfy their curiosity, or were at the same level of need as Three Hands. Slender Willow fell into both categories. She was in her twentieth summer and had lost her brave in a hunt two winters before. When she came to Three Hands' consultation lodge, he knew the time was right to introduce a "brother."

"Tell me, Slender Willow, what is the nature of the problem that brings you to my lodge?" he inquired.

"I come to Three Hands, great messin man of the Hiup, to seek the reason for my condition and also a cure for it," she replied.

"Explain your problem, and, with the help of the spirits, I may be able to eliminate it," he intoned.

"It was about twelve moons after my brave, Straight Spear, was killed that I noticed a strange force had entered my body. It must be the Spirit of Fire because my body seems to grows very warm about seven suns a moon. The spirit leaves my body for about twenty suns, then returns to cause great heat within me once again. Can this be an evil spirit and can you drive it from my body?"

"Is this force, or spirit, now present within your body?" he timorously inquired.

"Yes."

Three Hands' mind was soaring. The Spirit of Fire was also present within his body and rapidly making its presence known! This situation not only called for supreme body-parts control, but also for an awareness that very often the quarry can be lost by too quick a move by the hunter.

This was a perfect opportunity to call forth a "brother" to assist in resolving this dear child's problem. "I believe I know a way to drive the Demon of Fire from your body, but I caution you, if there is any weakness of heart on your part, once we begin, we may both be destroyed! Are you strong of heart?" he asked without the slightest trace on his face of the forces of exuberance, anticipation, hope, or desire that raged throughout his body.

"Yes, I am ready and strong of heart. I will not fail you. Do you have a powder to drive out the demon?" she replied.

"There is no powder strong enough to defeat the Fire Demon. We must call upon the good Spirit of Water to help us and pray that he is strong enough to overpower the demon. I must place myself in a trance and leave this world to meet with this spirit and seek his assistance. We must do as he commands and all will be well. I will be unable to speak once I enter the world of the spirits. When I am ready to return, I will raise my right arm to ask permission of the spirits to return to this world. Do you understand?"

"I understand and will do as I am commanded," she answered in a resolute voice.

Three Hands went into an impromptu, yet fascinating act, with hope in his heart and passion in his pit. He uttered a few incantations and then slowly collapsed to the ground, flat on his back, arms at his side, and feet together. He remained in this position as silence filled the tipi.

Slender Willow was sitting in a squat position at the side of the prone messin man and was concentrating on being strong of heart. She was startled by a deep voice. She glanced at the face of the messin man. His lips, although slightly parted, made no movement. The voice could not be his. "Has he made contact with the spirits?" she wondered.

The voice spoke her name! Confused, she glanced around the tipi and confirmed the fact that she and the messin man were the only human occupants.

"Slender Willow, this is the Spirit of Water. Can you hear me?"

"Yes, oh great spirit, I can hear you, but I cannot see you," she stammered.

"I am here in front of you. I have taken form so that I can see you and you me. I am behind the loincloth of Three Hands. Move it aside so that I may see you. Do as I command!" the voice roared.

The voice had the command of authority. With trembling hands she did as she was directed. Three Hands' mighty lodgepole sprang erect in all of its magnificent and awesome glory before her eyes. A slight lump formed in her throat, her face became flushed, and the heat within her grew and seemed to permeate every fiber of her body. The Demon of Fire within her must have been very angry, or afraid!

"I stand before you with an all-seeing eye and am struck by your beauty. My friend, Three Hands, who is with me now, tells me that my Brother of Fire has made his lodge within your body and is causing you much discomfort. Does he speak the truth, fair one?"

"Yes, Three Hands speaks true and is trying to help me," she whispered.

"Three Hands is good and I have answered his call for my help. I will speak with my Brother of Fire and try to convince him to leave your body peacefully, or I will fight him and cast him out. First, you must remove your robe."

Slender Willow was hesitant to obey, but seeing that Three Hands was still in the spirit world, she considered herself alone, so she obeyed the command. She must be strong for Three Hands' sake.

"Good. I see that you are sincere in seeking my help," the voice continued. "Now I want you to straddle the legs of Three Hands near me."

The lodgepole seemed to quiver as it spoke. After she had complied, the voice continued, "Now take me in both hands, for you must guide me to the nearest point of your body where my Brother of Fire is dwelling so I can speak with him," the voice directed.

Slender Willow placed both hands on the lodgepole like a raccoon floating downstream on a log with but one limb to hold onto. Her grip was timid at first, but she found herself increasing the pressure. Her breathing also increased as she found herself anxiously awaiting (and hoping) for the next command.

"Your hands are strong. That is good, for they must now guide me to the warmest part of your body so that I may begin to plead with my brother," the voice directed.

A second thought flashed through the mind of Three Hands after that last command, for it lacked specificity. The aim he desired might not be fulfilled, but it was too late to rephrase the command.

He had little cause for concern, for by now, Slender Willow had no misconception as to where the warmest part of her body was. With a strong grasp, resolution of purpose, skillful aim, and, of course, a strong heart, she raised her body and put the Spirit of Water where he could make the best contact with the Spirit of Fire!

A muffled voice seemed to come from within her as the Spirit of Water continued his commands. "I have met my brother. He says that he will not leave your body peacefully. Therefore, I am prepared to do battle with him. Do not let me out until the battle is over. Have I made myself clear?"

"Oh great spirit who is so good, I hear you and will do all that I can to assist you," she moaned.

The battle began. Slender Willow found herself bounced up and down like a pestle pounding grain. A glorious feeling engulfed her as the battle raged. She willed herself to continue the action until victory was attained. It took most of the morning to reach this point.

Finally, the sounds of battle were replaced by silence. Slender Willow's head hung down in exhaustion. For some time, she sat impaled and unmoving. At last she concluded that the battle was finally over and she rolled off Three Hands to let the Spirit of Water out. One look at him revealed that he, too, was exhausted and unable to stand erect, or even to speak.

Regaining her strength, she put on her robe and returned to her original position at the side of the messin man. She assumed that the Spirit of Water had returned to his own world, as no further commands were heard and the messin man's lodgepole lay limp against his body. She covered it with his loincloth and resumed her position. Her body felt quite cool. It was evident that the Demon of Fire had been defeated.

Moments passed. Three Hands' right arm began to rise until it was straight out from his body. It was the signal that he wished to return from the spirit world. Soon his eyes fluttered, then opened. He seemed to be in a weakened condition, for it took several tries before he could regain a sitting position.

"Was I successful? Were you able to speak with the Spirit of Water? Did he convince his brother to leave your body? How do you feel? What happened?" The questions tumbled from the lips of the messin man, giving the impression that he was totally unaware of what had transpired in his absence.

Slender Willow's mind was not as exhausted as her body. She intended to take full advantage of the opportunity at hand. Her reply was evidence. "You are truly a great messin man, Three Hands. The spirit you contacted came to see me and placed me in a dreamlike trance. He spoke to his Brother of Fire and convinced him to leave my body, but only on the condition that I return to your tipi in five suns. You are then again to contact him to see that his brother has not returned. I have never felt this good and I thank you for your help. I can see the strain that you have endured, yet I ask that you allow me to return, as the spirit has requested."

"I am happy of heart that I could be of help. We must never offend the spirits. I will look for you in five suns," a smug and self-satisfied Three Hands replied.

It did not then surprise him, knowing the power, speed, and range of female gossip, that soon he was receiving constant visits from squaws suffering the same malady as Slender Willow. He staggered his schedule selectively and cured himself of his own heat malady, as well as any need to marry.

Some squaws developed a faint heart after viewing the "rising spirit"; these women departed the tipi. Not one, however, admitted to not having completed the entire spiritual "cure." Others, of course, made the spirits battle long and hard before attaining victory. Three Hands could fail, but never lose.

The male members of the tribe were introduced to a "brother" (in a different way, of course) during the next meeting of the council. The special introductory activity was carefully planned by Three Hands. It was his plan to make a prediction in a manner that would startle, not panic, his audience. He dropped a hint to Bald Eagle that a prediction was forthcoming, and the word quickly spread. Interest in the meeting began to mount and reached the point where tribal business became secondary in priority to that of the prediction!

The evening arrived and the council got down to business in a most expeditious manner. The moment finally came when Chief Ten signaled the messin man that the council was ready for his prediction.

Three Hands took a carefully preplanned position. In his right hand, he held a lance. In his left hand, he held a bow and an arrow. Silence hung as heavy as a mist covering the ground on an autumn morn. He began to speak in a slow, deliberate manner. "I stand before our great chief, the council, and the many braves of the Hiup. I have read signs telling of an important event that is to take place on the fourteenth sun of the third moon. These signs say that the event is in relation to the hunt and that the spirit of the hunt, Fearless, would be involved. The signs were very faint. I will ask him to give clear signs that cannot be misread or misunderstood."

For several moments he carried out an incantation that rose and gained intensity. In a sudden move, the hands holding the weapons were thrust skyward as he shouted, "Oh mighty Spirit of the Hunt who knows no fear, who watches over our braves during the hunt, who sharpens their knowledge of trail signs, who instills contempt for fear, and who guides them to victory, give me a sign to read so that I can make your wishes known to my people!"

All eyes were focused on the messin man for the sign that he would receive. Instead of a sign, they sat aghast as a mighty voice seemed to come from the upheld weapons!

"Three Hands, messin man of the Hiup, your eyes have the sharpness of our brother, the eagle, when reading signs. Now I choose to speak directly with my people. I know that you will understand and abide by my wish.

"The braves of the Hiup are great hunters. I will be with you on the hunt and rid you of any fear. But hear you this: I will not protect those who act as fools while on the hunt. If you cannot concentrate on the purpose of the hunt and on your responsibilities, I will withhold keenness of eye, sharpness of hearing, and strength of arm. Those of you, if any, will be the ones that the bear, the cat, or the buffalo will approach unobserved and attack. These will be the only ones who fail to return from the hunt. Those who heed my words, I shall protect. I have spoken!"

The entire audience was immobilized by the event. It was the first time in memory that any of them had actually heard the voice of a spirit. Some, at first, had sneaked glances at the face of their messin man to try to discover if he was playing a trick, but saw no movement of his lips. It had to be the voice of Fearless!

Three Hands lowered his arms and placed the weapons at the feet of his chief. He then made his way to his tipi and entered. Once inside, he turned and peered out of the flap to view the reaction of his audience. As soon as he was out of sight, bedlam broke loose. The council area was buzzing like a swarm of bees around their queen. Everyone seemed to be talking at once to share their thoughts with anyone who would listen.

Seeing this, Three Hands smiled and turned to prepare for sleep. Far into the night he lay, staring at the top of his tipi with a smile of satisfaction on his face and a prayer of thanks on his lips to He Who Walks On.

Chapter Three

Man has little respect for a small stream that he can cross in one stride. When many such streams come together as one, their combined strength can arouse respect and fear in man.

The winds of social change usually begin as a zephyrlike breeze and slowly build to cyclonic force before those affected fully realize it. Action, or inaction, takes place to enhance or to impede this force. The action can be quick and clean like a well-placed arrow in a deer, causing a swift and merciful death, or it can be like an arrow in the hands of a novice whose lack of skill results in only a wound. This wound festers and does not heal, resulting in a long period of suffering before death.

The days of idyllic life for the Hiup were numbered. Like most people who live without fear, stress, or want, answers to questions regarding the future could be found in tradition. Tradition provided an uninterrupted continuation of the good life, since it was the all-powerful force behind the status quo. The Hiup believed that the next sun would be the same as today, as long as traditional customs that were in harmony with the Everywhere Spirit and Mother Earth were honored. It was the responsibility of their messin man to handle questions related to the future.

There would be no challenge to this honored belief if the forces of change could be shut out. In time, all civilizations and social orders have found this to be impossible. Unfortunately, the lesson is learned after the fact, not before it. The armor of the Hiup, in the form of tradition, was as fallible as all others before them. The winds of change were beginning to caress their ears and their minds. This invasion went unnoticed at first, but grew to become an object of great concern.

The change began as a trickle of information passed on by traveling tradesmen as they moved on the circuit. No matter which direction they traveled, the Huron from the north, the Seneca from the east, and the Aztec from the south all carried the same foreboding message: a new breed of man had arrived—one ruled by evil spirits. This new breed was of another color, had a different physical appearance, and held vastly different values. He called himself "white man," was very hairy, had little or no respect for Mother Earth, and spoke with a forked tongue. He had come to the lands of the red man in huge winged canoes over the Great Waters to the east and south. Their canoes then left, only to return bearing more hairy ones in unending procession. He also brought unbelievable weapons that he used on man as well as animals.

The Hiup listened intently to the stories of this new man. At first they were just curious and accepted the tales as entertainment, for there was plenty of food, water, and forests to accommodate this new addition. To them, there was no cause to worry, for these events were happening far away. The hairy ones remained of little concern to the Hiup until the tales grew in number. They were repeated by increasing numbers of families, even entire tribes moving through the pass on their way west to safety. No longer were they tales to embellish stories by traders on the trail. Now the actual terror faced by their brothers from the east was moving too close for comfort!

Chief Ten and the council came to the realization that the white man and the problems associated with him merited closer scrutiny. The reached this conclusion after a powwow with Sittin Pretty, chief of the Wiseolas. The chief had arrived at the pass with the five hundred surviving members of his once-powerful nation from the Creek area, just east of the Mississippi River.

Never before had the Hiup received such a large number of guests at one time. The strain was tremendous on the food supply, as well as the nerves. New Moon or not, Chief Ten called for a joint meeting of the two tribal councils, three suns hence.

The Wiseolas greeted this news with relief, for they had not been blessed with immunity from the byproducts of chico bean soup, which only added more misery to their aching bodies. Some had even gone so far as to inform their chief that if this was the end of the trail, they would rather turn back and take their chances with the white men!

Three Hands was kept busy looking after the trail injuries of the Wiseolas and subscribing to the aches and pains sustained during their forced march. He learned that the messin man of the tribe had been taken prisoner by the whites and held for practicing without a license, whatever that meant. Three Hands was mentally preparing himself for the added responsibilities he would face at the meeting. Another opportunity to impress was at hand and he meant to be ready.

Being an opportunist, organizer, and showman, Three Hands assumed that he would be called upon to interpret signs, to advise the chiefs, and to prophesy. He knew from the traders he had met, from He Who Walks On and now from Sittin Pretty, that the big question would be how to stop the white man. He was aware that he would be expected to come up with possible solutions. A great deal of his time was devoted to preparing for that moment. Anticipation, planning, and implementation comprised his basic formula for success.

The sun before the meeting found him with no answer. His mind seemed to desert him in his moment of need. "I cannot answer," was the thought that dominated each of his brain cells, with one exception. That one cell of resolution slowly ignited the adjoining cells until the roaring flames of ingenuity and logic crackled out the answer. If a great messin man like himself could not answer, then no mortal could answer. If no mortal could answer, then he must look to M.O.M.! All was well with the world of Three Hands for, as his fisherman friends would say, he was off the hook. The task now facing him was to lead his people and the Wiseolas to that point of explanation. No problem!

M.O.M. was the legendary Mystic of Mountains and patron of the red man. M.O.M. had been sent to Earth by the spirits to act as their interpreter when man became totally unable to find solutions to his problems. This legend lives on to this day to some degree, for, when faced with unsolvable problems, man still turns to his M.O.M. for solutions. M.O.M. was the highest level of shaman of the red man, and lived in the mountains north of the Hiup lands. M.O.M. had, according to legend, led the Hiup to this area and then left to make his lodge in the mountains, never to be seen again.

On the date set, the meeting of the councils began at the conclusion of the luk pot meal. All items of protocol were observed, the pipe passed, compliments exchanged, and so on, before the problem at hand was broached. Chief Sittin Pretty detailed the history of his nation, their great deeds, accomplishments, and experiences with the white man. The loss of their lands and the loss of so many of their people, including women and children, by standing and fighting the white man were meticulously detailed. They had proven to be no match for the enemy in numbers, the weapons he used, or the diseases he spread. Such diseases proved fatal for those who fought him, as well as for those who wanted to live with him in peace. The only way to survive was to give up their lands and get out of his way.

Chief Ten and members of his council presented questions and debated the issue until the dark sky was painted by the brush of the new sun. Only one question was left unanswered. How was the white man to be stopped? Surely the greatest of messin men, who had close contact with the spirits and who happened to be among them now, could lead them to the answer they sought.

On signal from his chief, Three Hands slowly rose to his feet and just as slowly made his way to his preplanned spot. His figure took on a commanding appearance. It was a spot where the ground was slightly elevated, at the edge of the fire's bright light where the shadows began.

Giving his audience ample time to be impressed by his appearance, he spoke: "Chief Ten, Chief Sittin Pretty, members of the councils, and braves of the Hiup and Wiseolas, I have listened to your words carefully. The uncertainties we face must be changed by actions on our part, actions not like the ones tried by our red brothers that ended in failure. The failures of our brothers were not due to a lack of courage, of compassion, or of deeds. Their failures were brought about by the use of evil spirits by the white man."

He took the buzz of voices in his audience as agreement with that possibility. He continued, "We have called upon our spirits for guidance, and answers have not been forthcoming. The meaning of this is that the solution rests not with the spirits, but with us. We have heard from our brothers what has not worked. Ours must be a new and successful plan. I will ask our Brother of Fire for guidance."

Three Hands slowly strode to a position facing the council fire where his presence could be clearly witnessed by all. He then sat, legs crossed, back straight, and arms at his side. For what seemed to be an immeasurable amount of time, he remained in that position, all eyes focused on him. When he began to hear a slight murmur of impatience from his audience, he knew it was time to make his move. Besides, he was beginning to feel a request from his own tailbone to change position.

Raising his arms and crossing them in front of his eyes brought an end to the murmurs and a silent prayer of thanks from his audience, since their tailbones had also reached the threshold of pain. He then rose to his feet and faced his chief. "I have looked long and patiently toward our Brother of Fire. I have asked him to act as the bearer of the answers we seek. He is our contact with the spirits."

Groans went up from the gathering and the murmurs began anew. "Our Brother of Fire went to seek an answer and returned with a sign. He says that within this sign is the answer we seek, but it is for us to find the answer within it. Our brother left me with the sign of a pouch at the end of a stick."

Instantly, shouts rose from the Hiup; the sign from the vision was clear to all: "The Spirit Bag! The Spirit Bag!"

Three Hands made his way to the tipi of the chief, followed by the members of both tribes. This was a moment when everyone could be involved in an act that would be part of a legend told by future members of the tribe. The opening of the Spirit Bag was to be accomplished in their lifetime. Their importance would be greatly enhanced by being present at this deed. They were to be the recipients of a direct message written by the spirits!

Reaching the appropriate spot, Three Hands bound his knife to a long stick and raised it to deftly sever the rawhide securing the pouch to the lodgepole. The pouch dropped into his waiting hands. He then walked to a position directly in front of Chief Ten and opened the pouch. Sifting through the decayed layers of deerskin pouches of the past, his fingers closed about the only solid object within. Withdrawing his hand, he saw that the object was a small flat rock, which he held up for all to see. "The answer is here!" he exclaimed.

Chief Ten and Chief Sittin Pretty stepped closer to view the rock. Three Hands dipped the rock into the chief's small pot that he used to heat water for his tea and cleared it of debris. A message had indeed been inscribed in sign language on the rock. The messin man read the signs:

THREE PUFFS WILL BE ENOUGH

What was the meaning? This was no answer to the problem of the white man. Did the message mean three puffs of the ceremonial pipe? Three Hands' mind raced to come up with a plausible interpretation, for his reputation was at stake.

The eternal light in his brain did not fail him. He casually handed the message rock to his chief and stated, "The message rock tells us to light a signal fire and signal three short puffs."

A chorus of agreement indicated that the tribes accepted that as a reasonable interpretation and were eager to carry out the instructions—but not before eating. Action was held in abeyance until the morning meal was prepared and consumed.

Once the meal was over, preparations for the ceremonial fire began and the stage set for the next step in the ritual. Chief Ten and Chief Sittin Pretty were given their rightful honor of holding the signal blanket. Three Hands stood by with a small pouch containing ochre and ground pitch from a pine tree. At the appropriate moment, he threw the pouch, which he had concealed in the wet boughs of the Ucumfastus tree, into the fire. The result was a striking dense orange smoke. The chiefs made three quick passes with the blanket, and then Three Hands extinguished the flames with a container of water. The three short puffs of orange smoke rose straight up into a cloudless and breezeless sky.

Their task completed, the two chiefs each selected a man to climb to the top of two tall trees to act as lookouts. The Hiup were convinced that a reply would be forthcoming, as this was the first use of the Spirit Bag. The Wiseolas were not as certain, yet they were optimistic. Members of both tribes sat in the great circle and exchanged points of view, expectations, and opinions. The sun moved across the sky and the shadows began to lengthen. The exchanges became less frequent and were replaced by stares and shoulder-shrugging. The women quietly began moving about to prepare a delayed meal.

Three Hands also experienced a growing concern with the passing of the sun. Had the Spirit Bag been kept too long without use? Had M.O.M. grown weary of such inactivity and moved to serve other, more needy tribes? The sun descended and only a glow in the western sky hinted at the direction of its passage.

Suddenly, a simultaneous shout from the two lookouts broke the stillness: "Message from the north!"

The entire group came to its feet as one!

"What is the message?" called Has It Made.

"Three short puffs. One red, one white, and one green," came the reply.

"From where does it come?"

"From the mountain beyond the Talking Waters."

Excitement brought muttering from many lips. The "I-told-you-so" prophets had to be heard. The Hiup wasted no opportunity in politely displaying to their guests their importance as the chosen ones by the spirits. The displays were not offensive, but there was a great deal of strutting!

Three Hands knew that he would now be expected to interpret the reply. There seemed to be no end to the demands placed on a messin man. Still, he thrived on these challenges and his mind again was equal to the task. He was keenly aware of the tactical importance of forcing the issue instead of waiting for it to be forced upon him. He held his hand skyward for silence.

"My brothers, having waited so long and so patiently together, are surely anxious to learn the meaning of this reply to the message of our chiefs. The red means to stop all actions. The white means to select a messenger who is pure in thought and the green means that this messenger should come with all haste to M.O.M. It is fitting that you, Chief Ten, should decide who your messenger should be."

"My answer to that, Messin Man, is to choose one who has served our people with wisdom, compassion, and integrity. The choice is easy. You, Three Hands, will be my choice. Prepare for your journey as quickly as the smoke fades in the wind."

Three Hands spent the evening preparing for his trail. This proved to be more of a mental exercise, since he had no frame of reference regarding protocol or even the direction, except for the reply of the lookouts. His mind was filled to overflowing with questions he knew must be answered before he broke camp. Which trail to take? How far would his trail take him? What provisions should he carry?

The anticipation of meeting the spokesperson of the spirits soared beyond the need for immediate answers. Within him boiled the determination to overcome any and all obstacles to reach that goal!

Legend, as told by the Rem A Nisser at council meeting "warm ups," provided some clues as to his destination. M.O.M.'s lodge was located in the mountains around the Lake of Talking Waters. Mother Earth used this body of water to produce and store the fish that swam in the stream flowing through Hiup lands. When more fish were needed, a ceremonial request would be made to Mother Earth, and she would release fish from this lake. The Rem A Nisser recalled that a messenger sent to M.O.M. must make his request for council with M.O.M. to the waters of this lake. If no reply came, it meant that the request was denied.

The first bristles of the sun's brush that stroked away the fine morning mist had just started their task when Three Hands took to his trail. The trail led along the edge of the stream and was not new to him, for he had traversed it many times on herb excursions. After traveling five suns, however, the trail was no longer familiar and each succeeding sun led him further into virgin territory. He was resolute in his course and took no time from the trail to explore for medicinal purposes, although he did make mental notes of promising areas.

Each day, the sun's gift of warmth grew less generous, and his decision to take his buffalo robe proved to be a wise one. The air took on a crispness that was evident by the creation of "smoke signals" with each exhale of breath. The forest grew thinner and the white tops of distant mountains came closer each day. His mind had but one thought: to reach his destination and return with solutions to the problems that confronted his people.

At the end of one moon's travel, he reached the edge of the Lake of Talking Waters and made his final camp. The next day, spirits willing, he would be in council with M.O.M.—sleep would be hard to come by this night!

Messin Man

The gentle warmth of the rising sun bathed Three Hands' eyelids, a natural signal that it was time to rise and greet the new day. Throwing aside his buffalo robe, he rose to a standing position and savored the panoramic scene of beauty surrounding him. Before him, the Lake of Talking Waters clasped a blanket of mist to her for comfort just as he had clung to his robe. The rising sun gave the same signal to the lake as it had to the eyelids of the messin man. Just as he cast aside his robe, the lake cast aside her mist to reflect the beauty around her in her watery eyes.

A quick bath in the water to renew his body, consumption of a dried rabbit leg, and a prayer to the Spirit of Wisdom found the messin man ready to face the challenge before him. Determined to present an image of strength, he strode boldly to the water's edge and in a strong voice stated his request: "Oh mighty Mystic Of Mountains, whose eyes can pierce the mighty oak to see the chewing ant at work, whose nose can pick up the scent of the sleeping bear in a log beneath the winter snow, whose hearing can detect the movement of the wings of a honey bee in flight, whose mind captures the movement of all things as they serve Mother Earth, I ask you to hear the voice of Three Hands, messin man of the Hiup, pleading for his people."

A voice that seemed to come from nowhere, yet seemed to come from everywhere, gave a swift reply. "Three Hands, whose gifted tongue I cannot help but hear, for it sings a melody pleasant to my ears, how can I help you?"

"Men of hairy faces are showing up in many places. Their words and their deeds are destroying my brothers and their seeds. They never give, just come and take, and that's why I'm shouting into this lake. The answers needed to survive are what I'm asking you to provide!"

"Enough! Enough! I will hear your plea if you will abide by mine. Come to me, but leave that 'corn' behind. Follow the path of the goat to the closest mountain top, but when you get there, you must not stop," instructed the voice.

Three Hands looked about him and saw what seemed to be a rough trail leading up the side of the closest mountain, and began his climb. He spent the better part of the day ascending the trail; its difficulty was evident by the cuts and bruises on his body. At last he reached a point on the trail where part of the mountain leveled off, forming a small clearing. He had not reached the top, however, as walls of sheer stone rose from two sides of the clearing.

Cautiously making his way to the edge of the clearing, he saw that the side of the mountain dropped straight down to a mass of boulders and rocks piled near the edge of the lake. He sat on a nearby rock to analyze his position. The voice had instructed him to get to the top, but not to stop. This was the top, as far as any further movement upward was concerned, since he certainly lacked even the basic skills of flight. Deciding to examine the clearing more closely, he started at the edge near the trail and carefully surveyed the wall of stone, not finding a hand or foothold for climbing. He came to the end of the wall and looked out to the space beyond.

He was on the verge of concluding that he had erred selecting this mountain when his acute peripheral vision caught sight of a slight outcropping from the side of the sheer wall overlooking the lake below. Closer examination gave him little cause for exuberance. There was a single ledge of rock, no wider than his hand, jutting out of the wallface and extending out of sight after about twenty paces. To use this ledge, one would have to hug the wallface while walking sideways on his toes. This was no trail for the weak of heart!

A myriad of reasons to disregard this trail as illogical and fruitless surged through his mind. Not one, however, could replace the priority of completing his mission.

Stripping himself of all articles that might be encumbrances to his balance, he made his way to the ledge, clad only in a loincloth. He even left his moccasins behind so that his feet would have the greatest degree of sensitivity to the ledge rock.

Extending his arm upward, he took his first step sideways onto the ledge. His hands and arms were of no value for gripping the rock face, but they were a positive influence in maintaining his balance. He flattened his body and his arms against the rockface so that only his heels did not have contact with the rock. His vision was limited to the small area at his shoulder formed by his right arm reaching for the wall. By casting his eyes slightly downward, he could peek through this limited space and see the ledge area about four paces to the right. His progress was measured by the width of his feet, not by paces. A glance upward would have broken his concentration, which was vital for any progress on this trail. His toes were the only source of guidance and his prayer was that they would continue to send the message that the trail continued and did not end in space.

To Three Hands' amazement (and total relief), the trail was a short one of about twenty paces, yet it seemed like a lifetime of sidesteps. The trail curved around the face of the cliff and ended at a grassy area similar to the one he had left, only larger. As he stepped from the ledge, he heard the voice that had directed him to reach this point.

"Well done, my brother. You have proven yourself equal to the task with courage and vision. You have earned the right to council."

Three Hands looked in the direction of the voice. He saw a figure seated in front of an opening in the rockface. A small fire blazed in front of the figure and a small stream of water fell from a ledge above, continuing across the glade to disappear over the edge of the clearing.

The figure beckoned him to come closer. As Three Hands approached, he saw before him a small man with long flowing hair as white as the snow on the mountain tops. His skin was wrinkled from the passing of countless suns so that his eyes and mouth seemed to be but miniature cave openings in the wrinkles. His only apparel was a loincloth, but Three Hands noticed a blanket folded on a rock at his side. The figure spoke again.

"Welcome to my lodge, Three Hands. I have looked forward to your coming since the reception of your signal fire. The winds have carried your reputation. I have lit the pipe and ask you to join me in thanking the spirits for guiding you here safely."

"Thank you, M.O.M., for your welcome. I come with a divided heart. Half is filled with joy for your prompt response to my signal fire, yet the other half is filled with despair by the problems my people face," replied the messin man.

They kept the formalities of the pipe, and the host moved to accommodate the needs of his guest. "I have some eggs that brother Hawk has shared with me. See that brother Fire does not leave us while I prepare them."

Three Hands moved to secure some wood for the fire from a stack near the cave entrance. At the conclusion of the meal, M.O.M. said, "We have fed the body, now we must rest the brain. At the next sun we will talk. Take this blanket to keep the night chill from your body."

The messin man awoke to find his host still seated on the rock next to the fire's embers. He had no covering, yet appeared to suffer no discomfort. The sun was presenting its early offering of warmth as he folded the blanket and returned it to its place on the rock. M.O.M. sat unmoving, with his eyes closed. There was no indication that the breath of life flowed within him. Three Hands placed more wood on the fire, took a position near it facing his host, and waited.

The sun had made such progress on its circle hoop that its generosity of warmth made the fire unnecessary. Then, M.O.M. moved. His eyes slowly opened and bound Three Hands' gaze to his. He spoke, "I have just paused from a journey within myself. I will rest from that journey so that I may hear the reason for the sadness in your heart. It is my desire that I can be of help in removing this burden. Tell me, what is the source of this suffering that has brought your trail to join mine?"

The messin man was eager to answer, but mental discipline compelled him to carefully choose his words of reply. There must be no mistake in presenting a clear definition of the problem. "My people are faced with a problem so great that the lands shared with us by Mother

Earth, under the guidance of the Everywhere Spirit, may soon be lost to men of another color if a solution is not found to prevent it. The very existence of our people is at stake. Our brothers from the east have lost their lands and the lives of many brothers to this invader. We have learned that courage, coexistence, or pleading is not the answer, and councils have not provided solutions to this problem."

"You come to me with questions and expect the answers? The answers lie within you, my brother. The secrets of the night skies are within one's own mind. To walk among the stars, one has only to open his senses and allow the questions to enter and be answered. One does not have to speak to communicate. Do the trees speak to tell you of the seasons? One's eyes and ears are entrances to the tipi of the mind. The answers will come to you if you remember the lessons learned by our brothers to the east.

"In dealing with the hairy ones, you must deal from strength, for your opponent will take anything less as cause for grasping the initiative. When one reaches the point of pleading, he has lost the argument. There can only be equals within your own circle. Your nation's hoop must never be broken. The hairy ones have weapons that can kill with sound. After you hear the sound, you or one of your brothers will be dead if their aim is true. They cannot be defeated in face-to-face battles. Illusion is your only weapon that is superior to theirs.

"The people of the hairy ones are ignorant of Mother Earth. They use the land, but put nothing back to continue her balance. They wish to call that land theirs alone and do not wish to share, yet they expect you to share with them. Give them nothing for they are like children, and unless guided toward the true meaning of the circle, will break it and cause destruction for all that follow. Guide them toward the knowledge that the Everywhere Spirit will be true to them only if they obey His laws. You must plan to guide them!

"Some men will come speaking of the Great Spirit, but giving Him different names. Some are honest and sincere, yet most will use these names to deceive you while they destroy you and your ways. The customs of the red man must not be cast aside as useless and replaced with customs of the whites!"

"I hear your words, oh Wise One, but the tipi of my mind must have no entrance," Three Hands reminded. "How can so few stop so many when tribes larger than the Hiup have failed?"

"You speak true when you say that the tipi of your mind has no opening. I have said that the answers lie within you and I will show you that my words are true. See the small stream of water near your hand?

Place your hand across it and try to stop the flow. What do your eyes observe?"

"The stream stopped and gathered its strength until it was able to run over my hand and continue its trail," replied Three Hands.

"Take this stick and draw two lines in the earth in different directions, yet both touching the stream."

Three Hands complied, then stated, "I see the stream sending some of its water to follow in the lines I drew in the earth."

"Is the force of the stream stronger or weaker than when you held your hand to stop its movement?" M.O.M. continued.

"It is weaker, for now it is divided."

"The water is not unlike the hairy ones. Is there now an opening in your mental tipi?" a hopeful M.O.M. asked.

"I have learned that one does not try to stop the water, but by dividing the path it takes, one can control where and how fast it can flow. My heart flows with gratitude for this lesson you have taught me!" Three Hands responded.

"I have taught you nothing. I have only guided your own power of observation to make the trail easier to take. Go now and let me return to the trail within me. This rest has refreshed me and I am anxious to be on my way. Beware of what is carried by the stream!" With these words, the ancient one's eyes seemed to lose their fire and his body became like stone. Three Hands quietly withdrew and returned to the ledge to begin the trail back to his people.

The return trail should have been faster than the trail to M.O.M., but it was not. The trail did not completely fill Three Hands' mental processes, for there had been opportunities to observe new territory and relate it to his medicinal needs. He also needed time to ingest his learning and move the components around until a logical structure took form. His pace was a mere byproduct of an internal gear system turned by his brain.

The priority set by his brain was to arrive at camp with an infallible presentation of his interpretations of M.O.M.'s lessons and advice. His arrival would not take place until all requirements were met. All loopholes must be closed before he entered camp. His presentation must not only magnify the need for a master plan, but also the sacrifices that would be demanded of all to carry this plan to fruition and success. Even though his eyes saw the trail, his pace was determined by this priority of his mind.

When he finally reached the camp, all components were in place. He raised his hands to a cupping position around his mouth and gave the "whoop of victory" to indicate his return. All camp actions stopped and each tribal member and guest moved to their assigned ceremonial position. Chief Ten, the only exception, remained in his tipi.

Three Hands entered at a quick pace, which brought murmurs from those gathered. Anyone's entrance to a group setting is measured by first impression. The significance of one's entrance is tantamount to success or failure with that group. A brave returning from a successful hunt would enter in a slow, deliberate manner to give the impression of survival courage. The quickened pace of Three Hands indicated that time was extremely important and an announcement of grave significance was to be made. The tribe and guests, being aware of his mission, grew apprehensive, as there was no sign of joy on the face of their messin man.

Chief Ten, waiting in the inner sanctum of his tipi, looked through the slit of the flap and also noted the face of his messenger. He heard the rising murmurs of the gathering as Three Hands approached the tipi entrance. Even the drummers, who normally loved to amplify the emotions of the event through their music upon hearing a "whoop of victory," observed the face of the messenger and muted their responses. When Three Hands reached the tipi of his chief, there was silence.

Chief Ten emerged from his lodge and greeted his messenger. "Three Hands, we welcome you back from the trail. I can read in your eyes that your trail has been a difficult one to travel. We are anxious to hear your news, but you have been long on the trail. Your mind and your body must be refreshed before you report. There can be no forgetting of any incident, no matter how trivial it may seem. Go, there is food in the luk pots and silence in your tipi. We will prepare the council fire and await your news."

"I thank you for your greetings and warm welcome," replied Three Hands. "It is true that my trail has been a difficult one, and I have much to tell. I heed your wise words and will report to you at the council fire."

He refreshed himself at the luk pots, at the waterfall, and finally at his tipi, where he sat to meditate and quickly review his coming presentation. Satisfied, he rose and made his way to the waiting audience. Every member of the tribe and every guest was curious to know if they were to be a part of future tales, since they would be firsthand witnesses to one who had personally spoken to M.O.M.

Three Hands began by reliving every detail of his trail to M.O.M. His ability to not only present the facts, but also incorporate his mental processes into situations, made the recitation come alive. There was no rush to conclude his narrative until he was certain that the ingredient seeds for planning were sown.

"M.O.M. has shown me that the answer to our problem lies within us, that we, of all nations of our people, must plan and act as one if we are to survive the objective of the white man—to drive us from our lands to starve. If we cannot bring our brothers to think as one, we must be prepared to die. Our lands, those of the Hiup, will be the lancepoint facing the white man."

"What do you mean by all nations?" asked Chief Ten.

"Every band, every tribe, and every nation west of the waters of the Mississippi and those east of the Mississippi who have yet to bow to the invaders," answered the messin man.

"We must council," said Sittin Pretty. Recalling the concern of his people regarding the chico bean effects, he added, "Let my people act as messengers and carry word of this council to be held in three moons. This will relieve your people of the heavy task of sharing your food and your lands. It will allow your people to make ready for the camp of great numbers that will come."

"You speak wise words, my brother. Let us prepare to act at once," Chief Ten advised. "Your people will be helped to prepare for this important trail. We do not know how much time we have to council and act before the white man comes."

Three Hands was pleased that he had presented the necessity for widespread planning and the urgency for doing so. Action to follow was the next priority on his list, for he was aware of the natural urge for initial action and enthusiasm and its tendency to wane if the action was to be delayed.

For seven suns, preparations were made to get Sittin Pretty and his people on the trail. Sittin Pretty was an exceptional administrator with remarkable insight. He had an excellent grasp of the total picture and of his available resources. The younger braves were sent, accompanied by their families and one older and experienced brave, to the most distant lands. They, as did the others, had the responsibility of igniting a chain reaction that would spread until all nations had received the message. Urgency was instilled in every member of the tribe. All would be reunited in three moons, here in the lands of the Hiup.

Three moons of waiting for the coming of the Grand Council was not time to be wasted. If the impetus were to be maintained, the Hiup had much to do. Three Hands went to his chief for council, then expressed his concerns. "We are not familiar with the ways and the language of the white man and know nothing of his plans, except what we have been told. M.O.M. has warned that the Hiup hold the most vital position in the success of this venture. We have no experience in battle and no weapons of war or action planning, yet we have been chosen as the lancepoint. Every nation and tribe will be looking to us for leadership and guidance in the role they must play in the master battle plan. Our ignorance will not likely instill confidence in our brothers. They may take our ignorance as a lack of courage."

"You have raised good points to consider," replied Chief Ten, nodding his head in approval. "To know for ourselves may eliminate many potential trouble spots. We must find a way to resolve these problems before the Grand Council, and I can see no other way except through direct contact. To take the war trail to do battle with no experience would cause the deaths of many braves, yet not assure obtaining the information we seek. What are your thoughts on this, Messin Man? What do you see of the future?"

"I have returned from a vision quest this day," answered Three Hands. "I saw my brother, the blue jay, among a family of squirrels. Brother Squirrel seemed skeptical and nervous at first in the presence of Brother Jay. Brother Jay observed the family as they went about gathering nuts to store for the winter, but he did nothing to interfere or alarm the family. He knew that if he attacked or presented a danger to the family or its food supply, he could expect retaliation from the squirrels. By using his eyes, he was able to see where the family was storing their nuts. When the squirrels left to seek nuts in another area, Brother Jay helped himself to the nuts from the hollow tree and transferred them to his own storehouse. He got his food and avoided danger to himself."

"Your vision quest has been most successful," beamed an exuberant Chief Ten. "We can send braves to observe the hairy ones, yet not do battle with him. They can return with the information we seek. It is but a matter of selecting those best suited for our purpose."

"Too many Brother Blue Jays may defeat our purpose if they appear at the same time," suggested Three Hands. "The squirrels were not alarmed by the one jay, but their response to additional jays may have alarmed them to the point of battle. I have a suggestion. Do you recall the performance of Loon Caller at the last corn planting ceremony? He made us all laugh when he pretended to be Tune, brother to the loon. He has a good mind and can appear to be something other than what he is. His voices of the birds and animals sound exactly like our brothers of the forest."

"I have a plan!" exclaimed Chief Ten, seemingly smitten by a non-binding force of genius. "I will send Loon Caller to the land east of the Mississippi. He can move among the white men and learn their ways, their language, and any plans they have that include us. He could report back to me before the Grand Council meets."

"You are the wisest of chiefs and one who does not wait for the rain to fall before planting," a demulcent Three Hands extolled. In his mind he crossed off another priority.

Loon Caller was an avid student of his brother birds and animals. His mind was quick to distinguish the different mating calls of the birds of the woodlands. With a little practice, he could master calls to such a degree of perfection that the birds responded instantly and naturally. His favorite was the loon that inhabited the small lakes and ponds that abounded in Hiup territory. This choice indicated a solid trait of humor.

The call of the loon is one that has enough peculiarity in sound that, when heard, causes spontaneous laughter in those who hear it (with the exception of a real loon). Many an unattainable goal of conquest with a serious-minded maiden was attained when he sounded the mating call of the loon. The sound acted as an icebreaker and usually brought a giggle or smile to the owner of a previously impervious defense. Who could resist one who appeared so innocent and harmless? Braves, too, were not immune to reacting to this inoffensive upstart. Loon Caller was liked by everyone.

It was this characteristic that came to the mind of Chief Ten when he mentally perused his choice of who would best serve the purpose of the trail. He wanted one who would never appear offensive and was sharp of mind, a skilled observer who could quickly learn the language of the white man. He summoned Loon Caller and detailed the mission. Loon readily accepted.

Three Hands amplified the importance of this trail when he went to give Loon a talisman pouch to keep him from harm. "This pouch will be of no use to you if the white man sees through your ruse and learns the purpose of your trail. You must know when to hold and when to fold back into the shadows. You will be of no use to your people if you do not learn and return. Be back as near the first moon as you can," Three Hands directed.

Loon made preparations for his trail, then headed east toward the Mississippi. The Hiup were busy in his absence, making preparations for the council and the large numbers that were expected to attend. Remembering the effect the large number of Wiseolas had upon their daily routine, they decided to locate the council camp at the base of the pass near the waterfall. The meeting itself would be held on the plateau, befitting the importance of the Hiup in any battle plans. The resources of the tribe would be less taxed if the guests secured most of their food supply from the plains below.

There was so much to be done that sun after sun passed with hardly a letup in the pace. Loon Caller's return to camp made the Hiup aware of the passage of time. Had he really been on the trail for a moon? "Not only a full moon, but part of the second," he reminded them.

The Hiup had worked so hard and diligently that only the final phase of the preparations needed completion. Chief Ten, Has It Made,

Three Hands, and the Gray Panthers welcomed the opportunity to slow down and examine Loon's report to see what changes had to be made in their original projections.

A council fire was made and the pipe passed before Loon rose to make his report. "My trail led me to the largest of the white man's camps on the eastern bank of the Mississippi. A Choctaw brave I met told me that it was a camp of ten thousand and that more whites were arriving every sun to add to that number. The number of red brothers in this camp were fewer than the fingers of my hands and all were considered savages of the lowest order by the whites.

"Red Mud, the Choctaw, gave me the same advice you gave me, Three Hands. Do nothing to alarm the white man and be constantly on the move if you wish to continue living. If a red man stayed in one place too long, the white man would find some excuse to kill him. I moved among them, observing their habits and customs. My movements and actions were such as to not violate their customs or focus attention on myself.

"I set as my first priority the learning of their language. I thought if any of my actions did arouse hostile feelings, I could speak with them and modify those feelings through explanation. I soon found the best resource for learning the language—the cubs. The natural curiosity of cubs, who have yet learned to hate, offered simplicity of language and a friendliness of exchange.

"My experience of talking with my bird and animal brothers was an invaluable asset in getting the cubs interested in talking with me." Chief Ten gave himself a mental pat on the back when he heard this. "A few calls of the redwing and mallard in the presence of the cubs aroused their curiosity, and they readily gathered around me. Once I had a group, we started to exchange languages: my sign language for their spoken word. A few suns of exchanges made excellent teachers and friends of us all. This, along with gifts of my special reed whistles, gave me the knowledge of enough words to communicate with the white man. I was able to move casually among the adults to listen and learn of any plans they were making.

"I soon learned which men I could speak to and which to avoid. The white man seems to have the habit of doing everything quickly, often without rhyme or reason. They walk from place to place at a fast pace, they eat their food quickly, their words come from their mouths quite fast, and they always seem to be in motion, with little time for rest. They remind me of our brothers, the ants, when one discovers food and runs around to spread the news. I found it best to avoid the fast-moving whites, as they become hostile when their intentions are interrupted.

"There are some whites who are the very opposite—not many, but some. They like to spend their time sitting around watching the others scurry about. These few are always males and they continually drink a liquid from a jar they call a 'bottle.' The speech of these men is very slow and easier to learn early in the day; it gets slower and more difficult to learn as the sun passes.

"When asked about my people and why I was in this camp, I told them that my people had not accepted my teachings and asked me to leave. As an outcast in the eyes of the whites, I was the lowest form of red man and the least dangerous. However, as a teacher, I held a position of respect among some whites, especially the younger adults and some females. I found it advantageous to change my name from time to time to upgrade my position as a teacher and to gain wider acceptance by the whites. I told them my name was Outta Tune, but later changed it to suit my purpose.

"The white man respects power and seems to be constantly working and planning to increase his own power or that of his group. He also fears power in the hands of others and will not challenge it until he is certain his power is greater. The only other fear he demonstrated was fear of the unknown. There seems to be a deep division among them that, for me, is difficult to understand. Those with power fear only the unknown, while those of little or no power seem to derive strength from a source of the unknown they call God.

"I tried to stay as long as possible and learn as much as I could before starting my return trail. The time finally came, as you predicted, Three Hands, for me to fold back into the shadows. To have remained longer would have endangered the final purpose of my mission—to return and report my findings to you.

"These things I have learned from my trail: many of the white man's words and symbols are not to be trusted; they live in large camps until it becomes too crowded and then they move; some thought the camp that I visited would grow to fifty thousand; the white man thinks himself superior to men of other colors; finally, there should be no movement by them in this direction before spring."

Chief Ten complimented Loon Caller on his report. "You have done well, Loon Caller. The information you have shared with us will be discussed in more detail and its meaning examined during the Grand Council. From what you say, we still have some time to meet and plan how best to greet the white man, if he decides to invade our lands in the spring. Until the council meets, you can use the time to teach us the words of the white man's tongue."

Activity continued unabated in preparation for the arrival of the potentates from the west. Smoke signals were observed and read; they stated the first arrivals would soon arrive in camp.

The third moon also would make its presence known, along with a challenge to the Hiup's first line of defense—the chico bean. Excitement was not the only thing building in the air, and the first arrival was not from the west but from the east! The new arrival slipped into Hiup lands unseen, but its presence soon became known to all who practiced breathing through the nose. There were a number of remarks passed regarding the new scent of the east wind. Humorous remarks became a part of daily conversation until the stench was so bad that it became a reason of concern for all.

The elders of the tribe voiced daily complaints to their chief about their difficulty in breathing. Chief Ten, now on guard against an invasion of any kind from the east, decided to act. If this smell was part of the white man's battle plans, council or no council, he was not going to be caught napping!

Calling his braves together, he explained his concerns for the elders of the tribe and the possible danger this scent could be to the entire tribe. The source of the odor had to be found and eliminated! He chose Wise Owl to be the leader of a party whose mission would be to seek and destroy the source of their discomfort. Wise Owl selected his men, put his nose to the sky, and inhaled some of the pungent odor. With outstretched arm he signaled the direction of his trail and led his men in that direction.

The Great Spirit's sense of humor was in evidence once more as He introduced another player to his game board.

⬅══ Chapter Four ══➡

There are no trails completely devoid of dangers that rise to block the trail and challenge the traveler. Since all trails are circles, the dangers must be removed for the trail to continue.

He had come wheezing and panting up the trail from the east and may have gone unnoticed, except that he was traveling upwind from the Hiup camp. After being on the trail for more than a month, and being a devout believer that water's only value was as a necessary ingredient in the creation of good whiskey, Angus' arrival in Hiup territory was announced by the wind. That wind carried the message that something was definitely rotten in Hiup!

Angus, until six weeks before, had been a distiller of the smoothest blend of Scotch whiskey to pass one's lips on its way to the body's catalytic converter known as the kidneys, but his love of adventure, the challenge of the unknown, and an overpowering drive to explore virgin territory kept him on the move. It was this latter aptitude, more than the others, that won him the nickname of "Jock." When he put this aptitude into action with Bonnie Kate in a hayloft near Glasgow, it led to his sudden decision to leave Scotland—that plus the pursuit of Kate's wild-eyed, vengeance-seeking, claymore-wielding father, Ian Stewart, who had accidentally discovered them in the hayloft entwined in a position that to him was uncompromising!

Jock's need for optimum speed in departing his beloved heather-covered hills left him with time to gather but three prized possessions: his bagpipes, a custom-designed tooled leather scabbard (lovingly referred to by Kate as "Jock's Strap"), and his Heritage. His Heritage was a "blend," the formula for which was needlepointed on the inner flap of his sporran by his dear, departed mother. She knew that this was the last thing that Angus would part with, even if it meant his life. His sporran was oversized and designed to hold samples of the Heritage, which was more effective than money when it came to bartering.

It was Angus' good fortune that there was a ship at the end of the quay, which he traversed at great speed (for Angus was a non-swimmer), that it was just hoisting anchor to leave port for the new country, and that the captain had a severe weakness for good whiskey. A sample keg got him aboard ship; two more for food, and two as antidotes for seasickness got him to New Amsterdam. Several additional kegs earned him the necessities of life as he made his way west to St. Lou E.

St. Lou E, at that time, was the last outpost of civilization and a fast growing town in this new country of America. Angus had gone as far as he dared (his aptitude as an explorer was limited to the female anatomy), so he decided to settle and enter the business world as a distiller. Surely Ian Stewart, though well known for his tenacity, as well as his ferocity when it came to defending his family's honor, would not reach him here. St. Lou E was to Angus as the edge of the world was to those skeptical of Christopher Columbus' theory. Only fools ventured this close to the unknown when they didn't have to.

Fate, at a single toss of the coin, had flipped two flies into his soup, so to speak. The first fly was encountering Reverend Tune, a real live, honest-to-goodness Injun who represented the feared savages occupying the lands west of the river. Angus had heard of the natives encountered by the English, French, and Spanish explorers when they came to this new country. Their numbers had been reduced to such a minuscule total by the westward "Christian" movement that he had not encountered any before Tune.

This "token" Injun explained to all who would listen that he was a former member of the Hiup nation and had dedicated his life to the real messenger of the Everywhere Spirit: the loon. His mission, he explained, was to convert others to this belief. By carefully and faithfully emulating the loon, his followers would be identified as recipients of any messages sent by this Everywhere Spirit. They lived their destiny as the "chosen ones."

Tune gave one the impression that he was not playing with a full quiver of arrows and was driven by a force of unparalleled optimism toward an obvious brick wall. He admitted that he had not one single convert to his credit among his own people. In fact, his tribe had labeled him a heretic and had implanted the suggestion in his mind that the great lands east of the Mississippi had uncountable numbers of true believers awaiting his call. He Who Thinks Himself In Tune was out of tune with his people. After casting the partridge bones to determine the direction of the trail, he had taken the one to St. Lou E. Now he was busy at work converting the white man from ignorance to the highest level of lunacy.

Tune's experience with the white man and his so-called "civilized" society began at St. Lou E. It did not take him long to figure out the white man's philosophy regarding Injuns. To them, a living Injun was a heathen who had to be converted to Christianity. Once converted, he was admitted to the white man's society at the lowest, never-to-be-raised level (but still accepted as proof of white supremacy, compassion, and morality).

The first act for true acceptance was to have a Christian name. This was easy. Outta Tune became Oral Tune. Oral was a well known and respected name in religious circles, and so it seemed a good choice. The second requirement for acceptance was to show that he was indeed a convert, so he formed his own religious group called the Loonies.

The ultraconservative nature of the white man had at its core the Ten Commandments, fear of God, and the firm belief that it was the white man's destiny to save all nonbelievers through conversion, immersion, or both. A man was considered a good Christian if he observed the rules. To twist these rules hypocritically to suit a purpose was an acceptable practice if it could be interpreted as in line with the local rules. A new religious order was accepted as good until it was determined by the "good townspeople" that the order's beliefs were contrary to local interpretation of the rules.

Tune's flock of converts numbered only five—three males and two females—but his reputation in the community was growing. The "good" people were taking notice. His flock of Loonies could be easily identified by their manner of moving from one place to another. With Oral in the lead, the group would move at a rapid pace, using baby steps for two hundred paces. This movement was accompanied by rapid up-and-down movement of the arms while emitting the mating call of their revered loon. The group would then return to a normal pace with no sound, but with a to-and-fro movement of the head, as if looking for a lost (or new) mate. The first procedure would then be repeated.

The initial consensus of most adults in the town was that this was just a fad and, like intestinal gas, would pass. One local humorist suggested changing the name of the town to St. Loonie, which brought a gale of laughter from bystanders. Another gained attention and instant gratification by shouting, "Here come the Loonie Tunes!" Still another, later to become a convert, stated with an air of intimate knowledge that he knew for a fact the sound produced by the Loonies was an ancient

Indian love call. When truly reproduced, the call acted as an aphrodisiac to the opposite sex. This raised a few eyebrows (and hopes) among many of the young citizens. However, the severe and thorough indoctrination of piousness by their parents destroyed any thoughts of change or experimentation.

Oral, in an effort to influence more of these susceptible whites, decided that another name change was in order. He thereafter introduced himself as the Reverend Loon. As the spiritual leader of the Loonies, the name seemed more in line with the establishment and the rules. Those who were tottering on the brink of decision might fall his way if his group projected an acceptable level of piety. Being led by a "reverend" might just provide the push needed.

To the youngsters of the town, his appeal was something else. The children thought his manner of movement was far out, and thus worthy of imitating. Like the Pied Piper, Reverend Tune and his group had a large following of children wherever they went; the children waved their arms and tried to reproduce the love call. For a while the group's actions and movement served as entertainment for the children, as well as the townspeople. In time, however, attention started to focus on the group in a negative way. Once negative comments are allowed to overpower common sense, even the most unobtrusive act can be changed to an unacceptable one by the mind, to be destroyed before common sense can once again prevail.

Some mothers, perhaps in a moment of personal jealousy over the attraction of their children to a perfect stranger, saw fit to point out to the town fathers the similarity to the notorious Pied Piper. Their fears and concern brought action. Reverend Tune and his group were politely, yet firmly, given the choice of leaving town quietly and promptly, or having their appearance changed to add more realism to their act through the application of tar and feathers!

On his way out of town, Reverend Tune met Angus. Angus had just completed a personal quality check of his latest batch of Heritage, and was in a very receptive mood for conversation. Angus knew of the reverend through conversation with others, but had never met him. His curiosity, perhaps influenced by the Heritage, led Angus to invite the reverend to sit and talk. They sat outside the entrance to the distillery and Angus listened halfheartedly as Tune spoke of his spiritual mission, his birthplace, his people, the fish, the chips, the frivolous white man, and the Everywhere Spirit.

Angus' mind was half a world away, roamin' the heather, as Tune spoke. The return trip was instantaneous as his homesick ears picked up the two dearest words in the Scottish language: fish and chips. (There are those who would leap to argue that the two dearest words are Scotch whiskey!) Did this strange-looking babbler say "free fish and chips in abundance?" The words "fish and chips" may have served as the transport vehicle, but to those who know the Scots, the word "free" must be given credit for the vehicle's speed. The picture of a Shangri La came to his mind, if only for a fleeting moment.

With a light heart and a sobered mind, he grasped the initiative in a manner that politely upheld his part in balancing the conversation. He literally oozed interest as he asked Loon to retrace his steps since leaving his tribe and coming to St. Lou E. Which direction did you go? Which trails were used? What means are used to identify a trail? Any particular dangers encountered? How long did it take? He filed each response in the back of his canny mind, then wished Reverend Loon the best of luck, success in his mission, and good-bye.

Angus recalled the directions to Hiup quite unexpectedly, just one week later, when the second fly landed in his soup. The event was a visit to Angus' distillery by an Irish aristocrat turned salesman by the name of Count Tee. The Count came to sell Angus on the finest corks known to man. Anyone familiar with the distilling process knows the value of a well-corked cask to the finished product, and a Count Tee cork was the pride of all Ireland.

The count, prepared for a hard sell to a man from an ethnic group known for its thrift, was pleasantly surprised when Angus became unusually attentive to his words. The reason, luckily for him, was his mention of meeting one of Angus' countrymen in Louisville. By coincidence, this man was seeking the whereabouts of a man called Angus MacDaniels. Could he be the one?

Angus immediately let the count know that his name was Jock MacDaniels, and therefore he was not the man mentioned. There could be some relationship in his blood line, but not to his knowledge. When asked to describe this man in Louisville, the count stated that he was one of the most ferocious, wild-eyed, and intent men he had ever met in this country. Also, this man carried a huge sword, with which he constantly slashed at some imaginary opponent. The strange man had mentioned something about "honor and vengeance, if it took forever!"

Wee Jock did two things almost simultaneously. He gave the count a staggering order for two thousand gross of corks (knowing that he would not be there to accept delivery) and he switched careers from distiller to explorer-adventurer. He urged the count to make haste returning to fill the order and to speak with no one regarding it. He then put his distillery up for sale, and it sold the very next day; it was well stocked with a product that was in great demand at local taverns. Filling his sporran with samples and a sack of barley seeds, securing his Jock strap, heaving his bagpipes under one arm and a five gallon keg of

Heritage under the other, he set out to retrace the steps of Reverend Loon to Hiup.

Having reached the pass, he decided to sit a spell and catch his wind. He had cast quite a figure coming up the incline to the pass: five feet two inches tall with blazing red hair growing profusely in all directions from his head, topped by a red and green tam-o'-shanter with an orange tourie. He matched the splendor of a brilliant rainbow. A beard and mustache that matched his hair all but hid his wee eyes and mouth. A once-white tunic was crossed by a grand green-and-black plaid and by a claymore scabbard. His bulging sporran hung before a once-flowing kilt that could now stand alone. Knee-high woolen argyle socks of black and blue covered each leg; each sock contained a trusty dirk.

The consumption of another sample keg of Heritage put Angus in the mood for a fling on his bagpipes. He reached for his beloved instrument, and it was at this precise moment that the Hiup braves arrived on the scene.

The braves had been given a specific directive from their chief to locate and eliminate the cause of the foul odor that was causing so much discomfort. This odor had permeated every nook and cranny of the Hiup camp, causing distress among the inhabitants. Particularly hard hit had been the elderly braves, who had spent hours in council meetings smoking the pipe. The weakened condition of their lungs made it impossible to expel this new odor properly, resulting in near suffocation.

The braves speculated about the source of this foul scent as they made their way on the trail. Drawing upon their experiences on other trails, they all came to the same conclusion. This was no dead and decomposing skunk or any other known animal; there was something unearthy about it. One brave suggested that the sun god, Uranus, had defecated as he passed overhead. After a brief discussion of the odds of this happening, they dismissed the thought.

The party had struggled to get upwind from the source in order to speed up the pace and clear their eyes, which were watering profusely. The strategy brought them to a point below the pass where they found the air clear. The consensus of opinion was that the source had to be on the trail at the top of the pass, so they moved up the trail.

Sharp Eyes was the first to locate the alien object. Signaling to the others, he fell to his knees and began to crawl forward. The dense brush at the sides of the trail provided excellent cover as they worked their way to within a hundred paces of the object on the trail before them. Through years of practice on the hunt, they had mastered the skill of moving leaves and small branches aside with undetectable movements.

Now all eyes could clearly make out the object, as well as the swarm of flies buzzing about it. The object did not move, so whatever it was, they considered it dead until Long Ears detected a wheezing sound coming from it.

The question in the mind of each brave (beyond the object's identity) was whether it posed a threat to them. After a whispered discussion, they decided to send Best Foot forward for a closer look while the others waited with their bows at the ready, a precautionary move that would later be referred to as the "volunteer" move.

It was just coincidental that the very moment Best Foot made his move, Angus reached for his bagpipes. To the dumbfounded group, the object under surveillance appeared to have arms which picked up an animal with long horns and stuck it in the area where a head should be located! This was taken as an offensive move that could be injurious to the health of the party. They arrowed up and prepared to shoot.

A split second before launch, the sound the animal made with the long horns after he pushed them into his head was of such a nature that it brought an instant chill to the spine of each brave. Their eardrums were subjected to such torture that weapons were dropped and hands moved to cover their ears in a desperate effort to gain relief! Their feet, fortunately, were not affected by the sound, so they were able to react on a survival impulse from the brain and speed away.

This sudden movement, resembling a flock of quail taking flight, was within range of Angus' peripheral vision, and he stopped playing. Turning in the direction of the flight, he tried to get their attention. This proved to be difficult, for the flock ran with their hands over their ears.

A short, yet safe, distance down the trail, the braves stopped and removed their hands from their ears. The sound had stopped, so they turned and looked back up the trail. The creature was standing erect and appeared to be signaling them with two humanlike arms. As a precautionary measure, they took positions behind trees and peered out from this defensive position to evaluate the situation.

Angus called out a greeting to them as soon as he saw them remove their hands from their ears. "Cum now laddies, ther-r-res na a need t' fear-r-r. I'm na a her-r-re ta do ye har-r-rm!"

The braves had seen and heard their first white man (although they hand not yet identified the creature as such). If the old expression regarding first impressions held true, the white man might never have expanded his domination beyond the Kie Ro Practic Mountains. It could be said that the one trait of the American Indian most responsible for his downfall was his acceptance of all men as equals. On the other hand, the white man preached the theory of equality, but never quite mastered the practice of it.

Messin Man

After a brief conference, the party moved back up the trail until they reached the perimeter of the scent circle. The smell was so overpowering that they covered their nostrils with the only available objects—their loincloths. Still, they were apprehensive and ready to attack at the slightest hint of an offensive movement on the part of the creature. This presented a dilemma to them, as they would need their hands to man their weapons. Even though the creature made sounds that seemed remotely human, they observed (through profusely watering eyes) fur on the face and head, and the colors on its attire. This creature resembled a walking rainbow!

Angus was also a bit apprehensive. His first impressions were not all positive either, for the group facing him stood with weapons cocked and at the ready. From what he could see, not all weapons were at the ready, but the sight of grown men standing with their only article of clothing covering their nose was more than he could ken. He reasoned that it must be the tribe's custom (strange as it may be). Reverend Tune had not displayed this custom, at least not in public. His mind entertained the hope that the females of the tribe also followed this custom.

Angus was aware that he was the intruder into the lands of these men and had to prove himself friendly to them—and quickly! He decided to use what little "Injun" tongue he had picked up during his conversation with Reverend Tune. He could not disguise his brogue, but he would give it his best shot. "Lower-r-r y' kilts men. Me fr-r-riend. Me cumum long way fr-r-rom land over-r-r yonder-r-r. Me knowum one of your-r-r countr-r-ry men, Loonie Tune. I cumum in peace!"

It was not apparent to Angus at first, but his manner of presentation was perfect to break the ice and set the stage for a friendly introduction to the Hiup. It is a little known fact, outside the Indian community, that they possess a great sense of humor. When the braves heard his attempt to communicate in broken English, only their extremely good manners kept them from indulging in uproarious laughter. Humor has always been a remarkable icebreaker when strangers meet.

Turning their backs on Angus to demonstrate the lack of danger to him, the braves knelt to discuss the situation and to plan their next move. The intended procedure was delayed when Splitting Sides snickered, triggering much holding of the sides and pounding of the ground in supreme efforts to keep from laughing out loud. In time, the group seemed to regain its composure until Sharp Eyes glanced at Bulging Pot, who giggled and started another round of silent mirth. Wise Owl finally signaled the group to get serious. "It looks like Loon found a fish to swallow his line. This must be what he described as a 'Loonie.' Did you hear that accent? Chief Ten and the others have got to catch this performance. Now don't say anything to spoil it before we get back to camp. I can hardly wait to see the expression on the chief's face."

"Hold on, Wise," said Splitting Sides. "We can't take him back to camp in his condition. We will have to lead and that will put us downwind from him, and personally, my nose has had it. Our mission was to get rid of the smell, remember?"

"Just leave it to me, and remember, I do all of the talking," replied Wise Owl. All in agreement, the braves turned to face Angus.

"Welcome, O hairy one of far-out colors. I, Wise Owl. You wantum to meetum our people? We takam you to our camp to meetum chief. You must first takum test of Niagara, god of waterfall. You passum test and we go see chief. You failum and you goum back to land you cumum from. You wantum to takum test?"

Angus mentally balanced the weight of his distaste of water and that of his love for living. The secondary reason for his endurance on this trail, an unending supply of fish and chips, was so close to reality that his answer came forth in a steadfast reply, "I takum test. Whatum me do?"

Wise detailed the rules. "You goum down trail. You seeum waterfall? Niagara watchum you. You must walkum across ledge at bottom of waterfall. You crossum, then go back ledge trail. If Niagara pleased, you cumum back here. Then we goum see chief."

Angus set his bagpipes, cask, and Jock strap next to a tree and set off down the steep incline to the waterfall at the base to begin his test.

"Wise, that was a stroke of genius," beamed Bent Arrow. "By the time he goes under that waterfall twice, he should lose most of that stink!"

"They don't call me Wise for nothing. But remember, the important thing is that we change nothing but the smell. When Chief Ten hears that accent, he's going to crack up. I hope he can make that sound again when he sticks those horns into his head. The pain must be terrific to cause a sound like that. It must be a way that the white man tests for courage. If so, this is one brave man. Three Hands will have to come up with some kind of a spell to cure the stranger, or earplugs for every member of the tribe and animal of the forest. Now let's get ourselves back into shape. We must have a plan to highlight our catch when we get back to camp!"

The group watched Angus as he made his way down the slope and to the waterfall. At one point, he slipped and fell. Unknowingly, Angus had experienced contact with his first "chip." He arrived at the waterfall and started across the ledge, Halfway across, the force of the falling water knocked him into the pool. Swim-crawling (the water was not over his head), he made his way to the bank and emerged to try again. This time he made it across and turned for the return trip. It took two more attempts before he successfully completed his task and returned to the hunting party. Picking up his possessions, while still dwelling on his opinion (silently, of course) of Niagara, he followed the braves into the forest on the trail to camp

What had been considered a routine, safe assignment was destined to be recorded in the annals of the Hiup and repeated around campfires for years to come. Wise Owl and his group of braves were determined to make the most of their never-to-be forgotten moment of glory. The return from the hunt was always show time in the Hiup camp, a custom originated to reward the hunters for their efforts on behalf of the tribe. A successful hunt would start a celebration that could last for days, with much singing and dancing, highlighted by the retelling of the rigors and dangers (whether real or imagined) overcome by the hunters.

Wise Owl stood at the entrance to the camp, arms outstretched to the sky; holding his bow and arrows, he gave the "Whoop of Victory!" The camp reacted instantly. The squaws and cubs stopped whatever they were doing and lined up on either side of the path that led to the tipi of Chief Ten. The braves continued this line right up to the tipi's entrance. Has It Made took a position to the right of the flap, while Three Hands stood to the left. Drummers took position with their arms poised.

Wise Owl carefully looked over the scene to make certain every detail was in place before he moved. Sharp Eyes and the other braves had been carefully placed, with Angus in the middle of their tight circle. Being more than a head shorter than the braves, he was hidden from the view of their waiting audience. Turning to Angus, Wise Owl cautioned him not to speak unless asked to do so by the chief.

Satisfied that all was in place, Wise Owl took a step forward, which was the signal for the drummers to throw themselves into their work. The group moved forward as one between the two lines, savoring not only the ego-inflating knowledge of being the center of attraction, but also the reaction of their chief and their people when they would open, flower-like, to present their tribute from the hunt. An unhurried pace would allow Chief Ten to change into an appropriate outfit. Chief Ten lived to dress and had no less than five resplendent changes hanging in his tipi.

Wise Owl led his group to the "ceremonial spot" (precisely five paces from the tipi) and stopped. The drummers, with perfect timing, stopped at that same moment. This was the signal to the chief inside that all eyes were focused on the flap of his tipi, awaiting his appearance.

Inside, Chief Ten's mind was actively seeking the reason the hunters had demanded the protocol of the "hunt's end" ceremony. He hoped they had not captured the smell and returned with it. Time would tell, but his first priority was a proper exit from his tipi. His sixty winters (forty as chief) had honed his showmanship to a flintknife's sharpness. With a gesture exemplifying innate dignity, leadership training, aloofness, and egocentricity, he flung aside the flap and stepped forward.

Not a sound was heard. Silence lay over the scene like a morning mist over a forest pond. Chief Ten's eyes moved slowly from left to right, surveying his entire audience. It was a deliberate move, not only to ascertain if protocol were being properly followed, but also to allow his audience the opportunity to examine him. Since all eyes were on him, they certainly would notice his perfectly color-coordinated attire. The beads on his snow white braids, necklace, bracelets, moccasins, and loincloth reflected the rays of the sun in a dazzling hue of blue that matched the near cloudless sky. They had cost him a bundle of pelts in a deal with a Cheyenne trader.

Satisfied that all objectives had been attained, he spoke, "Welcome, Wise Owl and proud hunters of the Hiup. Your presence has been missed and the hearts and noses of your people have longed for your safe return. I must say, in all honesty, that, to a man, we prayed that your efforts would be successful. The air has once more regained the freshness and fullness reflecting the scent of Mother Earth.

"We eagerly await your presentation revealing the evidence of success. The tale of your venture will be related over a pipe of my special mixture, 'sixty-nine,' at the council fire tonight. But now I can see it in your eyes that you have something of interest to us."

Wise Owl, with the true spirit of his own showmanship, was determined to play his role to the hilt. The presentation of Angus called for timing and flair. First, the protocol preliminaries: "Oh great chief of the Hiup, who favored us by selecting this group of braves from among all of the mighty hunters of our people, we express our gratitude. We also feel honored by this welcome from our people. From you we gained courage, strength, endurance, and steadfastness of purpose. The spells cast by Three Hands to ward off the evil spirits were as a blanket of security over us. For these good deeds we are grateful.

"We heed your words to share details of the hunt with you and our people at the council fire. It was at such settings that we learned many things about distant tribes, their lands, and their customs from those who came to trade with us."

"Wise Owl," interjected the chief, "is this another of your captivating, yet lengthy, "Brief Words of Wisdom to Live By" orations?"

Wise was primed. This slight hardly phased him, and certainly did not deter him from his prepared presentation. "Forgive me, O Patient One; I wish to be remembered as wise, not long-winded. I am merely giving a brief review to bring all of our minds to the point of oneness.

"The great Huron and Iroquois from the north, the Sioux and Lakota from the west, the Alabama and Coushattas from the south, and the Cherokee and Seneca from the east have shared tales with us. These tales have enriched our lives and increased our awareness of the bounties Mother Earth has provided for us. The Everywhere Spirit's reason for our being must be good.

"The traders from the east have told of strange men who came to their lands in great winged canoes. These men are known as the Hairy Ones, or White Men; they now move among the eastern tribes in great numbers. Some of these men have a scent beyond description. The agony and the pain these tribes must have endured from this scent must have been so terrible that the traders spared us this knowledge. These same traders have taught us a few words of the Hairy Ones' language, which Loon has expanded upon."

Wise Owl proved his mastery of timing and showmanship. "With the help of the spirits of air and water, we were able to neutralize the smell that took us on the hunt. Without further elaboration, but with a great sense of humility, we present for your viewing pleasure, a Hairy One!"

As one, the group of hunters fell to one knee, heads bowed and right arms extended toward their chief. This, of course, was the planned act and the effect was striking, to say the least. Angus stood alone in the center, as in a flower depetaled.

The entire tribe stood entranced, not moving and unsure of what the proper move should be if they had to make one. It was not unlike stalking the buffalo and reaching the point of arrow release, when suddenly the buffalo moves and you discover that it was your mother-in-law acting as a decoy. To shoot, or not to shoot—which would be the proper move? The tribe looked to their chief for direction.

Chief Ten was also momentarily in a state of shock, but only for the flicker of an eyelash. He was so cool and in command that the swallowing of his heart was barely discernible. Folding his arms, he began a slow deliberate circling of Angus. His eyes ran up and down and back and forth, covering every inch of the man before him. If there was any danger to himself or his people, he must so decide before returning to his original position.

His thoughts were many and varied as he made the circle: "I've seen bears with less hair than this one—and better looking. The Everywhere Spirit, in his great wisdom, must have had a reason for this creation, but it escapes me. The colors of his skin are gross. If this is a white man, where is the white? He must really be endowed to need a loincloth that big; Three Hands has something in common with this one. Can those be horns growing out of his armpits? Man, this fellow is just plain ugly! I hope he doesn't affect the unborn of our expecting women. I suppose I'll have to make him welcome, but he bears watching."

Having completed the circle, Chief Ten signaled Loon to his side to act as interpreter, then raised his right arm in greeting. "We welcome you, O Hairy One, to the lands of the Hiup. Our camp will be yours as long as you stay. What is your name and from where do you come?"

Angus had remembered his instructions from Wise Owl and had held his piece until now. He had been listening to and watching the preceding eloquence with interest, yet, at the same time, the wheels of his mind were churning in the formulation of some "showbiz" of his own. When the time came, he was prepared to move. That time came when the chief asked him to speak. "Me nameum is Angus Jock MacDaniels, but you can callum me Jock. Me comum fromum place crossum Great Waters called Scotland. You givum me greeting from your country. Me givum you greetings fromum mine."

With those introductory remarks, Jock drew his trump card. He deposited his cask on the ground and readied his pipes. Putting the chanter to his lips, he gave a few priming pumps with his left arm and went straightforward (with gusto) into the refrain of "Hail To The Chief!"

If all showbiz people suffered the same reaction experienced by Jock, the biz would fizz. Jock had not reached the second bar of the refrain when he raised his eyes to find himself completely alone.

The members of the tribe had been apprehensive from the moment Jock first came into view. They had looked to their chief for reassurance and guidance and found it. The male members had thoughts and evaluations that paralleled the musings of their chief. The females, however, were enraptured by the colors of his dress. They were instantly aware of the clash of colors, but assumed there was a logical explanation for the mismatch.

When Jock moved and appeared to put a horn into his head, the sound of agony he emitted was too much to bear. To a person, they had made tracks for the safety of the forest! Chief Ten's reaction was to take a step backwards and tumble head over heels into his tipi. Has It Made and Three Hands also bolted for the safety of the forest.

Wise Owl and his party were caught by surprise again as their heads were still in the bowed position. Being closer to the sound now than they were on the trail compounded their surprise. Once again, they reacted instinctively. They joined the flight of the others—with hands over their ears.

Jock realized the futility of continuing to pipe his welcome refrain when the recipient was no longer present. He strode to the tipi and pulled back the flap. "Are ye in there, Chief? Me meanum no harmum. 'Tis a blow to me heart that youm no likum my piping. I thought that I wasum pretty good at it untilum me meetum your kin. I'll puttum me pipes awa' 'til another time. Cumum now, let's sittum and talk."

Chief Ten cautiously stepped from his tipi. He was rather embarrassed that his reaction had made him appear to show fear before his people. Fortunately, they all had been running in a direction that prevented them from seeing their chief's reaction. He rationalized to himself that he merely tripped and fell while entering his lodge to procure some herb tea for the stranger.

Hearing what appeared to be an apology from Jock, he extended his arm. Jock took his hand and gave it a hearty shake. Both men laughed and Chief Ten casually signaled his people that all was well; their leader would protect them. The tribe members returned to their original positions.

Chief Ten continued his greeting, "We have welcomed you as a friend, Jock, and are eager to hear your words. I will make only one request of you: speak slow so we can translate your tongue to a point of understanding, with the help of Loon Caller. We have a little knowledge of your tongue, so the 'You talkom, me hearum is not necessary. It is a bad reflection on our language and our intelligence. We would like to serve you, as our guest, with a food of your choice. Is there a food from our lands that has special appeal to you?"

"There is one kind of food that people from my country consider the finest eating on this earth—fish and chips. I have heard that there is an abundance of them here. Can your women prepare this delicacy?" Angus inquired.

Chief Ten and every one present stood aghast. Could their ears be deceiving them? This man, a representative of the white men, was saying that fish and chips were the greatest food on earth? This new breed was illustrating savagery in its lowest form! Still, the chief had promised him that his favorite meal would be served, so in a voice that belied his sense of discomfort, he said, "We are familiar with the preparation of fish, but how do you wish your chips prepared?"

"Cut into thin strips and fried," came the response!

Shaking his head in wonderment, the chief spoke to Wise Owl, "Take our guest to lodge number six and see that he has everything necessary to be comfortable. Bring him to the council fire at the sight of the moon's rising." With that directive, he felt that he had fulfilled his obligation as host. He turned majestically and entered his tipi, which signaled the end of formalities. Some elderberry tea (on the strong side) would be just the thing to remove the sour taste from his mouth.

The entire camp exploded into a frenzy of motion in preparation for the council and the "cook fires" ceremony. Children ran to and fro, gathering dead wood for the fires and two were sent on the task of obtaining two choice "chips" for the stranger's specialty dish. Squaws bustled about gathering ingredients for the luk pot feast. Some, who had earned tribal recognition for their culinary expertise, would prepare their own specialty dishes. Those neophytes who had yet to reach that status carried out their responsibility for the main course. Some skinned fresh-killed deer, some butchered the meat, and others prepared the vegetables. The meat and vegetables would then be placed in the luk pots—great earthenware pots placed in a circle over red-hot fires. Each luk pot would contain a different offering.

Drummers were busy cinching up the skins of their instruments for peak reverberation level. Hiup drums fell into two categories: rhythm and melody. The rhythm drum was constructed from a hollow log with a piece of deerskin stretched over the top and cinched at the sides with sinew and notched pegs. These drums were of different sizes, some small and others very large. The rhythm drum was placed on the ground and struck with sticks to produce sound. This drum was usually played by two or more drummers.

The melody drum was also made from a hollow log, but skin was stretched over both ends and cinched at the sides. This skin, called the "foreskin," was cut from the front quarters of the deer. Only the most skilled drummers could play the melody drum, since the drum was suspended from the neck by a cord and the proper striking of each end required perfect hand coordination.

The drummers of the Hiup had learned long ago that the beating of the foreskin produced a superior effect and also produced the most sensuous results. The tightness with which the foreskin was stretched also became a factor in the quality of results. The foreskins were sure to take a beating tonight!

Dancers could be seen doing their limbering-up exercises. A Stare and He Who Walks Funny gathered up their best protégés for a last practice of specialty routines. A Stare's group had on the flat stone moccasins, and each dancer twirled a canelike stick. They would tap the sticks on the ground in rhythm with their tapping foot patterns. He Who

Walks Funny had his group place short round pegs in the toe of each moccasin and could twirl like tops. The maidens leaped into the air to be caught by their male partners. All were heady with excitement.

Braves and council members were also busy in preparation. Bodies were anointed with special oils, hair was braided and interwoven with beads, bracelets were carefully chosen to match necklaces, loincloths were rejuvenated, and moccasins were brushed with porcupine quill brushes.

Three Hands went over his notes and selection of incantations that would obtain the most appropriate results for this celebration of the coming of the first hairy one. A messin man must never be caught off guard and lose the respect of his people. Tonight, he would carry some aroma pouches to neutralize Jock's smell if it returned, plus some aurora pouches to put color into the festivities.

The sun set and the moon started to rise above the trees, signaling that "party time" had come. As protocol was a vital part of the red man's etiquette, everyone was seated around the fire according to their status. Chief Ten was seated with Jock at his right and Has It Made at his left. In order, on each side of these three, sat Three Hands, the four aged council members known as the Gray Panthers, the braves, and finally the artisans, who completed the circle.

The omen and children had taken positions, also according to status, and completed a larger circle exactly three paces behind their counterparts. Before each member and guest was placed a round, flat earthenware dish containing a long, thin flint knife, a piece of wood with a carved handle hollowed out at one end, and a short stick sharpened to a point. These served as eating utensils.

Chief Ten signaled the feast to begin by rising and making his way to the luk pots. Jock, as guest, was motioned to rise and follow him, utensils in hand. Others followed in status order until all were in line. The women and children remained seated. Each male adult passed by the pots and selected the items he wanted. Each was careful to take no more than he could eat. When the last male was seated at the circle, the women rose, also in status order, and led their cubs to obtain their food. The aroma that filled the air was proof that this was an exceptional luk pot dinner.

Hiup did not converse while eating, as it was considered bad manners. The time for talking would come after the pipe. The time needed to consume a meal was somewhat slower this night, for Jock was allowed to finish first so that his favorite dish could be served as the highlight of the feast.

Apprehension was the prevalent mood. The suspense mounted with each passing moment. Seeing that Jock had cleaned his dish, Chief Ten gave the signal for a squaw to bring the guest the dish he had requested.

"I've enjoyed your food, Chief Ten, but I must say I hae been looking forward ta my favorite fish and chips. It has been a lang time since I hae eaten them and my mouth is watering ta have such a delicacy pass through it once again."

The entire audience leaned forward as one to witness this event.

"Strange looking chips," thought Jock when served. "But what the hell, it has been a long time." He cut off a bit of the boiled brook trout and popped it into his mouth. It was heavenly. Swallowing to clear his throat, he sliced a chip and popped it into his mouth—to the astonishment of the tribe! The chip popped out just as quickly as it had popped in, with Jock's face turning beet red to match his hair. He quickly reached into his sporan and brought forth an antidote, then drained his last sample keg. "What are ye trying ta do, poison me?" he bellowed.

The tribe was still in a state of shock from observing a man place a buffalo's reject into his mouth as food. The reaction of their guest only heightened their disbelief. Chief Ten hastened to explain that, although they were hesitant to fulfill his wishes, they were duty bound, as hosts, to satisfy the wishes of their guest. If chips were requested as part of a meal, then chips it would be! It was not their place to reason why.

Jock explained that, in Scotland, chips were made from slices of potatoes and cooked in hot oil. The chief in turn explained what the word "chip" meant to his people. Jock, who had a great sense of humor, saw the experience as extremely funny and burst into uncontrolled laughter. The tenseness in the air evaporated as the entire tribe joined the laughter. The Hiup also had a tremendous sense of humor as part of their character; since this joke was on Jock, not them, the situation was even more humorous!

The time came for the pipe. Three Hands took the pipe from its sacred pouch, filled it with Chief Ten's "sixty-nine" blend, lit it, and presented it to his chief. From the chief it went to each member of the council to lift it in offering to each spirit of direction, East, North, West, and South; each took a puff, then passed the pipe to the next in line. Jock took one puff and passed the pipe to Has It Made. Each brave had the privilege of passing the pipe, which was then emptied of ashes. Three Hands would place the ashes into an aurora bag and cast it into the fire as a token of oneness. He then returned the pipe to its pouch, which signaled that the time to talk had come.

Chief Ten turned to Jock, and, in a strong voice that could be heard clearly by all in the two circles, said, "The four spirits have indicated by the pipe ash that all is well to talk. The winds carry only the scents of Mother Earth, and there is peace in the air. We are honored by the presence of a guest from lands to the east, and it is obvious from our first meeting that we have much to learn from each other. From what we have seen and heard, his customs and manners are certainly new to us, but we are a patient people and are eager to learn new things." The chief indicated to Jock that the audience was his.

Between the morning interlude and the evening meal, Jock had spent time reflecting. If he were to "hide out" among these people, he should do his utmost to avoid offending or upsetting them in any way. He realized that everything about him was new to the Hiup, and he would have to go slow and avoid any impositions—like playing the pipes without adequate forewarning or introduction. He was determined to go slow and neither say nor do anything that could be interpreted as unacceptable or insulting to his hosts. With Loon at his side translating, he spoke.

"O great Chief, leader of the brave hunters of the Hiup, I give thanks for your welcome. Your hospitality is from the heart and your women have prepared food sae delicious that my stomach lies in pure content. I'm sure that they cou'd prepare a proper haggis if given the recipe. However, let us, like the buffalo, let the 'chips' lie where they fall. I would like ta offer a slight token of my appreciation ta you, Chief, for this warm welcome." He reached into his left stocking and withdrew a dirk, which he presented to Chief Ten. To his audience, he had reached into the black and blue hair on his leg and taken out a short pointed object, which he gave to the chief.

Chief Ten was somewhat dubious about Jock's move, but when he held the dirk in his hands, his face beamed with pleasure. It was the first metal knife he had ever seen, and as he ran his finger lightly over the blade, he nodded his approval. He held the gift up, then passed it along for all to examine. Jock had a good rebirth in the minds of the Hiup.

"Chief Ten, I know that our customs are different, and quite noticeably our dress. I will explain my articles of dress. First, my head covering, which is something ye dinna use. 'Tis called a tam-o'-shanter and has a tourie on the top." He took it off and let it pass among his audience. Until then, it was thought to be a part of his skin. Next came the "Jock strap." He unsheathed his claymore and held it aloft. "Ye have bows and arrows, spears and clubs. This is all of those weapons rolled inta one for me. I use it only ta defend mysel'." He strode to a pile of firewood, picked up a sapling, and tossed it into the air. As it fell, he swung his claymore and cut the branch cleanly in two, which brought a gasp from the audience.

The next item for introduction was the plaid. When unpleated, the resemblance to a blanket was plain to see. The sporran followed and was passed about. The tunic and blouse did little to dissolve the image of a "Hairy One," as Jock's arms and chest were covered with a thick growth of flaming red hair that flowed in the breeze like a crimson tide. "I'll na bother ta remove my kiltie, but ye'll see that it serves the same purpose as your loincloth." The women were disappointed, for the one question of greatest interest to them was to remain unanswered!

Jock ended his modeling activities with his stockings and shoes. The audience examined each item and returned them to their owner. The only remaining item was his pipes. Now Jock was aware that his presentation had been successful in allaying the mistrust these people must have had regarding him. Strangers and their appearance always seem to bring feelings of mistrust to the surface of any group of human beings who regard theirs as superior. Strangers are considered "invaders" to some degree until actions are examined, explained, and either accepted or rejected. Jock had not presented anything that could be considered a danger to the Hiup.

Only one item on the minds of the Hiup needed explanation before that final fear was put to rest. Chief Ten brought that item up for discussion. "We thank you for sharing your manner of dress with us, Jock. We are but a simple people and have had no experience with the dress and customs of your people. We will share some of our customs later, as other festivities are presented. But first, we ask you to share your reasons for selecting this trail to our lands."

The real success of his venture lay in his response and Jock knew it! He paused for a moment, then replied, "I lived wi' my people in a camp east of the wide river. There were many tribes in this camp that spoke many tongues. I was nae happy in heart for there was much arguing and fighting among us. We are of the same color, yet we come from many lands beyond the Great Waters where our customs are as varied as our tongues. We look ta the Great Spirit for guidance, but His laws are interpreted differently by each tribe, which causes much fighting.

"My wish was ta seek peace in my own mind and heart. I knew that I cou'dna find it among my brothers of such disharmony, sae I sought a place where I cou'd be alone. Only in such a place cou'd I find the answers ta peace of the heart. It was my guid fortune ta meet a man of peace who helped me ta learn a little of your tongue. He tauld me of his lands and his people, who were gentle of nature. It sounded like the place I was seeking, sae I decided ta tak the trail here. I was beginning ta think the trail had na end and that Reverend Loon had made the story up. Then your braves found me."

There was a pause while his audience digested those thoughts and shared their interpretation with their brother on either side. Chief Ten looked at Has It Made and then Three Hands, saw their nods, and then looked to the Gray Panthers. He witnessed their nods of approval, then spoke, "Again we thank you for sharing the voices of your heart. My people will meet and discuss how we can best assist you in keeping to your trail. Now, let the festivities begin. I know that our young people are anxious to demonstrate the harmony among the Hiup." He gave the signal and the party began.

Everyone had an opportunity to participate in the festivities, but once again it was in status order. The braves started with ceremonial dances related to hunting and acts of bravery. Three Hands gave an interpretive performance concerning the Everywhere Spirit and Mother Earth. He Who Walks Funny and A Stare presented their innovative routines, the neophytes danced whatever routines they had mastered, and finally the women and children began milling and racing about doing solos.

The drummers, who gave full support to each group of dancers, seemed indefatigable. As a gesture of appreciation, the tribe gave the drummers an opportunity to present routines of their own. Everyone returned to their circle position and gave their full attention to the drummers. The spotlight, or rather the firelight, was on them.

The group gave very stirring presentations that ranged from the low vibes portraying the wind moving through the forest, bringing scents of Mother Earth, to the stirring description of the hunter picking up the scent of an animal, then stalking it to the kill. The kill was apparent by the abrupt cessation of all drums after reaching an earsplitting peak followed by a rousing "Whoopeee!"

There was a slight pause in the action and each member of the tribe looked about, exchanging knowing glances and smiles. The best was yet to come and they knew it. It was time for the battle of the drums! No one had reached the status of "best drummer" since the all-time great, Fiddle With Sticks, had passed on to the big drumland in the sky. For three winters, two young men had vied for this honored position—one named Clean Kroo Pa, and the other, Budding Birch. The two were so adept that they played, not one, but three drums! In addition, they had objects like small, hollowed-out logs suspended above their drums by sinew, plus half-round stones, meticulously chipped until they were but a thin, hollow shell, laid out in a line on a log placed between two of their drums.

The signal for the "battle" to begin was given by the chief, and begin it did. In order to determine a winner of such a contest, there was a set procedure. The two contestants would play while seated on a stump surrounded by their instruments. They would use sticks instead of their hands to create sound. Finally, one player would play a challenge routine, then allow his opponent to repeat it. After five challenges, their roles were reversed. Each would then be given an opportunity to display his best skills with a solo. The audience was to act as judge.

Jock had some experience as a piper to relate to the skills of a drummer, but these two young men surpassed the most skillful drummer he had ever known. Playing their three drums and making rhythm sounds by striking the logs and rocks added dimension beyond his ken.

The battle raged back and forth until each had performed his solo, then each in turn stood and received the 'Wow! Wow!" whoop from the audience. The Hiup knew a good thing when they heard it. When the last drummer stood, they were careful not to exceed the "Wow! Wow!" for the first drummer. In so doing, a future rematch was assured.

The festivities were halted to give everyone a recovery period. This time was used to return to the luk pot line and rejuvenate one's source of energy, or to take care of the body's other vital needs. After eating, the braves were given a chance to speak with the guest as individuals or in small groups. Chief Ten then signaled the festivities to resume.

Jock reached the point of explaining his pipes where he decided to show off his musical talents. Hoisting his pipes, he ran through a sample "soft" refrain without startling his new friends, then worked his way up to the old standards. Soon he was marching around the council fire followed by host of dancers trying to synchronize their dancing to the beat of the pipes. Their efforts were beyond description.

The partying and eating continued until the rays of the sun cleared the treetops and warmed the participants to a state of drowsiness; the festivities yawned to an end.

The Great Spirit, Wakan-Manitou, was not a bit drowsy. He smiled as he motioned for the Dilemma Bull to sharpen his horns in preparation for action.

Chapter Five

It is important to beat your own drums for your message to be heard, yet not so loud as to drown out the reply of others.

There was no letdown after Jock's "coming out" party. The mood changed, however, to one of complete seriousness. The camp area near the base of the waterfall was rapidly filled by the constant arrivals from the west. There had been little social intercourse with the visitors beyond visits by the neophyte Hiup to their counterparts from the west. Protocol held that meetings at the chieftain level would not take place until the third moon, so that the later arrivals would have equal opportunity for introduction.

Representatives of the different tribes established enclaves independent of each other, but all shared in the abundant food supply on the plain, so the visitors did not impose upon the food supply of the Hiup on the plateau. The main migration of the buffalo to the south left plenty of space for encampment, more than enough chips for fires, and enough stragglers to provide meat.

Jock became an integral part of the Hiup preparations. He had made a bargain with Chief Ten that was strictly enforced by every member of the tribe. It was agreed that he was never to be seen by any visitors to Hiup territory, nor the knowledge of his presence shared with any visitor. His purpose was to insure that knowledge of his location never be shared so as to inadvertently reach the ears of Ian Stewart! In return, he would act as teacher and advisor to the hierarchy of the Hiup regarding the language and ambitions of the white man.

Three Hands made it clear that the importance of such a resource as Jock was vital to the success of the Hiup in a leadership role. The realization and awareness by the leaders of the tribes involved in the Grand Council that the Hiup not only knew what they were talking about, but that they had mastered the language of the white man, would have tremendous leverage in decisions that had to be made. Their role would be "leaders of leaders!"

Although his mind was busy sorting and organizing the priorities of his role in the council, Three Hands did not miss the significance of the arrangement between Jock and the tribe. Jock had been welcomed by the tribe and was free to share the hospitality of the tribe for as long as he remained. Why was he so adamant about the absolute secrecy of his presence? Could it be that he was a messenger sent by the whites, as Loon had been sent by the Hiup to learn the plans of the enemy? The answers must be learned before the council began!

Jock was housed in a secluded area north of the Hiup camp, but with easy access when needed. His needs were attended to by members of the tribe so that his full attention could be focused on his teaching sessions. Three Hands spoke with Swift Feet and requested that she supervise the details necessary to meet Jock's needs for food, hygiene, and lodging. He wanted to have close communication with one person in his quest to discover Jock's secret. Though none would express it, a number of squaws noticed her making extended visits to service Jock's needs. Soon the visits ceased as such, and she shared his tipi on a permanent basis. It saved her from making so many trips, she explained. Her reasoning was accepted with smiles by understanding females.

Chief Ten, Has It Made, Loon, and the Gray Panthers went to Jock's lodge daily for long sessions of language training. The sessions provided linguistic mastery for both parties; English for the Hiup, and Hiup for Jock. To insure his acceptance by the tribe, Jock spoke only Hiup when conversing with tribal members.

Jock not only worked with mastery of English, but added history and mapping. The history lessons gave his students an invaluable awareness of the white man's movements to date, as well as projections of the trends he had set in these movements. All were necessary in formulating battle plans. The map sessions greatly extended the mental image of the lands east of the Hiup encampment. Visual images allowed location of the tribal lands with drawn landmarks known previously only through oral description by traders. These points would be important components of the master plan.

Three Hands' concern regarding Jock's purpose for secrecy was resolved by the determination of Swift Feet. Three Hands had scored again! There was nothing like a slight indulgence in the Heritage, fish and chips (the real thing), a warm fire, and a warm body next to his to put Jock in a relaxed and talkative mood. He confessed to Swift Feet that he was born with a terrible affliction—women just couldn't keep their hands off him. The urge to fondle him was so strong in some women that they followed him relentlessly wherever he went. If these women, driven by the lustful need for his skills and staying power, ever learned of his whereabouts, they would travel any distance and overcome any obstacle to be with him. Now, thanks to the generosity of the Hiup, he needed no women to interfere or dilute the attention he wanted to give to her alone.

Three Hands, after his experiences involving the Brother of Fire, could appreciate (and accept) Jock's dilemma, and concluded that the red-haired one posed no threat to the Hiup.

The time for the Grand Council arrived at last, and Three Hands had been delegated the responsibility of organizing the event with meticulous adherence to protocol. No visitor could be offended in any way, no matter how slight or unintentional the offense. Every visitor was considered vital to the success of the planning and implementation.

This responsibility would have given any ordinary messin man nightmares and fits of depression, but Three Hands was not an ordinary messin man. He had no delusion about his role in the history that was about to be made, and he looked forward to the challenge. His role as organizer would be minuscule compared to that of manipulator. He must inject the proper thought at the proper time to persuade the chiefs to accept various components of the plan. There could be no divisiveness or indecisive attitudes. Consensus must be reached and accepted by all!

Power was not alien to the red man. Until the power holder was identified and accepted, little progress would take place between two or more groups. Even then, the seat of power was constantly under challenge and attack by those who sought to usurp it.

The trail to power is usually created by manipulation. To be a successful manipulator, one must concisely determine the existing seat of power, then focus his total energies to move and manipulate this power, according to his own priorities. Losing control of this power could quickly result in the demise of the manipulator's influence.

Three Hands, although confronted with a problem of great numbers, had no delusion as to where the seat of power would lie. It would not be the chiefs that he must control; the real power would be in the hands of the messin men of all of the tribes represented at the council!

As his first act to establish his role as power broker, Three Hands sent a relay message calling for a purification council, to be attended by every messin man. This council would be held in a neutral location so as not to offend the visitors' sense of equality. The Canyon of Fire, so named because the rays of the setting sun highlighted the natural redness of the canyon's walls, was chosen. Two hundred messin men gathered in the amphitheater setting, where optimum speaking conditions prevailed. The struggle for power and position would begin and be won there!

As host, Three Hands began the ceremony by lighting the pipe, introducing himself, taking the ceremonial puff, and then passing the pipe to his left. Each messin man repeated this procedure until the pipe returned to Three Hands. This took many fillings of the bowl and disposal of the ashes into the fire. Three Hands had come with an adequate supply of ceremonial tobacco pouches.

As the messin men deposited the ashes into the fire at the last puff before refilling the pipe, there had been no outstanding action. Three Hands, however, being the last recipient of the pipe, was prepared to demonstrate a change in that condition. When he deposited the final ashes into the fire, a slight of hand deposited an aurora bag along with them. The multicolored smoke ball that rose from the fire got the attention of the two hundred in attendance!

A casual observation of the results brought just as casual a remark from the instigator: "The spirits have accepted our purity of hearts and minds." He allowed that thought to tune the minds of his audience for a moment, then began to outline the role his fellow messin men must accept in the Grand Council.

As each messin man rose to introduce himself and pass the pipe, Three Hands put his sociological and psychological expertise to work. He began to categorize the group to pinpoint those who might later rise to challenge his position as leader at the council. Those who rose quickly and spoke quickly he placed in the "reactionary" category; those who rose slowly, spoke only after giving the entire gathering a good opportunity to view them, and spoke in a deliberate manner, he placed in the "challenge" category. Crooked Arm of the Sioux, White Cloud of the Cheyenne, Eagle Feather of the Apache, and Straight Arrow of the Comanche stood out above all others as possible challengers.

"My brothers, we each face a responsibility to our chief and to our people," Three Hands stated. "The very survival of all red men will depend on decisions made at the Grand Council. Although our chiefs are the wisest and bravest of men, they are not the greatest interpreters of signs. I'm certain that Crooked Arm's chief has disagreed with his reading of signs at times and was later proven to be wrong. Am I right on this, my brother?" Crooked Arm, hearing his name mentioned in a personal and positive way by his host, smiled and nodded his head in the affirmative.

"And I am certain that many of my brothers, like White Cloud and Eagle Feather, have saved an entire hunting party led into danger by their chief because their chief had ignored their reading of the hunt's unseen danger signs," Three Hands continued. Again came the smiles and nods of affirmation by those mentioned, along with many others who had experienced similar situations.

"If each of us could speak to support instances where we read true signs while our chief read false ones, I'm sure that several suns would pass before we were through. Do I speak for all of us?" Again, full support was indicated.

Straight Arrow signaled a request to be heard. It was granted. "Three Hands does indeed speak true. We have come a long distance with our chief to assist him in the formation of strong battle plans. We must all be alert, for there can be no misreading of signs from the spirits, no matter how small. We must concentrate all of our energies on this grave responsibility" A thunderous reply came in the form of shaking messin gourds!

Three Hands rose, prepared to act according to his plan to mold his seat of power, now that the role of the group had been defined and accepted. "There will be many of us reading the same signs. What if the smallest sign were not read true by all? Would not some of our chiefs be in disagreement within the council?"

Silence blanketed the group. The self-confidence of each messin man had pushed this possibility into the realm of impossibility. This inquiry traveled the length of the umbilical cord between possibility and impossibility. Three Hands paused long enough for that distance of mental travel to be traversed before pressing his point. "I have a thought for my brothers: when we speak to one another, can there be any false readings of meanings spoken with straight tongues?"

Crooked Arm rose quickly, as Three Hands knew one or more of the "challenger" group would. "Does my brother suggest that only one is to read a sign, interpret it, then inform the rest of us of its real meaning? Can any one man have such superior powers that he can do this? Who would choose him?"

"The mind of my brother, Crooked Arm, is as sharp as the claws of the bear. Perhaps he will assist me in bringing each of us to the same point on the trail of our minds. I ask you, Brother, does Wakan-Manitou speak directly to you or does He give you signs to read?" asked Three Hands.

"He gives me signs to read and interpret."

"What if you read them falsely?"

"He gives me other signs."

"If He spoke to you, could there be any misunderstanding of His wishes?"

"Wakan-Manitou does not speak to man!" snorted Crooked Arm contemptuously.

"But if He did favor you among all men to speak to, would not that be a sign that His words are so important that He would not chance misinterpretation through signs?"

Crooked Arm could not fathom, for the moment, the reason why Three Hands was raising such an issue. Since Wakan-Manitou had favored no man in this way, he could not lose face with his peers by answering, "There can be no doubt of it."

"Then I can share with my brothers what I have learned of Wakan-Manitou's wishes. I have counseled with M.O.M., who told me that Wakan-Manitou will be with us so that there can be no mistaking His wishes. There will be no signs to be read falsely or to cause disagreement between us. If we speak in opposition to His wishes, He will tell us so."

Crooked Arm looked around the group with a look of disdain on his face. He now had a glimpse of the direction Three Hands was moving and his purpose in doing so, but he was not about to relinquish his desire to assume the top position of power in coming events to this upstart! He stood to speak in rebuttal, "Our brother, Three Hands, is a great messin man, as are you, but to think himself spokesman for all of us leaves some doubts in my mind. He speaks words of truth, but they are only words. Wakan-Manitou has not spoken to him, although he says that he has had council with M.O.M. We know that M.O.M. is one who relays the words of the spirits. When M.O.M. spoke to you, did he say that the spirits had spoken with him and directed him to speak only with you, or did you have to read signs?"

Three Hands' evaluation of his opposition was proving to be very accurate. He must act in a decisive manner to eliminate the challenges of others! "I answer you with words of truth. M.O.M. spoke to me, but I cannot say that Wakan-Manitou spoke to him, or gave signs, for I did not ask. The feeling in my heart told me that it was not my right to question one who speaks with the spirits!"

There was a murmur of approval from the audience, but Crooked Arm was not about to give up the struggle. He continued the attack in an effort to shake the foothold his opponent had made on the others to swing them over to his line of reasoning. "You were right in your heart, and I do not challenge the words of M.O.M. I only seek clarification of his words so that all of us will think as one in carrying out his directions. You say that, at this council, one of us will speak for all, through contact with Wakan-Manitou?"

"That is the message M.O.M. gave to me." Three Hands replied.

Crooked Arm pressed on. "Where did you hold council with M.O.M.?"

"In the mountains to the north."

"How long was your trail there?"

"One moon."

Crooked Arm felt that his moment had come to strike hard and fast to eliminate Three Hands as a power. He had led him to this point and moved in for the kill! "One moon to M.O.M. and one moon back. If you are the chosen one, and an important question arises that you cannot truly answer as the spirits would wish, are we to wait two moons for you to go back to M.O.M. and return with the answer? Surely the spirits would not agree to the wisdom of such an arrangement! If the problem facing us is of such magnitude, why has M.O.M. not come in person?"

The words of Crooked Arm struck responsive chords, and the reactionaries leaped to their feet, shaking their messin gourds and shouting encouragement to him. The conservatives sat and took time to reflect on the arguments set forth by both men. They chose the middle ground for their stance and remained silent. Straight Arrow, Eagle Feather, and White Cloud were uncertain, at the moment, as to what action to take, since alignment with either of the two combatants could dash their own hopes of assuming the power role later. "Let these two destroy themselves," became their strategy.

The web that Three Hands had so cleverly woven snared its first victim. Like Iktumi, the spider, he moved swiftly to encase his prey and render him helpless. He raised his arm for silence, saying, "It is well that we share our thoughts, for it has been proven that there is not oneness of our hearts. This is bad messin. Our brother, Crooked Arm, has raised good thoughts, but he has put wet wood on a fire that has no flame. I do not speak for all of my brothers, for we are equals, so one should not try to stand taller than his brother. I only wish to show the need for us to speak as one so that there will be no false thoughts. If Wakan-Manitou wishes to choose one of us as His spokesman, who are we to challenge His wishes?

"I have said that M.O.M. has spoken to me and directed me to tell my chief to call a Grand Council," Three Hands went on. "He said that if the need was there, Wakan-Manitou would speak to eliminate false thoughts. M.O.M. spoke to me because I was the messenger sent to ask his guidance in the resolution of the white man problem. If one of you had been there, perhaps you would have been chosen as messenger.

"M.O.M. does not travel in body, but in mind. The spirits, who see, hear, and know all, converse with him. It is our responsibility to solve our own problem through the reading of signs. If we cannot do this, we must seek help in clarifying the signs. Would you cancel this council on the grounds that Wakan-Manitou had to be here in body for it to continue? Think on my words!

"Our chiefs will make the decisions that effect us all. Our responsibility will be to guide them to wise decisions. We are the experts in the interpretation of signs. May our eyes be as sharp as the finest lancepoint, and our hearts as one!"

There could be no argument with this reasoning from any member of the gathering. It certainly had appeal, since the possibility that one of them would be given the highest honor by the spirits could be real! If they were the chosen one, they would certainly want the backing of all present.

"Are my words and thoughts in agreement with yours, my brothers?" Three Hands asked as he anchored the last segment of his web. The unanimous nodding of heads confirmed the trap was ready. "Then I will share our unity with the spirits!"

With the fervent hope that He Who Walks On had not encountered any of those present and displayed his talent with "voices," Three Hands lifted his arms to the sky and set the stage for his master stroke! "O mighty Wakan-Manitou, guider of your sons in binding our moccasins to the Hoop of Life, we seek your guidance now in making this council of your many brave leaders one that will sustain us in our efforts to make the hoop strong and unbreakable. The strength of each of us is bound as one in our resolution to make it so. We cannot survive without your patience and guidance to keep us strong. Make your wishes known that we may follow them without failing your purpose. Make your signs clear and our eyes sharp!"

Three Hands lowered his head to his chest and arms to his sides. There was silence over the gathering, in reverence and hope that such a well-spoken prayer would be accepted by the spirits.

The brief silence was broken by a thundering voice seeming to originate from the huge boulder behind Three Hands and echoing throughout the canyon. "I hear your words, Three Hands of the Hiup, and those of my sons with you in council. I have listened with a strong heart, for you have all shown strong hearts and an awareness of the importance of this council. Three Hands spoke true when he said my signs could be read falsely by some eyes that are old and weak. I have chosen one of you who will hear my voice and share my words with you until the threat of the white man is past. The voice that repeats my words must be strong and clear. I have heard many strong voices at this council, but one has risen above all others to speak sure and true to the target as the straightest of arrows.

"My choice is Three Hands. He will pass my words on to you and each one of you will carry them out as one. Your courage will be needed to keep the hoop strong. If you fail me, my wrath will make the danger of the white man as insignificant as a charging ant would be to a buffalo! As I am one, you must be also. I have spoken!"

A silence descended upon the group as minds raced to absorb the significance of the message. This was the first time for all, with one exception, that the actual voice of Wakan-Manitou had been heard! Crooked Arm set his gaze on Three Hands. He was caught on the "horns of the Dilemma Bull," for he wanted to believe that Three Hands had presented a masterful trick, but the lingering doubt from traditional awe of the spirits kept him from issuing a charge of trickery. If this was no trick, then he stood the chance of facing the promised wrath of Wakan-Manitou. He had closely observed the face of Three Hands while listening to the words of Wakan-Manitou and had not seen his lips move, so he decided to bide his time before issuing any challenge.

The silence was broken by the voice of Three Hands. "Through no choice of my own, I will carry out the wishes of Wakan-Manitou. I will stay here this night to purify my heart and mind to receive any messages."

The gathering dispersed slowly, but with a great deal of exchanges between the participants regarding this momentous occurrence. Each man was eager to report the details of this historic council to his chief!

Three Hands waited until all had left the canyon, then began to evaluate the events of the council. He was certain that the majority of the messin men accepted his performance as genuine. Some would have doubts and require further convincing. A few would not relinquish their power and influence and place it in the hands of one man. They would work tirelessly to expose him. His priority had to be to concentrate on the latter, as they posed the greatest threat to his plan.

The next morning, Three Hands sent word to Crooked Arm, Straight Arrow, Eagle Feather, and White Cloud that he would like a council with them at the canyon. This council would test his ability to lead, or would increase the voices of opposition. They, too, would have spent the night analyzing the past council, and have plans they might reveal in a smaller group setting. His plan was to attack first and further narrow the number of opponents before they could ally others to their stance of opposition.

The group met, as requested, and the formal ceremony of the pipe was performed. Three Hands then made his move. "My brothers," he said, "the time is short, as the Grand Council is to begin in two suns. I have spent the darkness purifying my heart and mind. When I became totally at peace, I began to glide among the stars, as the owl glides among the trees. I had completed this journey just as the sun parted the shadow of night. I heard a voice, as near to me as you are, White Cloud, speak my name. The voice said, 'I know that you are not happy to be the chosen one, for you feel in your heart that it sets you apart from your brothers.

"'The responsibility is great and will cause some jealousy among the weak of heart, but fear not! As I have spoken, those of weak heart will feel my wrath until their hearts are strong once more. My reasons are not to be challenged, and I, not you, will always be the one who stands taller than his brothers, which is as it should be. The importance of the Grand Council is so great that no one voice will dominate it, but one voice will communicate my wishes! Your heart and mind are now pure and ready for my message.

"'First, you must select the strongest and purest of heart of your brothers to assist you in carrying out my wishes. It is extremely vital that your choices be wise ones, for the strength given to them will bring every messin man together to bind an impregnable hoop. Their power will grow, as my wishes make more demands upon my people to keep the hoop strong. You are my messenger for this council, but they must learn from you, for they, in turn, will become messengers in moons to come.'

"That was the message given to me and that is why I have asked you for this council," stated Three Hands. "To make decisions is beyond my power, as Wakan-Manitou has indicated. You have risen above all others at our last council and spoken strong and sincere words. I ask you to share this heavy burden with me so that the wishes of Wakan-Manitou be carried out with no deviations. If you accept, your burdens will be increased until Wakan-Manitou relieves you of them. What are your thoughts on this matter?"

Eagle Feather was the first to respond. "I have spent the darkness, as did you, making peace in my heart and mind. I left the council with a heavy heart, for I could not see the reason for one brother to be chosen to stand above the rest. Our brothers all heard the voice of Wakan-Manitou as clearly as you. Why, I asked myself, could He not have continued to speak to each of us when the need arose? He must have reasons, but my mind could not share them with me."

"The reason may be that you are trying to raise your mind to the level of the one speaking. Are you prepared to equate yourself with Wakan-Manitou?" responded Three Hands.

"No! No!" came the hasty reply. "You have returned my mind to peace with your words that His words are not to be challenged. I accept them and am ready to help shoulder the burdens needed to keep the hoop strong and unbroken."

"I, too, accept the wishes of Wakan-Manitou," stated Straight Arrow. "I am honored that you have chosen me to share this burden. Tell me my responsibilities, and I will carry them out."

"Straight Arrow speaks my heart, also," added White Cloud.

Three down and one to go! Only Crooked Arm had yet to respond. How had the time of darkness been used by this final chip on the lancepoint? The answer was not long in coming!

Speaking slowly, with carefully chosen words, Crooked Arm presented his thoughts. "I, as had my brothers, spent the darkness in purification. I thought long and hard on the words of Wakan-Manitou and on those of my brothers. Questions filled my mind, as I had left the council confused. Now my mind is clear and my eyes as sharp as the eagle. There are still questions that linger in my mind like a dragonfly over a summer pond. If these questions can be answered by our brother, Three Hands, my mind will be as clear as the waters of the lake. Let me review what my mind has absorbed so that, with your help, any false thoughts will be cast out:

"Wakan-Manitou has chosen to speak with man through a chosen messenger, who then conveys that message to his brothers." Crooked Arm paused, then went on, "A Master Plan will be designed at the Grand Council to stop the white man's advance into our lands. This plan will remain in effect for our lifetime and beyond. We have no concept of this plan, yet we must advise our chiefs in decisions necessary to construct such a plan. If this plan fails, we face certain death. Are these the facts as my brothers know them? If not, tell me which are false."

The group nodded confirmation. "Then my questions are these," he continued. "Our brothers to the east have faced the same problem as we with the white man. If they were unable to stop him, why didn't Wakan-Manitou release his wrath against the white man and destroy him before he could continue to destroy our people? The second question is, why has Wakan-Manitou waited until this time to select a messenger to speak for Him when He could have done so and united all tribes when the white man first came to the lands of the red man? The last question is, if we are to be given power above all other brothers, what is this power and how do we use it?"

Four faces turned toward Three Hands for his response. The same questions had arisen in the minds of the other three, but they had expeditiously placed them in the backs of their minds, thinking the answers would come with the passing of suns.

Three Hands was aware that his answer must be swift in coming, for if he could not answer without hesitation, his role would not be convincing or vital to his brothers. He was ready! "You offer good questions that must be answered to clear your mind," he said in compliment. "The answers will not be mine, but those guided to my mind by M.O.M., for I asked these same questions of him at our council. His reply was that the answers were already in our minds. We must seek them with strength and determination, or they will elude us.

"Our brothers to the east opened their arms and their hearts in welcome to the white man. Without their help, the white man would have perished. The whites mistook this generosity for weakness, for their minds were filled with greed and conquest, as proven by their actions of injustice. The white man spoke with forked tongue when he promised to live in peace with respect to his red brothers.

"The vision of the magnitude of the problem did not come to our brothers until it was too late," Three Hands went on. "Some decided to fight, but found the weapons and the numbers of the whites overpowering. The whites cleverly created situations that inflamed jealousy and turned brother against brother. Each tribe thought only of itself, instead of uniting and acting with the strength of one. They formed small hoops, which the whites surrounded and crushed, as the stampeding buffalo tramples the grass.

"Why did Wakan-Manitou not destroy the white man for these acts? I cannot answer for Him. Our people have learned that the white man has a Great Spirit that he looks to for guidance. Perhaps this spirit told Wakan-Manitou that He would destroy us if Wakan-Manitou destroyed His people. This may be why Wakan-Manitou has chosen to guide us rather than act for us.

"Wakan-Manitou has spoken to us because we have asked for guidance. We have learned from the unfortunate experiences of our brothers to the east and have come together in council united as one. M.O.M. has always been available to us as a relay to the spirits. Did our brothers seek his help, or did they think themselves stronger and wiser than the spirits, able to solve their own problems without their help? Perhaps this level of thinking displeased the spirits. Again, it is not for us to question the reasoning of the spirits, for we have been assured that they are with us for strength and guidance.

"Your question regarding the power beyond that of any other messin man will be answered by your actions. If we construct the basics of a workable plan that fulfills the requirements of the spirits, we will have already risen above the others," suggested Three Hands. "If we fail, our disgrace may result in the death of us all—and not by the white man!"

"Your words make sense and my mind is clearer now," said Crooked Arm, "but we still do not know if this plan we are to form will meet with approval by the spirits. Can you share your council with M.O.M. so that we can have something in place before the Grand Council? Time is short, and there is much to be done!"

Three Hands proceeded to relive his council with M.O.M. for his select group. He began by demonstrating the lesson of diverting the stream and stressed the importance of it in the master plan. His expertise in organizational skills kept the focus on "prioritizing."

"This we know," he outlined. "The white man has superior weapons, and he constantly probes his enemy's weaknesses before striking. His battle plan is to encircle, then crush his enemy, and he respects strength. To defeat him, we must demonstrate our strength through illusion, never allow him to encircle us, and never allow a direct confrontation in battle.

"From our scouting of the white man's camp on the eastern banks of the Mississippi, we have learned that they are preparing for a crossing of the river into our lands. The whites are lazy and will not come in numbers by foot. They travel in large white tipis that move and are called 'wagons.' These wagons cannot pass among the trees of the forest, so they cut down trees like beavers making a dam. The clearing provides a trail for their wagons."

Three Hands went on to emphasize, "The whites have little or no knowledge of the lands or the people of these mountains, or beyond. We must maintain this level of ignorance and use it for creating our illusion. Each red man must project this illusion to every white man to maintain the strength of our hoop."

"Your people have acted wisely in preparation for this invasion," commended White Cloud. "I can see clearly why Wakan-Manitou has chosen the Hiup to lead us in council."

Nodding his head in recognition of the compliment, Three Hands cleared an area of ground between them. With a stick, he drew lines forming a map that illustrated what Jock had demonstrated in his map sessions. He marked the critical areas to show the white man's movement since his arrival. He identified tribal areas, as well as where tribes met their demise or moved west in accommodation to the white man. His mapping stopped at the Mississippi River, and the stick lay on the ground parallel to the river. "This branch indicates our mountains, and that is the extent of my knowledge. You, my brothers, must now pick up the branch and mark where your lands lie."

"It is true that your people have acted wisely," stated an impressed Crooked Arm. "They have not sat in their canoes in a dry stream bed waiting for the waters to flow. Let us complete the drawing so that we may all be of one knowledge."

Each of the four messin men took turns with the stick and drew critical landmarks and tribe locations, until they had illustrated the area from the river to the western great waters. The map included the rivers and the Mountains of Great Rocks, as well as the desert areas; the land components of the great plan became clear to all.

"When the whites cross the Mississippi, they will have to clear trails for their wagons. They will experience little difficulty until they arrive at the base of the Kie Ro Practic Mountains," observed Crooked Arm.

"That is true," agreed Straight Arrow, "but there are only three passes they can use to cross with their wagon trails: the northern pass to Dakota lands, the pass here of the Hiup, and the southern pass of the Natchez. Once they move through these passes, their trail is clear to the Mountains of Great Rocks. Once they cross there, they will be able to continue to the Great Blue Waters."

"Remember the words of M.O.M.," Three Hands injected. "They must not be allowed to travel as they choose, but only on the trails of our choosing, which is the trail of the circle. If they come from the east, then they must be led to return to the east!"

"Their trail must not be an easy one, for this would tempt them to continue the trail with more determination," suggested White Cloud. "A thought has entered my mind that will fulfill the requirement of M.O.M.'s words. Let the Dakota and Hiup passes be used only for trails west and the Natchez pass only for their return."

"Your thought has served as a breeze to clear away the fog from my mind," expressed an excited Eagle Feather. "To limit the range of the circle trail, can we not use the Mountains of Great Rocks to turn their trails to the south? The Gray Waters to the south could be used to turn them through the pass of the Natchez. By using the desert, their food and water supply could be controlled and any urge to settle eliminated. In fact, through this control, the illusion of an undesirable area could be instilled in their minds."

"The words of M.O.M. have guided us to a plan of simplicity itself!" stated Three Hands. "The words of Wakan-Manitou regarding power are also becoming clearer. Those who pass into the lands of the Dakota will be your responsibility, Crooked Arm. Those who enter the

Hiup lands will be my responsibility; and guiding all return trails through the Natchez pass will be your responsibility, Straight Arrow."

"But what of my responsibility?" asked Eagle Feather, who certainly did not want to be left out.

"And mine?" entreated White Cloud.

"The inside of the trail will be the responsibility of Crooked Arm, Straight Arrow, and myself," replied Three Hands. "The outer perimeter of the trails, which will be the most demanding of bravery, will be the responsibility of you and White Cloud. The messin men of all tribes in your part of the circle will answer only to you, as will those in our areas. Are we of a single mind on this?" All nodded in agreement, for each would have power like no other messin man before him. Indeed, all were satisfied!

"One other problem has yet to be discussed: the lands between the Mississippi River and the Kie Ro Practic Mountains," observed Straight Arrow. "Is the white man to be allowed to settle in this area? If so, he may build numbers that could overpower those guarding the passes, and our plan would disintegrate."

Each man intensely studied the map, seeking a solution.

"You say the white man has no knowledge of the lands west of the river's bank?" asked Straight Arrow.

"That is true." replied Three Hands.

"Then he is certain to send scouts to report the best areas for trails. Can we not make it the responsibility of our brothers near the river to guide them to the passes? They would see only what we want them to see. They would have to report back to their people that they can move in peace, but only on these trails. Any other trail would be met with force at the water's edge. From what you say of their habits, they would choose to move in peace."

"Your thinking is clear and that should please the spirits," commended Three Hands. "Send word that another council for messin men will be held here at the setting of the sun. Their response may resolve further problems before we meet with our chiefs and advise them for the Grand Council. Do you have any other thoughts to add before we leave this council?" Each shook his head in the negative, and the council ended.

The sun was gone, with only the redness on the horizon to mark its trail, when the council of messin men convened at the Canyon of Fire. The pipe was passed once more, then Three Hands rose to address the members. "I stand here with my brothers to share the strong messin that has been passed to me since our last council. I remained here after the council to purify myself. A voice as gentle as the breeze that passes to announce the awakening of the moon spoke to me. It was joyful that we had met and shared our hearts. The spirits were pleased with our words and our thoughts.

"The voice told me that there was much to be done," Three Hands went on. "It instructed me to call a council of four and to form the basis of our battle plan to guide our chiefs at the Grand Council. This we have done. It is a simple plan, but includes all of the words of guidance from the spirits and from M.O.M. I share this plan with you, for you are many and may see dangers that we have overlooked.

"We must all leave this council as one in heart and spirit if we are to guide our chiefs to also be united in their decisions. That you were not one of the four was not because you stand less tall than they, for the success of the plan depends not on the efforts of the planners, but on the strength and courage of those who carry it out. The spirits have chosen the planners. Now they have chosen you to make the plan work! Let me share the plan with you."

Three Hands went over the concept and components of the plan. The other four remained silent to reinforce the concept of one voice speaking for all. Many rose to suggest variations to be considered, but in general the plan was adopted as presented.

Three Hands stood with head bowed, to once more give praise to the spirits and to ask approval of the council's plan. Those present longed for a repeat of the communication from Wakan-Manitou to strengthen their hearts (and ego). They were not to be disappointed, for Three Hands had planned to bind the hoop in a forceful manner!

The mighty voice boomed forth to shake the branches of the Ucumfastus trees on the canyon rim, and to ignite the fires of determination and resolve in the hearts of those present. "I have listened with a happy heart to the council of My children. The white man, with deceit in his heart and mind, will be defeated by the strength of the purest hoop in the hearts of My children. The words of the chosen five are never to be doubted, for they are My words. They will be the messengers. You will be the wind that receives their words, the embers in the hearts of all My children until it is a raging fire from which the white man will retreat in fear and wonder. Those are My words!"

After a respectful period of silence, Three Hands continued (in his earthly voice), "You have heard our words and those of Wakan-Manitou. We must share our joy of His approval with our chiefs. Those who have accepted these words will place a stick into the fire as a sign of oneness. Those who do not share our thoughts as one will show their minds by passing the fire so the spirits can see the doubt in their hearts."

Each messin man threw a stick into the fire as he left. The fire became a raging inferno, for not one passed without casting his stick into it. Three Hands was last, and deposited his stick with a prayer to the spirits for forgiveness for his actions. He reasoned that if the spirits disapproved, he would have received the clearest of signs to indicate their displeasure.

Returning to his camp, Three Hands went directly to Chief Ten to apprise him of the past events. He carefully went over each council, including the reception of Wakan-Manitou's messages and the plan itself. Chief Ten could hardly contain his excitement over the significance of the councils to himself and to his people. His messin man had been chosen by the spirits, above all others, and it followed that he naturally would be the most envied chief at the Grand Council!

One special thought did creep into his mind: whenever the name of Three Hands was recalled by the "Rem a Nisser" of every tribe, his own name also would be included! This thought was pushed aside (with great difficulty) to a place in his mind from which it could easily be recalled; now he must concentrate on his responsibilities. The Grand Council would begin at the next sun.

Three Hands knew full well the importance of Chief Ten's presentation before his peers to the success of the plan. In his role as adviser, he went over every facet of the plan, and suggested possible points that could be raised in objection. However, there was a safety valve built in: if someone raised a point to which a chief could not respond, it was his prerogative to confer with his messin man.

Chief Ten retired to his tipi to review the events and to select an appropriate vocabulary for his presentation. The council would weigh each of his words, so his choices must be made in accordance with the priorities of the goal. He was in tune with the plan and with the reason for it. There was no doubt in his mind that, with his usual eloquence, he could convince his brothers to act in accordance with the wishes of the spirits.

Three Hands went to his tipi with but one purpose: to sleep! The Grand Council was to begin at the next sun, and the evaluation of his actions and guidance would be measured at its conclusion. If the messin men had thoughts contrary to the plan, they would voice them through their chief during the council. To the best of his ability, he had prepared his own chief for the role of leader, and had done all he could to unite his brothers as one. He had been true to them and to his M.O.M. His sleep this night would be deep and untroubled.

There were many who did not sleep with a contented heart. Casual attitudes and indifference had permeated the entire encampment. Many had traveled great distances and were weary from the trail. Those who had arrived earlier from short trails had to entertain themselves, and that had begun to lead to boredom. Feelings of great expectations began to be replaced by complacency. Tribes that had differed to the point of battle in the past could share a camp in peace for only so long. The question became, could they share a camp in peace long enough to remain peaceful through the Grand Council? If the present atmosphere continued, the issue would be in doubt.

The lingering doubts in the minds of many were completely eradicated when the messin men returned from their purification council. By sharing with their chief their experience with Wakan-Manitou (with a respectful degree of embellishment), they created a complete change of atmosphere, like a Chinook wind racing down from the north. The tired were no longer trail-weary; the complacent became recharged with zeal for action; and a common thread of unity began to needle its way throughout the encampment below and the Hiup camp above. The entire area became sacred ground!

Each chief eagerly awaited the return of his messin man from the second council. The past event, as momentous as it was in itself, became even more important as the unifying agent for all chiefs of the Grand Council. Any battle action could only be initiated by a chief. Input by the governing members of any council (Gray Panther, messin man, et cetera), be it tribal or national in scope, was an integral part of council proceedings. The final decisions, however, were made by the chief.

The ears of the chiefs also were eager to receive information regarding planning, for planning preceded action. Thoughts of action increased the flow of adrenaline, causing the blood to flow like waters released by the crumbling of a beaver dam. The messin men returned with the basic components of a battle plan, and each chief consulted with his entourage to prepare himself for his role at the Grand Council. Each was like a cub bear getting his first scent of a honey tree!

Each chief also was becoming aware of the opportunities that lay ahead. This was probably their once-in-a-lifetime opportunity to participate in a council directed by the spirits! Their name would be sung at councils far beyond their own tribe for as long as the sun moved across the sky. Each chief took pains to plan actions that would bring his name and that of his people to the fore, so that when songs were sung and tales told, they would be included. When they left on that trail to the Camp of Many Lodges, they would be recognized and welcomed with honor upon arrival!

While each chief was intensely involved with thoughts and deeds that would insure his importance in the eyes of his peers, each messin man was just as intently involved in formulating actions that would uphold the unsung creed of every messin man: "Behind every great chief stands an even greater messin man." The power of the messin man in a tribe could be equated with the response of his chief in a council of his peers. To advise unwisely could result in embarrassment for his chief and certain reprisal to himself as the cause. He also would lose face in the eyes of his peers. For certain, he wanted his name to also be included in those songs and legends!

Sleep was not a priority for the aforementioned tonight! The sudden change from boredom and complacency to the challenge of battle led by Wakan-Manitou, and the honors it would bring, pushed sleep to a lower priority.

The Moon of the Frost was rising!

Chapter Six

For the fool, glory is dying in battle with his enemy. For the wise man, glory is living in harmony, with no enemies!

The first rays of the morning sun, lovingly caressing the leaves of the Ucumfastus trees to gain access to their branches and finally to the ground below, found the campground bustling with activity. The Hiup, as hosts, had rehearsed their role to a lancepoint sharpness. Chief Ten and his council were at their usual location by the fire. Loon was at the entrance to the camp with Clean Krupa and Budding Birch at either side. Braves lined each side of the trail to the council fire area, while squaws and their cubs busied themselves preparing food.

The tribal representatives below also had readied themselves for the part they would play at this monumental event. The first priority was to impress, so, bedecked in their finest skins and ornaments, they moved to the pass like a long snake that had been segmented. Each segment moved at a pace that provided ample opportunity for individual recognition.

As each group, led by a messin man, arrived at Loon's position, he would ask their identity. The messin man would give the name of his chief, the tribe, and a few outstanding qualities of his chief, then he would step aside. Loon would then turn to face the area where Chief Ten stood and call out a flowery introduction that included the praises of the chief. The two drummers would then conduct a long stimulating roll on their drums, while a brave stepped forward and escorted the group to their designated seating area. This procedure was repeated until all guests were seated, then the formal ceremony began.

Chief Ten gave Three Hands the signal to begin the pipe ceremony. Drawing an ember from the council fire, he lit the pipe for his chief, who took his puff and exhaled to each of the four winds, then passed the pipe to his left. Three Hands had requested that his four associates be seated next to him, which was granted readily by their chiefs, for it was an added honor.

When the last puff of the first pipe had been expelled, the chief with the pipe signaled that it was empty, and Crooked Arm rose to empty the ashes into the fire, refill the bowl, give it to the next chief in line, and light it for him. This procedure was repeated until all of Three Hands' cohorts had ample opportunity to participate and be seen in an important ceremonial role. When the last chief had participated, Three Hands retrieved the pipe and emptied the ashes (along with a palmful of concealed aurora dust) into the fire. Each chief nodded in agreement that the resulting multicolored smoke ball was a good sign.

Three Hands' sharing of this ceremonial responsibility with the other four was by design, not by generosity. This sharing not only served to reinforce the status of those who were to play the greatest role in the battle plan, but would also raise their status in the eyes of their peers, who would be called upon in supportive roles. Their close proximity also gave him some control over their words and actions.

The attention of the entire gathering now focused on the host, Chief Ten. The success of Three Hands' efforts to prepare his chief for this vital function was about to be put to the test. Would he highlight the essential need of putting aside tribal differences and attitudes to the point where a common cause would guide the destiny of the red man? Three Hands and his messin men were prepared to move in such a way that would continually provide fuel for this "Fire of Destiny!"

Resplendent in his sky-blue coordinated dress, necklaces, and beaded braids, Chief Ten, the personification of chief, rose to greet his guests. "My brothers of the skin and heart who have come from all directions of the wind, I give you welcome to the lands of the Hiup. As I watched you moving to places of honor reserved for ones of great deeds, I saw strength in your faces and resolution in your eyes. This made my heart sing with gladness and pride to be your brother.

"Your trails have been long and have kept you away from your people for many suns. You have heard the call of your brothers and answered it without question, yet seeking in your minds the possible reason for a call of such magnitude. There is but one answer and it is a simple one: we have been called together to decide, as one, as to how we wish to die!"

An undercurrent of response rippled through the gathering, and Chief Ten paused for the effect to subside before continuing, "We have all faced death many times on the hunt, and our show of great wisdom and courage has caused the Walker of Death to look us in the eye, then move aside to let us pass. Only those who fear the Walker as he moves among us and cannot look him directly in the eye without fear or hesitation are the ones he chooses to walk with him forever, or until they conquer their fear. Then, and only then, will he allow them to leave his side and move on to the Camp of Many Lodges.

"The Walker has taken the form of man to confuse those of weak hearts, and thus adds to his number of followers. He must be very lonely, for he has found few of our brothers to walk with him. Now he calls himself the Hairy One, or White Man, and walks in great numbers to confuse brave men. He has moved among our red brothers to the east of the waters of the Mississippi like the wind over the buffalo grass leaving a wide trail. His trail is wide, because there were many who listened to his forked tongue and walked with him in innocence until they saw through his disguise.

"Many brave brothers rose to oppose him and, being lonely, this angered him greatly. He cast a spell that caused even the bravest of our brothers to lose their strength and fall to the ground, too weak to rise. Their messin men had no spells greater than those of the Walker, so these brothers began the trail to the Camp of Many Lodges. Even their squaws and cubs came under this spell and walked with their brave on his last trail.

"Some who fear the Walker now walk with him to deceive other brothers into thinking there is no danger and nothing to fear. The strength of the Walker, or Hairy One, is great, and he possesses terrible weapons of death, but his greatest weapon is deception. His words are tempting like the sap of the maple. If you accept this sweetness, you are caught as fatally as the mosquito in the web of the spider. Are we to be men of courage, who can bare our chests and challenge the Walker to release his arrow in an attempt to penetrate our strong hearts? Or will we run like the inexperienced cub to savor the sweet sap?"

The response to this challenge was not in the form of murmurs. A shout went up as though one mighty voice to signify that the former was their answer! Chief Ten had adeptly set a spark to the dry timbers in the hearts of the chiefs! Still, the fire there was not the desired inferno, so he started to fan it. "Are we to be like the rabbit who depends on his speed to run to safety from the fox, but his brain leads him in a circle back to where the wise fox is waiting for the kill?"

A strong response to the negative from his audience!

"Will we be the fox and make the white man play the role of the rabbit?" he went on.

A very strong response to the positive! Chief Ten was on a roll and the adrenaline coursing through him was contagious to his listeners. He picked up the pace. "In times when game is scarce, will we be the buzzard who soars lazily without courage while the fox and the wolf fight over the kill before leaving the skin and bones for us to pick?"

"Never!" came the response like the strongest of winds rattling the leaves of the trees.

"Can the fox and the wolf join in the hunt as brothers to combine their strength, courage, and cunning to shorten the hunt and increase its rewards?"

"We hunt as one!" came the thunderous reply. The fire was beginning to roar!

The chief issued his final challenge: "When the hunt is long and challenges the strength of the fox and the wolf to continue, will the fox end the hunt and watch his brother carry on to the kill, then expect to share equally?"

"We stay to the kill! We stay to the kill!" came the roar as the fire was heated to a fever pitch!

The master speaker had his audience in his hand. "Good! Your voices have proven that my eyes and heart have not misjudged your courage and wisdom. From this council must come proof of your words in the form of a battle plan. This plan will allow our people to look the Hairy One in the eye and make him move aside so that we can pass.

"Let me call forth our brother, Sittin Pretty, who has faced the Hairy One and those who walk with him. He has served as the messenger to the Hiup to warn us of the wind that was blowing our way. He has given us time to analyze and respond to this danger. His wish that he and his people continue to spread this message has resulted in this council. We give him our thanks, but let him speak in his own words of his experiences with the Hairy One."

Chief Sittin Pretty rose and immediately captivated his audience by recalling events and experiences that had reduced a once proud nation to the size of an average tribe. Every ear was tuned to his message, and the sadness in his heart was shared by all. When he had ended his diatribe, the resolve and purpose had been solidified in the mind of every red man present!

Chief Ten stood once more to give direction for purposeful organization. "My brothers, whose hearts beat as one to bear the sorrow of the Wiseolas and our brothers to the east, we must decide on our plan of battle. The Everywhere Spirit watches over us to give us wisdom and strength, but reminds us that the solution to our problem lies within us. Our messin men have heard His voice and have been chosen to guide our voices. We will heed their words!

"We will divide our numbers like the four winds so that all voices can be heard. Two suns will signal the time for us to return to the council fire to form one wind of such force that the Hairy Ones cannot stand before it. Crooked Arm, White Cloud, Eagle Feathers, and Straight Arrow will call those of you who will meet with each of them as a Council Wind. They and your messin men will share the words of Wakan-Manitou to guide you. Each council will plan the actions and responsibilities it will carry out. All will then return to join our blood as one!" Chief Ten concluded.

The four leading messin men took a separate position and began to call out the names of the tribes that would meet with them. When that task was completed, all agreed that the time for council was ended for this day and so turned in the direction of the luk pots. The remainder of the day was spent in feasting and socializing.

Once the feasting was over, the entire gathering, including the women and cubs, descended the incline to the campground below, where the entertainment began. The tribes of the plains had brought their other four legs, their ponies, and began demonstrations of skill and daring never before witnessed by the Hiup. The men were entranced by the speed and actions this creature created before their wondering eyes. The horse had totally captured the imagination and admiration of every male Hiup!

The male visitors took full advantage of this opportunity to impress their hosts. Their willingness to share brought joy to the hearts of the male cubs, who were hoisted to the backs of the ponies and taken for short rides around the campground. Neophyte braves, who had just passed the rites of the Spring Awakening, were eager to demonstrate their ability to gain instant mastery of the art of riding. This led to many flying bodies, as some ponies also sensed an opportunity to demonstrate their ability to quickly unseat a strange rider. There was much laughter and many bruised limbs and egos, but all was taken in good spirits.

There also were many contests between the visiting tribes that highlighted mastery of the pure art of riding. Individuals, as well as groups, vied for recognition of their prowess on the pony. The training and respect given each pony by its master portrayed an image of oneness in these demonstrations of skill. The people of the Plains were known as the "People of Six Legs," because they and their mounts were inseparable. The ownership of ponies was a status symbol of great importance to them.

The mornings and part of the afternoons involved serious council activities. With Three Hands constantly moving among the attendees to weave the thread of continuity and focus, segments of the master plan took shape. Each council outlined its responsibilities to be carried out, and added their pledge to do so.

On the morning of the third sun, they returned to the council fire to share their comments and to refine them according to the outline of the master plan. The guidance of Three Hands and his messin men had been so thorough that, after each Council Wind had reported, the plan came together as smoothly as the petals of the cactus flower to form a perfect circle.

Chief Ten then presented a summation of the plan for final corrections or improvements. "The success of our plan lies in simplicity itself. M.O.M. has cautioned us that to try and meet the advance of the white man with hostile actions would end in failure, for we do not have the numbers to defeat him. We must present the illusion that our numbers are without end, and mystify him as to our location. We must appear everywhere, yet never come into such close contact that he can cast spells or weave webs of deception to trap us. Only spokesmen will come into contact with him and only then when it is absolutely necessary.

"Our shows of force must constantly remind the white man that he faces superior numbers wherever he turns. We will appear and then disappear, only to reappear at another time and location. They will send scouts to find us, but we will never be where they seek. Our eyes will watch their every move, and we will be prepared to move, according to plan. They will not stand and fight if they see that our numbers can trample them like a charging herd of buffalo. They must never be allowed to stop with a feeling of security from attack. When whites are allowed to remain in one place too long, their instinct is to start building lodges and expand their holdings. Their camp must be limited to one sun!

"We must guide their trails inside our hoop," Chief Ten continued. "They will be guided to the passes of the Dakota Sioux and Hiup. Their trails will then follow the sun to the base of the Mountains of Great Rocks. The Apache will meet them and guide them south to the lands of the Comanche, who will again turn their trail east to the pass of the Natchez. Their trail must end in the lands where they started—east of the waters of the Mississippi. At no time will their trails meet with others to increase their numbers, their strength, or their feelings of security!

"It has been suggested by some—and we are pleased to hear the voices of all brothers—that a better plan would be to stand and fight at the passes where our strength would be greatest. To do this, every tribe would have to leave their lands and relocate at the passes. Our food supply would not support our increased needs for long, and our supply lines would constantly be lengthened with each passing sun. Our strength would then be reduced at the passes.

"I ask of these voices who favor such a plan: Who is ready to give up the lands so dear to their hearts to come to the passes? Who is ready to set aside their traditions of peace to become a warrior race? Who is ready to commit themselves, their sons, and even their sons to the battles of the passes? Who is prepared to oppose the words of M.O.M. and Wakan-Manitou? They have spoken that, if their words fall on deaf ears, we will be destroyed before the coming of the Hairy One. Let those among us who favor such a plan stand now with strong voices, for surely the ears of the Hairy One are tuned for any signs of weakness or dissension between us! The ears of Wakan-Manitou need not hear your voices, for his eyes can see the weakness of your hearts!

"The Walker stands at the water's edge to move at the first sign of weakness," the chief went on. "He is ready to move at the first voice of the Spring Awakening. Are we to look him in the eye as one, through the plan of the spirits, and make him move aside? Or do we stand and die like the rabbit and let the buzzards pick our bones for the Hairy One to trample unmolested as he enters our lands?"

The gathering rose to its feet as one, with arms extended skyward, shouting, "We obey the Spirit! The Walker will move aside! We are brothers! We are one! Let the Walker and the White Man hear our words! They will cower in fear!"

Chief Ten allowed a respectable amount of enthusiastic response before he raised his arm for silence. "The Everywhere Spirit, Wakan-Manitou, will have a happy heart to hear your words. Our battle plan is strong, and our minds are one. We have had a good council, and now we can return to our people and share the word. If there is a weak heart among us, the spirits will show their displeasure and punish it. Go in peace!"

The formal council ended, as all participants broke the circle and formed small groups to add final words. The Hiup were busily engaged in socializing for the last time with friends made during the time of council. They would not miss this final opportunity to be close to the object of greatest fascination to them—the pony! There was still time for riding while the squaws packed for the return trip.

The entire encampment reflected the feelings of satisfaction, of accomplishment, and of camaraderie. Reality would soon dampen these feelings, as tribes returned to their own lands and the true test of togetherness tested by ageless customs. For now, however, the strain of the council, the longing to begin the return trail, and implementation of the battle plan were replaced by exuberance. The young participated in games of skill and prowess. The braves, the chiefs, and the messin men engaged in exchanging gifts and in casual social discussion.

Chief Ten had developed a strong affection for the pony. He stood mesmerized as the activities involving ponies flowed before his eyes. When he saw a chief in full regalia, sitting atop his pony with the feathers of his war bonnet and coup stick flowing in the breeze, the sight instantly aroused feelings of envy and longing in his heart. His euphoria climaxed when Chief Running Bear invited him to mount his war pony! The view from this added height seemed to instantly expand his vision to enormous range and depth. The strength and beauty of the animal flowed forth to encircle his rider and bind him as part of the animal itself.

Chief Ten now knew why the men of the Plains thought of themselves as "six feet." Like the neophyte who had culminated his first experience of plucking the bud of womanhood from his female counterpart, he was enraptured! He posed the one question that still plagued him to Chief Red Sky of the Tonkawa: "How can it be that my brothers to the west own such an animal, as does the Hairy One to the east, while it is unknown to the Hiup?"

A smiling Chief Red Sky replied, "Legend has it that the pony was used by the sun god, Uranus, to move swiftly across the sky. When he reached the end of his trail in the west, he would leave his pony to rest and began his next trail with a fresh one. The ponies that he left became so great in numbers that he gave man permission to use them until he needed them again. When ponies are missing, the owners know that Uranus has taken them for his trail across the sky.

"The Rem a Nisser recalls men of another color coming to our lands long ago. These men rode ponies and their skin reflected the light of Uranus. Our people thought they were sent by Uranus, so they treated them as gods. These men were so evil that our people grew angry and drove them from our lands. In their haste to leave, they left their ponies, which the red man learned to breed until their numbers were great. Our ponies have become as brothers to us.

"You, our brothers of the forest, would have little need for ponies, since game and water are plentiful and close by your camp. In our lands, the game and water are scarce and the hunt may take us many suns from our lodges. If we had to travel by foot, our people would always be moving and hungry. The pony is strong and can carry great weight on his back and even greater weight if pulling the "two sticks." Our lives depend on our pony!" Red Sky concluded.

When the day's activities had drawn to an end and preparations were finished for the final night's rest at this encampment, Chief Ten made his last farewell to his new brothers, and was ascending the slope to the plateau above. He held his head high and his spirits soared, for he was making the return trail as a "six feet." Chief Roaring Wind of the Comanche and Chief Rolling Thunder of the Pawnee each had presented him with one of their ponies as a sign of their respect for his leadership of the council and for a new brother.

Those who were making this return trail with him exhibited their individual admiration by continuously contesting their Hiup brother for a position next to a pony in order to run their hands over its hide. Chief Ten rode slowly, not only to impress his people waiting on the plateau above, but with the knowledge that a pace faster than a walk by the pony required a skill that he had yet to master. He was, however, still a master of the art of impression, and the image he was building in the eyes of his people above would have been obliterated instantly if he lost control and fell from his mount. He rode straight and tall as he observed his people vying for the best position to observe their beloved chief. Although every fiber of his body was aflame with pride and self-satisfaction, Chief Ten could only portray coolness and aloofness, for he was chief! His people shared his moment of ecstasy.

The first rays of the next sun highlighted the change in the valley below. The area that had bustled with activity for more than a moon now reflected solitude. There was no evidence of past habitation. The respect shown Mother Earth by every tribe made it their top priority to return the area to the exact condition they had found it upon arrival. Tracks of the travois were the only visible signs that the area had been visited by humans. Small bands of buffalo could be seen eating their way through the grass toward the waterfall. This atmosphere of normalcy would be of short duration.

The Hiup camp slowly settled back into the unhurried pace of daily living. The plan was ready to be engaged the moment their scouts detected the Hairy One moving into the pass. The lone exception to this atmosphere of normalcy was Chief Ten. His every waking moment seemed to be centered on his new "brothers," his ponies. He spent most of his day atop one or the other of his two steeds. He spent the rest of his time feeding and grooming them.

The animals' dispositions differed as much as a placid pond and a roaring cataract! The former, a mare, the chief named Surefoot. The other pony, however, was a stallion, and proved to be of stout opinion and attitude. The plateau area was too confining to him, and he longed for the wide open and unrestricted spaces of the Plains. He was as swift as the wind and longed to relive the times when he ran with mane and tail flowing in the wind created by his speed. The parameters of the canyons and forest stifled his desires. His displeasure surfaced the moment Chief Ten mounted him and held him to a demeaning walk. He stood resolute in his determination not to be so demeaned, and only the strongest of nudges from Chief Ten's heels in his ribcage would make him move at all. He was appropriately named Mind Of His Own!

The chief was so enamored of the image he projected when riding his ponies that his days were spent riding among his people; his people were good and deserved this honor. He mentioned to Has It Made that, upon his death, he wished to ride one of his ponies into the Camp of Many Lodges so that all there would know of his greatness as chief. He asked of his son to see that the pony he was riding was Surefoot, for if Mind Of His Own was his mount, he might never make it to the Camp! At the time he made his request, he had no inkling of the coming event that would deny Has It Made the opportunity to carry out his request.

Twenty suns after the council, Chief Ten, atop Mind Of His Own, rode up the trail to visit Jock. The horse was nothing new to Jock. He could see the pride in the eyes of the chief and dutifully extolled the pony and the fine shadow the two cast whenever they visited him. True to his plan, Jock had kept a low profile among the Hiup. He kept out of sight while the council was taking place, but willingly served as adviser to the Hiup whenever they requested his opinion as to the expectations of the white man. Now that the council was over, he went back to his favorite pursuit: concocting his "Heritage."

Jock's farsightedness had paid off beyond his wildest expectations with the assistance of the spirits of nature and with good fortune. In a clearing Jock had created with sweat and claymore along the bank of the stream, Swift Feet planted the sack of barley seeds Jock had tucked into his sporran. The soil, aided by buffalo chips and fish dug into it by Swift Feet, had produced a fine crop of barley grain, a basic ingredient of the Blend. Swift Feet also had planted a crop of grain called maize, with which Jock was experimenting to create an emergency blend, in case of a barley crop failure. He found the water from the stream lacked the degree of purity necessary for that ultimate smoothness in taste of the Blend. However, all things considered, Jock was content to suffer this minute imperfection.

Jock was, by nature, neither selfish nor greedy, yet he definitely was a practical man. The primitive conditions under which he labored to create the Blend did limit the amount of finished product. "Just enough to service the needs of one bonnie Highlander," he rationalized. Fortunately for himself and for his hosts, this rationalization was in the best interests of all.

His strong and continuous desire to live undetected by the outside world became the determinant in his brewing procedure. The natural flow of wind was from west to east, but at certain times of high pressure, the wind moved from northeast to southwest. It was at these times that Jock fired the barley in the pots to cook the mash, then quickly followed with the distillation process. He feared that the wind would carry the readily identifiable scent to the nostrils of Kate's father, or to someone who might recognize the scent and share the fact in passing with Ian Stewart. This could send Ian on the trail to Hiup territory and discovery of Jock!

He also had to concern himself that a north wind possibly could send the scent into the Hiup camp. An unfamiliar scent (his) had led the Hiup to him once before, and he did not care to answer questions regarding his brew. This endeavor took a great deal of organization, planning, and patience, but it was necessary for his survival.

When the chief arrived at Jock's lodge one day, Jock was nowhere to be found, for he and Swift Feet had taken a walk to explore the sight and pleasure of the Canyon of Fire. Chief Ten was about to leave when he spotted one of Jock's sample kegs on a stump next to the entrance to the tipi. Out of curiosity, he picked it up. He was curious about the container and its purpose, but he was bound by a code of honor to respect the property of others. The binding of the code was slowly unraveled by the intensity of his curiosity. What could the contents be? The question swirled around his thought processes like a bee in a field of prairie flowers trying to determine the choicest morsel, when in fact they were all the same. "Oh well," he thought, "it really is none of my concern . . . or is it?" The curious bee was about to alight!

Curiosity has a way of creating movement, and not always one that has a logical explanation to the mover. Rationalization then charges forth to provide support to one's decision-making process, which supposedly is based on reason, e.g., "It would do no harm to examine the container to determine the reason for the strange scent. Perhaps it is the wood that it is made of that produces the scent, although it does smell like wild grapes that have been left unpicked and fermenting on the vine."

The chief then saw that the container had a hole in it that was plugged by a small round substance like a cut portion of a small tree branch. He shook the container and heard the movement of a liquid inside. What could this liquid be? There was no need to store water, for it was so plentiful and near. He mused further, "If I remove the plug and determine the contents, I can replace it and no harm is done." (Proof that if one really puts his mind to it, some degree of rationalization will be acceptable, for the moment, to investigate items usually avoided.)

Messin Man

The first obstacle had been shunted aside, so he pulled out the plug and the scent rose to titillate his nostrils. It did have the tang of fermentation, but the identity of the other elements escaped identification. The web of intrigue slowly encircled his entire being, but completely unnoticed. Its force seemed to overpower the movement of the hand to replace the plug. The fire of curiosity was burning the bastions of reason slowly but completely!

The chief visualized the times he had seen Jock tilt his head back and swallow the contents of containers such as this. It was impossible to know this as fact, for the hair on Jock's face concealed any positive evidence of his swallowing. He was aware, however, that each time Jock went through this procedure, he became friendlier and more talkative. Perhaps this was a magic potion of the white man that could be used to change character. One could only speculate on the matter, for Jock had never offered to share this experience of power with any member of the tribe.

Reasoning always prevailed. If this object or its contents presented a potential danger to him or his people, he must be aware of it and take action to prevent it. How could he do this without violating the code? "This code is applicable only to red men," reasoned the chief. Jock was a guest, not a red man; then again, he was a white man and, therefore, somewhat suspect. The truth must be known, for the protection of his people! There was just no other way. Placing the container to his mouth, he tilted his head and swallowed the contents in one gulp.

The passage of the liquid down his throat to the stomach was made with the speed of a falling star and with the heat of a cooking fire! The chief tried to dissipate some of the intense heat that spread to every part of his body by expelling air from his lungs. He actually expected to see a tongue of flame spurting from his mouth as he exhaled, but none came.

A fleeting awareness of panic was quickly replaced by a mellowness of attitude as the heat of the internal flame became a glow. He was relieved that this adventure had shown the container's contents to present no danger to his people beyond a possible overheating of the body. He tossed the container and plug over his shoulder with the casualness of indifference to the possibility that his action had violated any code.

As had Jock, he suddenly felt the urge to talk, but there was no one around. He decided to return to camp, where there would be plenty of ears receptive to the endless words of wisdom from their distinguished chief. To return meant that he had to mount his trusty pony, Mind Of His Own. This requirement, he found, was not to be accomplished with ease. To his chagrin, he found that complete control of his faculties and motor coordination were less than organized. A feeling of euphoria encompassed him, accompanied by double vision, a questionable sense of depth perception, and a control of balance so sensitive that the slightest breeze (and there was none) seemed to push him from his selected course.

Under normal circumstances, the chief would evaluate such symptoms as a cause for concern. Today, however, the chemical and biological influence of the Blend, while meandering through virgin territory, had replaced concern with an air of total indifference! Fortunately, one characteristic had not been replaced, but in fact had been subtly reinforced—determination! He intended to mount his beloved pony and ride back to camp to converse with his people.

The trail to where Mind Of His Own was grazing was a short one of twenty paces, yet for some reason, his pony not only kept changing location, but had increased in number from one to two. An awareness that the spirits of good fortune had smiled on him and had presented him with an exact duplicate of his pony was accepted as just reward for something or other that he had done. He couldn't recall a reason, at the moment, so he accepted the gift without question. However, the gift did pose the problem of which pony to mount for the ride to camp. The expediency of logic provided him with the answer. He would mount the first one he could put his hands on.

The mounting of a pony could be accomplished in various ways, depending upon the skill and showmanship of the rider. The chief had witnessed various methods during the past social activities between council meetings. One rider might take his mount's mane in one hand and, in one motion, leap upward, turn his body one-quarter turn in midair, and spread his legs so that, upon landing, he would be facing the head of his pony with legs gripping its sides.

Another method was the reverse mount. The rider approached his pony from the rear and, while leaping forward, place both hands on the rump of his pony to propel himself forward onto its back.

A third method was to grasp the mane of the pony and, while running, leap completely over the animal to land on the other side, where, as soon as the feet touched the ground, the rider would leap back over his pony. This back-and-forth process ended when the rider decided to land on his pony's back. This procedure demanded the greatest skill and, therefore, was a favorite when wishing to impress an audience.

Chief Ten had spent a considerable amount of time in seclusion practicing the skills of mounting. The third method he eliminated, for it demanded the skill of youth. The second he had tried once and found that the landing created a tremendous pain in the groin area of the body that was not in sync with the demands of this procedure. The first method he found to be less taxing on his body, as well as on his ego and, thereafter, became his standard mounting procedure.

Back to the problem at hand. The chief finally succeeded in grasping the bridle of one of the ponies, but mounting the animal proved to be another challenge. His customary leap and body pivot lacked his usual grace; it culminated in his pinwheeling over his mount and landing on his backside on the ground. He took a brief moment to analyze his action and decided that he had moved too fast. Grasping the mane of Mind Of His Own Number One (or was it Number Two?), he lifted his right leg over the back of "Whoever." While pulling on its mane, he slid his body up and onto the animal's back. Not flashy, but effective. A second effort was needed to attain an erect sitting position. Once mounted, he looked about for the second pony, but it was nowhere to be seen. He would return for it later. With that final decision made, he put his heels to the ribcage of his mount and rode back to camp.

The time involved in this return ride allowed the Blend to achieve its greatest degree of influence. Chief Ten was feeling absolutely no pain! His mental state had reached a high level of reckless abandon; he was soaring! Just before reaching the camp, he decided that this was an appropriate time to impress his people with his riding skills. He would no longer walk his pony around camp, now that he had mastered the skill of the trot.

The rider's heels served to convey signals to the mount regarding its master's intent for speed. If rider and mount were in perfect harmony, the response of the steed would mirror the rider's intent. Chief Ten's condition at that moment was simply not accurately tuned to his intent, resulting in an excessive application of heel pressure to communicate to his steed his wish to trot.

Mind Of His Own was somewhat short in his ability to read minds. He was, however, quite skilled in reading heel intent. When signaled to walk, he complied, even though he rebelled inwardly at such an insult to his talent for speed. When he felt the chief's application of severe force to his rib cage, he wasted no time in debating the possibility of false intent. This was the signal he had long been waiting for from his new owner. The request for top speed had been delivered, and he complied instantly. Straight through camp he sped like the wind, exuberant over this long-overdue opportunity to display his talent!

Chief Ten, even with his new total commitment to an attitude of casualness and indifference, found his position in need of quick review. This fool pony had been signaled to trot, and now he was running at full speed. The unexpected change caused him to lose his grip on the bridle. His first reaction was to get a firm grip on his pony's mane and try to maintain his balance. He then tried verbally to send a revised communiqué to his steed to cancel the heel signal. Mind Of His Own's ears were laid back to minimize wind resistance, so they did not pick up any meaning from the slurred vocal sounds of his rider.

The camp residents were just as surprised as their chief. Those at the near edge of the camp caught just a fleeting glimpse of the two performers as they sped past them. If they had not heard the frantic shouts of Chief Ten, they would have missed the spectacle entirely.

Those at the far end of the camp were in a perfect position to reap the thrill of the vision heading their way. From their point of view, their chief was putting on a superb display of horsemanship. His legs were flying up and down on each side of his mount, as if urging even greater speed; his right arm was flailing the air as if to pull himself and his mount through the air, while his body was moved up and down, scarcely making contact with the back of his mount! It was as though their chief was emulating the efforts of Brother Eagle to leave his perch and become airborne.

This illusion, as presented by their chief, couldn't have been more emphatically shattered when the ride came to an end. Mind Of His Own's focus was not on the quality of the ride, but on the sudden realization that he was reaching the end of running room. His exhilaration was cut short by the sight of the Canyon of Returning Voices before him, indicating the necessity to stop. The strong legs that had propelled himself and his rider with the speed of the wind now acted as one, coming to an abrupt stop at the canyon's edge!

Chief Ten's vision equaled that of his mount, for he, too, saw the approach of the canyon's edge. Unfortunately, he, as passenger, did not have the option open to his transport of using his legs as a braking device. Consequently, though not by choice, Chief Ten, with arms and legs flailing and voice rising, continued in a not too graceful arc into the void of space until the slender finger of gravity beckoned to him. Choiceless, his response was a vertical, stonelike descent to the canyon floor!

← Chapter Seven →

Through the eyes, the greatest of dangers hold little fear for the strong of heart, yet when seen only through the mind, even the strongest of heart can grow fearful through doubt.

The Canyon of Returning Voices continued to send back the last echoes of the chief's voice to the audience on the plateau long after his flight had terminated on the rocks below. Members of the tribe rushed to the canyon's edge to gaze down upon the body of their chief. In stunned silence, each tried to relive the scenario that had unfolded before their eyes in an effort to find a logical explanation for the final scene. The other main character in the scene grazed peacefully nearby.

Comprehension was long in coming, for it had to await its turn in the order of priorities. Realization was first, followed swiftly by despair of the heart, portrayed by the lament of his squaw, and joined by the voices of other squaws as comprehension's turn came to be recognized. The men, whose hearts were heavy also, turned to listen for the assignment of retrieval.

The tribe was faced with a not-too-uncommon dilemma for humans. They had relied on the fact that Chief Ten would lead them until age prevented him from doing so. They expected that the slowness of the aging process would allow ample time to train his son to take over his responsibilities in a smooth transition. The absence of life-threatening forces in the lands and lives of every Hiup chief of the past had perpetuated this belief.

Messin Man

At the age of thirty-seven summers, Has It Made was introduced to a new psychological and physiological force: stress. Under normal circumstances, to move from son of the chief to chief would not be too traumatic, for the role and its demands were not of an earth-shattering nature. Now, however, the entire western populace of Indians faced a trial of survival or destruction. The role of chief of the Hiup, and its accompanying responsibilities, took on more serious overtones in light of the challenges to be faced and decisions to be made. The Hiup were in a critical position; they were the first line of defense that would be tested by the enemy.

Fortunately for Has It Made, the transition would be smooth and the responsibilities kept to a minimum under the guidance of the great manipulator, Three Hands. The tragic loss of Chief Ten did not find the messin man at a loss to formulate appropriate actions and procedures. He had long before placed several options in his mental storehouse to await instant recall when needed. Although the timing and manner of Chief Ten's demise were totally unexpected, Three Hands' recall of an appropriate option provided a suitable plan for meeting the demands of the present problem.

A suggestion to Has It Made to return to his lodge and to seek a vision quest of his spirit brother was accepted. Orders were then given to those chosen to retrieve the body of Chief Ten. The remaining braves and the Gray Panthers were directed to prepare for the ceremony that would set their chief on his trail to the Camp of Many Lodges.

The camp scurried to carry out his directives. The messin man was looking beyond the procedural tasks of the ceremony. It would be his strength and vision that would guide his people through their period of grief and apprehension, and to focus their strength on the top priority—the coming of the white man. The time for mourning must be appropriate, yet not too extended, for time was growing short!

The initial lament of the women at the canyon rim, and the repetition by the "returning voices," had been heard by those who were in the forest hunting and fishing. They hurried to learn the reason for such sorrow. Among those to return were Jock and Swift Feet. On their way back to camp, they stopped by their lodge to deposit some berries they had gathered. Jock, the organizer, even in his haste to get to the main camp, did notice one item out of place; stooping to retrieve the keg, he sadly acknowledged the loss of its contents. Speculation over the reason for this loss weighed heavily on his mind as they continued back to the camp.

When they arrived, the recovery group was just entering camp with the body of Chief Ten. As the group passed them, Jock's keenly developed sense of smell picked up the undeniable scent of his cherished Blend coming from the body. His analytical mind quickly solved the mystery of his empty keg.

Three Hands' sense of smell, though not as finely tuned to the scent of the Blend as Jock's, still picked up the out-of-place scent emanating from the body and permeating the air. His mind groped to recall where he had experienced this scent before. The process ceased as Jock moved close to him to request an update on the tragedy. An identical scent radiated from Jock! What was the connection? The two men had a common scent, yet they were far apart when the event had taken place. An explanation definitely would be sought at a more appropriate time. Now the litter on which the chief's body had been transported had to be suspended from the branches of a tree to await the burial ceremony at the next sun.

Under the direction of Three Hands, the tribe moved to set in motion the requisites for the ceremony that would set their chief on his final trail to complete his hoop. The body had been retrieved from its perch in the tree, lovingly bathed by his squaw, and clothed with his favorite garments. His hair was braided and inset with color-coordinated beads, and his feet enclosed in his finest beaded moccasins. His favored possessions were placed in a bearskin pouch, and pots of his favored food sealed for his journey. He would be well-fed on his trail, and his entry into the Camp of Many Lodges would be impressive.

Ceremonial fires were stoked, and the tribe members took their places when Three Hands began the ceremony. His oration, projecting the wisdom, the courage, and the concern for the welfare of his people that Chief Ten had shown, was well received by the tribe. The ceremony culminated in a request that Wakan-Manitou and his helper spirits guide the trail of their chief true. The lament of the squaws rose and fell with each laudatory comment.

A buffalo robe was placed to cover the litter and its contents before it was lifted to the shoulders of the honor bearers. The procession, led by the messin man, headed in the direction of the Wall of Caves. It would be there, in a small cave, that the litter would be placed to await the arrival of the spirit chosen by Wakan-Manitou to guide him on his final trail. The entrance was sealed with rocks to prevent disturbance by animals.

Upon return to camp, Three Hands conducted still another ceremony—the installation of the new chief. For emergency contingencies, Has It Made was already chief, but the installation ceremony was an important component of the formalities for tribal acceptance. Preparations were being made by all, according to the role they would play when the ceremony began at the next sun's rising.

Installation ceremonies and the accompanying festivities were not limited by time, as were burial ceremonies. The warm climate's tendency to hasten decomposition placed speed highest in the order of priorities. Three Hands prepared the pipe; Has It Made prepared for his appearance in his best finery; the Gray Panthers practiced their oratorical presentations; and the braves, dancers, and drummers fine-tuned their skills, while the women busied themselves preparing the feast of feasts.

Only after every detail was in place did the ceremony begin. Three Hands lit the pipe, blew a puff of smoke to the four winds, then passed the pipe to Has It Made. The pipe made its rounds with several emptyings of ashes (along with aurora bags) into the fire. Three Hands had taken pains to concoct aurora bags that gave new colors for this occasion.

Oratory extolling the virtues of Has It Made and his past deeds was rather brief and sparse, since he had developed in the shadow of the accolade receiver, his father. Members of the Gray Panthers recalled their observances of the appointee as he grew up, and some braves shared their experiences as they related to Has It Made (which needed a great deal of embellishment to hold the attention of the audience). When Bear Claws groped to highlight how his life was possibly saved by Has It Made's heroic throwing of water on him when his loincloth caught fire as he was warming his backside, Three Hands mercifully stepped in to conclude the "oratorical" portion of the ceremony.

Has It Made was formally installed as chief of the Hiup when the messin man placed the sacred buffalo scalplock (with horns attached) on his head. Chief Has It Made stood and delivered an exceptionally fine bit of oration. Upon completion, and after the adulation whoops of his people, he gave the signal (by sitting down and folding his arms) for the festivities to begin. The dancers, the singers, and drummers capped the memorable event, in turn, until the first light of dawn.

Camp life returned to normal after a well-needed sleep-in following the celebration. Three Hands returned to servicing the needs of his people, which naturally included the needs of several maidens afflicted by the Brother of Fire. Their placement on "hold" because of recent events seemed to serve as time for Brother of Fire to increase the need for the messin man's remedy. Once these "emergency" cases were attended to, Three Hands took time away from his practice to advise the new chief regarding the need to be ready to implement the battle plan on short notice.

Three Hands also took time to visit Jock to resolve the unexplained behavior of Chief Ten. Jock long before had come to the conclusion that Three Hands was the real power broker of the Hiup, and the one to be reckoned with. He welcomed the visit and the opportunity to converse, but planned to offer no information that was not solicited.

Jock's value as a resource during the Great Council had not been forgotten by the messin man. It was his belief that Jock's value to the Hiup and their allies would be greatly increased once the white man appeared on the scene. Questions that would require quick answers as a show of strength and understanding might be readily available through Jock. This advantage would highlight the thinking ability of the Hiup in the minds of any enemy with whom they came into contact.

The game of wits began after the formalities of greeting were over. "I have thought long and deeply on the events that surrounded the death of our late chief," said Three Hands. "There are two questions that lie heavy and unanswered on my mind. The actions and behavior witnessed by my people were alien to Chief Ten. He was a man of thoughtful planning, somewhat showy perhaps, but never reckless or out of control. A man seldom lives to such an age as he by being foolish or careless, yet his actions were indeed reckless and out of control. The question is, why? I know you to be a man of analytical thinking, and so ask you to share any thoughts you may have on this matter."

"Aye, I have thoughts," replied Jock. "Chief Ten was here to pay me a visit on the day of his death, but Swift Feet and I were gone. The chief evidently returned to camp on a pony that was possibly frightened by an animal and became uncontrollable to ride. I have never seen the chief ride faster than a walk, so when his pony bolted, he was unable to stop him."

"Your point is well taken and has provided a possible answer to my question," intoned Three Hands, "however, it has, in turn, raised another question. How did you know that the chief had visited your lodge on the day in question? You and Swift Feet did not arrive in camp until after the event. Not one Hiup was privy to knowledge of his visit."

Jock inadvertently had placed himself in a position he had hoped to avoid—he had offered information! His mind raced to create a plausible answer without repeating his error.

"I see that you need time to recall the events of that day. Perhaps the answer to my second question is part of the answer to the first," stated Three Hands as he moved quickly to maintain the initiative. "When the body of our chief was returned to us, I detected a strong scent from him that was alien to my nose. When you arrived in camp, my nose picked up the same scent coming from you. What was the source of this scent that was common to both of you? This is the question for which I have no answer. Would you share your thoughts as to a possible solution to this mystery?"

Jock realized he was hooked on the horns of dilemma; he decided his best approach was to share his inadvertent responsibility in the events that led to the tragedy. Three Hands was too clever to accept untenable postures, and Jock saw that in this man lay his chances to remain alive as a guest of the Hiup.

He decided to take his chances on speaking true. "You see with the eye of the hawk whose vision can penetrate the heaviest layer of pine twigs to detect the movement of the mouse beneath them," Jock stated in a most flattering manner. "I know that you can also see the heaviness in my heart over the death of my friend and brother, Chief Ten. This heaviness is increased by the thought that my carelessness may have played a part in his change of habits."

Three Hands listened to Jock's reply with great interest, musing to himself, "This is one fast learner, and one of great intelligence. He is also capable of matching my manner of portraying innocence to win a sympathetic ear. This man uses a good style of flattery and sounds more like a red man than a white. This should prove very interesting."

Jock continued, "Swift Feet and I were at the Canyon of Fire enjoying the work of Mother Earth and planning for that great moment of gladness when our first cub is born in the spring. We heard the sounds of sorrow from the Canyon of Returning Voices, and immediately began our return trail. We came past our lodge and I noticed something had been disturbed in our absence, but not by an animal."

Jock went into his tipi and returned with an empty sample keg. Removing the cork, he held the keg near the face of the messin man. "Is this the scent you picked up from Chief Ten?" he inquired.

Three Hands' nostrils sampled the odor radiating from the hole, then closed quickly in rebellion against the smell! "A bit stronger from your container, but nevertheless the same," he coughed. "My mind seeks answers to its composition and the purpose for which it is used. Can it be a potion for the sick? Is this an instrument created by the white man to be used against my people to disorient them and to bring about their death? Speak true, Jock, for my ears will close like the nostrils of my nose if they detect false words."

Jock's mental processes were churning to devise a progression of intelligible utterances that would sound plausible to his listener without jeopardizing his need for seclusion. Fortunately, his sense of survival was so acutely honed that it was able to pick out key words from Three Hands' questions to serve as a catalyst to organize a progression suitable for his needs. "Your words of concern for your people fly straight to my heart like the surest of arrows, Three Hands, only to find an open wound there. The wound was caused by the death of Chief Ten. A liquid similar to what was in this container may have been the source of your chief's erratic behavior, but I cannot say this as truth, for I was not here with him. I do say as truth that the contents were not created for use against your people.

"You ask if it is a potion for a sickness of the white man," Jock went on. "If I said yes, it would not be a full truth. I ask your patience in hearing my words and helping me to close the wound in my heart so that it may never open again. As a messin man, you have proven your greatness in mixing the proper herbs, roots, and other ingredients for specific illnesses of your people. Would you give a small cub the same portion you would give a brave or a squaw?"

"No," came the reply. "The cub would not need the same amount as the full grown even if the sickness was the same. The needs of each individual must be carefully determined before my medicinal help is prescribed."

"Your awareness of this difference is the basis for your greatness as a messin man," stated Jock. "Even though I know the answer, let me put another question to you, even if it tries your patience. If you discovered a berry-laden bush in the forest that was completely unknown to you, would you gather the berries and eat them all?"

"Never!" chuckled Three Hands at such a preposterous inference. "I depend on my experience in taste to determine if the berry was a gift from Mother Earth to her children, or if it was a reminder that all of her gifts were not meant as food for man. She has led us to see that we can add to the beauty around us by making use of such berries to make dye for our blankets. One must sample such unknowns carefully and use one's senses to determine the best use of such gifts. If such a gift proves to bring pain or sickness, then we do not use it as food, which pleases Mother Earth."

"A very wise procedure," complimented Jock. "The contents of this container were like the unknown berry to Chief Ten. For some reason, instead of sampling it, he consumed all of the 'berries' at one time. Now, I can drink the liquid and it does me no harm, for I am used to doing this. It is a prescription that fills my needs, but, I fear, these needs and those of Chief Ten differed vastly; our reaction to this messin was just as different.

"You say that you have experimented to discover a specific messin for a specific need. I, too, have experimented to find a specific messin for my specific need. Many white men have the same basic need as I, and use this same messin, but not of the same portions. If I said that this messin was for a sickness, it is not any sickness as you know it."

Jock went on to explain, "Your people are blessed by Mother Earth, for your streams run clear and water is plentiful in your lands. In the lands from which I and other white men come, water of such purity is not readily available. We have made a bad habit of discarding our refuse into our streams and poisoning them. One takes a chance on illness if he drinks this water; therefore, the need to develop a substitute for water became necessary. Some selected the grape as the basic ingredient, because they were plentiful in their lands. Others, like myself, chose a drink made basically from grain, which grew easily in our lands. Both drinks serve our needs as a water replacement. They can be stored for long periods of time in containers like those I use to store the drink I make from grain."

"I can understand your words and the reason you give for making such a drink, or messin, but I do not understand the reasoning of your people to destroy the gift of purity given your water by Mother Earth," Three Hands interjected, shaking his head. "The fact that they do raises an alarm in my mind if such a habit is continued by the white man when they come to the lands of the Hiup and beyond. You say that you make this drink now, even though pure water is near for your use. Why is this so?"

"It is a spirit that is so captive of the body that its will is hard to break. The pain that such intent delivers to the body is so great that one's mind suggests captivity rather than substitution or abstinence. It is a disease of the mind and spirit that is liquid servitude," continued Jock, hoping that his explanation was being accepted.

"Do all white men suffer this affliction?" asked Three Hands.

"Nay," replied Angus, "although the majority do, there are a few who practice abstinence as diligently as those who must use the drink."

"Then it must be well to determine to which group I belong, as representative of my people," the messin man stated in a move to test the truth of Jock's words. "I wish to sample your water substitute to see which spirits guide me!"

The request sent Jock's thought processes from the spillway of confusion to the placid, controllable stream of logic. His most dreaded position at this time would be castrated by the horns of another dilemma. The request of the messin man had to be honored, or all of his words would be taken as false. If, by some stroke of misfortune, the messin man developed a liking to his Blend, his secret would be ended and his life once more in peril. If, on the other hand, Three Hands could be guided to reject the Blend, his immediate problem would be solved. The influential power of Three Hands was not to be taken lightly, so therefore his actions must be appropriate to bring resolution to his problem.

One could hardly honestly credit Jock's decision to respond as he did entirely on his mental capacities. His response was influenced to a great degree by subconscious tradition. "If ye wish to impress someone highly, ye brings out your best! If ye wishes to create the worst impression, ye brings out your worst!" Jock went into his lodge and selected a sample keg of his greenest, most recent brew; in so doing, he bypassed his store of "vintage" Blend. Reappearing outside, he handed the keg to Three Hands.

"I do not intend to follow the procedure used by Chief Ten to evaluate your drink, Jock," declared Three Hands. "I prefer my own method." So saying, he removed the cork and took a mouthful of the liquid. His evaluation was not long in coming! After a brief try at sloshing the liquid around his teeth and gums, he hastily (and forcefully) ejaculated the liquid from his mouth! A fast run to the stream and handfuls of water sloshed around in his mouth soon allowed his power of speech to return.

"This is the foulest-tasting substance I have ever placed into my mouth!" the messin man gasped. "Your drink has fire in it! If I didn't know better, I would think that a fire stick had been placed in my mouth. Your drink is indeed water of fire!"

Jock could hardly contain his relief. Only a follow-up was needed to cement his point. "As you wisely stated, my friend, the same messin for all does not have the same effect on all. From its effect on Chief Ten, my heart beats with gladness that you did not swallow the drink. From your facial expression, I would say that this messin would not be of benefit to your people; in fact, it seems to be bad messin for the red man!"

"That is true, my brother. If you wish to remain as brother to the Hiup, you must see that the opportunity for any Hiup, or any red man for that matter, to drink this water of fire, either by intent or by accident, never occurs! I would suggest that you destroy this potion, but I honor your need for it. Heed my words on this matter!" cautioned the messin man.

"Heed his words on this matter." To Jock's ears, these words were like the musical sounds of the finest pipes—pure ecstasy! To be sure, this was one subject sealed by mutual agreement. "I heed the words of my brother," he promised. "My heart cries that I did not have the knowledge that I have now, for it would have saved the life of your chief. That carelessness will not happen again!"

"Then let us get back to the problem at hand: the coming of the white man," Three Hands requested. "Can you spend more of your time in teaching your language to my people? Everyone must be a spokesman if the white man breaks our defense at the pass. Our first encounter will set the pattern for appropriate reactions to the presence of the whites."

Jock, still enjoying the psychological high of his successful efforts to preserve full control over his Blend, was most benevolent in his willingness to accept this added task. "I will be most pleased to do this and any other task that will benefit my brothers, but there is one problem that causes me pain."

"Share this problem with me, and the pain that goes with it, so that I may know and share your discomfort. Together we may cause the Spirit of Pain to leave you and return peace to your heart," suggested Three Hands.

"My brothers of the Hiup have accepted me as one of them and have given me the choice of sharing the many bounties of Mother Earth here in your lands," said Jock. "You have even allowed me to take one of your women as squaw, which has given me much happiness. The problem is a divided heart. I am white, and the white man your people have named as their enemy. I cannot turn against my white brothers to side with my red brothers. I have agreed to teach you my language, in hope that both of my brothers can communicate in peace and live in peace. If there is war between the two, my heart would break with sadness!"

Three Hands could not deny the truth in the words of Jock, for they would be his words if their roles were reversed. Jock's value to the cause of the red man could not be underestimated. His fears must be laid to rest if his value was to reach its full potential.

"I can understand the heaviness of your heart, my friend, and the thought lies heavy on my heart that we would ask you to desert your white brothers and lead them to harm." Three Hands paused, then continued, "We will soon meet white men in increasing numbers as they come into our lands. We will wage war against them to protect that which is ours, but this war will not be a war of death. We plan a war of minds and, if successful, there will not be one drop of blood shed on either side. If there is to be blood shed, it will be through the act of the white man, not us. Your sharing of your knowledge of the habits and thinking of the whites can only strengthen our resolve to avoid the shedding of blood. We will defend our lands, but through the weapons of our minds, not our lances. Your counsel will greatly assist us in this endeavor."

"I know you to be a speaker of the truth, and the weight of the sorrow in my heart has been lifted by your words," replied Jock. "Let the experience of the water of fire be well learned, for the white man will use it as one of his weapons if he discovers its effect on the red man." Jock could see no harm in hammering in the last brad to secure the band on his monopoly of the Blend.

"The lesson has been well learned and will not be repeated, if we have both spoken true," confirmed Three Hands as he turned to make his way back to his camp.

The time of snow in the mountains was the Time For Sleeping in Hiup lands. The climate was mild enough that snow did not fall in quantity and accumulate. It was, however, a time for hibernation by many animals and rest for the trees of the forest. The Hiup spent this season of the year tanning hides to be used for clothing, making new lancepoints, et cetera. Activities were of a restful and unhurried nature, except those activities of creation which seemed to take up the slack of other seasons. New cubs would be introduced, not only in the forest, but also in the camp of the Hiup.

There was considerable council activity by the men to hone their preparedness for the expected introduction to the white man, which should come at the time of the Spring Awakening. Jock was deeply involved in those councils. Patience was a virtue of the red man, but even the most patient began to feel their hackles rise as the season drew near. Ears were tuned to detect sounds that would indicate the moment was here. They took no chances on an accidental meeting with the enemy. They stayed on the high ground, posting lookouts to warn of encroachment.

The time for rest ended; the arrival of the Spring Awakening also brought the arrival of a party of Quapaw. Their leader, Listing Canoe, reported to the Hiup Chief. "The people of the Quapaw have kept to the plan. The whites have sent scouts across the Big Water, whom we intercepted. They were informed of our intent to allow passage only on a trail of our choosing. Their leaders have accepted our terms after hearing the consequences of not doing so. They say that they will come in peace and do not seek war with us."

Chief Has It Made spoke for the Hiup, "We welcome our brothers of the Quapaw to our camp. Their words are as welcome as the rain upon the seed of the corn. Your people have acted wisely and with bravery. The white man saw no fear in your eyes and knew better than to treat you as he does our brothers to the east. With bravery such as you have shown, our plan cannot fail. The white man will also see no fear in our eyes when he comes to our lands or the lands beyond. When you return to your people, share our words with them and the singing in our hearts that they are our brothers."

The time of waiting was to end, for soon the sounds of the trail-making whites would be heard. The hearts of the Hiup beat like the sound of Clean Krupa's drums at a Hop! Finally the first sounds of trail activity could be heard by placing one's ear to the ground; the sound of crashing trees was clearly discernible. As days passed, the sound increased until it was unnecessary to place the ear to the ground. Soon the hacking sound of the ax and the rasping of the saw was audible. Although still unseen, a small wagon train was slowly making its way toward Hiup Pass

The wagon train was smaller than when it had started west from St. Lou E. The rigors of the trail had taken its toll on a number of wagons, and their occupants had returned by foot to the point of origin. Of the twenty wagons that had started this trail, only fifteen had managed to reach the base of the pass or the lands beyond. Even then, several were in a questionable condition of reliability. The procession moved at a snail's pace, having to wait until trees, rocks, and other hazards were cleared before moving forward. Now, emerging from the forest, the ascent to the pass began, but the pace was still slowed by the boulder-strewn area—and by the drums!

According to plan, the Hiup were not to show themselves, yet would make their presence known to those approaching the pass. From their vantage point high above the trail to the pass, all eyes watched as the first wagons, led by a lone figure on horseback, emerged from the forest and gained the rocky slope to the pass. At this precise moment, Three Hands gave a hand signal that was relayed to a group of drummers stationed in the Canyon of Returning Voices. The drummers began a slow, modulated rhythm that reverberated through the canyon and was repeated and amplified by perfect acoustics!

To each member of the approaching caravan, each day on the trail found two forces constantly at work to challenge them. During the day, the physical force of clearing the trail so the wagons could advance occupied their minds and their bodies. In the evening before sleep, psychological forces gnawed relentlessly at them. Each day's advance stretched the umbilical cord that connected them with the security of the womb of St. Lou E, and found the surgical knife—fear of the unknown—an ever-present reality ready to sever the cord!

Panic clutched the train in an immobilizing grip when the sound of the drums reached them. For what seemed like hours, everyone assumed the likeness of statues. This reaction was replaced by an attempt to turn the wagons around and retreat from the sound. The leader of the train broke from his trance and quickly rode to the rear of the train, entreating his followers to hold their positions. He instructed each adult male to leave their wagons and group for a council.

The Hiup reacted to the action below with glee. There was much laughter and backslapping over their first act of battle. There could be no question that their first move had been a success, but Three Hands was quick to remind them that one success did not mean the battle had been won. The white man's first reaction would have a follow-up, and this would determine the next move of the Hiup. A signal was given to the drummers to stop.

The reaction of the group below was to evaluate their present status and to reach consensus on their next move. They were aware that, once across the Mississippi, they were in the lands of the red savage. Most had little knowledge or experience with the red man in numbers. They only knew that the worth of the red man, in the eyes of the white man, was equal to that of a worthless animal. No member of this train had ever encountered the red man in numbers greater than a band anywhere east of the Mississippi. Now, judging from the sound of the drums, it seemed there must be thousands of the savages ahead. The moccasin suddenly was transferred to the other foot.

A number of men expressed their belief that the best move was in the direction of St. Lou E. The leader of the train, having shaken off his first reaction (which would have been in agreement with the "returnees"), used a logical approach; he urged the group to evaluate their status. He reasoned that they had come too far and had extended too much energy in clearing the trail to give up their quest just because they had heard some drums. Had they not been given assurances by the tribes at the river that they could move in peace if they kept to the conditions set forth by those tribes? They had encountered no hostile actions on the trail thus far; they had violated no condition, so why jump to conclusions that may not be warranted?

The points raised by their leader, Big Mik McDermott, seemed plausible enough to overrule the attitude that no savage could be trusted to keep his word. They agreed to return to their wagons and continue the trail. Even the persuasiveness of their leader, however, could not dispel the one new addition to the trail that would now be with them every day to probe at their resolve like a knife in the small of the back. The bravado built by their experience of superiority over the red savage was totally destroyed by the sound of those drums and replaced by fear of the unknown! Caution would govern every move they made. The battle plan of the red man was working better than realized. The wagon train started to move again toward the summit of the pass—and the drums!

The first creak of the wagon wheels signaling the advancement of the train triggered the return of the drums. This time the beat was of a slow cadence to match the movement of the train. Has It Made gathered a council to determine what, if any, action would be needed when the train reached the summit. The Gray Panthers restated the object of the plan: not to be seen unless it became unavoidable.

Three Hands pointed out that to let the whites pass with no contact would let an opportunity pass to learn more about them. Knowledge could strengthen future corrective actions.

"Our only contact has been with Jock, and we cannot be certain that he represents all white men. If he does not, then our plan may have a negative effect. I suggest that one spokesman meet the white man and remind him of the conditions for safe passage in our lands. We could not only gain information regarding his attitude, but our people could see them up close while hidden in the forest. It could be a valuable learning experience for us all."

"Your words are wise," agreed Has It Made. "I will meet the white man."

This was not the messenger Three Hands had in mind! The greeter would have to be sharp of mind and tongue, and intensify the illusion, not shatter it. (Someone like himself would be perfect, he thought).

He hastened to voice his rejection of his chief in that role. "Spoken like the brave chieftain you are, but our ignorance of possible reactions by these whites might place you in great danger. A witless reaction brought on by any member of their party might result in your death. We have just recently lost one chief, and our people would be leaderless at the time of their greatest need. Someone must take your place as spokesman."

Has It Made may not have been too swift of mind, but his messin man's suggestion of the possibility of fatality struck home. After all, he reasoned, he had waited a long time to gain the position of chief, and he enjoyed the role, so why take a chance on losing it if it could be avoided and the tribe's objective still be attained?

He made a wise decision. "Your words of concern touch me deeply and, as usual, come from the wisest of thoughts. We need a spokesman who can weave our web of deception even tighter around our prey. Can I call upon you, Three Hands, to be that man?"

Three Hands had once again demonstrated his ability to have supreme control over his facial expressions. The laughter from within was displayed as a mask of concern on his face. He quickly responded before someone else in the party could devise an objection because of his worth to the tribe. "It would be my honor to speak for you and for my people," he replied.

Word of the plan was relayed to all members of the tribe, and emphasis for concealment amplified. The adrenaline was coursing through every member of both parties now as the wagons moved toward the fulcrum—the crest of the pass.

Down below, Big Mik's mind was less on the clearing of boulders from the trail than on visualizing what lay ahead at the crest of the pass. His days, except for meals and sleep, were spent atop his horse. As leader of this train, his role was to choose the direction of the trail and to supervise the clearing of it for the passage of the wagons. The choice of direction was easy, since the savages had made the parameters of the trail clear. An innate distrust of those savages guided his thoughts as to possible defensive reactions available if hostile actions were taken against his train. The safety and welfare of his charges were uppermost in his mind.

Big Mik's stature befitted his name. Big and brawny, he was never one to run away from a fight; although slow to anger, once aroused he became a dangerous opponent. Craving a lot of elbow room, he was one of the first to depart the colonies and head west into the dark and bloody grounds of Kentucky. He had fought the native sons and respected them as opponents in battle. The edge given by his trusty long rifle to him and others like him had proven too much for the red man. The experiences gained as a frontiersman had made him an equal to the red savage in woodland combat. His eyes were trained to the signs of the trail, and his every move was guided by instinct. If the red men he would soon face were like those he had fought in the past, he would survive this trail.

He had experienced their drums before and recognized them as a means of communication. The usual procedure was to hear a single drummer, who sent a message that was picked up and relayed by another drummer down the trail, and then relayed by other such drummers until it reached its destination. The sound of the drums ahead was not the same as message drums. It seemed the number of drummers ahead was enormous!

Big Mik knew he was soon to gain additional experience. His train was out in the open and vulnerable. He knew that he could not gain the crest before darkness. He decided to camp far enough from the crest and woodlands to be out of weapon range. If there was to be a fight, the enemy would have to leave the protection of the woods and meet them in the open.

That evening, he shared his plan of action with his men. Now that the train had stopped, the drums had stopped also. The quietness was welcomed. "By high sun tomorrow, we will reach the crest. I will ride far enough ahead to scout the trail; if I encounter any hostiles, you will have time to form a defensive position. You are not to advance until you see my signal that all is well."

An undulating blanket of uneasiness covered the camp that night as thoughts of the next day prevailed. There were no guards posted, because the white men accepted the fallacy that red men were so afraid of the dark and the night spirits that they never attacked at night. The time of rude awakening lay ahead!

The sun's first rays found both camps stirring and preparing for the unknown. Big Mik was busy supervising the clearing of the trail, as planned. Just before high noon, they reached the point where the train was to stop. After the noon meal, Big Mik mounted his horse and slowly rode toward the crest, eyes ever vigilant for any sign of movement, his rifle in readiness across the pommel of his saddle.

Reaching the crest, he reined in his horse and his eyes took a survey of the scene before him. The forest ended about a stone's throw on each side of the trail, except for a single line of towering trees at the far end of the clearing where the pass seemed to end. At the edge of the clearing to his right, a stream coursed in the direction of the towering trees. A wagon master of little experience might be deluded into bringing his train into the clearing to set up camp—a perfect spot for an ambush! Here they would be easy prey for hostile action, to be disposed of so the trap could be reset for the next train.

Urging his horse forward, he made his way slowly toward the trees. His eyes moved right and left, and detected no movement or sign of habitation. As he approached the shade trees, a spectacular scene began to unfold before him. The trail did not terminate here, but continued in a sloping drop to his left. The sky began to end as a horizon appeared as an endless line of waving grass dotted with countless numbers of grazing animals. To his right, a spectacular waterfall plunged effortlessly from the forest's edge to a pool below, where its force from the fall was dissipated, allowing it to continue on as a stream that disappeared into the side of a sheer wall of rock. There was joy in his heart, for from what he could see, the long arduous days of dropping trees and moving boulders were past. From this point on, as far as the eye could see, there would be a smooth trail.

Big Mik turned his horse and was in the process of returning to give the signal to advance, when a figure, hardly ten paces to his right, appeared from out of nowhere. His eyes had long been trained to detect all unnatural aspects of his surroundings at all times, but this figure had blended so harmoniously into the surroundings that it had gone undetected. How long had he been there observing him? How many more were waiting unseen, and what were they thinking?

His finger moved slowly toward the trigger of his rifle as his eyes traveled slowly up and down the figure of the man who had moved to stand before him. He was definitely an Injun, and of a build that equaled his own. Glistening black hair fell below his shoulders; his only garments were a rather long loincloth and beaded moccasins. His skin was copper in color and completely devoid of paint, and he carried no weapon—which were all good signs. The savage's eyes were traveling about Big Mik's person slowly, in a purposeful, evaluating manner equaling his own. Their eyes met and locked!

The savage slowly raised his right arm and gestured for Big Mik to dismount, which he did. He knew that, before any council with such savages could begin, one had to be on the same eye level with them. He dismounted with rifle in hand, but the savage pointed to the rifle and indicated that it be returned to its scabbard. Big Mik obliged this request, then turned to face his host once again.

Big Mik had a basic working knowledge of Iroquois and Muskhogean, and so began the greeting procedure and explanation for his presence in the lands of this man. He was hoping that the savage could understand him and accept his words. He was completely taken back by the reply from this man before him!

"I ken what ye are a sayin, but there's no a need ta search for words frae two tongues when I am comfortable speaking and understanding your own. I am Three Hands, messin man of the Hiup. We hae witnessed your entry inta our lands wi' a wee bit o' curiosity. We canna but wonder as ta your intent."

The reply was some time in coming, for Big Mik was so startled that coherent speech did not win mental priority until his mind answered its own questions. This man, savage or not, if one closed his eyes, could be a rebellious brother like himself, who hated the English, a highlander from the hills of Scotland! How could this be? Could it be possible, like the lost tribe of Israel, he was from a lost tribe of Scotland?

Speech regained priority and he replied, "I am Big Mik, leader of the wagon train. Forgive my hesitation, but I am filled with wonder that you are so versed in my tongue. I have never experienced such a wonder with red men in the east. Let me hasten to assure you that we come in peace. We travel to the west to find land that will accept us and allow us to live in peace. We are gentle folk and seek to live in harmony with our brothers. We were told by the red men at the Mighty River that we could travel this trail if we proved our words to be true. We keep to our word."

"Your words mak our hearts sing," said Three Hands, "and if true, ye will find the trail ta be as true as those words. Tell your people ta cum so that I may speak wi' them and all will understand our intent ta be true ta our word."

"My people will also be happy to hear your words of assurance," replied Big Mik as he mounted and turned to ride to the point where his people could see his signal to advance.

Each wagon, pulled by oxen and trailing a cow behind, creaked its way up the slope to the crest and into the glade. Big Mik directed them to form a semicircle with the wagons, leave their weapons in them, and then assemble near the line of towering trees. Once there, all eyes were on the figure before them. Big Mik allowed them to gaze briefly at the land beyond and its beauty before requesting them to be seated for council.

While the wagon-master was returning to signal his people, Three Hands signaled his people to come to a point where they could see and hear, yet not be seen. He was rejoicing over the impact his speech had made on Big Mik. Jock's value was proving to be immeasurable! He waited patiently and silently while Big Mik instructed his party where to sit for council. He did not underestimate the importance of his words to them, therefore, he would choose his words carefully!

Big Mik spoke to prepare his group for the observance of protocol, which he knew to be vital for a good relationship with their host. His sense of humor stayed the urge to prepare them for the shock he had experienced when the red man spoke—he was eager to see their reaction! "This is Three Hands of the Hiup, and he is spokesman for his people. His words will guide us and give us direction and comfort on the trail ahead." He then took his place at the side of Three Hands, where he was in a prime position to observe the reaction of his men as the first words rolled from the tongue of the messin man. He was not disappointed, for they all, to a man, sat in disbelief!

"I bid ye guid welcome ta this council of the Hiup. My people watched your approach wi' mair than curiosity in their hearts. We hae heard of the Hairy Ones ta the east of the Mississippi and how they came ta the lands of our brothers and were warmly welcomed, as I welcome ye. These men, your brothers, betrayed, killed, and took their lands awa frae them. Our hearts are filled wi' sorrow for our brothers, but we hae learned well the lesson of their foolishness.

"Your leader, Big Mik McDermott, has telt me that ye seek land for a new hame. I ask mysel' if those same words were heard by our brothers ta the east before their hames were taken frae them and made the hames of the white man. Do all whites speak wi' such forked tongues, we ask? The sound of the wailing squaws of our dead brothers is carried by the wind ta our ears wi' the same answer: aye! We heed their voices."

Unaware of the impact his brogue was having on his audience, Three Hands continued, "My people and our brothers ta the west, whose numbers are greater than those of the buffalo below, have studied the lessons of our brothers ta the east. The voices of those who spoke ta kill every white man who crosses into our lands west of the Mississippi were many. Others of us asked, 'Wud we then no be savages like the white men who dealt thusly wi' our brothers? We are a' na men who kill wi' out reason, for that is against the laws of Mother Earth and Wakan-Manitou who guide us.

"Think ye bak ta the lands frae which thou comest. Once these lands belonged ta the red man, whose numbers were as great as the trees of the forest. How many hae ye left ta count? Our brothers welcomed ye ta their lands and called ye brother. What name did ye call him? Brother? Na! Savage? Aye! Wud ye also call me savage? Look inta your hearts for the answer, and I dinna think ye'll find another name there!

"Hear my words and weigh them carefully, for your days will be numbered by the number of days ye remember them!" the messin man stated emphatically. "Ye are judged by the lesson of our brothers. We dinna welcome ye ta our lands, only ta council sae that all will know and remember this. We have agreed ta allow ye safe passage through our lands under certain conditions. Your trail will end in lands where other white men, like yourselves, live. Your trail through our lands will only be as wide as the tracks of your tipis. Ye will na stop except ta rest your animals and even then na longer than it taks one moon to rise and follow its trail across the sky before the sun rises. Stay not twa, or ye'll no awauken the morrow! Our eyes will be on ye every step ye taks. Breaking the conditions set forth will be cause for us ta think ye wish ta tak our lands like your brothers took the lands of our brothers ta the east. Your destruction will be as swift as will that of every white man ta follow. These are the words of my people, who dinna speak wi' forked tongues! I have spoken!" With this, he sat down.

Big Mik rose to speak for his people. "We hear the words of Three Hands and wish him to know that we are heavy of heart for the injustices to the red man by others of our color. We are men of straight tongues and will prove it by abiding by every condition you have set forth for us. Judge us each day on the trail, and you will see that the kindness you show in allowing us passage through your lands is justified. Those who will follow must be judged by their actions alone, for by our actions we will prove our search for peace with our red brothers."

Three Hands stood, signaling the end of the council. Big Mik extended his right arm and was met by the extended arm of the messin man in a sign of peace.

"Ye may camp here until the rising of the sun, then ye must break camp and move on. Your tipis must sta' on the trail, but your hunters may leave the trail ta hunt. The buffalo are everywhere, so the hunters can no a' go beyond the sight of those on the trail." With those words of summation, Three Hands turned and quickly disappeared into the forest.

The camp activities that night were quiet and subdued; every adult was deep in thought and their apprehension was reflected in their movements—with one exception!

Messin Man

A young Hiup maiden, at a loss of purpose after the evening meal, decided to visit the pool at the base of the waterfall for a refreshing swim. The whites were camped for the night in the glade at the top of the incline and presented no danger to her.

Alas, the hand of Fate also caressed the shoulder of Brother Lustafter, a self-ordained missionary traveling with the train. Brother Lustafter, however, was not at a loss of purpose this evening. He had decided to walk down the incline to the prairie below and to the solitude it presented for his voice to be heard by his maker.

As he walked, Brother Lustafter talked. He practiced his thoughts aloud in order to refine meanings and improve his power of persuasion. He asked for divine guidance in keeping the thoughts and deeds of the settlers pure, and also for guidance in converting any savage he encountered on the trail. His prayers were partially answered when he inadvertently came upon the maiden who was swimming in the pool.

Practice paid off! His persuasive manner soon convinced the young girl that he presented no danger to her. She was somewhat cautious, for she had never been this close to a white man and had been warned by the messin man to avoid them. It was difficult to avoid this one—he stood on the bank of the pool right next to where her clothing lay. Emerging from the pool, she dressed and was soon in conversation with Brother Lustafter. The language barrier was kept to a minimum by the substitution of hand signs when needed.

The missionary worked patiently and diligently at the task of converting this young and supple savage, in accordance with the objective of the missionary position. Once this position is assumed, a plunge forward to fulfillment, regardless of surrounding influences or objections, is paramount to the success of this objective. Only when the pinnacle of ecstatic awareness is reached is the position retracted. Many missionaries feel that their way is best and all other positions are inferior, or at best, merely supplemental.

The maiden was so successfully and totally converted to this position that she later, after several additional sessions to make certain of mastery, returned to the Hiup camp, and with the passage of time convinced other maidens to accept the better way of life it provided. The males were the target for conversion and were soon joyful practitioners, unaware that this new position they assumed was to lead to their demise in days to come!

Meanwhile, at the first rays of dawn the drums began to stir; so did the members of the train. With Big Mik directing, the process of movement down the steep incline to the plains below began. A team of eight oxen was hitched to the front of a wagon by ropes. The wagons went down the slope backwards, with the oxen acting as anchors. The driver handled the wheel brake in case the ropes broke or some other accident occurred to increase the speed downward. It was a slow, laborious task, for when the wagon reached the plain, the oxen had to be unhitched and returned to the crest to be hitched to another wagon. One team was always on the way down while another was on the way up. The safe delivery of a wagon to the plain was paramount, as it was the only means of transport from this point.

By the end of the day, all wagons were on the plain except one. One had reached its capacity for trail torture, and had disintegrated beyond repair. The remains were left at the bottom of the slope and salvageable items transferred to other wagons. If not for the generosity of other train members, the occupants of that wagon would have been faced with a return trail by foot to St. Lou E. They set up camp by the waterfall, and at dawn the train moved west and out of sight, to the accompaniment of Hiup drums!

The passage of time and continuous trail challenges would soften their memory of their first encounter with the red man and his Scottish brogue. Time, and interaction with following whites, would also soften the brogue of the toll-collecting red man!

←═══Chapter Eight═══→

Visions come only to those of imagination, interpretation, and action. To all others, they are merely dreams or fantasies.

Covered wagons were of a basic design, but with individual differences and strengths. These differences were sorely tested by the rugged trail west from St. Lou E. Rains washed out ruts and craters that constantly tested the mettle of the drivers, as well as their wagons.

Some wagons never made it to the Hiup pass because of equipment unequal to the rigors of the trail. Breakdowns caused many to admit defeat and return to St. Lou E. Those who did make it to the pass viewed the easier-going aspects of the trail ahead with relief.

Still, the movement down the steep incline had to be accomplished before that feeling of relief became a reality. For many, this was the point of return, as they were not successful in overcoming the demands of the steep incline from the crest to the prairie below. This was due in part to their own shortcomings; but it was also due to the ingenuity of the red man.

If the descent was made with patience and good planning, wagons usually arrived at the base intact. However, human nature is variable. The appeal of the plains, the grass, and the nearness of game below highlighted a flaw in the reasoning process of some drivers. Instead of the slow process involving the oxen as an anchoring device, some drivers chose to guide their wagons down by reins attached to the shafts.

Messin Man

They depended on their wheel brake for speed control. Due to impatience, greed, lack of skill, rocky terrain, or the absence of good fortune, shafts sometimes struck the ground, resulting in broken shafts and sometimes a complete flip of the entire wagon. A lack of equal concentration on shaft control and brake control led to the success of one, to the detriment of the other. The result was a wagon that descended with shafts raised and intact, but at a speed whereby negotiation of the gentle curve near the base was impossible; the wagon would self-destruct against the boulders beside the curve.

Some wagons never reached the plain intact, due not to a failure of equipment or driver skill, but to boredom on the part of the Hiup. Like so many exciting enterprises, when novelty wears off, sharpness is worn to dullness. This is a facet of human nature that is not a monopoly of the white man, as proven by the Hiup.

As wagon trains came to Hiup Pass and were greeted by Three Hands, every member of the tribe would be concealed in the forest to observe the whites and their ways. This procedure became so routine that boredom began to impact upon the numbers concealed. Since boredom challenges active minds, the Hiup rose to the challenge with gusto and innovative actions. Cubs, the first to be afflicted, saw not only an opportunity to change the process of "downhilling" by the wagon drivers, but at the same time put the drivers' "crisis-reaction time" to the test.

To create the proper conditions, they waited until the white encampment had bedded down for the night, then descended to the plain, where they collected buffalo chips—the fresher and mushier the better. The chips were transported in woven slings and deposited across the incline about halfway down from the plateau. To prevent premature drying out, they poured water in amounts sufficient to offset this possibility. Then their "bull-chip-slip" was ready!

The first driver, be he a "shaft driver" or moving with an oxen "anchor," was relieved of any sense of complacency by this additional tribulation on the trail. If he was the former, the wheel brake was useless as a slowing device, for the locked wheels slid through the bull-chip-slip zone at an increased speed!

When the wheels, with brakes locked, exited the zone and entered dry ground, varied reactions were observed. If the brake pads on each wheel held evenly, the wagon's speed changed abruptly upon entering the dry zone, and the driver, much like Chief Ten, responded to the scientific principal of "action-reaction" and became airborne. The driverless wagon continued on to the bottom of the slope, if fortune smiled upon it, in salvageable condition.

At times, some "bulla-manura" would get on one brake pad only, causing an uneven drag that caused the wagon to enter the dry zone at an angle. In such cases, the wagon made the remainder of the descent in a number of spectacular rolls before disintegrating. To the cubs, the beauty of the scene was that no two consecutive trips were the same. The following drivers, after long discussion, trail examination (and many expletives), and option evaluation, made the necessary adjustments for a safe descent.

Cubs' minds are fertile fields for inquisitiveness, exploration, and answer-seeking; the Hiup cubs were no exception to this phenomena. They had spent many hours observing the habits of the people of the trains. They observed that the method used by train members to exit their wagon offered promise of "action-reaction." The men exited the wagon by placing one hand on the seat rail, then leaping with a pivotal motion to the ground. The women and cubs made their way down in a backward movement, with the aid of handholds.

After a train bedded down for the night, the cubs utilized skills learned as neophyte hunters to set baited traps at the proper location near the front wheels, disguising them to blend into the natural surroundings. The following morning, the pioneers, be it man, woman, or child, upon descent from the wagon, stepped or leaped into the trap—the baited "bulla-manura," of course! The reaction of the pioneers did not enhance the mental image of the Injun in the minds of the "trapped," but the device did increase their desire for a hasty departure from the area!

The adult members of the Hiup were not immune to boredom. They devised some entertainment of their own. When a train made it to the plain and reassembled for the movement west, the notion of perhaps delaying that move to gain some much-needed rest may have been entertained by some drivers. That notion did not linger long enough to solidify, due to the entertainment arranged by the bored adults.

A wagon train usually took most of the day to manage the slope and assemble to evaluate and repair damage incurred in the process. Tired and hungry, the members would refresh themselves at the waterfall, while hunters moved a short distance to the nearest buffalo herd and returned with fresh meat for the evening meal. Just as the last chore was completed, darkness set in and the camp prepared to bed down, the braves chose to strike.

The unique characteristics of the Ucumfastus tree were put to use by these braves in a sport designed to keep the peace of mind of the pioneers in turmoil. By using a bow drill, a hole was made through the bark of a tree and into the sap center. When the drill was removed, internal pressure caused the tree to ejaculate a stream of gum that was caught in a bowl. The force of the ejaculation and the amount were determined by the age and size of the tree. Some trees could ejaculate three or four times, after which they were plugged, and the tree allowed to recover. The drilling procedure could be repeated, usually after ten suns, when the tree had manufactured new sap.

The collected sap was mixed with shredded buffalo grass, formed into a ball, and allowed to harden. The ball was then placed into a woven reed sling secured to the top branch of a Ucumfastus sapling that had been bent and secured to the ground by sinew. A reed whistle was attached to the ball with strands of reed. This gumball was highly flammable; it burned with such intensity that it left no residue.

The procedure was to bend the sapling in the direction of the train below. When all components were in place, the ball was ignited and the securing sinew quickly cut. As the sapling snapped to an erect position, it propelled the ball away from the forest and sent it wailing toward the train below! Members of the train saw only a highly illuminated ball traversing the night sky like a comet, heading directly toward their wagons and screaming like a banshee!

The first pioneers to witness this spectacular sight thought it to be a shooting star. When more of the same appeared and were noted to be heading in the direction of their canvas-covered wagons, panic surged forward to take charge of their mental processes. Water brigades were hastily set up to contain any fires caused by these objects. There were none, because the fireballs burned out before reaching the wagon area.

Water brigades were maintained throughout the night, in case of further attacks. The braves had ended their fun and were blissfully asleep, while the brigade stood a sleepless watch. At first light, the unnerved men would seek clues as to the composition of the fireballs, but found not one scrap of evidence. This harrowing experience left them with no desire to tarry in this spot on the trail and risk destruction.

With the passing moons, wagon trains of various sizes moved on the trail through Hiup Pass. Each was met by Three Hands and given the directives of the trail before being allowed to move to the plain below. Some were subjected to entertainment activities by the cubs or adults, while others were allowed to pass unmolested. If a train passed, for example, during the time set aside for celebration of tribal customs, such as the Spring Awakening, priority was given to customs and only explanatory time given to the trails.

The opening of the trail west was similar to a break in a dam. Like waters held back by the strength of the dam, once a crack appeared, wagon trains poured forth in a stream through this crack. This stream caused erosion of the terrain it passed through. Chief Has It Made, Three Hands, members of the council, and Jock stood under the

Ucumfastus trees, gazing out over the Plains where the last wagon of the most recent intrusion was disappearing at the horizon.

There was despair in the hearts of the red men as they evaluated the scene before them. The debris of wrecked wagons at the base of the incline was a point of beginning for a line of abandoned items stretching to the horizon. The red men shared their despair with Jock. "The white man comes and the white man goes," mused the chief. "I wonder if Mother Earth views his passage with as much sorrow as we?"

"Mother Earth has known him much longer than we," responded Three Hands. "The sorrow in her heart must be greater than that which we feel. I now know the meaning of M.O.M.'s warning to beware of what is carried by the stream."

"The trail he leaves wherever he goes is made with no shame. He leaves a scar on the earth that will be slow to heal," added Piercing Eyes.

Bulging Pot was less generous in his evaluation. In a defiant act of frustration, shaking a fist toward the trail taken by the trains, he shared his thoughts with the others. "They are savages of the lowest level of intelligence. They foul our waters by pissing in our streams, and it is a constant test of one's skill to walk in the forest. It is hard to find one tree or bush that does not have a pile of shit at its base!"

"We have not lost one man through hostile action, yet seem to be losing our lands, as we know them," Has It Made stated in summary. "Brother Jock, must we continue to accept the desecration of our lands as the price to pay for our generosity and peace?"

Jock had not come up the Clyde in a wheelbarrow! He knew how much the red man revered the balance between man and nature. Their distaste for the obvious lack of such reverence by the white man had to surface; being the only white man present, questions would be asked of him. And questions require answers, so, while gazing at the scene before him, he had been directing his thoughts in preparation for this moment. If his value to the Hiup was to be maintained, he had better have some answers!

The security blanket separating Jock from the one fear (Kate's father) that guided his near-paranoid evasive maneuvers, was still being provided by his red brothers. His constant study of their language and customs had given him insight into their thinking processes and expectations. He had taught them the English language as requested, but never spoke it in conversation with them. He conversed in Hiup, and their respect for his doing so gained his acceptance as an equal. It was to prove invaluable to him in the future.

His response was slow in coming, for he had learned from his hosts that rash acts or words were held in disfavor. His choice of words would be instantly evaluated by his red brothers; they were carefully chosen. "My ears hear the gentle voice of Mother Earth, reminding me that the shame of my white brothers is also mine. My heart is heavy, and my eyes weep for what they see. I ask your patience if the words to answer your thoughts are slow in coming because of my sorrow for my red brothers.

"The plan of my red brothers must not change, for it affects every red brother. The illusion of uncountable numbers holds the white man's ambition in check. To break your word will be a signal to the white man that you have fear in your hearts, and they will come in even greater numbers to make war with you. The choice, to come or not to come, must still be left to the white man, for now. There are ways to discourage his eagerness to move west of the Mississippi. The bear and the bee live in harmony within the forest, yet the bee does not stand by and let the bear take the honey he has worked hard to store to sustain his life. He cannot kill the bear, yet he makes it painful for the intruder and hastens his departure."

Chief Has It Made and the others were mildly surprised at Jock's words. They were more the thoughts and words of a red man than those of the white, as they reflected wisdom, compassion, and reverence. Jock's response was well received by Three Hands for an additional reason. It reinforced his importance in recommending Jock's retention as a valuable resource in planning and dealing with red-white interactions. The prelude having been presented, the answers were eagerly awaited.

"The greatest weakness of the white man is his greed. His desire to possess governs his every move. The taking of his possessions is the greatest loss he can suffer; therefore, we must exploit this weakness."

"How can we take his possessions without doing battle with him?" asked Three Hands.

"When the traders come to exchange goods with you, do you do battle with them or do you give them something in exchange?" Jock inquired.

"We give them something they want for something we want," the messin man replied, still unsure of Jock's purpose.

Jock continued, "And what possession of yours does the white man want?"

"A trail through our lands."

"And what of his possessions do you ask in return?"

Jock's last question was thought-provoking, yet the reply seemed common to each red man.

"Nothing! We have want of nothing the white man possesses," Three Hands shot back in reply.

"And that is why the white man leaves a trail of his castoffs that foul your lands. He has contempt for your refusal to ask for something in exchange for the privilege of passing. He thinks you place no value on your lands. You must do something to change this feeling in him. Sting him like the bee stings the bear!" Jock hissed, his voice rising to emphasize the importance of his suggestion.

"And what is this possession of the white man that we must demand?" asked Bulging Pot.

"Money!" The canny Scot had played his ace.

"Money? What is money?" inquired Piercing Eyes.

"Money is a form of goods to the white man. It is made of metal and can be carried in a pouch, much like your messin pouch. He uses it in exchange for other goods," Jock explained.

"We have no use for the white man's money!" snorted Has It Made. "Why demand something that is worthless to my people? We should demand a pony dog or something of value to us. "

"The pony dog is considered an item of great value by the white man, and he would refuse. If he refused your demand, you would have to fight or lose face. This confrontation is what you have planned to avoid. No, the demand must be of such value as to be acceptable to the white man, not to provoke him to fight," Jock explained. "This money can be bartered for blankets, knives, or other trail items offered by them, just as you barter with trail traders."

"How do you make the whites give us their money, and how will it slow the numbers passing through our lands?" questioned Three Hands, still lacking total understanding of Jock's scheme.

"I will make a sign for you. This will be in the words that the white man uses to communicate, and so he will know the cost to travel through the pass of the Hiup. Word of your demands for passage must be taken back to those still waiting to cross the Big Waters. There will be many among them that think the demand is too much and will not cross. That should solve the first part of your problem."

"The first part?" the chief inquired, eyebrow raised.

"Yes. You asked me if you had to allow the desecration of your lands without response, did you not?" Jock replied.

"That is true." Chief Had It Made admitted, nodding his head.

"Then you may wish to consider allowing one white man to remain on your land at the base of the pass. Now hear me out!" Jock added quietly as he interpreted a flush on the face of Bulging Pot to be a hostile retort to his suggestion. "This man would be carefully chosen as one who could make the wagons continue on the trail instead of lying broken at the base of the pass. This man would be allowed to stay only if he obeyed the laws you establish for him."

There was a long period of silence as the red men mulled over Jock's suggestions. Chief Has It Made polled his men with his eyes and saw a nod of agreement from each. He turned to Jock with his decision. "We respect the words and wisdom of our brother, and will follow his suggestions. Tell us what you need to carry out your plan, and we will assist you."

"I ask only one thing, my chief. Since Three Hands meets each train, I ask that he assist me in carrying out our plan so that the white man cannot fool him and spread the word that the red man is stupid and easily fooled," Jock requested.

"It shall be as you wish," replied the chief.

Jock and Three Hands immediately began to construct the sign. By salvaging boards and nails from the wrecked wagons below, Jock was soon able to construct the signboard; he used his dirk to carve out the demands of the Hiup. When this task was completed, Three Hands sought the strength and zeal of several cubs to dig holes and lift the sign into a position of prominence in the center of the trail at the entrance to the glade. The group stood briefly to admire their work, and then the cubs were dismissed. The explicit nature of the sign would eliminate any misunderstanding by users of the pass.

Jock's next priority was to educate Three Hands for the role he was to play as toll collector. He produced coins to match the values stated on the sign; after several acts of role-playing, Jock declared the messin man ready for the real thing.

The next objective took on a more serious tone, as there would be no margin for error in this endeavor. "Your selection of the man to stay on your lands is vital to our plan," said Jock. "He must not only have the skills to repair wagons, but must also be lacking in curiosity. One who questions will constantly find time to wonder where all of the Hiup are camped and why they do not make themselves seen at the pass. He will constantly question why he must obey your laws if no one appears to enforce them. He could exploit knowledge of the situation for his own use and could influence others to join him in ignoring your laws and settling on your lands.

"You will be looking for a "smithy," as he is called by his brothers; he will carry a large, heavy piece of metal called an "anvil" in his wagon. If he does not carry this item, he is not telling the truth and should be told to move on," Jock cautioned.

"I heed your words," replied Three Hands, "but there is one question that lingers in the back of my mental tipi."

"And what is that?"

"How is the word of our collection fee returned to those beyond the Big Waters to deter their crossing and so lessen the numbers coming to our lands?" the puzzled messin man asked.

Jock thought for a moment. There would be a few Scottish men on the trail who would balk at the payment of a toll out of their sense of thrift, or of principal, and turn back to St. Lou E. Their numbers would not be enough. Some hostile feeling had to be developed that would insure retention of this hostility once the Mississippi had been recrossed.

A light went on in his head as he simply put himself in their place — what would offend him most? "There are broken wagons at the base of the incline, and there will be more until you find a smithy, for the white man does not learn easily from the mistakes of others. When these men, their squaws, and their cubs come back up the incline to return to St. Lou E, charge them again for passage through your lands to the river."

"This will cause anger in them?" the messin man asked in disbelief.

"You can take my word for it. Do not succumb to their pleas of injustice, and they will not forget it," snickered Jock. "You are about to learn, firsthand, of the lengths the white man will go to before he will part with his money!"

Three Hands was a man of patience. Although he looked forward to the mental challenge of this added role, he still had to fulfill his duties as messin man. Jock returned to his seclusion with Swift Feet, to be seen only when needed.

It was ten suns before the next train appeared on the trail. The drums had performed their usual ritual, and the train stopped below the glade. When the wagon-master arrived at the crest to survey the situation, Three Hands and the sign were there to greet him. He gave the man the sign of greeting and signaled him to dismount. "Ye are in the lan' of the Hiup. Those who pay can gang forward on the trail. All others weel gang bak the way they came," he stated.

The usual routine explanation of the requirements of the trail followed. The wagon-master listened and then replied, "I will return to my people and share your words with them."

Three Hands watched him return to the gathering below to consult with the drivers. Soon he remounted and led the train to the glade and to the waiting toll-master. The wagon-master was first to pay. Three Hands approached each wagon and accepted the coins from the driver, placing them in a large deerskin pouch. He noticed that one wagon had turned back toward the river.

It was a good beginning! Pouch in hand, he returned to camp, leaving the wagons to make their way down the incline. There had been no evidence of a smithy, but perhaps one would be with the next train.

Since the coins held only a symbolic value to the Hiup, they were placed in jars and stored in one of the messin man's tipis until a use for them could be determined. Jock was informed of the truth of his words—not all wagons chose to pass. It was a small beginning and spirits were high.

Jock passed on one added bit of information to the toll collector. "Bite down on the first coin and examine it closely when all can see. This will show the white man that it is useless to try to fool you with false coins. Remember, I told you how devious he can be when it comes to money," he added, grinning.

Each wagon train proved to be a learning experience for Three Hands, yet the taking of tolls soon became routine, and he found time to examine those who passed before him. He observed that not one man passed coins to him in a spirit of friendliness. Their faces reflected hostility; though he heard no words, they seemed to mutter a lot. He discovered that the hostile look on their faces could be intensified by smiling at them as the money changed hands. He smiled a lot! The white squaws never spoke, but stared straight ahead, as if he were not there.

There were some exceptions to this rule regarding the white squaws, which made his smile even wider. Some, he noticed, dropped their eyes to quickly examine the "savage" before them. If their eyes met those of the messin man, a flush came to their face, and their eyes returned to a forward stare and remained there. Their cubs stood silently behind them, or on the seat beside them. The pull of curiosity held no restrictions on the movement of their eyes.

Jock's words rang true, as new learnings surfaced. On a day when his messin duties were light, he returned to the glade to observe the activities of those who had progressed to the plain below and were filling their water barrels at the stream. His eyes wandered to the activities of the cubs. As he watched, he became aware of two things. First, their games and work activities were not unlike those of Hiup cubs. Second, there seemed to be something wrong about their numbers. In the back of his mind, a thought struggled for recognition and finally received that priority. There seemed to be more cubs below than he had counted as he collected the tolls. There would be no peace of mind until the puzzle was solved.

When the next train arrived, he was determined to see if the cub puzzle was real, or if his mind was playing tricks on him. As each wagon toll was paid, he counted the cubs and placed an equal number of coins in a separate pouch. Later, he counted the cubs at play and compared that number to the coins in the pouch. The puzzle had returned! There were four more cubs than coins! How could this be? His talent for logic strode forth to take charge of this challenge.

The priority of this new challenge moved ahead of the need to locate a smithy. The devious white man was secreting some of his cubs when paying the toll and retrieving them at the plain. After much thought, he came to the conclusion that the wagons had a false bottom, which hid the cubs from him. He would examine the next wagons to see if this was true.

The next train that arrived was subjected to a new procedure of examination. Before collecting the toll, Three Hands walked around each wagon, peering not only under but into each one. There was no evidence of a false bottom, or of cubs hidden inside the wagons. He counted the cubs and compared the numbers as before, with the same result. The thought of magic powers possessed by the white man entered his mind, but he dismissed this assumption as illogical.

Mother Earth must have decided that, although she enjoyed a good laugh, the consternation of the messin man had gone on long enough. She, in her gentle fashion, would provide the solution for him in her usual manner of generously allowing the mortal to think the solution resulted from his own endeavors!

As Three Hands canvassed each wagon of the next train for the solution to his dilemma, his ears picked up the sound of a muffled sneeze coming from a water barrel tied to the side of the wagon. Three Hands immediately accepted full reward for Mother Earth's generosity, and a smile of triumph formed on his lips. "Perhaps it is time to see if the white man has a sense of humor," he mused. It was obvious that he was not about to pass the generosity of Mother Earth on to the whites. He strode to the front of the first wagon, where the wagon-master stood. "My people have signaled that they wish to speak with me. I shall hear them and return." With those words, he strode majestically into the forest. The wagon-master was left to explain the delay to his people.

Three Hands entered the forest and quickly moved, unseen, to an area familiar to him for his purpose. The area was sunny and rocky. His eyes moved about until they rested on the object of his search, a large hog-nosed rattlesnake sunning himself on a rock. Deftly grabbing his unsuspecting victim behind the head, he popped him into his collection pouch and headed back to the train. On the way, he broke off a supple branch of a Ucumfastus sapling and put it into the pouch.

Reaching the glade, he took a position where he could be easily heard and, more importantly to his plan, be seen by all. He laid the pouch on the ground to his left, with the drawstring purposely loosened. "My people hae observed your comin' and have sent me ta greet ye. As ye came closer, they felt the danger of an evil spirit that had taen lodging in your tipis. They were fearful of the harm he could do ta ye, our respected guests. It would bring dishonor upon my people if we allow this spirit ta do sae in our lan's. My people have provided me with a gud spirit that will drive awa the evil spirit from each wagon, and ye may continue your journey in safety. When the evil spirit is chased away, our gud spirit will return ta his natural form."

The members of the train had observed the return of the savage, and they watched him place the pouch on the ground. There was a great deal of movement within the pouch, but no clue as to its contents. Although they heard the words of the savage, their eyes remained focused by curiosity on the pouch.

A strange-looking head was seen to emerge slowly from the pouch; after a pause to test the air, it was slowly followed by an enormous body of great length. At the end of the body was a series of rattles. Once out of the pouch, the snake coiled itself in a defensive position, with its head poised to strike. After a brief pause, it assured itself that there was no danger presented to it, and so made its way back toward the forest. The members of the train were not aware that this movement was, fortunately for Three Hands, going precisely as planned.

The "savage" appeared unaware of the snake's escape from the pouch, for he picked up the pouch and headed in their direction. The pouch was not empty, for it appeared (by clever hand movement) to contain more snakes. He stopped at the first wagon, where he had heard the sneeze. Dead silence engulfed his audience. Lifting the pouch toward the heavens, he shouted, "Enter, O spirit of gud, and kill the spirit of evil within!"

With a flourish, he loosened the drawstring, placed the opening of the pouch over the hole in the top of the barrel, and began to lift the other end so as to empty its contents into the barrel. The silence was shattered by a screech from the squaw on the wagon seat. The man beside her leaped from his position on the seat next to her to land on the ground. Running to the rear of his wagon, he shoved Three Hands aside and threw off the lid to the barrel. He withdrew two small cubs from the barrel. His squaw lifted another cub from the barrel on the other side of the wagon.

All of the cubs set up a wailing that matched that of their parents. There was also scrambling among the parents of other wagons to duplicate the retrieval of cubs from their water barrels! The puzzle of the missing cubs had been solved!

Three Hands, still enveloped by self-satisfaction, walked to where all could observe him. (Mother Earth possibly regretted her generosity by this time.) Lifting the pouch high over his head, he opened the drawstring and turned the pouch inside out, whereupon the branch of the Ucumfastus sapling dropped to the ground. "Sometimes the spirit of evil hides in the hearts of men!" he spat. With that, he went to the wagon-master and accepted his toll.

This was the first train that paid full price. It was also the first train that had wagons turn back after reaching the glade. The jubilation of the toll collector was in direct contrast to the consternation of the white men caused by the fact that they had been humiliated by a savage. The swallowing of pride was too much for three drivers, who turned their wagons and made a hasty retreat toward the river. They concluded that, if all of the savages ahead were like this one, "to hell with it!"

Three Hands returned to camp and shared his experience with his people. There was much glee exhibited for the lesson taught to the "white savage." The tale's ending was yet to be told, however.

The next morning sun found the messin man taking his place on his favorite ledge to observe the activity on the plain below. The train was forming to move on, according to the trail rule. He noticed a reduced number of wagons and, glancing to his left, he observed the remains of three more wagons at the incline's curve. He then observed three separate groups leading oxen and heading back up the incline. In a short time they reached the glade. The most valued possessions were either secured to the backs of the oxen or carried in packs on the backs of the parents and cubs.

As they approached, Three Hands took a position by the sign. He placed his toll pouch in position and held his hand out for the toll. The groups stopped as one and stared at the figure before them with unbelieving eyes. They thought, "This savage expects us to pay toll again, after his trail caused the loss of our wagons and valuable goods? Incredible!" One of the men stepped forward and inquired if their concern had a basis of truth—why the outstretched hand?

"The cost of the trail is clearly described by the sign in a manner that ye understood when ye passed it before. Are these same words holding a different meaning, one sun later?" came the reply from the messin man.

"But we paid for the use of your trail already!" the spokesman retorted.

"Ye paid for the use of the trail west. Now ye wish ta use our trail east. Ye hae paid ta use the trail west and are free ta use it, but if ye wish ta use the trail east, ye must pay for it," the toll-master stated with a wide smile.

"We cannot continue west, for we have no wagons. The only possessions we have are those we are carrying, thus we cannot pay you for the use of the trail east!" stated the indignant spokesman.

"My ears hear ye hint that the reason ye no longer hae wagons is the fault of the Hiup. If this be true, all of your people would be with ye now instead of moving west, as they hae done. The sign states that ye can be charged for the litter ye hae left below on the trail. Mak your decision now, or my people will mak it for ye!" replied the toll-master, still smiling.

The three men met to discuss their situation. This savage was as crooked as a moneylender, even if his logic could not be argued. Their remaining goods were more valuable than the toll, so they paid it. They were furious, but dared not to risk the consequences if this savage called forth his people to settle the debt.

"Wait until we tell our people how the Hiup make the unfortunate pay unjustly for the use of this trail. No one will ever want to use your damn trail!" shouted the last man after he was well down the trail and felt safe from reprisal. His words were welcomed by Three Hands as he hastened back to camp to repeat the tale's ending and its promise for the future.

There must have been some truth to the words of that last threat, for the trail was free of travel for one moon, after which there was also a change in the traffic pattern. Instead of large trains, the white man came in a mixture of patterns. Most trains were made up of fewer than fifteen wagons and many of only two or three wagons. This was a welcome change, particularly to Three Hands, for now he had time to concentrate on locating a smithy.

The role of toll-master was becoming tedious and unchallenging. The ever-innovative messin man devised ways to enliven the task. One of his favorite means was to intimidate the squaws, not with words, for he never spoke to one, nor by a fierce appearance. He accomplished his goal by perfecting a manner of walking that exaggerated the normal movement of his oversized pendulum beneath his loincloth. A slight, hardly noticeable twist of his hips brought the item to a point where its arc almost extended beyond the cover of his loincloth.

Another technique was to walk in the stream, which was waist deep, and emerge with a well-soaked loincloth. This gave the loincloth a gluelike quality as it fastened itself to the groin area (and the pendulum, in particular), leaving nothing to the imagination.

Without exception, Three Hands found the crucial time to ensure success of his endeavors was when the driver left his seat on the wagon to pay his toll. Until that moment, he would stand near the sign and his appearance gave no hint of his "intimidator."

The moment the driver was distracted by his dismount, Three Hands began his hip-swinging walk toward the wagon, his eyes locked on the eyes of the squaw. He followed her eyes as they traveled from the upper torso downward and, upon reaching the area of the pendulous appendage, paused and seemed to widen before returning upward. The eyes of Three Hands were waiting for this moment, for they again locked on those of the squaw, seeking an unspoken answer to a question he had in mind. The reply was, without exception, movement of the head and eyes to such a tilt as to avoid his eyes, accompanied by a red flush of the face and a nervous clasping and unclasping of the hands. These motions were analyzed by the messin man after each experience. He was used to Hiup squaws observing the movement of his body parts as he walked, but their response was always limited to either a smile or a giggle. Could it be that his moves were offensive to white squaws, or were they perhaps less easily aroused? He had plenty of opportunities to continue his experiment to learn the answer.

One day a single wagon, pulled by two ponies, made its way to the glade. Three Hands was in position and motioned the driver to leave his seat and pay the toll. As usual, he began his walk toward the wagon with his eyes on those of the lone squaw on the seat. She was, in his estimation, a squaw of about twenty summers, and her eyes were definitely on the move examining him! Her eyes arrived at the groin area and remained there until he was next to the ponies; they then rose to meet and lock with his in a steady gaze. He intended to put her to the ultimate test, to see if his interpretation was in error.

The driver was reaching to produce the toll when Three Hands stopped him with the suggestion that he water his ponies and rest them in the shade. The man did not reply, but did unharness his team and lead them to the stream for water. Three Hands followed him, strode into the stream, and crossed to the other side, pretending to retrieve something. He then recrossed the stream and walked back toward the wagon.

His loincloth did its part to spectacular perfection. The eyes of the squaw were observed moving slowly to the area of perfect performance; they remained there until he was close to the wagon. Her eyes moved upward to once again lock on his. A slight smile was on her face, but no flush. Her lips appeared to be dry, for she moved her tongue slowly back and forth over her lips to moisten them. Her actions were certainly not out of fear or insult!

Still musing over the reactions of the squaw, the messin man continued past her to make his inspection of the wagon, since no cubs were in view. Could the actions of the squaw be a diversion to keep him from discovering her cubs? A check of the water barrels showed them to contain water, but no cubs. A perusal of the wagon's interior showed only the usual goods, with the exception of a large, heavy object in the rear. Could it be the anvil of a smithy? The situation held promise in more ways than one, but he needed to evaluate it fully. There could be no margin for error.

Strolling back to the stream and the driver, he began his final evaluation. "I noticed a large item in your wagon. Cou'd it be an anvil?" he asked.

"It could," came a curt reply.

"Ye are a smithy?" the messin man continued casually.

Another curt reply: "I am."

"Why do ye choose ta travel far from your people who need your services?"

"My reasons are my own."

Three Hands continued the questioning. "Ye travel alone. Are ye not fearful of attack frae my people?"

"My word was given to obey your laws. I keep my word! Do your people keep theirs?" the stranger countered.

"Always!" Three Hands stated emphatically.

It was a good beginning. Only one more point to cover before a decision could be made. Walking across the stream for another pretended reason, he turned and made his way back to the wagon. His freshly moistened loincloth cooperated fully in the retest.

Once again, his eyes moved to those of the squaw, and saw them locked on the movement of his central highlands as he moved to the wagon and stopped before her. Her eyes rose slowly, as if regretful of leaving a prized view, and again met those of the man before her. The smile came simultaneously to both faces in a signal of understanding.

Three Hands watched the driver return and hitch his team to the wagon. He introduced himself. "I am Three Hands, messin man of the Hiup."

"I am Seth Brimstone, and this is my woman, Fireanda."

"Walk wi' me, Seth Brimstone, for I hae something to show ye," requested Three Hands as he walked to the edge of the incline. "What do your eyes see afore ye?"

"Grassland covered with junk," Seth replied.

"Ye are a mender of broken wagons?"

"Yes."

"Then look and tell me wha is missing below."

"You could use a good smithy!" a now-smiling Seth replied.

The evaluation was complete! He had a smithy—a man of few words and evidently a loner. His decision was made. The messin man made his pitch. "My people hae concerns about their decision ta allow white men ta travel in our lan's, but they hae gien their word. The white man has kept his word ta obey the laws of the trail, ta keep moving, and no set up his lodge on our lan's. His passage, however, has left a trail below that dishonors Mother Earth. Ye can help your brothers erase this dishonor with your skills as long as ye obey our laws. Wha are your thoughts on this?"

Seth was a man of few words, but not brains! It would be folly to continue a trail toward the unknown when a potential fortune and thriving business lay just before him. "I give my word and will stay," came the short reply.

"Build your lodge at the base of the cliff, beyond the path of the buffalo going ta the water," Three Hands directed.

Seth moved to pay his toll, but Three Hands waved him off. "Ye are our guest. Ye pay only if your word is nae true."

The message was clear, and Seth began his descent to build his new home, while Three Hands made his way back to camp to update his people. His heart was singing!

Seth and Fireanda worked together to build their new home, for they expected, and received, no assistance from the red man. By salvaging materials from the debris at the base of the incline, they had enough wood for construction of crude living quarters and a workshed for Seth. They also found enough items, such as rims, spokes, et cetera, to compile a stock of spare parts. Their efforts completely eliminated the pile of debris, including wood scraps that were piled for use as firewood.

Has It Made, Three Hands, members of the council, and Jock once again stood under the Ucumfastus to observe the plain below. There was a soaring of spirits, especially Jock's, for his star was rising among the Hiup. He knew the wisdom of not resting on his laurels, but to stay ahead of demands. These high spirits would soar until reality grew weary of the charade, clipped their wings, and returned them to face it, for the smithy had eliminated a positive asset as well. Broken wagons had been removed from the trail, which was good. However, broken wagons also had caused whites to return east and spread words that caused others to believe the trail too risky. The numbers moving west were reduced. Now, thanks to their ingenuity, the smithy was repairing wagons and sending them back on the trail west.

Jock was back to phase one, for he had no ready answer to this dilemma. They seemed impaled once again on the bull's horns. Fortunately, man easily accepts rationalization as a means of freeing himself from the horns, so after a lengthy discussion, it was agreed that, since it was their actions that allowed the white man to travel to their lands, they must accept responsibility for the offenses he heaped on Mother Earth. It was more important to please Mother Earth than to slow the numbers of travelers, at least until they could think of a better solution!

Chapter Nine

The guile of a squaw can cool the indignation and ego of a man as easily as an evening breeze on a hot scalp.

Seth did a thriving business as wagon trains came and went. Between trains, he spent long hours at his forge, manufacturing parts to resupply his inventory. Three Hands was also busy. During a break in his schedule of messin his people, toll collecting, and extinguishing maidenly fires, he traveled to the plain below to witness firsthand the operation of the smithy. There had been several complaints to the chief regarding the constant banging noise from below. Three Hands went to see if Seth was keeping his word, and if the eyes of Fireanda would keep theirs. His priority was weighted heavily in the direction of the latter!

After a brief pause to greet Seth, he observed Seth stoking the fire to a white hot level before starting his banging technique on the anvil. He then meandered to the rear of the building, where he saw Fireanda hanging out her wash. She looked around and watched him walk toward her; he noticed his "walk" again produced that magnetic effect on her eyes, for they became fixed on his loincloth once more.

When he came close, her eyes broke away and met his. "I was beginning to think you did not get my message," she said in a soft voice.

"'Tis my responsibility ta read signs, but I hae had little experience in the signs of the whites. It was my hope that I had read your sign true," he replied.

Emitting a soft chuckle, she retorted, "That is one sign that defies color!"

Her statement brought a noticeable flush to her face and a simultaneous rising of the messin man's loincloth. Motioning him to follow, she made her way to the door of the house and beckoned him to enter. He had barely cleared the doorway when he felt her hand drop to push aside the last obstruction to her long-sought goal. With gentle movements of her fingers, she examined the prize in a thorough manner. It was apparent that while Seth was building a white-hot fire in his forge, he was neglecting the white-hot fire in his woman! While Seth was busy forging out new items on his anvil with his hammer, Three Hands was just as busy forging out a new item with his hammer. The "extinguisher of fires" was at work; fortunately for Fireanda, the fireman was always on call!

The relationship continued undiscovered as, luckily for them, Seth was a workaholic. The frequency of the messin man's visits did bring the question to Seth's mind on one occasion, and he put it to his visitor.

"I gae to the sacred Canyon of Fire, just ta the west, ta appease the spirits there with my offerings," came the reply.

The messin man certainly did not speak with forked tongue, for he did visit a canyon of fire, and his offerings did appease the spirit there. Had Seth an inquisitive mind, or had he taken the time to verify these words, he may have discovered the truth in the double meaning, but fortune favored the two participants, for this was not the case.

During one visit, Seth informed Three Hands of his need for raw materials to continue his work. This would necessitate a return trail to St. Lou E to procure them. He asked two questions of the messin man. Would this violate the agreement with the Hiup, and, if not, would the messin man check on the well-being of Fireanda as he passed on his way to his ritual at the canyon?

Three Hands could hardly contain the laughter from within at the irony of this request. With his stoic expression, he replied, "Your word is still strong. Gae in peace. Your woman will no a' come ta any danger. Ye have my word." He faithfully kept his word, for his "religious zeal" took him to the canyon at each new sun.

Wagons came and went in Seth's absence, and wagons were wrecked on the incline. This proved Seth's trail to be of value to the Hiup, for it meant additional tolls that sent more angry whites back to St. Lou E. Upon his return, Seth cleared the area of debris, and Mother Earth was happy once more.

Three Hands was aware that the horns of the "dilemma bull" were in close proximity when Fireanda demonstrated her need for female companionship in the form of irritability. It had a dampening effect on her "furnace."

"A basic female need is conversing with another woman," she explained. She pleaded with Three Hands to allow another couple to settle so she could have the female companionship needed to regain her good nature.

The horns became more menacing with the passage of time, but a victim had yet to be impaled. Three Hands relished his relationship with Fireanda and was reluctant to bring it to an end. Still, the plan of his people remained the top priority. He would not jeopardize the plan for a white woman's priority! The intercession of Wakan-Manitou averted certain impalement. He wisely played on the weakness of both the red man and the white man. For the red man, it was vanity. For the white man, it was money. He put His plan into action.

Three Hands met a small train of three wagons at the pass. It would have been a normal passage except for three key factors. One factor, of course, was Wakan-Manitou. A second was that one of the wagons was different from the others, in that it was much larger and drawn by a team of six pony dogs. The third was that when the messin man went into his "walk" while collecting tolls, only two of the women on the wagons resorted to the "look high and wring the hands" routine to ignore him.

The woman on the large wagon did not. Her eyes locked on his loincloth when her man left his seat to pay the toll. When he came near, her eyes sent the same message as Fireanda, and the message was accepted by Three Hands. He used the tried-and-true device of suggesting that the drivers water their ponies, while he waded the stream and returned to the big wagon. There was no misinterpretation of the previous message. How was he to take advantage of this message and still comply with the battle plan? Leave it to Wakan-Manitou, for He had not played his top card in His game!

Walking around to the rear of the wagon, Three Hands looked inside and saw the same kinds of objects as in other wagons, only more of them. His thoughts returned to the woman seated at the front of the wagon: interesting possibilities—and also a solution to Fireanda's irritability. He dismissed that thought, for personal pleasure could not be placed before the battle plan as top priority.

Wakan-Manitou then played His top card! When the driver of the big wagon hitched his team, Three Hands stood ready to accept the toll. The driver did not reach into his pouch to produce the coins. "Will you accept goods of equal value instead of money?" he asked.

This was the first time that coins were not offered as toll. "What will the white man offer?" Three Hands wondered.

The driver continued, "My toll comes to eighty cents. Let's see what we have in that price range." Motioning the toll-master to follow, he went to the rear of the wagon, climbed up, and disappeared inside. Moments later, he reappeared with several objects in hand. "How about this hunting knife, or hand ax, or even this string of bona fide rubies?"

Three Hands was very impressed by the objects before him. A decision would be difficult, for all of the objects were magnificent. Seeing the indecision on the part of his customer, the man went back inside the wagon and returned with more goods. "Perhaps this hoe to turn the soil of your garden, or a bit of cloth for your women to make clothing, or needles for sewing?"

"I will tak the knife," decided Three Hands. "Your wagon carries much mair than those of most other white men. What need cou'd ye hae for sae much?"

"These goods are not all for my use. I am a trader of goods," explained the driver.

"Ye seem ta have all that most men wad want. What cou'd ye possibly accept in trade that ye dinna already hae?" inquired the puzzled messin man.

"Money," came the reply.

Wakan-Manitou stoked up the fire in the Three Hands' mental tipi, and in so doing started the dissolution of his dilemma through rationalization: "Money? We have collected many coins we thought to have no value to us. On that, Jock is very clever. This man is willing to exchange goods of great value for something that is of no value!" He pressed his advantage before the man could change his mind.

"I am Three Hands, messin man of the Hiup."

"And I am Goodson Ware. This is my woman, Bea Ware."

Three Hands was on a roll and gathering momentum. Motioning Goodson to follow, he led him to the edge of the incline and made the same pitch he had made to Seth. Goodson saw the logical advantage of this location and agreed to the terms of the red man. He made ready to descend the incline and prepare for his role as a general store proprietor. The messin man directed him to locate next to the smithy, and then returned to camp with the knife to explain to his people the value of his move.

The impact of precedents are so often overlooked when things seem to be going right. It seems to be their nature to come back and haunt those with poor memories. The new addition was another violation of the battle plan to keep all whites on the move, and it would not be the last! Rationalization does not necessarily mean justification. In this case, it meant a crack in the plan, a crack that would widen under the pressure of further rationalizations and accommodations.

The weakness went undetected, for Three Hands was as busy as a tomcat in heat scheduling visits to appease the spirits of the canyon. His basic problem was to visit one without the knowledge of the other. Fireanda's flame had been heightened now that Bea's arrival and companionship had dispelled her irritability. The messin man found Bea's flame to be as equally intense as Fireanda's. To the great improviser, scheduling was as pleasurable as carrying it out. The two couples became fast friends, and even gave their location a name—Chip Dip!

All seemed well as time and trains passed. The men were treated to his toll pouch, while the women were treated to his "walk." He still got an ego-satisfying pleasure out of tormenting the women with his act, and all responded with the "high eyes" act; all except the one who came in the strange-looking wagon about three summers after Bea Ware.

Three Hands was returning from a "spiritual appeasement", and had just reached the glade when his eyes and ears detected a movement on the trail. He stopped near the sign and waited for the travelers to reach him. He would collect the toll, then proceed to carry out his second priority of the day—collecting specimens to replenish his messin stock.

As the travelers came closer, he could see that their vehicle was unlike any that he had seen before. It contained three occupants, who could be easily counted, because there was no white top over it. He studied the occupants as the vehicle drew closer. The driver, a male, was of the color of a fire stick that had not been entirely consumed by the flames. The two passengers were female, and were seated facing each other in the center. The one behind the driver was obviously of great weight and size; Three Hands gave her only slight notice, as large squaws held no appeal to him.

It was the squaw on the seat facing the driver that captured his full attention. She was of slight build and very light-skinned, yet these were not the features that riveted his gaze—it was her clothing! Her body covering was of a color brighter than the yellow maize, her moccasins greener than the spring leaves of the Ucumfastus. Her white arms ended in green hands the color of her moccasins; they held what looked like a miniature tipi on the end of a lodgepole. On her head was a green covering like an inverted luk pot with an enlarged lip around it. From this covering protruded two enormous maize-colored feathers. On her lap lay a miniature black panther.

Three Hands' face mirrored his amazement. This party, all together, looked like a moving rainbow that was headed his way!

The vehicle stopped in front of the messin man, but the driver made no move to get out and pay the toll. He remained on the seat. Three

Hands took the initiative and decided to "walk." Strolling toward the visitors, his eyes rested first on the driver and his color. His eyes met those of the driver, whose own eyes had been giving him a visual going over. The driver's face broke into a wide smile, exposing gleaming white teeth. Three Hands' eyes then moved to the squaw seated behind the driver; her back was to him. Her head slowly turned to face his. Her eyes gave him a quick but thorough examination before her face also broke into a wide smile, accompanied by a low chuckle.

His eyes moved on to the final subject for examination. The examination began at the feet and moved slowly upwards. Her hands, he saw, were not really green, but covered with a cloth of many holes that allowed the cool breezes to enter. In one hand she held the miniature tipi on a stick that shaded her head. Her other hand held an object like the wing of a butterfly that fluttered in front of her face. His eyes continued upward to lock with hers. Her mouth was firm, but there was laughter in her eyes. She did not flinch from his stare, but held firm before casually moving downward to re-examine that remarkable loincloth.

The priority of restocking his messin stores was relegated to a lower level as Three Hands found it difficult to concentrate on anything but the squaw before him. He knew that he must collect the toll, as well as his thoughts.

He turned to the driver and made his introductory speech. "I am Three Hands, messin man of the Hiup and collector of tolls." He went on to detail the rules of the trail, and at the conclusion held out his hand for the toll. The driver sat motionless on the seat, making no effort to pay. Three Hands repeated his demand for the toll. There was still no movement by the driver.

"Either this group has no sense of hearing, or they do not understand the language," he thought. Well, he was a master of signs, so he pointed emphatically to the sign, then to his toll pouch.

"No need to get your dander up, big boy," came a voice as soft as an evening breeze. It was the rainbow squaw speaking. "Zeke, come help me out so that I can stretch my legs," she continued. The driver sprang from his seat and first helped the rainbow squaw, then the other squaw from their wagon.

Three Hands observed his actions, noting that they violated the basic code of the red man regarding squaws. Men did not leap to serve squaws—squaws leaped to serve men! He decided to voice this observation. "Why do ye do the work of a squaw?" he asked the driver.

"Because I belong to her. I'm her boy," came the reply.

"Belong? Is this squaw your mother?" an incredulous Three Hands stammered.

Charles V. Kirk

His question brought a peal of laughter from the three before him. The rainbow squaw regained her composure and moved to explain, "Mister Three Hands, my name is Miss Lynn Gweeney, and this is my girl, Lotta Lasagna, and that is my boy, Ezekiel, and this is my cat, Satan. No, they are not my children, but say, do we have to stand out in the sun? Why don't we walk to the shade, and I'll tell you all about it." She handed the black panther to Ezekiel.

Three Hands had no objection to her request, but his body tensed when Lynn casually linked her arm in his and began to stroll in the direction of the Ucumfastus trees, talking as they walked. "Lotta works for me, but I own Ezekiel. This may seem strange to you, but it is part of our customs. If you have the money, you can buy anything. Be a good boy and call me Lynn. 'Squaw' sounds so degrading and unimpressive."

The two arrived at the stand of trees while Lotta and Ezekiel began the task of watering the horses and checking the baggage. They knew that Lynn was a mistress of manipulation, and would soon have the savage eating out of her hand. Unknown to them, their mistress was facing one whose specialty was also the art of manipulation, and the battle for supremacy had begun!

Lynn Gweeney came from a well-to-do shipping family in Boston. She had the best of schooling, possessed a beautiful singing voice, and dreamed of becoming an opera star. She was a natural beauty with social charm, but her iron will often brought her into conflict with others, especially with her parents and their plans for her future. Upon reaching the age of womanhood, she had developed, in addition to fine features and a fine voice, a fine figure.

Music hath its charm, but Lynn learned that her physical attributes gained her far more (and faster) recognition from the opposite sex. Her rebellious nature peaked when she became aware of her parents' plan to wed her to society's most eligible dullard, Claude Balls III. The prospect of a life of childbearing and endless dull social functions lost out to her independent attitude and dreams of adventure.

By the time Lynn reached St. Lou E, she had gained a lot of experience, some of which could be classified as adventurous. Her fine social manners and decorum had not been destroyed, but the veneer had been hardened by reality! Favors once exchanged in the name of adventure or love were now exchanged for cash. Through backbreaking effort, she established one of the largest and most respected brothels in town. As an entrepreneur, she began to hire others to do the backbreaking work.

Lynn had learned her lesson well, and knew everything had a price. The price to remain in Boston—to wed Claude Balls, III—had been too high for her to pay, so she left. When she found the price of staying in business in St. Lou E was becoming too high to pay, she planned her next move. Greasing palms was an expected part of doing business, but the game was getting out of hand. Everyone from the mayor down to the lowest level of the constabulary held out his palm. Soon they were not only holding out their palm, they were holding out (so to speak) their manhood for "freebies" whenever nature got a rise out of them.

Everyone and his dog seemed to be getting into the act. Dogs are mentioned only because Lynn's watchdog, Laidback, got in the family way yet never went outside unescorted! While these demands were irritating to Lynn's sense of independence, and did affect the profits, they were only some of the underlying reasons for moving on.

St. Lou E was growing rapidly, which was good for a business such as hers, but it took a lot of patience, managerial skill, and manipulation to make it successful. Business became too good! The girls she recruited, after several months of apprenticeship involving intensified instruction and on-the-job training, were striking out and forming businesses of their own to avoid paying Lynn a percentage of their earnings. As the number of "independents" grew, prices went down (something to do with the law of supply and demand).

The handwriting was on the wall, and Lynn was a good reader. After reviewing the facts of life known as the Time Line Curve, Lynn decided that she could not, under present circumstances, remain at the top of the curve and avoid a degrading slide to the bottom, entwined in competition and graft.

Her dream of opening an opera house, where she could engage in more refined and cultural activities, was shattered by reality. Many of her regulars were moving west, where land was free for the taking and the stress of city life unknown. It was said that an empire was possible for those who dared to answer the call of adventure.

Lynn had the business acumen to realize that, where the men went, their needs also went. The final decision was made, the business sold, and a carriage outfitted for transportation to the new "lands of plenty." The nucleus for her new start was Lotta and Ezekiel. Lotta was well-suited for "service," as she was a true lover of life. In addition, she was a good cook. True, most of her specialties were of Italian origin, and therefore fattening, but the taste was worth the risk! Ezekiel was a slave who would provide muscle for the physical demands of the journey.

Ignorant of the demands of trail travel, Lynn chose a carriage as her vehicle of transport, for it allowed the beauty and breeding of the occupants to be clearly seen. Besides, those old covered wagons chosen by the "ragamuffins" were hard-riding, and their constant creaking would upset her nerves and "wear [her] to a frazzle!" They started out as part of a train, but gradually fell behind, as the fragile carriage had to move slowly over bumps and potholes in the trail, so as not to jar or tire the ladies.

Several weeks of trail travel reality had totally demolished her spirit of adventure and romantic dreams. She had it up to her cleavage in trail travel. Only her stubbornness to refuse to admit defeat kept them going, but her thread of resolve was wearing down to the snapping point: how far was this old West anyway? Surely they should be there by now!

She was fed up with the trail and its gratuities of insect bites, ticks, dried food, wild animal noises at night (which prevented a good sleep), and the lack of even a minimal level of physical hygiene. She decided that city life, with all of its drawbacks, was paradise compared to this. When they reached the top of this hill and rested in the shade of those tall trees, they would turn around and begin the return trip the next day.

As they had approached the crest, the sign came into view, and Ezekiel pointed it out to the ladies. Their first evaluation was that someone, perhaps also disenchanted with the trail, had created the sign as a humorous prank. When their eyes picked up the moving figure of a tall man clad only in moccasins and loincloth, the humorous supposition was replaced with one indicating possible danger!

"Drive on, Ezekiel, but say or do nothing that will aggravate the savage. There may be more in the forest. I will do the talking," commanded Lynn. She was in the perfect position to observe the closing distance between the carriage and the red man. Her eyes moved up and down over every visible part of his figure. She could see that he possessed no weapons and perhaps posed no danger to them. As a normal reaction (for her), she focused on his loincloth and the movement behind it. As an expert on male anatomy, she was impressed!

They stopped in close proximity to him, and he spoke—in English! Well, this was not only one more surprise on the trail, but finally something that was favorable to her. It would be far quicker, though not necessarily more pleasurable, to communicate vocally rather than through sign language. She had no prior experience with Indians, but what the heck, she thought; he was a man, and men could be persuaded to agree with her way of thinking!

Even as she walked beside the savage with her lips busily engaged in idle chatter, Lynn's mind was formulating actions to enhance the opportunity presented to her. For three weeks, she had endured the tortures of the trail; she had proclaimed her evaluation of it with appropriate invectives at the time. Perhaps the trail was trying to correct its malevolent design by introducing this tall, handsome, and virile man at her side.

Messin Man

Her thighs were beginning to respond to that possibility in the form of a warm glow. Her body had never turned down an opportunity to unleash its powers of persuasion to bring about the rise and fall of a targeted male. She had no intention of bringing an act of seduction to fruition with this savage for, after all, she was a lady. To tease him unmercifully might be the respite from the trail she needed before heading back to St. Lou E. Her charms would have the savage on his knees before her in no time! There was much truth in this thought, but it would come about after the shoe had been changed to the other foot!

The teasing began, "Now, isn't this better than being out in that old hot sun? Let's walk over to that stream so that I can refresh my face and get a cool drink. Come along now, we'll sit a spell, and you can tell me all about this toll of yours," the rainbow squaw directed.

Three Hands' mind also was busy on the way from the carriage to the shade and to the stream. "This squaw talks more than a magpie courting a mate," he thought. He had concluded the action necessary to satisfy his priority for the day, and was in a relaxed and receptive mood.

For all her talk, this rainbow squaw might serve as a respite from an anticipated busy afternoon of seeing to the messin of his people. Perhaps a little teasing to bring a redness to her face, then he would collect his toll, and leave her to go about her tasks. It had been pleasant walking near the woman, for her scent was not unlike the sweetness of the honeysuckle in bloom!

His usual technique of walking in a manner designed to highlight the pendulous movement of his appendage could not be utilized because of the squaw's closeness to him. Perhaps the old "walk-in-the-water" routine could be used. When the squaw requested a drink from the stream, his opportunity to utilize this technique arrived, and he offered no objection to her request.

Arriving at the stream, she sat down on the bank and carefully arranged her dress in a manner to avoid soiling it. Taking out a tiny handkerchief, she wetted it with some cool water and applied it to her brow. "My, but that feels fine. I think I will loosen my blouse and cool my neck a bit, too."

Loosening the fastenings, she pushed the neck of her peasant blouse down so that its upper limits just barely covered the outermost limits of her breasts. The handkerchief again was wetted and applied to the newly exposed area, as Three Hands watched with interest and amusement.

"Now that is so delightful and refreshing. Mister Three Hands, would you get a lady a drink of water?" she asked.

"Lynn Gweeney get her own drink," came his reply.

"But I have no cup to drink from," responded a demure Lynn.

Charles V. Kirk

Three Hands cupped his hand and placed it in the water, then withdrew it and placed it to his lips to drink the water, as a demonstration of his words. "Each of us carries a cup for drinking cool water. If we are thirsty, we use it," he responded.

Lynn cupped her hand and bent over to reach the water. If her action was designed to provide the messin man with an unrestricted view of her breasts, it certainly attained that objective! If it was to provide her with a drink of water, it failed, for the water disappeared between her fingers before reaching her lips.

She tried this three more times before Three Hands decided that he had been rewarded enough and acted to help the rainbow squaw. Taking Lynn's hand in his, he formed a cup with her fingers and held them together with a firm grasp that prevented the water from running out. After two such dips, Lynn's thirst had been quenched, but Three Hands' fire had been ignited! In a paradox, water had, in effect, started a fire.

Now refreshed, Lynn continued to converse with the savage beside her, noticing an increasing twitch in his loincloth. "Mister Three Hands, we were with a wagon train, but fell behind. How long has it been since it passed?" she inquired.

"Come," the savage replied as he gained his feet and motioned her to follow. Her expectation of gentlemanly help to her feet evaporated, so she got to her feet and followed him to the edge of the incline. Pointing to a gathering below, he stated, "There is your train. It will leave with the next sun."

Lynn's eyes swept the scene before her. She was awed by the panoramic view. Her eyes moved to the buildings on the other side of the dip in the ground below. Those looked like the buildings of white men, or did these savages live in the same type of homes? Questions sought answers, and Lynn saw an opportunity to have two questions answered at the same time, if her aim was true.

With a seemingly innocent move, she lifted her parasol to point to the buildings. In doing so, the tip caught the loincloth of Three Hands and raised it to a horizontal level before it slipped off and returned to its original position. The brief interim provided Lynn with a complete and unobstructed answer to one question, but the second required verbalization. "What is that?" she asked with the pointing parasol.

"Chip Dip," came an abbreviated reply, which did not serve as a comprehensible answer for Lynn. Three Hands had no time to react to the action of the rainbow squaw's parasol. He had no proof that the act was deliberate, but he leaned toward the assumption that it was not beyond this woman's realm of design. Since she had taken him by the arm, a supreme act of familiarity, he had nursed a curiosity of what lay beneath her colorful covering. She had satisfied part of that curiosity when she got her drink. Then again, he had spent enough time toying with her and should be back attending to the needs of his people. Before he could turn to the subject of toll, the squaw had resumed her role of magpie.

"Chip Dip—what an unusual name. Now whoever lives down there?" she questioned in a seemingly innocently manner.

"Seth Brimstone and Goodson Ware," came the reply.

So there were whites living there. Surely this could not be the great West, the land of dreams and adventure that she had suffered so to reach! Four buildings? In a play for time to sort out the truth, she resumed her game of tease with the savage. "Tell me, Mister Three Hands, how did you get such an unusual name? I can only see two hands on you, like everyone else."

Unlike the white man, Three Hands had yet to develop a hang-up on the subject of sex, so he told the story of his Spring Awakening.

"Well, I must say that, from my point of view, Three Feet would have been more appropriate," she giggled. She was about to continue her questioning when the messin man held up his hand for silence.

"You pay the toll now, for my people hae need of me," he stated.

Well, the nerve of him! It might just as well be that she could use his services, too! She planned to have the last word. "Well I declare, I have been rambling on and had completely forgotten the toll, for you have been such interesting company. Now, according to your sign, that will be forty-five cents. You can take it out of this?" she asked.

The rainbow squaw handed Three Hands a piece of paper with pictures and some marks on it. He was puzzled, for it was the first paper money he had seen, yet he could not lose face by showing his inexperience. "Have ye no coins?" he asked in a bid to gain time and regain command.

"Oh, I never carry coins if I can avoid it. They are so heavy. Just give me my change and we will be paid up."

"Change? What is change? Jock never told me about change. I've got to see him about this," he thought. His quick wit provided him with the perfect cover-up. "I must gae ta my people for your change, as I, too, dinna like ta carry the heavy weight of coins. Ye gae ta the wagon train and wait. I will meet ye there."

"That will be fine with me," Lynn replied as the savage started toward the forest. Even if it was a ploy to skip out on change-giving, she thought, it would be worth it to see and learn more about Chip Dip. If this was the end of the trail, she was more than eager to go back to the city. She turned to signal her companions to join her so she could bring them up to date on what had transpired.

Charles V. Kirk

Meanwhile, Three Hands was making a fast trail to Jock's lodge. Arriving there, he poured out the story of the rainbow squaw and her paper. Jock listened and chuckled, "That is another form of the white man's money. It is true what the woman says about being more convenient to carry. I never thought anyone on the trail would have that much money in paper. That is a twenty dollar bill she gave you, so she expected change, or rather enough money to balance the value of the paper after the toll. Let me show you how to measure the equivalent of paper money with coins. When the train leaves, we will change the sign to read, 'Exact Change Only' and avoid such complications as this."

In the meantime, Lynn moved down to rejoin the train below and its umbrella of protection, and to explore Chip Dip before the savage returned with her change, if he did at all. Tomorrow she would make the dreaded trail back to the city.

By the time Lynn had visited the Brimstones and the Wares, she was beginning to have second thoughts about the return trail. When the 'Chip Dippers' learned the nature of Lynn's business, they went out of their way to convince her that St. Lou E was the best place to reinvest her future.

To downplay Chip Dip, they invented alarmist tales, such as being surrounded by hostile savages and living from day to day at their mercy. Death was staring them in the face constantly; the pain of the constant drumming, coupled with the fireballs, made life unbearable. The long periods between trains would bore to tears a refined lady like herself. Even if she wanted to stay, that decision was the Hiup's, and they did not deviate from that decision for any whites.

Lynn only faintly heard their arguments against staying, for her mind was examining the opposite side of the ledger: if things were so bad, why did they stay? They hadn't indicated that they were being held against their will. The bottom line was that, if she could convince Three Hands to let her stay and she became bored, she could always go back to the city.

Her dread of returning on the trail so soon guided her mental reasoning. She added three further points to her side of the ledger. First, there would be less business, but that would be balanced by the lack of payola. Two, there would be no competition—the policy of the savages would see to that. Third, the challenge presented by Three Hands' third hand could eliminate boredom.

The Hiup had chosen those who could stay strictly on the basis of need, therefore Lynn knew that her main obstacle would be to convince the Hiup that she could provide a needed service. She had but one service to offer, and she was not too confident that it would be a vital one to the Indians. She had to learn more about their nature and needs. She decided to take the initiative.

The first priority of the messin man after the luk pot meal was to return to Lynn and give her change from her twenty-dollar bill. As interesting as it had been, and as curious as he had been, it was time to send her on her way west. Her change was in coin, for no paper money had been collected, which presented a problem of weight. Jock had suggested that he take the coins to Goodson and exchange them for paper, which he did at first light before the train activities began. Three Hands then consumed a good meal and was on his way back to deliver the change.

He had just left the forest and was heading for the incline when he was stopped by a dulcet voice coming from the stream. "Mister Three Hands, if you are looking for me, I'm over here."

Three Hands turned and made his way toward the stream and the voice. He found Lynn immersed in the water, with only her head showing. Her rainbow clothing was neatly arranged on the ground nearby. "I decided to take my morning bath while waiting for you. Why don't you come and join me?" she suggested.

Three Hands had taken his daily bath before his meal, as was his custom. The whites had strange customs, if men and women bathed at the same time in the same waters. "Men dinna bathe with women," he replied.

"Why not? Do men fear harm from women when immersed in water? Does the water change us into animals who bite and tear the flesh of men, or grow horns to bring death to men? Look, I have no horns or long teeth to harm you. I give you my word that you have nothing to fear," she chuckled.

The messin man admitted to himself with a grin that she had a point. He had never challenged custom, but had taken it for granted that men never bathed with women. The words of assurance that she would not harm him turned the grin to laughter. Perhaps it was time to create another custom! Removing his moccasins and loincloth, he leaped into the stream.

Once in the water, a relaxed atmosphere prevailed, punctuated by an exchange of idle chatter. Lynn remained submerged, but the clarity of the water left little for the imagination to cull. Chatter led to play when Lynn splashed water into the face of Three Hands, and the act was reciprocated by the messin man.

The play accelerated when Lynn shouted, "I take back my words to do you no harm!" and promptly shoved the head of Three Hands under water. This action was also reciprocated by the red man and continued until both were weary. They pulled themselves from the water and lay side by side on the bank in the sun to dry.

Lynn turned on her side to face her playmate and said, "You are the first savage—"

She was stopped in mid-sentence by the upraised hand of her partner in play. "Call us Hiup. Savage sounds so demeaning and unimpressive!"

Lynn erupted in laughter as she heard her own words being returned to her. This was truly an interesting man, who was not only intelligent, but had a good sense of humor. She felt very relaxed in his presence. How could anyone be intimidated by these red men? "You are absolutely correct, Mister Three Hands. You are the first Hiup I have met. Where are the rest of your people?"

"They are everywhere—in the woods, the canyons, the plains, and the mountains," came his reply. "They want nae part of the white man, for they hae found him ta be a savage, and one who has nae respect for the trail, the streams, or the land. They feel that if they witnessed the white man's selfish ways constantly, they wou'd hurl aside their patience and bring death down upon those who desecrate our lands. That is why Chip Dip is allowed. They clean the trail of the white man afore my people can see their spoilage," came his reply.

Three Hands, deciding that there had been enough talk, rose to retrieve his clothing and give Lynn her change. Lynn rose also, but did not reach for her clothing. She stepped forward and ran her fingers lightly over the arm and chest of the red man. "I wonder if all of the Hiup are as handsome and strong, yet gentle in nature, as you?" she crooned softly.

The movement of her fingers continued on downward until the caressing fingers reached, then explored, his namesake. There was no reaction from Three Hands, but there was definitely a reaction from his namesake, which was striving mightily to demonstrate its handsomeness, its strength, and perhaps its gentleness. "If I had been chief and given you a name, it would have been Five Hands!" she groaned. Then she moved to place the namesake next to her pubic area, and began a slow undulating movement against it.

A continuous moan came from her lips as she slumped earthward, with her arms urging the messin man's body to follow. The silent plea of his namesake to comply with that request did not go unheeded by the mind of Three Hands. He proceeded to put the poker into the firepit of Lynn Gweeney, and stoked the flames until they roared out of control and consumed every ounce of her energy. The sun was well on its trail to the western horizon by then.

Messin Man

When the ashes had cooled and conversation was once again possible, Lynn's mind was made up—she had to stay. She decided that a straightforward approach would be her best bet. "The men of the Hiup must be strong and great warriors if they are like you. Every man that I have known would have given up long ago in exhaustion, and never have known the thrill of the climax and victory.

"You have said that your people do not wish to associate with the whites; that they have allowed the Wares and Brimstones to stay because they keep the trail clean. I would ask you to speak with your people on my behalf for permission to stay."

Three Hands stood and dressed in silence. He waited patiently for Lynn to complete her dressing before he spoke. "Come," he directed, and led her to the edge of the incline before he spoke again. "If I am ta speak for ye wi' my people, use your eyes ta find a reason ta make the trail better for them. Only then will I speak for ye."

The messin man had been mulling the same objective around in his mind. He would like her to stay, for she had taken his body to heights of pleasure that no woman had done before. Still, he would have to have a better reason than his own personal pleasures.

Lynn looked around desperately, trying to identify some logical reason to offer. It could have been due to fate, or it could possibly have been because the messin man's benefactor, Wakan-Manitou, was in another of His humorous moods, that Lynn's eyes caught the bright reflection of the sun's rays on a nearby object. She walked to inspect the object and lifted a shard of glass from a broken whiskey bottle.

It was a long shot, but it was all she had. Lynn spoke in her most sincere voice, "See, here is some glass that has been left on the trail by someone in a train. This glass could cut through the moccasins of your people and cut their feet as easily as a knife. I could have Zeke pick up all of the glass and other dangerous objects along the trail. I could see that all white men who pass on the trail will not throw glass on it again."

Three Hands took the shard and ran it gently across his arm, drawing a thin line of blood. Bulging Pot had stood nearby in suns past and remarked how bad the trail was being desecrated by the wastes of the whites. He could offer the glass as proof, but only his people would determine if it was reason enough to allow her to stay.

Noting a slight hesitancy, Lynn moved to reinforce the strength of her argument. "Ask your people if we could stay only until the leaves turn brown, to prove our worth, and then we will return to the banks of the Mississippi."

The thought of a temporary stay might not be rejected by his people, Three Hands rationalized. She would be gone before the bear began his sleep. "I will speak with my people. Ye can stay until their decision is known. We will gae and tell Seth Brimstone and Goodson Ware that ye will stay, unless my people decide against it." It was with a light step that Lynn descended the incline at the side of the red man.

Seth and Goodson agreed to house Lynn and her companions until the Hiup decision was reached. If the decision was favorable, they would assist Zeke in erecting living quarters of their own; if not, they would bid them good-bye.

Seth and Goodson decided that the time was right to make a request of Three Hands. They each wanted to erect a house west of Chip Dip where they could have more privacy and be able to plant a garden for fresh vegetables. Three Hands saw this as a request of major proportion; this new arrangement would allow him more freedom of movement in his scheduling of "ritual" time. The request was granted.

When the sun was setting in the western sky, Chip Dip had, in reality, three new inhabitants; they would not be the last. There was still one more to come.

In the eastern sky, a dark cloud was heading in a direct line for the Hiup and for Chip Dip. Fate, or perhaps someone else, was once again toying with the Hiup!

Chapter Ten

Those whose vision is limited to discerning boulders will spend most of their time on the trail stumbling over pebbles.

The humorous mood was replaced with one of seriousness when the war council met. All were anxious to hear what had taken place. Chief Has It Made and the council offered no objection to Three Hands' presentation of temporary visitation by Lynn and her companions. He had argued their value to the cause with a demonstration of the shard of glass.

The planning and energies of the Chip Dippers were focused on the new latitudes granted by the Hiup. Their first priority, shelter for Lynn and her entourage, presented a problem. There was only enough lumber to erect temporary shelter next to Goodson's store. New homes for Seth and Goodson were impossible.

Input of suggestions at a general meeting brought consensus on a plan for a solution. The men would return to St. Lou E and purchase needed items. Milled lumber was out, since it would require too many trips to haul. Seth suggested they mill their own, for trees were readily available and the waterfall could be used for power. Lynn offered to pay for the equipment in exchange for the men doing the heavy work.

Seth and Goodson were to use the trip to resupply, while Zeke was given a list of materials (wine, whiskey, and beer) to get Lynn's business into operation. The interior decorations and furniture would be purchased from Goodson's store. Seth and Goodson were to drive their wagons, while Zeke would purchase a new one to haul Lynn's needs. The men informed Three Hands of their plan and left on their journey.

The messin man was not idle in the absence of the three men. He could periodically be seen loping down the incline toward Chip Dip on "ritual" rendezvous. He found, with the added number, that his schedule gained more flexibility through after-dark visitations. The two trains that came through during this time were only minor distractions.

When Seth, Goodson, and Zeke returned, each driving a heavily loaded wagon, they stopped at the glade and tethered their horses. Seeing Three Hands standing below with the women, they hastened down the incline at the fastest pace possible, for a "dark cloud" had followed them back, and was hovering over their heads!

After greeting the women, the men informed Three Hands that they wished to council with him on a matter of great concern. Three Hands was intrigued by their request as they made their way in silence back to the wagons. White men seemed so emotional and given to hysterics that his alarm button had not been triggered. To Three Hands, very few whites seemed to possess the patience of the red man.

Reaching the glade, the horses were watered and set out to graze, and then the men sat to speak in council. Goodson Wares assumed the role of spokesman, "While we were in St. Lou E, we heard rumors that the government was sending the army to this pass. We all moved around town to get as many details as possible. It seems that those in charge of the army have heard stories of great wealth in your lands and in the lands to the west. Word must have gotten back from people of the trains that settled in the far west. They are sending soldiers to destroy the red man and build forts for the many Blue Coats to follow. We heard that a force of about two hundred men was on its way from Washington to St. Lou E!"

Three Hands listened to Goodson's words, trying to grasp what Goodson was telling him, then moved to clarify what appeared to be a warning. "Army? Washington? Government? Blue Coats? Forts? These are words unfamiliar ta me, but I see a look of apprehension on your face, which disturbs me, for I dinna understand the reason for it. Explain, that I may understand."

"The Army is a large number of braves who train only to fight. They wear blue coats and carry many thunder sticks to carry out the laws of Washington. Washington is a camp, like St. Lou E, where all of the tribal chiefs meet with the great chief in council. They make the laws that all white men must follow. Wealth is what white men call their valuable goods; land, money, furs, and horses are examples of wealth," explained Goodson.

"What I hear ye saying is that the great chief wishes ta tak the lands of the red man from him, and is sending large numbers of braves here ta attack us. Do I hear ye true?"

"That is right," agreed Seth. "Once the army moves through this pass, wagon trains of numbers without end will follow them. And if the red men try to stop them, they will be destroyed."

"The great chief and his council mak the laws for the white man. Our chief and his council mak the laws of the red man. Ours are laws of peace and should be welcomed by your great chief. He will regret his thoughts of war with us. I thank ye for your words and will inform my people," said Three Hands. He knew that the reaction of Chief Has It Made and the council to this news would not be as casual. To disguise his concern, he casually strolled away. Once out of sight, however, his pace increased to a run!

The rumor carried back to Three Hands did have some substance, in fact. The first of the wagon trains from the Hiup and Dakota Sioux Passes had been led, according to plan, in a half-circle back to the Mississippi River and through the Natchez Pass. The settlers were so embarrassed by being outsmarted by savages that they told no one of their travels. They moved into and settled the lands of the southeast. The climate was warm, and the land was there for the taking.

Word actually got back to the east via the disgruntled drivers who had wrecked their wagons at Hiup Pass and had to return to St. Lou E and beyond. The loss of their stake for a new life in the west, plus the loss of face at paying the return toll, was a bitter pill to swallow, and these few sought revenge to cover up their own shortcomings. They spread the word that lands west of the Mississippi held untold riches.

"What about the Injuns?" was a question often asked.

"We only saw one Injun on our trip." This was, in fact, the only truth in their words. Politicians picked up on the stories and suggested using the army to open up the west to place those riches under their control. A small force was en route to overpower the lone Injun and open the west. This force was only two hundred men—in case there was more than one Injun!

Three Hands arrived at camp with his concept of the problem and its possible effect on his people. He requested a council meeting of Chief Has It Made for that night after the luk pot meal. The chief could see in the eyes of his messin man that the subject at the council would be of great importance. Three Hands continued on to inform Jock of the meeting.

The specter of war hung over the Hiup camp, for a force of trained warriors was en route to engage them in battle, to test their defenses and to overrun their position. The Hiup battle plan was working, to date, because it had avoided confrontation with the whites. The Hiup were not fighters, and they knew it! They also knew that their weapons were inferior and would pose little danger to the enemy, as they had witnessed the use of the thunderstick on the buffalo by hunters on the trains. There were feelings of apprehension, but not of fear. The Hiup might not have been great fighters, but, led by the mind of their messin man, they certainly were innovative thinkers!

The council meeting lasted until the sun strode forth to take charge from the night. Chief Has It Made had accepted input from his advisers. Jock had no say in the meeting, but his mind was once again anticipating the time when his red brothers would turn to him as a resource of the white man's thinking. Three Hands was well aware that it would be Jock, the only one experienced with the white man's techniques and thinking, who would be the tactician in their planning.

Chief Has It Made, at the advice of his council, sent two messengers to the Quapaw to request observation of the movements of the Blue Coats, to keep him posted, and to relay battle plans once they were formulated. With his war council, he went to the glade to evaluate potential defensive positions designed to deal with the advancing Blue Coats. It was at this point that Jock's input was requested.

Jock had thought long and hard on the logistics and possible defensive tactics. He put himself in the place of the leader of the Blue Coats. When his force exited the confines of the forest, he likely would set up camp. The scouts he had sent out would have indicated the presence, or absence, of any Injuns. The move from the forest to the top of the hill would place his troops in the most vulnerable position, and he would want to plan the move in detail.

If the lone Injun had brothers, they would hold the high ground. Their numbers must be known before any advance was made. A plan began to unfold as Jock's mind returned to his role of adviser. "The Blue Coats must be stopped before they begin the climb to the pass," Jock stated as their first priority.

"And how do we stop him?" inquired the chief. "We have only bows and arrows, and the strongest arm could not deliver arrows from here to the forest's edge."

"That is true," agreed Three Hands, "so we can forget the arrows. Do you have something in mind, Jock?"

Jock had indeed! He drew upon the history of his country. After all, the pass was not unlike a castle and its moat. The moat was the castle's only line of defense, and the enemy knew that before the moat could be crossed, his force would have to survive a rain of projectiles. He also knew that arrows did not have the range of a pistol, rifle, or cannon, so the problem was how to keep the enemy's weapons out of range. His memory was illuminated by the "fireballs" of the Hiup.

"Aye, I have a thought," he replied with a canny smile as he barked out orders. "Wise Owl, bring me a rock the size of your head. Gray Fox, weave me a fireball net. Bulging Pot and Three Hands, bend that Ucumfastus sapling and secure it to the ground."

His orders were carried out in quick order, for curiosity is a prime mover. The rock was placed in the net, which was secured to a fork in the sapling. "Now watch the trail below," he directed, as he proceeded to cut the thong holding the sapling down. The rock flew skyward in a tremendous arc, to land on the trail near the forest's edge.

A shout went up from the group at the success and significance of the experiment. A beaming Jock turned to the chief. "Have every man, squaw, and cub here after the noon meal; there is much to be done before we are ready!"

The area was a beehive of activity under Jock's supervision, as he wanted to check his plan, down to the smallest detail of every option. Three hundred saplings were fitted with a rock and net, then tied down. When all was ready, Jock and the war council moved to the cover of the forest below, where Jock gave the signal to release the first rock. The spot where it landed was marked on a crude map drawn on doeskin. The rock had been coded with a dab of ochre paint, and the sapling that delivered it marked with the same color. When all of the rocks had been delivered by their sling, Jock's map indicated a wide band of coverage across the trail. Anyone caught in that area could be destroyed! Each rock was retrieved and placed at the base of the sapling matching its code.

Jock and the war council sat to evaluate their first defensive activity. Three Hands was the first to comment and inject logical inquiry. "Once the rocks are released, our defense is gone. What if the Blue Coats send only a portion of their force, holding the rest in the forest? The survivors could then proceed to the pass. Would our arrows be equal to their thunder sticks?"

Jock's mental process had been honed to a fighting edge. A gun was not discarded once it had been fired—it was reloaded and fired again. "We can be ready to repeat our defense as long as we have rocks. Time must be spent gathering rocks so that each sapling can be used as fast as it can be bent. Even stones the size of my fist can be used, and if the Blue Coats hold some of their force in the forest, these smaller rocks will find them like the falling rain. Our defense will only be as good as our planning for its use."

The council agreed, and it directed the squaws and cubs to gather rocks and stones and to place them in position. When the messengers of the Quapaw arrived and were fed and rested, they were sent back with the directive not to interfere physically with the movement of the Blue Coats. They were to observe, but not be seen. "Use the calls of the birds and animals of the forest all around the intruders to make them think we are everywhere, and could attack at any moment." The Quapaw also would alert the Dakota Sioux to this new situation, in case there had to be a change in the master battle plan.

The Hiup were now as prepared as they could be, for all that could be done at this time had been done, and life went on as usual. The Quapaw would warn them when the time for battle was near. Three Hands went to Chip Dip to instruct the men and women as to their status. "If the Blue Coats come, we will deal with them, hopefully in a peaceful manner, for that is our wish. If the Blue Coats do not want peace, they will die. You are not to interfere if you wish to remain here in peace. There will be no more trains until this matter is resolved, but you have much to do. You will not be harmed."

It was true that they had much to do, for new homes for the Brimstones and Wares had to be erected, as well as Lynn's home and business. They assured the messin man that they would abide by his directives.

Very little time had passed after work on the defenses had been completed before two Quapaw braves arrived in camp. They gave Chief Has It Made and his council a description of the force that had landed on this side of the great river. They had counted two hundred Blue Coats (ten of whom were on ponies), ten wagons, and six black logs on wheels. The Quapaw had observed them for two suns and estimated their arrival at the pass to be in less than twenty suns. The Quapaw would shadow them until they entered Hiup lands.

The war council met to review their plan and map strategy for using it. Chief Has It Made stated that when the Blue Coats arrived, he would go forth and demonstrate the bravery of the Hiup before returning to the glade. Three Hands glanced at Jock and rolled his eyes, which brought an unseen smile to the face of Jock (unseen because of the heavy growth of hair on his face). It was time to maneuver the chief back to reality before orders for that destructive strategy were carried out!

"Let us not forget the words of M.O.M. and the strength of our battle plan," Three Hands reminded them. "Our strength lies in deception and not being seen. Would not a greater sign of Hiup bravery be to have only one Hiup meet them? This Hiup would act as spokesman to present our objections to the breaking of our laws by the whites and the consequences of doing so."

Jock moved quickly in support of Three Hands, because he was right on the money! If their defense was to hold, the Hiup must send their most intelligent and experienced representative to speak with the leader of the Blue Coats. He must be equal to or superior in cunning to any white man he had known in the area of persuasive reasoning; that man, of course, was the messin man.

He raised his hand for permission to speak. It was granted. "Three Hands is right. As a white man, I would consider this a great act of bravery to face such a force and certain death alone. Three Hands has worked long and hard with love for his people. It has been his experience with the white man and his language that have guided you so successfully to make wise decisions, my chief. You may wish to give thought to his selection as that lone Hiup."

The chief may not have been a genius, but he was alert to avoidance. He removed himself gracefully from contention. "My heart is warmed by the words of Three Hands and our brother, Jock. I, as chief, should be the one to face the Blue Coats, but I have yet to master their language fully, which could show weakness in council with them. A wise chief sends only his most skillful and experienced hunters if the hunt is to be successful. Jock, you will remain in the Ucumfastus forest to lead our response here. Three Hands will meet the Blue Coats. The two of you must work together closely, so that no signal will be falsely given or misunderstood. So it shall be!"

Three Hands and Jock spent entire days together at the edge of the glade to hone their strategy. "The first Blue Coats we see will be their scouts. You must meet them below and let them know your demands for council, then send them back to their leader. Now if I was their leader, and learned that only one Indian came to meet me, I would think the rest of his war party would be concealed and watching me. I would want to display my power for all to see, and strike terror in their hearts. Perhaps my enemy would turn and run for their lives from certain death. He has cannon—the black logs—and would probably fire once or twice to reinforce that thinking.

"Now if this is the case, his force would be in the range of our rocks and suffer casualties, but, on the other hand, he might hold some of his force in the protection of the forest. Then we must use our stones. The cannon is his most powerful weapon, for it can kill at distances farther than our stones. You must try to draw his complete force out into the open. The range of our rocks begins at a line even with those two birch trees straddling the trail. Remember, battles are won by outsmarting your opponent," Jock stated in summation.

His opponent would be Colonel Buford Ulysses Lamar Dozer, commonly referred to by his men and superiors as "B.U.L." because of his ruthless desire to win battles by running over his enemy and annihilating them without mercy. At that very moment, he was leading his forces toward just such an objective—to run over the Injun and crush him without mercy.

As he led his force forward, his mind turned over the significance of the constant calls of animals and birds coming from all sides. They could be natural noises of the forest, but a good soldier would not eliminate the possibility that they were signals used by his enemy. The Injuns were masters of the art of imitation, yet his scouts had yet to report an actual sighting of any red man.

From the information supplied by his superiors, the distance from the river to the pass was three weeks' travel. The cannon was slowing his pace a bit, but by forced march and determination, he should arrive at the pass the next day. He was anxious to leave the confines of the forest, for his experience and that of his men had been in open battles, not forest warfare. His scouts were out ahead to locate the enemy.

The nearness of the enemy was whispered in the ears of the Hiup by the winds from the east. The noises of clanking caissons and cannons were carried along the thin line of the trail as it snaked its way from the river to the edge of the forest at the base of the slope. When the noises came within two suns' range, Three Hands went to the slope to meet the expected scouts. A master of improvisation, he knew that he was about to be put to his most severe test. He was eager to accept the challenge!

When the scouts did emerge from the forest and looked up the slope, they saw a lone figure with arms folded, standing and observing their approach. He was simply dressed, and no sign of a weapon could be seen. Priming their rifles in case they would be needed, they rode forward. When they came within five paces of the figure, he raised his hand and signaled them to dismount.

Before them was a man over six feet in height, of strong build and fine features. They themselves were mostly of English descent, and averaged a head shorter than this savage. They had seen and even fought some redskins east of the big river, but none were this tall. Perhaps he was the "Goliath" of his tribe! He spoke in English, although burnished with a strong Scottish accent. "I am Three Hands of the Hiup. I am tauld your leader hae guided ye here ta do battle with the Hiup. It is insulting that he hae brought but two hundred Blue Coats. 'Tis such a pitiful number and unworthy of our warriors taking time ta put on paint when the squaws cou'd defeat them afore preparing our food. 'Tis like sending an ant ta devour a buffalo! Inform your leader that I will meet with him when the sun is overhead!"

The scouts returned and reported their experience with the red man to Colonel Dozer. By noon the next day, they would be at the meeting place, so he called a meeting with his two officers to discuss strategy. His next in command was Captain Arlo Popoffski, commander of his artillery, who was renowned for being hot tempered, with a lust for maiming his enemy. He had been chosen for this mission because his reputation was well suited for their objective. Lieutenant Manley Walker, his junior officer, was in command of the foot soldiers.

Colonel Dozer was uneasy after hearing the report from his scouts. That his enemy was aware of his exact strength and had expressed a lack of concern about fighting could be a cover-up. Still, the Injuns were aware of the exact numbers of their enemy, while his count of his enemy totaled one!

Captain Popoffski was not concerned with numbers and sought to reassure his commander of the killing power of his cannon. "The enemy will not get close enough to be counted until after the slaughter," he boasted. "If any are left alive, Lieutenant Walker can send his men to complete the killing and secure the pass."

The company continued its march the next morning; by ten o'clock, it had reached the edge of the forest and looked into the open space beyond. The lone figure could be seen standing halfway up the slope.

Colonel B. U. L. Dozer barked orders for his men to deploy. "Captain Popoffski, set your cannon to the right, in line with those two birch trees and facing the ridge! Lieutenant Walker, set up my command tent here in the center of the trail. Set your bivouac area behind the cannon and post your men to my left in line with the cannon. I want these savages to see us in full battle force! Private Gofer, put the kettle on for my tea! We have until noon to get into position before the meeting—if the savage is still there!"

Three Hands watched the soldiers' activities. There was a great deal of rushing about, like ants around a dead bug. He counted the participants and saw that the leader of the Blue Coats had taken his entire force from the protection of the forest. They were in full view— and in line with the birch trees! His admiration for Jock's intelligence soared!

At 11:30, the colonel's forces had been deployed, in line with his orders and facing the ridge. The open space leading to the ridge presented both assurance and doubt. Their position was out of range of arrows, but if Popoffski's boast of his firepower proved to be hot air, then the troops would have to cross this open space to reach the ridge. During the move, his forces soon would come into range of the enemy weapons. They easily could conceal a thousand men in those trees along the ridge, but he was satisfied with his position for now. He waited for the savage to come to his position for the meeting. He would have a long wait before that came to pass!

Messin Man

The three officers sat waiting in the shade of the tent. Colonel Dozer was sipping his tea, while Popoffski was diligently working over his chew of tobacco, occasionally arcing a stream of juice to the ground in front of him for test purposes. Manley Walker, visualizing his first battle, nervously fingered the sword lying across his lap. "Why didn't the savage move?" they wondered. "He's probably trying to overcome his fear of what is facing him."

Just the contrary was true, for Three Hands saw that the formation before him had played right into their hands. To destroy them would have been easy enough, but the victory would serve little purpose for their plan. Someone had to return to their great chief with word of the invincibility of the Hiup! Besides, it was not yet high sun, and the longer the men below were exposed to it, the less sharp would be their brain—and their aim.

When the sun had reached its zenith, Three Hands moved slowly down the trail and stopped about fifty paces from the tree line. The officers had expected him to come all the way to their tent. "Why doesn't the bastard come on?" snorted Captain Popoffski. "I think he is afraid!"

"I think he is showing us that he will come halfway to meet us," said the colonel. "Come."

The three officers, under the watchful eyes of their men, moved to stand before the savage. The three would stand in the shadow of the messin man, for he was the tallest of the group. Dozer was 5'9", Popoffski was 5'6", and Walker was 5'7". Two factors evened the discrepancy in the eyes of the Blue Coats. First, the officers were white, and, second, the tall man was an ignorant savage. Dozer decided to press this "advantage."

"I am Colonel Buford Ulysses Lamar Dozer, commander of the thirty-third battalion, army of America. These are my officers, Captain Arlo Popoffski and Lieutenant Manley Walker. We have come in peace to open this territory to the people of the United States. What do you call this territory?"

"Ours!" came the reply of the red man. "I am Three Hands of the Hiup. Ye said ye come in peace, yet ye come with weapons. I meet wi' ye without weapon, for the Hiup are lovers of peace. Our lands hae been open ta travel by the white man, but he canna stay mair than one sun in one place."

Popoffski was so eager to display his contempt for the savage before him that the brogue went by without notice. He ejected a stream of tobacco juice that landed precisely between the feet of the red man. "No savage tells us if we can move or stay in these lands. Our great chief wants these lands for his people, and we are here to see that he gets them. You and your people can move aside, or we will move you by force."

The messin man had been analyzing the men before him as they spoke. The leader had not spoken since the introduction, yet allowed the loud one to speak without asking permission. Obviously, he was without manners. The leader he compared to Chief Has It Made—not too swift of mind and easily persuaded. Popoffski was impetuous, quick to anger, and dangerous! The third man had not spoken, but had demonstrated a nervousness that could lead to unpredictable actions.

The game had just begun, and he was happily involved in the battle of minds and purposes. "Your great chief obviously placed little significance on that objective, since he sent such small numbers ta accomplish it," he said calmly, ignoring the insult of the tobacco juice. "My great chief also believes your purpose ta be insignificant, for he chose only me ta face ye and hear your words."

Popoffski's temper exploded at this obvious insult by this heathen! Manners and protocol were shattered by the necessity to rebuke this insulter. "Why, you son of a bitch, you're too stupid to see death staring you in the face! Your ignorance is pronounced by your choice of words. Colonel, let me show this nincompoop a sample of our killing power. If he is so obviously unable to comprehend our words, then let us put them into action he can understand. My men can send a round to the ridge and scare the hell out of them. They'll eat their words while they are running," he suggested.

Dozer thought perhaps that would be better than wasting time talking, for this ignorant savage did not seem very impressed by the significance of their power so far. He assented to the request with a nod of affirmation.

Three Hands looked on as Popoffski hissed orders to his men and they scurried about to carry them out. One cannon was loaded and turned to fire toward the ridge.

"Ye point your weapon in my direction," he stated calmly. "Am I ta understand that we are now at war? My people hae been waiting for some signal ta unleash their weapons and destroy the ants that have invaded our lands."

Colonel B. U. L. Dozer had not intended the demonstration as a battle action. He quickly amended the approval to his officer. "Turn your cannon so that your demonstration will be seen as just that; not as an act of war at this time." He then turned to the savage, stating, "We wish to demonstrate the power of just one of our weapons, to destroy only that which we wish destroyed. In doing so, we hope your people will see the wisdom of laying down their weapons. You may proceed, Captain."

Captain Popoffski barked the change to his number one cannoneer, "Private Parts, show us your skill by removing that tree with the yellow blooms on yonder canyon wall."

The order was carried out with a ground-shaking roar as the cannon discharged its missile. Several seconds later, the tree on the canyon wall disappeared in a cloud of smoke. "See that, you ignorant savage!" shouted a gleeful Popoffski. "By the time your people hear the thunder of our cannon, it will be too late to run, for our messenger of death will be among them!"

A cloud of white smoke drifted from the cannon to the conference area, its strong acrid smell penetrating the nostrils of the four "conferees." Popoffski could not resist hammering another nail of intimidation into his threats. "Smell that? It is the smell of death. Tell your people that you have smelled it, and lived only through our generosity!"

Three Hands was prepared for the thunder of the cannon, as he had been forewarned by Jock. Popoffski observed the red man carefully, but could not detect the slightest of flinches when the cannon fired. The Blue Coat rooster had made his point through threat. It was now time for Three Hands to make his. "I will carry your words ta my chief and prepare mysel' for his laughter at hearing them. I will meet with ye when the next sun is overhead." Turning on his heel, he strode majestically up the slope,

Popoffski was livid over this obvious insult and pleaded with his leader to kill all the bastards with his cannon—now! Colonel Dozer still had reservations. The tactic of overpowering the enemy was not clearly the most logical at this time. "You know the location of your target?" asked the colonel. "If so, you have more information than me, and if not, our ammunition would be wasted by firing blindly. Three Hands is just a scout and does not have the authority to make decisions. We may have convinced him, although he didn't show it, that their weapons are no match for ours. No, we will wait until tomorrow to act, after we hear his words—if he shows up at all."

Three Hands was welcomed in the woods by Jock and the Hiup. When Chief Has It Made saw the elation in the eyes of his messin man, he broke into a wide smile. "Come, let us return to where warm food is waiting to fill our stomachs, and eager ears await to hear of your meeting with the Blue Coats."

Three Hands went to Jock and thumped him on the back. He chortled, "They are ours to do with as we please!"

The humorous mood was replaced with one of seriousness when the war council met. All were anxious to hear what had taken place below. The visual display by the Blue Coats had been very impressive and noisy, but the question was, how did it affect their plan? They had stood patiently by their saplings for a signal to release them, for it would have been the beginning of their very first battle!

Every member of the council, as well as Jock, knew that this had been a day of each side measuring the other's strength. The next sun would not be the same. One of the groups would act and draw retaliatory action by their opponent. Their plans had been formed, so little could be offered as a suggestion to Three Hands at this time. Three Hands knew that his people had been on edge for some time, and his mind brought forth a suggestion to relieve their anxieties. "The Hiup have never gone to battle an enemy, and there may be uncertainty in some as to their worthiness in battle. The Blue Coats need a lesson that demonstrates the hunting skills of the Hiup. The first action of battle can be ours!

"The Blue Coats have set up small tipis that they possibly use for sleep, as they are too small for living," the messin man conjectured. "They have probably set up guards as the wagon trains have done to protect them from our possible attack at night. Until now, our sleep has been more important than thoughts of acts of violence at night, for we are a peace-loving people. Now we can and will attack, and our weapon will be the soft chip of the buffalo! Our skill will be tested to see if we can place chips just outside the entrance to each Blue Coat's tipi, undetected by their guards."

The entire camp erupted with laughter. The idea was unanimously accepted, and a scout sent to determine the location of the Blue Coats' guards. There were two in position on the slope. Unseen, an antlike stream of shadowy figures made their way from the plains up the incline to the pass and then down the slope. Hugging the walls of the canyons, it moved past the guards to the bivouac area. The chips were placed, and the "ants" retraced their trail to their "nest."

Once all had returned, Clean Krupa and Budding Birch were sent to the Canyon of Returning Voices, where they demonstrated their skills with their drums. The walls of the canyon vibrated and echoed their performance again and again. The drums brought the expected reaction from the Blue Coats. Their startled exit from their tipis brought them into instant contact with the soft chips. There was a great deal of cursing, but little sleep for the Blue Coats that night! A side effect of the action involved the Chip Dippers. Because they were close to the canyon, they also spent a sleepless night.

Sleep came slowly to Three Hands as well. His mind was going over his objectives and options for dealing with the Blue Coats at their next meeting. After the morning meal, he sat with Jock on the bank of the stream at the glade. He spoke of the insulting words and of the actions of Captain Popoffski with his tobacco juice. He shared an idea that might avenge the insults, yet still advance their purpose.

He had observed that the three men had stood in the same position without change. If they gave orders to the other Blue Coats, they did it by shouting from where they stood. They seemed wary of turning their backs on the "savage."

Going over Jock's coded map, the two determined what they thought to be each man's position, if they could be guided to the same positions they had held the previous day. The sapling for Popoffski was to carry soft chips held loosely together by prairie grass, equal in weight to the rock it replaced in the sling. At a given signal, Jock himself would release the projectile.

Jock was convinced that the Blue Coats would use their cannon, first to intimidate and then as a weapon. The act of intimidation had already occurred, so the cannons had to be eliminated before they could be used again. Fortunately, they were in perfect range of the "rock artillery."

Three Hands then suggested, "When I signal, do three things. At the first signal, release the chip ball. At the second signal, release the rocks. At the third signal, the men, women, and cubs are to eat the chico beans that are prepared and drink the spring water. The women and cubs are to go to the Canyon of Returning Voices—the beans should react by that time. The men are to return to the glade and form a half-circle facing the Ucumfastus trees. Remember, timing will determine success!" Jock could not conceal his laughter and eagerness to put the plan into action!

The four men met at high noon, as before. From the faces of the Blue Coats before him, and of those to his left, the soft chip battle had been won in the darkness. Popoffski could not wait to show his anger by dispatching a stream of tobacco juice between the feet of the red man.

Three Hands did not flinch at this act, but a smile did flicker across his lips as he said, "The great chief of the Hiup says that, if the Blue Coats are wise, they will return ta their great chief and inform him that the Hiup had no a' thought of moving east ta recapture the lands of their brothers that hae been taken by the whites. But the threats your chief has spoken, through you, may encourage tha Hiup ta change their mind."

"Why you arrogant bastard!" gasped Colonel Dozer, his face turning red as a beet in indignation. "My men are prepared, not for any more demonstrations, but to move forward and destroy your people if they do not lay down their weapons and surrender! They await my orders!"

The officers looked around to see that everything was in place, then turned to accept the capitulation of the savage.

Instead, they heard a voice to their right saying, "These arrogant sons of bitches need another demonstration of the displeasure the Hiup feel for those who offend Mother Earth!"

Turning in the direction of the voice to identify the speaker, they saw no one!

"Who the hell was that?" stammered a nervous Lieutenant Walker.

"Stamping Bear," answered Three Hands. "He is quite annoyed at your offense ta Mother Earth when ye destroyed her tree."

"I don't see any Stamping Bear!" stated a dubious Dozer.

"Of course not, for he is a Hiup brave. The Hiup are invisible ta the eye of the white man. Did ye, or your guards, see six hundred braves march unseen past ye last night and leave their symbol of agreement with Stamping Bear? They cou'd easily hae slit your throats, but we are a peace-loving people, unless pushed too far," explained the red man.

"Let me have this lying idiot, Colonel!" Popoffski implored of his leader. "Turn me loose, and I will blow him off the face of the earth!"

A sound of quiet laughter came from behind Colonel Dozer. He was startled, for this invisibility problem could not be rationalized, and he turned about, hoping that someone would be there to bring sanity back to the situation. Again, there was no one there. Not wishing to appear rattled or confused, he asked, "Stamping Bear?"

"No," chuckled Three Hands, "that was Snake Dancer. Stamping Bear is there, by your thundersticks, but he, too, is smiling at the smallness of the Blue Coat's boast."

The three men stared intently at the face of the red man before them; while so engaged, another voice came from behind Captain Popoffski. Not one of the three noticed any movement of the lips of the red man. Apprehension began to replace bravado when the voice was heard to say, "Turn me loose and let me hae these idiots!"

Three Hands had mimicked the words of his opponent as a form of ridicule. He played his hand with great delight and with an ego-satisfying performance! "No, Strong Arm. The Hiup dinna stoop ta the level of these savages," he replied scornfully.

Popoffski said nothing, but displayed his anger and frustration by ejecting another stream of juice in the direction of the red man's feet, part of which struck his moccasin.

Glancing down, the messin man shook his head, ordering, "Very well, Strong Arm, gae ahead. The idiot is yours." With this, Three Hands knelt to the ground to wipe the tobacco stain from his moccasin. The signal had been given! Now if only Jock's map and the strength of the sapling would be true. Moments passed before he heard a thud and,

Messin Man

upon looking up, saw a startled Popoffski covered from face to waist with soft chip dip! "Thank you, brother Jock!" he said to himself with a grin.

The barrage so startled the poppycock Blue Coat that he swallowed his chew of tobacco! With one hand, he pawed at the slowly dripping chip covering his face and eyes. The other hand tried frantically to dislodge the fireball that had just passed the point of no return in his throat! A searing volcano poured into his stomach. His screams alerted his men, who broke ranks to try to save their leader from apparent death.

Three Hands rose and looked Colonel B. U. L. Dozer straight in the eye. There was no humor in the eyes of the savage! "Your rooster not only offended Mother Earth, he offended me, the representative of the Hiup, as well. 'Tis an insult ta all of my people and did nae gae unpunished.

"Strong Arm is nae as patient as me, and sae took it upon himself ta avenge this dishonor directed ta me by filth from your captain." The messin man spoke slowly; the intent of his words unmistakable. "'Tis your belief that your weapons instill fear in the hearts of my people. Ye hae closed your ears ta the words of peace and threaten our people with death by your thundersticks. We will hear the sound of thunder, then die, ye say. Stamping Bear has returned ta my great chief wi' your words. We will await his answer!"

The three men stood in silence. Captain Popoffski soon returned, clean but subdued, to join his leader. Three Hands turned his head in the direction of the slope and said, "Stamping Bear has returned. What is the reply of our great chief?" A voice could be heard whispering next to his ear. "So be it!" replied the messin man, and he immediately sat upon the ground in front of the three officers.

Colonel Dozer, not wishing to be a standing target like Popoffski, also sat on the ground. Taking their cue from their leader, the other two sat on the ground next to him. Being smaller than the red man, they felt somewhat protected from any further barrages of manure.

The movement to sit, however, was not the signal for more chips. In its place came a shower of rocks that struck the line of cannon and caissons, tearing them asunder and burying them! The Blue Coats looked on in astonishment at the destruction. The three officers started to rise, but Three Hands held up his hand and issued a stern order, "Wait!"

The three stayed in their position, which signaled the rest of their forces to do likewise. They were in full expectation of another fusillade of missiles, but silence was the only thing to descend upon the group.

Five minutes passed, which seemed like an eternity to the soldiers, when the sound of thundering cannons rolled endlessly down the slope from the ridge above. Three Hands rose and signaled the others to do likewise. "Ye are most fortunate," he said in a strong voice that could be heard by every Blue Coat, "for our weapons are not as generous as yours. Once released, our enemies never hear their thunder, for they are dead. Your thundersticks were destroyed, not because we fear such toys, but because they were offensive to Mother Earth."

"But where are your cannon? Where are your people? I have seen only you," a confused Dozer asked.

"Our cannon, as ye call them, are in the clouds of the sky, awaiting such mortals as ye, who come with threats and with ignorance of the laws of Mother Earth and her children, the red man.

"My people, the Hiup, are all around ye at this moment," Three Hands stated. "For every Blue Coat, there are five hundred Hiup. I have taken form, at the direction of my great chief, ta communicate with ye. Would ye heed my words if you cou'd no a' see me? Think on this! If ye wish another demonstration, Sharp Knife stands beside the third man in the line ta my right and is quite willing ta slit the man's throat and the throats of as many as necessary ta erase any doubts in your mind!"

The third soldier and others around him had some anxious moments, and the colonel hastened to assure the savage that another demonstration was unnecessary. To add to their woes, the timing could not have been more perfect to reinforce the words of the messin man, for the chico bean by-product had drifted down the slope from the half-circle of braves assembled in the glade to encircle the Blue Coats. Now their attention was focused solely on trying to breathe and see, for the nostrils had closed at the first whiff, and their eyes began to water profusely to wash out the irritant.

The "immune" messin man stood patiently observing the consternation of the soldiers; the cloud and its effects had passed before he spoke, "Now ye can carry the word back ta your people that ye have smelled the Hiup's cloud of death and live only through our generosity!"

Three Hands went on to solidify his position, "My great chief has spoken! Hear his words carefully, for ye are ta return ta your great chief and tell him that the laws of the Hiup must be obeyed! The wagon trains may pass as long as they obey these laws. The words of your great chief and those ye have spoken, along with your actions, hae offended my people. My great chief says that if any Blue Coats are sent ta these lands, there will be nae talking—only death for every one of them!"

The messin man picked up a stick and drew a line in the trail in front of the colonel. He then pushed the stick into the ground in a vertical position. "Ye may leave in peace if ye do so afore the shadow of the sun crosses this line. Stamping Bear and Sharp Knife will go with ye. If your great chief ever sends Blue Coats ta cross the mighty river, Stamping Bear will slit his throat. At the same signal, Sharp Knife will slit yours as a reminder that the Hiup keep their word! They will always be at your side—that is my promise!" With these words, the messin man stepped back and squatted on the trail near the stick.

Colonel B. U. L. Dozer had seen, and he had heard! Signaling to the now somewhat presentable Captain Popoffski and to Lieutenant Walker, he turned and entered his tent to confer on the matter.

Three Hands listened to the heated murmur of their voices coming from the tent. The time of crisis was here. If the Blue Coats called his bluff, there could be a great loss of life, with the real possibility of greater numbers of Blue Coats being sent to avenge the deaths of those before him. If they decided to attack, he would signal the release of more missiles to destroy them.

The men emerged and walked to where the large number of Blue Coats were waiting. They evidently had given their orders, for the three officers mounted their horses and rode toward the line. They stopped about ten paces from the squatting messin man. The Blue Coats on foot formed lines behind their leaders. Behind these men were the supply wagons. All remained in their position in silence.

"It looks like the decision has been made to attack," thought Three Hands. "They are formed to run over me and move to the pass. If that is their decision, so be it! There can be no peaceful solution to avoid death." He sat, prepared to give the signal when they made their move.

The two opponents remained in position as the shadow slowly approached the line. The time for war was at hand. Colonel B. U. L. Dozer had instructed his men to keep an eye on him for their next order and to follow it to a man.

Just as the shadow reached the line, his order came, *"Retreat! Let's get the hell out of here!"* With that, the entire party wheeled and scurried toward the trail through the forest. The bluff had worked! The colonel wanted to test the resolve of the savages to the last instant to see if they broke in the face of his forces. If not, he was not about to attack an enemy who was invisible and who had proven the effectiveness of their weapons.

A jubilant Three Hands trotted up the slope to the shouts of praise by his people. The Hiup had won their very first battle and were in a mood to celebrate!

Colonel B. U. L. Dozer returned to Washington and reported to his superiors and to the president. The intimidators were so intimidated by the invisibility and invincibility of the Hiup that a special communiqué was issued: travelers going west of the Mississippi River would do so at their own peril. The U.S. Army would neither support nor rescue them!

The joy of their brave exploits was celebrated long and completely by the Hiup, for they were now part of a legend. They were exuberant that their battle plan was now back on target, with the black cloud of trouble blown away by the wind of victory. Winds, however, are notoriously fickle and unpredictable—as these "legendary" Hiup were soon to learn.

⬅ Chapter Eleven ➡

Seekers of peace must begin the hunt within themselves. If they cannot focus their efforts on this part of the trail, they will surely go astray, until the need to seek is no longer a need but the object of excuse.

The battle plan seemed to qualify as a grandiose one. It had purpose, objectivity, total commitment by those involved, checks and balances, and provisions (or options) for all known or anticipated contingencies. There was consensus among the tribes that the plan was working and was serving the end intended. As in most cases, however, it was the unknown, sitting unnoticed in the background, that would evoke consternation when it chose to make its presence known.

The unknown force for the Hiup was complacency. This force moved like a gentle mist, hovering unnoticed until it made its decision. Then it dropped like a blanket, covering everything and obliterating all landmarks from view. Movement by all creatures was either nullified or attempted only by the desperate who placed their faith in their ability to grope. The hairline crack in the battle plan was continuing to widen at the Hiup position. As planned, when a wagon train left one tribe's area of responsibility, that tribe would send a number of men to join the next tribe's forces to present the illusion of large numbers to the whites. When the train passed out of that tribe's area, the "loaned" braves would return home to await the next train. In this procedure, no tribe's welfare was infringed upon.

The Hiup contribution to this part of the plan was nil, but not by choice. Once the trains left the pass area, they were on Plains, the realm of the pony, of which the Hiup had but two. The efforts to live up to this obligation produced increased pressure on the fissure.

The Kansas, who picked up the trains when they left Hiup lands, were keeping to the plan. On occasion, after they completed their tasks with a train, a group of riders would make their way to the Hiup camp to inform them how well the plan was working to the west. Their stories of the means they took to intimidate and harass the trains were shared with the Hiup. The Hiup in turn shared the "Bull-Chip-Slip" and "Fireball" techniques with their visitors. There was a great exchange of laughter.

The Hiup, especially the younger braves, were enthralled by these tales of the Kansas (who did not avoid the opportunity to embellish them to the hilt), and their imaginations began to work overtime. Visions of racing with the wind on the back of their very own pony made their activities pale in contrast. The concept of adventure and endless opportunity to display bravery became a passion.

Chief Has It Made and Three Hands were not oblivious to the words of the visitors and to the impact they had on the youth of the tribe. Their visitors' words also subtly underscored the lack of support in the form of "loaners" to their brother Kansas, so, as a matter of pride, as well as obligation, the Hiup made changes in their routine. They had but two ponies, and if used, even in principal only, honor would be served.

A council meeting was called, and it was decided that the two ponies left to Chief Has It Made by the demise of his father would become the nucleus of a training program for their young braves. Upon completion of the training, two braves would be sent to fulfill their obligation to the Kansas and to the battle plan. Such a program also would serve as a pacifier to the imagination of their young. Standards for qualification to the program would allow for maintaining a competitive, but fair, standard of entry.

Chief Has It Made spoke to the leader of a Kansas group about the plan and requested his advice in setting up the program. The leader immediately offered the assistance of one of his men to act as trainer. This man would remain behind and guide small groups in the art of learning proper riding techniques. When the two top "graduates" were ready, they would join their brothers of the Kansas.

The leader of the group spoke of his eagerness to return to his camp and spread the news that the Hiup soon would be riding at their side to keep the trains moving. His words pleased the Hiup, and their plan seemed to counteract the force of complacency and mend the crack — not so!

The training program proceeded without delay, and soon two graduates were ready. When the next train moved out from Chip Dip, the two left the Hiup camp, accompanied by their tutor. Parents and friends shared the usual advice as to safety and conduct. Amid the sound of the drums, they rode west.

It was really a momentous occasion, as it was the first time that a Hiup had left his people as a warrior. They were expected to return in about one moon and would be welcomed by a celebration. A Stare and He Who Walks Funny were already involved in mental musing as to new dance steps they would introduce to highlight the occasion.

One moon did pass before the two young braves returned to camp, and their return created increased excitement for they rode into camp with four ponies in tow. The usual protocol of reporting to the chief was carried out after the Whoop of Triumph. The council fire was lit, the luk pots filled with the finest delicacies, and each member of the tribe was busy planning his role in the celebration activities to follow. Three Hands was planning special incantations to highlight his importance, while Has It Made fussed over the attire that would best highlight his attributes.

After the feasting, Three Hands lit the ceremonial pipe and offered incantations of thanks to the spirits for the safe return of the two braves. An aurora display of five colors set the stage for the report to follow.

The two braves were primed for their moment of glory. Their return trail had been spent in rehearsal for this moment, and their choice of words had to be deliberate to present each action with clarity (and embellishment).

When the wagon train had started west from the pass, they had shadowed it by riding along the rim of the canyons, then dropping down to the plain and out of sight of the train. They had met members of the Kansas and accompanied them to their camp. The chief had said that, since the numbers of the Hiup were small and their importance at the pass so great, the fact they had sent two braves to ride with his people made his heart sing with happiness. Messengers were then sent to the Pawnee to join them there, as a train was on the way.

By the time the train had come into view, the Pawnee had arrived, and together they presented a force of a thousand braves. This force would appear at a distance, sometimes to the right of the train, sometimes to the left, or even to the rear. To those on the train, their numbers appeared endless, which necessitated constant guard against attack and possible annihilation. There was no inclination to break the agreement with the red man by stopping to settle!

When the train reached a set point, the Pawnee were met by members of the Arapaho, while the Kansas, with their Hiup brothers, returned to camp to await the next train.

The report by the returning Hiup braves, so far at least, appeared routine and contained no awe-inspiring action, which prompted questions from the audience. Answers were needed to confirm visions of a west that provided excitement and adventure: "What did you do while waiting for a train? Were there feasts of celebration upon your return to camp? Was the pony truly as great as we thought him to be? Did you encounter danger? Were the tales of the Kansas merely tales?"

Strong Arm saw that the time for focusing on individual achievement had come. "We have shared activities with you that relate to the purpose of joining our brothers to the west. Our battle plan is working well, and that is the priority. Although your activities at the pass may seem routine, they are critical for establishing, in the minds of the white man, the need to adhere to our laws of the trail. The actions of our brothers to the west are intended to present the illusion of numbers. Every member of every tribe is vital to the success of our plan."

Piercing Eyes made his move to continue the response. "The words of Strong Arm ring clear like the mighty waterfall. Our brothers did tell tales and they were speaking true." The audience leaned forward; the meat was about to greet the fire! "They also had ways to frustrate the whites, and we participated willingly. One night, thirty of us approached the camp of the whites by crawling on our stomachs so that we would not be seen by their guards. We slipped a buffalo hide 'moccasin' on the feet of each of their ponies. Moving as silently as shadows, we left their camp with the ponies. It would have been easy for us to have taken these ponies for our own, but this would have prevented the wagons from moving on. We would have also broken our word to the whites.

"We led the ponies to a distant point, tied them together as one, and removed their 'moccasins.' The next sun, we observed the camp as it awakened to find the ponies missing. Men were sent out to locate and return with the ponies. Finding them tied together made them realize that they had not just wandered off, and that the red man could move at will among them as invisible as the wind."

The audience gave its approval of this example of courage by emitting a series of whoops. Strong Arm spoke to maintain the plateau of interest. "I remember the night we made our way to another camp after the whites were asleep. On the plain, the whites form a circle with their wagons at the end of the day, thinking this will ensure their safety while they sleep. At a silent signal, we rode faster than the wind in single file toward the circle.

"When we arrived, we did not slow our ponies, but sent them leaping over the front of one wagon, across the circle, and out the other side, whooping as we went. There were several guards near fires in the center of the circle. They had thundersticks, but we knocked them from their hands as we swept by. I think we brought their sleep to an end that night!"

Again, many whoops responded to the story. Piercing Eyes resumed speaking, "We also learned to use a coup stick on our brother Omaha to the north. Sometimes, while waiting for a train, we went to the lands of the Omaha, and if we could enter his camp undetected, strike one of them with our coup stick, and then leave the camp without being struck ourselves, we could add a feather to our coup stick. I must say, our brother Omaha came to our camp to test his skill on us and, if struck, cost us one feather from our coup stick." The two then displayed their sticks with several feathers attached, which brought more whoops.

The questions and answers continued for some time, giving all a chance to be heard. Three Hands asked one final question. "You have made our hearts swell with pride! You have shown courage and wisdom on your trail. You have returned with four ponies. What is the explanation for that?"

Strong Arm replied, "We returned with the two ponies of the Hiup. Of the two remaining, one we claim for ourselves, having won them by deed. The other we give as a gift to repay the honor our people bestowed upon us. If it is the will of our chief, we will train others to ride. They can then represent us at the side of our brothers, the Kansas and the Pawnee."

Later, after much discussion, Chief Has It Made decided there could be no harm in allowing the two to conduct their training sessions. Unknowingly, this decision extended the hairline crack in the battle plan. When the next train left the pass, Strong Arm and Piercing Eyes, accompanied by four neophyte riders, rode to the west!

The hairline crack grew steadily wider with the passage of time. A precedent had been set by the decision to train riders to join their brothers in the west. As each group returned, they had ponies of their own, plus those they brought back to give to the tribe.

Two problem areas were gradually highlighted until they grew too bright to be ignored. One, the numbers leaving grew larger each time a party returned to train others and then leave again with them in tow. Two, not all of those leaving were returning, having made the decision to remain where the action was. The result was a manpower shortage impacting on the tribe, especially in the area of contented women. For harmonious living, their needs must be met. The ratio of men to women was rapidly increasing on the side of the women.

Three Hands did his best to nullify the impact, but he was growing older and was not as eager to call forth the Spirit of Water as in days past. He made his concerns known to the chief (from a medicinal point of view, of course). Women had been coming in greater numbers and frequency, requesting "messin bags" to relieve them of their "condition." He could not reveal their words because of a client-messin man relationship, but the chief got the message.

The situation presented a dilemma, for the chief could not order braves to remain in camp. His position was limited to a guidance role. He could request the young to stay, but he was working against the lure of adventure.

Three Hands played his reserve card. He would ask the guidance of M.O.M., whose word was law; all would obey or suffer the wrath of Wakan-Manitou. The chief agreed that it would be proper to do so. The messin man sent a signal, received a favorable response, and left on the trail to M.O.M.

Arriving at the lake, Three Hands shouted his greetings as before and heard the reply to advance. Although not as nimble in youth as he was on his last visit, he made his way along the rock face, with arms outstretched and feet inching along the narrow ledge. At last he was able to step off onto the grassy landing.

M.O.M. was seated, just as Three Hands had left him many summers before. "Our trails cross once more, Three Hands," said M.O.M. in greeting. "Surely the tipi of your mind has allowed proper actions to come forth to eliminate the problem of the white man!"

"It is not the actions of the white man directly that close the flap of my tipi," responded Three Hands. "The white man's movement in our lands is the basis of my problem, but not the direct cause. The plan to combat the white man is working well—perhaps too well. Our cubs are no longer content to seek comfort in their lands and their customs. Their hearts hear the songs of their brothers to the west and the sound of the wind made by their ponies, and some are leaving our lands to answer this call, including older braves."

"I hear your words and remember," mused M.O.M. "I regret that you have forgotten mine since we last joined in council. "

"Your words were the wind that blew open the flap of my mind's tipi. I remembered and used them as a guide for our plan of battle against the whites. If I had not remembered your words, would the plan be so strong and so true?" asked Three Hands.

"You ask a question of me that is the real proof that you have not remembered my words," a disgruntled M.O.M. replied. "Perhaps a stronger wind, like a Chinook, is needed to clear the web Iktumi, the spider of confusion, has woven to secure your flap in the closed position! My words to you, evidently so easily forgotten, were that the answers you seek are now blowing in the wind. Let your mind soar like the eagle until it finds this wind where no flapping of the wings is needed to soar."

The messin man was humbled by awareness of the truth of M.O.M.'s words. He had let the problem become the total focal point. It had blocked out the solution that was waiting its turn for recognition. The "spider of confusion" had indeed secured the flap of his mental tipi.

Three Hands sought to regain credibility. "Your words are like the fire stick that sets flame to the spider's web and releases its hold over the flap to the tipi of my mind. The wind is already at work, cleaning out the web inside. You say you are willing to guide this wind, if needed. Hear the words of confusion flee from my mind like falling leaves before the wind of autumn.

"We, the people of the Hiup, have lived in the same lands for more winters than a tree has leaves," the contrite messin man continued. "We have strong ties to our customs and those of our fathers before us. We lack neither courage nor pride and have been content to live and die in these lands. We have had many visitors who left tales of their lands with us, yet no Hiup has left our lands to live elsewhere."

"I hear you say your problem is that none of your people wish to leave their lands — that is a problem?" M.O.M. asked, not quite sure if he heard correctly.

"No, the problem is just the opposite," Three Hands explained. "Too many of our young braves have responded to the call of their brothers and their ponies to the west. The excitement of the coming of the white man has worn thin. The tales told by visitors from the west have made the eyes of our young shine like the stars in the sky. Even some of our older braves have left our lands to answer the call of adventure and excitement. The call to those who have left must be stronger than the call that pulled them west, if they are to return to their lands and their people."

"That is the answer you seek?" questioned M.O.M.

"No, all of the debris has not exited the flap," the messin man admitted. "To know that one must kill the deer before eating it is of no value if one does not have knowledge of the weapon necessary for the killing.

"Our women mourn the absence of their braves, who have not returned to them. They have needs that go unsatisfied, which makes them as mean as the bear who has been awakened prematurely from his winter sleep. Some braves may have gone west to escape their meanness. The problem is to find an attraction of such appeal that it will draw our braves back to keep their women contented and bearing cubs.

This would return peace to my people. That is the weapon I seek: not to kill, but to bring peace."

"This is the answer you seek?" asked the aged one.

"I have found the answer, but the trail does not end there. I must find a solution to the answer," responded a mind-weary Three Hands.

"The solution may be nearer than you think," advised the man of skin with endless wrinkles. Then he smiled. "You say that, if you find some means of pacifying the women of the Hiup and of arousing the fervor of the men to such a height that the desire to leave their lands is forgotten, your problem will be resolved?"

"It is so," an apprehensive messin man responded.

This man, M.O.M., who had appeared in the past to be cast of stone, was having some degree of a control problem, for he was shaking with inward mirth. Several moments passed before complete control returned, and with it, his speech.

"Tell me, eaglet who longs to soar, do you have a squaw?" M.O.M. inquired.

"No," came the messin man's reply.

"Then you do not have a restless squaw problem?" M.O.M. stated presumptuously.

"But I do, for as their messin man, these squaws come to me seeking relief from their afflictions," Three Hands explained.

The control problem was precipitously close to becoming a lost cause for M.O.M. "And do you provide relief for them?" he chortled.

"Some, but the demands are far greater than my ability to accommodate them," admitted the messin man.

"The Hiup number how many squaws?" M.O.M. inquired, whose self-control had returned.

"Seventy, not counting the Snow Hairs."

"How many braves?"

"Fifty, again not counting the Snow Hairs," Three Hands calculated.

"Why do you not count the Snow Hairs?"

It was Three Hands' turn for silent laughter, but he regained control before his eyes betrayed the laughter within. He replied, "Only the minds of the Snow Hairs can react to the memories of days when they could keep a squaw's fires raging to the point where blankets were unnecessary to stay warm. The changing of hair color brings a feeling that snow has been placed on the fire. It can no longer give warmth and eventually goes out. Blankets are then the only source of warmth for them."

"And if each Hiup brave could keep the fire burning until he sets foot on the trail to the Camp of Many Lodges, would this please the squaws?" M.O.M. asked, with just a hint of a twinkle in his eyes.

Three Hands was perplexed at this point. He knew the words of M.O.M. were always true, so there must have been a purpose for such a question. He gave his humble, yet doubting reply, "Yes."

"And if the message were delivered to the Hiup who have left your camp that every Hiup brave remaining in the lands of the Hiup could keep his fire burning until his first step on his final trail, would they wish to return and greet their brothers and squaws again?" the aged one (with eyes now blazing) asked.

"I believe they would mount their fastest pony for the return trail and probably bring some of their Kansas brothers with them," claimed Three Hands.

"Then observe my actions with the eye of an eagle and see if your wings need more flapping to soar!" With these words, M.O.M. rose to a standing position, the frailties of his body seeming to offer an open invitation to a gentle breeze to lift him and carry him away. He reached into a messin pouch secured around his neck, withdrew a pinch of powderlike substance, and placed it into his toothless mouth. Several moments passed. To the "eagle" gaze of Three Hands, nothing was happening.

But the action that exploded before his eyes left a slackness in his jaws! Slackness, however, was not the word to describe M.O.M. With a flourish of his hand, he cast aside his loincloth to display a rock-hard erection of admirable girth and length.

His entire body was rejuvenated, and a gleam appeared in his eyes. "What say you to this, eaglet? What would your Snow Hairs say to this? I will await your answer at a later council, for I must leave you now. I will return before the sun hides behind the horizon. Refresh yourself until my return." With these words, he turned with the agility of a rabbit and scurried into the opening in the wall of stone.

Three Hands slowly regained his senses and the ability to rationalize. M.O.M., who was as old as the mountains (and looked it), had undergone a sudden, tremendous, and unbelievable transformation right before his eyes! Questions already were tearing at his senses for logical answers, but his mind went blank. His eyes had witnessed a sight that resisted plausible or rational analysis. He decided to make his meal while awaiting the return of his senses, as well as his host. Neither returned before sleep overtook him.

The new sun's warmth awoke him. He opened his eyes to find his host had arrived with the new day. M.O.M. strolled back to his rock seat and sat with legs crossed. A thin smile of satisfaction meandered across his face, which was once again relaxed with folded skin. His loincloth drooped with its only task, to cover a similarly drooping member.

"Well, eaglet, have you had your body refreshed with food and sleep?" inquired a smiling M.O.M. "My body also has been refreshed and looks forward to a long trail of rest. Do the eyes of the eaglet, which see in all directions of the winds, see an open flap to the tipi of your mind? Can a possible solution to your question be coming forth in the warmth of the sun? Are you ready to soar?"

"My eyes have seen, O wise one, yet the heat of the vision before them has been so intense that reason is slow in approaching this heat in a logical manner," the messin man replied.

"And what did your eyes see? Be not quick to answer, for the soaring wind is near and ready to accept your wings if they are strong enough. The wind may never be so accepting to you again!" M.O.M. cautioned.

The mind of the messin man did not miss the significance of M.O.M.'s words. "I have been favored with a vision that possibly no earth being has ever witnessed," he thought to himself. "There has to be a reason. If I can make the proper interpretation, my solution will be clear. If not, M.O.M. will think me unworthy of a solution and go on his trail of rest."

Since M.O.M. accepted no questions, he decided to continue his analytical approach to receive further guidance. The termination of this council must be avoided. He chose his words carefully. "My eyes have seen the transformation of a spirit-human, who is as old as these mountains, into a figure emblematic of youthful actions with exceptional rigidity of manhood. This transformation took place after he had placed a powder into his mouth. This spirit-human then left me to my thoughts. Those thoughts raced into my mind like water into a split canoe. I came to this spirit-human in council, seeking guidance of my thoughts, and have learned that solutions come to seekers of truth if their hearts are true."

Three Hands became flushed, the vision of truth rapidly coming into focus in his mind. Discipline made his reply continue in a slow, deliberate manner, so as not to dislodge one stone on the trail of logic. "My wings grow strong, and the soaring wind is beginning to lift me. I sought solution to my problem, and it has been shown to me. If all of our people, the Snow Hairs as well as the young, could enjoy the fruits of youth until the sun they begin their last trail, they would never leave; their squaws would be forever content. I have been guided to this solution by one whose heart is filled with concern for our people."

"Your words were those of an eagle who has begun to feel the joys and rewards of soaring," M.O.M. pronounced majestically. "You have learned your lessons well. I am ready to share my solution to your problem, as we are one in thought. This solution, if not used for good, can become evil and lead to the your destruction, as well as that of your people. I believe you to possess the wisdom and strength to keep this a good force."

"It shall be my will that your trust never be violated," Three Hands vowed.

"I believe you," M.O.M. said in acceptance of his words, then went on, "I have in my messin pouch a potion that awakens the natural urges of man, even if he sleeps the deepest of sleeps. This urge is not endless, for it, as all things do, needs time to rest. The amount of potion used will determine the reaction time and duration. The younger the receiver, the faster the reaction time. If given this spirit of awakening, how would you use it to help your people?"

Three Hands reflected on the countless possibilities, but again remembered that M.O.M.'s every word had meaning beyond what the ears received. The spoken word was merely the catalyst for mental projections, so his reply was slow, yet organized, in hope of acceptance by M.O.M. "The spirit of awakening should never be involved with cubs, or with the young, for they have a natural spirit within them to guide such urges.

"Those whose hair continues to harbor the snow even after winter has passed would be the ones who need their natural urges extended. The young are not impressed with the loss of the natural urge until they reach the age of Snow Hair, and so would not benefit by use of the spirit. When they observe that the age of Snow Hair does not affect their urges, they will not wish to leave their land of opportunity. This spirit must be shown to inhabit Hiup lands only. The spirit would be used to keep this legend strong in the minds and memories of all Hiup!"

"How would you administer this spirit, in light of the precautions you have listed?" M.O.M. asked.

"At a time and in a way that was unknown by my people, I would place it in the food of those chosen, while asking the favor of the spirits on this food," the messin man replied.

"Your reply tells me that your mind has found the soaring wind and can be trusted to use the spirit wisely," M.O.M. decided, then went on to detail the ingredients needed to create the spirit. "I call this spirit, 'Span Ishfly,' after the wide wings and skill of the soaring eagle. When your older braves, whose natural urges have turned to memories, experience Span Ishfly, they will rejoice!" M.O.M. removed the messin pouch from his neck and handed it to Three Hands.

Messin Man

Three Hands accepted the pouch. He opened it and felt the composition of the powder within. It was a finely ground mixture that could be easily slipped into a luk pot undetected, he thought.

M.O.M. uttered a precautionary bit of advice, "Take this pouch to use until you can concoct your own supply, but . . . don't use it now!"

The warning was too slow in coming! After his examination of the pouch, Three Hands found traces of powder on his fingers; using the natural method of cleansing them, he placed them into his mouth and cleaned them with his tongue. His youth and abstinence during the trail to M.O.M. were factors that caused instant results, for the spirit definitely moved him! He rose to his feet. At the same time, his "lance" rose to a state of magnificent arousal. Heat permeated his body, but his mind was still in control. He took one step in the direction of M.O.M., stating, "I wish to . . ."

At that moment, M.O.M. had not only witnessed the lateness of his request to the messin man, but also the power of the spirit at work within him. As Three Hands rose to a standing position, so did the largest member he ever had seen on a mortal! Here before him was a young stallion who had been long on the trail without a source to relieve natural urges, and who was now walking toward him!

Even with all of the wisdom of the ages, M.O.M. panicked! The sight of Three Hands' weapon moving toward him called for a decision to be made. Two choices came to mind: to be gored by this "bull buffalo" or to catch the wind and soar like the eagle, out of danger.

He made his selection; to Three Hands' wondering eyes, he ran to the cliff's edge and propelled himself into space, with arms waving in a frantic effort to soar. His looked-for wind was not there to receive and assist him, for it was occupied with carrying the words of Three Hands as he completed his request,

"cool
     off
          under
               your
                    waterfall."

The last words of his request were but a whisper as his astonished eyes witnessed the actions of M.O.M., plunging out of sight. He ran to the edge of the cliff and looked down, expecting to see M.O.M. soaring like the eagle. M.O.M. had soared, not like the eagle, but like the proverbial rock! His remains could be seen among the rocks at the base of the mountain.

Three Hands' quivering body, the natural urge completely negated by trauma, sagged to the rock seat and sat long and deep in thought, trying to rationalize the tragedy. The pressure of his conscience began to crush him as the full realization of the event's significance became evident. He failed to rationalize M.O.M.'s reaction for some time. Reliving that time frame resulted in the conclusion that M.O.M. had misunderstood his intentions. M.O.M. had reacted before he could complete a simple request for a cold shower under the waterfall!

Two realities rushed forward to demand priority of thought. First, M.O.M. was mortal when he leaped into space, and mortal at the conclusion of his brief flight. Had he been in spirit form, he would have soared like the eagle and returned to his perch whenever it suited him. Second, the Hiup and all other tribes in this area depended on his availability when his guidance was needed. Who could they turn to now? What would their feelings be when they learned that a Hiup had been responsible for his end? Where was he to turn now? He sought a vision quest of his spirit brother for guidance and forgiveness.

For five suns, the messin man sat on the rock seat conversing with his spirit brother. The brother was long in coming, for his brother in this quest was M.O.M.! He had arisen from the rocks to be with him in a final act of guidance. His words were comforting, yet somber. "Do not fear what has happened, as I leave you with the soaring wind to always carry you to heights where keenness of eye will show you the trail to take when you seek strength and guidance. This strength will be tested often, but your concern for your people will be the lifting wind. Break that faith, and your wings will be clipped to soar no more!"

With the arrival of the third sun, Three Hands prepared for his return trail. Choosing to explore the possibility of avoiding the narrow ledge, he moved to the opening in the face of the rock wall that M.O.M. had retreated into after using Span Ishfly.

He found himself in a cavern with a series of small roomlike indentations in the walls. In these rooms were food in storage containers, blankets, firewood, and other supplies. M.O.M. may have presented the appearance of agelessness and spirituality while seated on his rock, but there was evidence that not too much of his time was spent outside in the elements—inside were the comforts of the best lodge!

A trail led down the side of the mountain from the well-concealed exit from the cave. Upon reaching the base, Three Hands sought the remains of M.O.M. After locating him, he carefully and lovingly prepared the "spirit man" for his trail to the Camp of Many Lodges, or wherever spirit-mortals made their last camp.

His trail back to Hiup lands seemed long, because his mind was not on the trail, but rather on the situation ahead. He now needed a plan that would not fail, for now there was no M.O.M. to turn to. Slowly the vision of a plan focused in his mind.

Upon return to camp, after the ceremonial procedures were carried out, he met in council with Chief Has It Made and the council. He narrated his trail (deleting the last segment, for practical reasons) and prepared them for the words that would guide them. "M.O.M. instructed me to go on a vision quest to ask my spirit brother for guidance," the messin man revealed. "My spirit brother came as an eagle and carried me on his wings to soar to great heights, far above the tops of the mountains. We saw the lands of the Hiup, the Kansas, the Dakota, and our other brothers to the west; also the Mississippi River and the lands to the east.

"As we soared over the mountains, though the valleys, and over the trees, I saw that the trees in the lands of our brothers were smaller and had no leaves. Only the trees in the land of the Hiup were tall and green with leaves. I asked my brother why this was so. His reply was that the trees of the Hiup were Wakan-Manitou's trees of life; they were green, no matter their age. The trees of our brothers live and die, as do our brothers themselves, but those in the land of the Hiup, like your people, will never feel the decay of age. The spirit of youth will always be with them as long as they live among the trees of life. That tree was the Ucumfastus!"

The vision raised many questions among the members of the council as to its meaning, but no hint of answers. This vision was full of promise, for their lands and name were mentioned. An interpretation was sought from their messin man. Three Hands was ready! He continued, "In my vision, I saw the trail of mighty moccasin prints between the tallest of trees, and each tree had a fine dusting of snow on its branches. Along the trail, small branches had been cut off and placed beside each moccasin print. From these branches, new roots were sprouting. I read this sign to mean that Wakan-Manitou wants us to walk this trail through the Ucumfastus, as their leaves hold the secret of staying young in spirit."

Questions and challenges for explanation and interpretation were not long in coming. Slow Walker was the first to rise and pose a question. "I have lived for fifty winters in these lands, and each winter adds a chill to my bones. I no longer hunt, for the game outruns me, except for Brother Skunk. The blanket of my squaw is as cold as mine; it adds no warmth. I, like my father, will grow older until I begin my last trail, for walking among the Ucumfastus has not allowed me to keep my youth!"

There was an undercurrent of approval for Slow Walker's rebuttal to the messin man's interpretation of the vision. Snow Braids rose to present another challenge. "You have been on the trail to M.O.M. and returned. It was my understanding that your trail was to seek solution to the problem of our young braves leaving our land for the land of our brothers to the west."

He went on to remind his listeners, "Our numbers grow smaller. If the white man learns of this, he will plan to come at us in great numbers and overrun us. What influence does your vision have on this problem? We all grow old and accept that as the law of Mother Earth, but we can't replace our young to maintain our numbers. Let us seek answers to that question!"

Three Hands allowed sufficient time for the flames of rebuttal to glow, sputter, and then die into silence as his audience awaited his reply. Delaying any action a few added moments, for effect, he finally rose to respond, "Does the snow lie so heavy on our heads when we reach the age of Snow Hair that it smothers the brain beneath? Does the fact escape your memory that M.O.M. has guided you, through me, to a vision? Are we to reject the vision and its signs before using our minds to interpret them? If so, then we have lost faith and so deserve the trail of the unfaithful, which leads to destruction.

"I believe this vision and its signs to be true, as they have always been in the past. The signs are clear. The snow on the leaves are the ones among us with snow in their hair. The broken branches and leaves are to be used to produce new growth. As messin man, I will try to find the answer. Only the purest of believers will be invited to join me in carrying out this vision to the end!"

With that final statement and its underlying tone of threat to nonbelievers, Three Hands left the council to its own devices to agree with, or to oppose, his remarks. Some would have to be brought into line to strengthen harmony of purpose. This option had been already conceived and awaiting its need for injection.

For three suns, Three Hands could be seen scurrying about the forest, gathering leaves and branches of varying sizes from the Ucumfastus trees. He was in and out of his "lab" tipi, calling for boiling water, drying mats, and other items, then disappeared inside for long periods of time. He continued this charade until he thought curiosity had peaked among his people, and any action on his part would hold center attention.

On the evening of the fourth sun, Three Hands instructed several squaws to build a separate luk pot fire, with a small luk pot of spring water suspended above it. While others of the tribe were seated and eating with the small luk pot in full view, Three Hands began to tear some Ucumfastus leaves into small pieces and drop them into the pot. Stirring them and offering incantations added to the mystique. He

Messin Man

covertly deposited a small amount of Span Ishfly along with the leaves. All the components for the test were in place except for one: the consumers.

With an air of disdain, Three Hands left his luk pot and made his way to the food luk pots, then returned to his position in the council circle to eat. All others were finished before him, so they had to test their patience and manners until he was finished. When the luk pot concoction had enough time to cool for consumption, he rose for the kill!

In a solemn voice, the messin man began his plea, "I have been faithful to my vision and followed the signs given me to read. If my eyes have been true like those of the eagle, then the results will also be true. I ask only those who heard my words in describing my vision, and knew those words were for them, to step forward. Those of you who do not accept my words will not be held in disfavor by your brothers, but you must live with your own feelings. Only those with snow in their hair will take part, for that was one of the signs. Come!"

The invitation was not given without risk. Failure to draw at least one participant would have been disastrous for the messin man as a power within the tribe. There was no stampede to come forward. There were some who had faith, but feared ridicule by their peers; some who rejected the sign of the leaves; some who saw no relationship, as did Snow Braids, between this invitation and their problem. There were four who, either through the deepest of faith or through a "What do I have to lose?" attitude, went to drink from the pot.

The entire camp followed the movement of the four with an intensity that forbade the eye to blink, lest some detail be missed. One by one, the four took the gourd from the messin man, took one big swallow, then passed it to the next man, and finally back to the messin man. The eyes of the audience were once again allowed to blink, as it was obvious the "spiritual offering" had produced no change in the four. They were still Snow Hairs, and their messin man had been wrong in his interpretation of his vision.

The nonbelievers retired to their tipi with a feeling of self-satisfaction and wisdom for not taking part in the senseless ceremony. Sleep came quickly to them, for they had peace of mind.

The tranquillity of their sleep was soon shattered by strange sounds that reverberated throughout the camp! An attack by the hairy ones was the dominant thought in the mind of each brave as he leaped from his tipi, weapons in hand and seeking a target!

There was no enemy to be seen. Further investigation found the sounds coming from the tipis of the four Snow Hairs who had accepted the offering of their messin man.

The braves outside were poised to enter each tipi to aid their brothers in their fight against an unidentified intruder. Focusing on the voices within, however, they heard not the sounds of pain, but of pleasure! Perplexed, the braves returned to their own tipi to recount the event to their squaw.

The following morning, the eyes of the entire camp, including those of Three Hands, were on the tipis of the "Sound Makers." The morning activities were well under way before the Snow Hairs emerged from the flaps of their tipis, followed by their squaws. No words were exchanged, but the Snow Hairs could be observed walking with head held high, straightness of back, and a strong step. They ate with the appetite of youth and with the shadow of a smile of satisfaction on their lips. Their squaws also walked with a light step as they joined their peers at the luk pots. The squaws were immediately surrounded by the other women, and a rapid exchange of conversation began, punctuated by giggles.

Three Hands also had a smile on his lips, for he knew it would only be a matter of time before his medicinal lodge would be visited by new "believers" requesting a sip of the gourd, and he was right, as usual! However, if the plan was to succeed, word would have to spread to the west to lure the young braves back to the camp of their people.

The most recent young braves who had returned to boast of their exploits with their western brothers would be the messengers. The past night's exploits of the four Snow Hairs would captivate the amorous portals in the minds of those "returnees." The exclusive potential for expanding every Hiup's amorous pursuits would certainly be shared, upon their return to the west. The problem of wooing the Hiup back from the west seemed well on its way to resolution.

Any smugness on the face, or in the heart, of the messin man would later be replaced with despair when the side effects of the potion became known and had to be reckoned with. This "elixir of resurrection" for the Hiup would also serve as the instrument of their demise!

Chapter Twelve

Man has become so efficient in the use of his brain that, very often, he outsmarts himself.

The forces of manipulation, once set into motion by the manipulator, seem to acquire perpetual motion. The manipulator has little time to rest on his laurels and enjoy the fruits of his labor before the motion activates other motions that demand their share of the manipulator's attention and energies.

Three Hands had set into motion a force, Span Ishfly, that was intended to resolve the problem of survival of the Hiup; and it seemed to be doing so. He was the regulatory instrument of control of this force, and he would keep his word to M.O.M. in this regard. His attention was brought back into focus regarding his responsibility for the demise of M.O.M., as his brothers had no one to turn to for solution to their problems when all else failed. Who could they turn to now? The dilemma was his to resolve—and quickly!

As dilemmas are a toy of Wakan-Manitou, he had absolute control over manipulations, as well as the manipulator. He was toying with the horns of His "dilemma bull" like the greatest of toreadors, but was now growing weary of the sport. With His great feeling of compassion, He was about to enhance the ego of the messin man by slipping aside the flap of his mental tipi and inserting the seed of resolution. Three Hands, like most mortals, regarded this seed of resolution as a product of his own mental capacity.

Messin Man

The germination of this seed began during his observation of passing trains. As trains stopped and tolls were collected, the seed's runners guided his vision to sheets of paper tacked to the sides of water barrels.

The vine's emerging leaves caressed his curiosity to the point of asking a driver the meaning of this paper. "Oh, that," replied the driver, "is an offer of a reward for information leading to the whereabouts of a Scottish fellow by the name of Angus MacDaniels. It seems that one of his countrymen is so anxious to locate him that he is offering fifty dollars to anyone who will tell him where Angus can be found. The poster gives a description of him and who to contact for the reward. Take the poster, and if he comes through here, you can be fifty dollars richer."

"Thank ye," said Three Hands, "I will keep my eyes open for him."

The words on the paper were too much for the messin man to ken at the moment, but the mention of Jock's name acted as a gentle breeze to clear his mind. Wakan-Manitou's smile must have been a mile wide at this point; he had scattered some fertilizer to ensure rapid growth of the emerging bud and to crowd out any weed growth that might hinder the blossoming of enlightenment. The pace of Three Hands' moccasins increased as he made his way to Jock's lodge. By the time he arrived, the "blossom of dilemma resolution" was in full bloom and ready for harvest!

Jock was outside instructing his young cub, Ian Coyote, in the art of fingering the kanter as a prerequisite for playing the pipes. Swift Feet was grinding corn, and Three Hands noted that she was swollen with another child. He greeted them and dutifully listened to Ian's skillful finger work, then complimented him when he was done. Protocol completed, he signaled Jock that he wished to council with him. The two walked from the clearing into the forest. Jock was totally unaware that his nightmare was now a reality.

Three Hands introduced the subject by telling of his experience while collecting tolls. He handed the paper to Jock, who read it and fell silent. His shoulders sagged and his strength seemed to flow out of him. The messin man saw this change and moved to assist his friend.

"This man who seeks you is not a friend. Is this not so?" he asked.

"Aye, he is not a friend," came the soft reply.

"Does he pose a danger to you?"

"Aye. He believes that I have done him an injustice, many summers ago, and seeks revenge upon me for it. I was a young buck then, and restless," Angus explained.

"So this is the reason you did not wish to be seen by your white brothers," Three Hands stated, as understanding came into focus.

"Aye," Angus said, his tone reflecting his internal turmoil.

"But you have nothing to fear, as you are surrounded by friends. This man will never learn of your presence here," the messin man assured him.

"I have lived among my red brothers in peace, yet have never had peace of mind. There was always the danger of this man's threat being carried out. I have a family now and seek only to live in peace. It may only be a matter of time before a mistake is made, or a word spoken, that will lead him here. I do not wish to pose a danger to my red brothers for that which is mine to face," Jock replied in obvious sincerity.

"Jock, my brother, you have done much to help your brother Hiup. Your wisdom has helped us plan for survival against your white brothers in such a way that causes no injury to either side. You have turned the Blue Coats back, and even my role as messin man has been enhanced by your guidance, yet you have asked for nothing in return. I ask now that you allow me to help you in your time of need," requested the messin man.

Jock's curiosity was aroused by Three Hands' words of praise. But curiosity was soon replaced by incredulity as the messin man recalled the details of his meeting with M.O.M. and the impact his demise created on the messin man's responsibility to his red brothers. As the story ended, Jock asked the one recurring question that occurred to him. "I hear your words and understand your concern, but how does it affect me, a white man with problems of his own?"

The question locked into place still another segment of the web of manipulation being woven by the industrious spider in the tipi of Three Hands' mind. The spider's efforts continued. "You have proven to be a man of great wisdom whose words have practical application. You have need of a lodge that only the eyes of the high flying eagle can find. What better refuge than a sacred place where visitation is by invitation only? The only visitors would be red men, including myself, of course."

Jock's mind, confused by thoughts and images tumbling out of control, sought to form one question that would bring stability and order. "But I am white. What red man, besides yourself, would accept my words upon seeing my skin was not of his color?" he questioned.

The tension of the subject was broken by the surfacing of an uncontrolled chuckle from Three Hands. "Just how much of your skin can be seen, my fire-haired brother? It would take sharp eyes indeed to penetrate that dense forest of hair on your body to see your skin. The sun has darkened your nose, ears, and hands, so that it would stretch one's imagination to label you white! One additional point in your favor is the fact that to my knowledge, no mortal has ever seen M.O.M. Who is to say that the spirits are of any specific color? You have a red squaw, and Ian Coyote could pass for red."

"Your points are well taken," replied a receptive Jock, "but you have raised another problem. How do I explain this to Swift Feet and Ian?"

"It is not a squaw's place to question her brave's decisions. She need only be told that you have had a vision and have asked an interpretation by me. I will explain that the spirits have chosen you to lodge atop the tallest mountain to watch the movement of the white man so that no harm will come to your red brothers through surprise. My interpretation will also satisfy the questions of our brother Hiup. Your name will only be spoken by the Rem A Nisser in sacred meetings," explained Three Hands.

The manipulator was on a roll! His creative imagination and follow-through had erased any and all problems. With a light heart, he prepared Jock for his move north. Map sessions were carried out daily until Jock was totally familiar with the trail to the Talking Waters and the mountain lodge beyond.

In council with Chief Has It Made and council members, Jock told of his vision, and Three Hands shared his interpretation of it. There was consensus of the honor being bestowed upon Jock by the spirits, and its light reflected on his Hiup brothers.

Jock, Swift Feet, and Ian Coyote said their farewells to their chief and their people, then set out on the trail north. Three Hands met them down the trail to make sure there were no questions left unanswered, then broke off and took his own trail to gather messin specimen. He noticed the enlargement of Jock's eyeballs when he mentioned the purity of the waters of the Talking Lake; he knew that Jock's trail would be a swift one.

Swift Feet and Ian Coyote soon would discover nearby inhabitants and form new friendships. Jock, however, as the new M.O.M., would not have the same privilege to make friends, which suited his wishes. He was obligated to assume the role of loner, but his life certainly would not be dull. The pure water of the lake seemed perfect for the Blend, but only time would verify that. If nearby clearings could sustain the growth of grain, he could free his mind and energies and devote time to tutoring Ian, his successor. Jock was determined to live up to the great responsibility given him by Three Hands to be a M.O.M. to all who needed his services.

Three Hands returned to camp with a number of specimens and with a feeling that he had mastered still another great challenge to his mental capacities through logic and organized planning! Now for some well-deserved peace of mind and the pursuit of more enjoyable endeavors, like the squaws of Chip Dip. He had only to wait for the signal that Jock had reached his destination. The one red puff of smoke (an aurora bag provided by Three Hands) came in less than one moon. With a smile of contentment on his face, the messin man continued his activities of just plain messin!

Three areas of concern kept the mind and body of the messin man active: messin his people, collecting tolls, and his missionary position in Chip Dip with Fireanda, Bea, and occasionally, Lynn. The picture would appear to be the epitome of tranquillity and harmony, devoid of dangers or circumstances that once again would challenge the mental capacity of Three Hands. But not so, for, with a single stroke of his brush, Wakan-Manitou, the artist, amended the scene.

The three newest inhabitants of Chip Dip had not been idle since the incident with the Blue Coats. Lynn had organized a combination of endeavors to pacify the two main needs of the weary wagoneers: thirst and rejuvenation of the spirit. She also lived up to her promise to keep the trail clear of dangerous items. Zeke tended bar while the trains reformed at the base of the incline; after the wagons left, he would scour the trail for debris. By having a bar available, glass was kept on the premises, which eliminated the problem of broken glass on the trail.

To keep herself and Lotta occupied, Lynn offered a room for rent on a short-term occupancy schedule. Lotta was the basic source of rest and relaxation for the customers, but when demand exceeded availability, Lynn graciously (and profitably) offered her services.

Periodically, some young client was determined to either get his full money's worth or to reinforce his super ego by showing off his staying power, resulting in a slowdown of business opportunities. At peak levels of demand, Lynn felt it necessary to inject her surefire termination factor to cool the ardor and staying power of such clients.

When her decision to activate this factor was made, she simply dangled a homemade cloth mouse filled with loco weed seeds over the buttocks of the client. This movement caught the eye of Satan, who was always languishing on the back of the settee. His natural urge to hunt was ignited and displayed by a twitching of his whiskers and the swishing of his tail. As silent as a shadow, he made his way from the settee to the sideboard, then on up to the topmost shelf. From there he had a perfect view of his prey and began the meticulous calculation of perfect timing that would lead to conquest.

That time arrived when Lynn saw him in position and ceased movement of the mouse. At that instant, Satan made his move! In a magnificent leap to gain still more height, he arched perfectly toward his target with legs outstretched and claws extended. Lynn's timing was also perfect, for at the last instant, she jerked the mouse away and

Messin Man

Satan's claws pierced, not his intended prey, but the buttocks of the unsuspecting lingerer!

Satan's action accomplished two objectives. First, it brought about instant termination of any thoughts by the client to continue his activity. Second, the natural and instantaneous reaction of the buttocks to move away from the source of excruciating pain caused full penetration of the distended digit, which brought about some gratification for Lynn. The ear-shattering scream of agony from the victim was softened somewhat by the noise from the next room, where the next client, or victim, was waiting. Life, like Satan's claws, was not dull in Chip Dip. It was to be further enlivened by the arrival of the final entry on the roll call of its inhabitants.

It was one of those hazy, lazy days when nothing important enough was occurring to command one's total attention and planning. Travel on the trail had been light for the past moon; there had been ample opportunity for Three Hands to visit the new lodges of Bea Ware and Fireanda Brimstone, the Snow Hairs were content, more members of the tribe were returning from the west, and not a single sign of potential danger was evident in the lands of the Hiup. Then Wakan-Manitou changed that scene with another stroke of his brush!

Three Hands was halfway up the incline from Chip Dip when his ears detected movement on the trail leading to the pass. It was the sound of a single horse and rider. The hooves of the horse were plodding in a laboring step, which indicated that he was ascending the trail. That the horse had a rider was evident by the deliberate and steady pace, as opposed to the meandering rhythm of a free-moving animal. The messin man attained the top of the pass and stood among the Ucumfastus trees to watch the approach of the traveler.

As the two reached the edge of the glade, Three Hands wiped his hand over his eyes to fix what he suspected to be a possible problem affecting his vision. The horse and rider that stopped at the edge of the glade stood no higher than the level of his eyes!

Seeing the messin man standing in the shadows, the rider urged his mount forward. As they came slowly toward him, Three Hands confirmed his sight to be true—this was the smallest combination of man and beast he had ever seen. Was this child on the trail alone? Was he lost? Where was the rest of his family? There was no other movement on the trail.

When the horse and rider reached Three Hands, they stopped. The rider's gaze locked with that of the red man. His eyes were not those of a child, but of a man of twenty summers. Shading those eyes was the wide brim of a tall beaver pelt hat atop his head. The man remained in the saddle, seemingly unsure of his next action or the action of the man before him.

The "savage" made the first move by offering his hand in greeting. "If ye come ta the lands of the Hiup in peace, I, Three Hands, welcome ye. Ye may refresh yourself and your animal at the stream. If ye come as an enemy, turn back now or prepare ta die."

His brogue caught the rider off-guard for an instant, but he recovered his poise and replied, "I come with no thought of harm to you or your people." With that statement, he dismounted and led his horse to the stream.

The messin man observed the visitor with disbelief. That feeling quickly turned to one of humorous astonishment. The newcomer, once dismounted, stood no more than twelve hands high and walked with his body at such an acute forward angle that it appeared that he would fall on his face at any moment! His head preceded his body by at least three hands. His stride was short; his arms, bent at the elbow. swung alternately across his body in a pendulous motion. It seemed that his body was tense and that his total concentration was centered on maintaining his balance. Two belts were angled across his waist, each affixed with a large handgun in a leather holder.

As his gaze traveled downward, Three Hands saw the legs encased in what appeared to be animal skin that flapped as he walked. Finally, he saw the boots—boots like he had never seen on any white man, or any man, for that matter. The heels were nearly a hand high, which had a great deal to do with tilting the body forward. The guns were worn slightly over each buttock; they apparently acted as a counterbalance that kept the body from toppling forward.

The messin man stood patiently until the rider tethered his animal to graze and returned to where he waited. "I thank you for the refreshment of your stream for me and my horse," the rider said in appreciation.

Three Hands motioned him toward the shade of the Ucumfastus trees and said, "Come, let us enjoy the refreshment of the shade while we talk. I am curious as ta your reasons for this trail."

The two made their way to a grassy area and made themselves comfortable. The rider took off his hat, which caused Three Hands to lower his estimate of the rider's height even more. He took some deer jerky from his pouch and offered it to the stranger, who readily accepted it. Although his curiosity was highly activated by the appearance of the stranger, his hunger for answers was controlled by the laws of protocol. One never solicited information of a personal nature from a stranger. Personal information had to be offered voluntarily; still, protocol did not eliminate the use of subterfuge, such as flattery, to encourage voluntary information. He began by saying, "I have seen many horses on the trail, but none as strong for its size as yours."

"He is a Shetland and of English breeding. I bought him from a man who traveled from town to town back east entertaining for money," explained the stranger. "He and I are brother outcasts."

"Outcasts? 'Tis a word unfamiliar ta me," admitted the messin man, hoping for definition.

"An outcast is one who is rejected by his own breed—someone who is made fun of and never accepted as an equal. My height has always brought me ridicule, which has been hard for me to accept," explained the stranger.

"Being a man is nae determined by height," the messin man intoned. "Is the pin oak less a tree than its brother, the white oak? The roots and trunk of one are just as strong as the other ta support it in the strongest of winds."

"Your words make sense. I have never thought of it in such a way," the small one stated in agreement. "I spent most of my time fighting to defend my honor and pride. My anger prevented me from seeing the logic of such reasoning. I could not think of such appropriate responses to those insulting my dignity as a man."

"Fighting? Did nae this response bring pain ta your body, as well as the mind, in upholding your honor?" asked the curious messin man.

"I can see the picture in your mind of a flea attacking a bear," chuckled the small one. "No, I used an equalizer to eliminate the disparity in size and to reduce all argument to an even battle of the minds."

"I am intrigued by your method of resolving your problem of honor, but I fail to understand the meaning of 'equalizer.'"

"An equalizer is something used to eliminate any disparity in opponents. The disparity in my case was size, and these were my equalizers," responded the small one as he stood up and gently placed his hands on the guns at his side. With a motion that defied the eye to blink and still follow his speed, the two guns were out of their holsters and into the hands of the small one in firing position! "Having these guns pointed at the balls sure brings a man down to my size in a hurry," he said in a soft, but firm voice.

The action and comment brought a laugh and a slapping of the thighs from the messin man, as he visualized the look on the face of any man who had ridiculed this gamecock behind the thundersticks! He formed an admiration and an instant liking for this pin oak of a man. Not wishing his actions to be misunderstood as an offense, he hastened to clarify his behavior. "The look on their faces must have been something to see, but tell me, if you will: I see thundersticks on many white men who pass here. Can they not be used against ye, as ye do against them in such instances of confrontation?" Three Hands inquired.

"Speed of draw determines who is in command of the situation, and stories of my speed of draw have made many men think twice before insulting me," the small one replied.

Tremors of apprehension rumbled through Three Hands' mental tipi. These thundersticks and the reason for carrying them presented an introduction of a possible unstable element while the small one was in Hiup lands. He pursued this thought. "Have ye used your weapons against many men?"

"Yes, many men, but never to kill, for that is a far greater offense to me than an insult. If having my guns pointed at a man's balls did not cause a recall of the insult, I offered my opponent a practice draw. I emptied my weapons but allowed him to keep his loaded. If he beat me to the draw, he could shoot me. If I won the draw, I would reload and offer him the chance to withdraw the insult or try once again to outdraw me. Each man was beaten so badly on the first draw that he lost the nerve to try again and so withdrew his insult.

"It was my reasoning that my problem would end either way, through a retraction or through my death. So far, I have never lost a draw, and I agree with your thought. Violence is no way to resolve problems. I decided to head west to find a place where people will accept me for what I am, not how I look."

"A wise decision," nodded Three Hands, who found himself captivated by the small one and his tale. Reluctantly, he decided it was time to bring this council to a close and see the traveler on the trail once more. He would escort him as far as Chip Dip, then return to his tribal duties.

"There are some of your people below who can provide ye wi' anything needed ta continue your trail. Tell me the name ye are called that I may share it with them," he requested.

"My name is Percival Ignatius Poindexter Squeek, but let me warn you, I have found that my troubles always start when my name is spoken," came the reply. "Men seem to identify my name with less-than-manly acceptance, and that's when the insults begin."

"If one's name is the basis for troubled relationships wi' your people, hae ye no a' thought of changing it?" Three Hands suggested.

"Our laws and social customs impede any desire to do that, for it would be an affront to our parents. I tried to use only my initials, P. I. P., which worked until someone asked my last name. That brought laughter, followed by the insults," explained the small one.

"I fail ta see the cause for laughter from the name PIP, but I dinna fail to sense your torment." The sympathetic messin man went on, declaring, "Ye are now in the lands of the Hiup and are subject ta our laws and customs as long as ye are in them. It is our custom ta change a name when a given name is no longer fitting. With your permission, I offer ye a name that is more appropriate and will never be the cause of insult in our lands!"

Such a promise and its rewards caused the curiosity of the small one to soar! "What is this name?" he asked.

"Short Tree In A Big Wind," replied the messin man. "You hae shown that even the mightiest of insults of your brothers cannot cause you to topple. You are as strong as the strongest of oaks!"

"I like that!" beamed the newly named as he repeated it again and again on silent lips to test the sound in his mind.

"Come, let me speak this new name for your brothers below; ye will see their feelings upon hearing it," the messin man suggested as he turned to lead the way.

With Short Tree In A Big Wind leading his pony, the trio descended the incline to Chip Dip. Seth was the first to notice their approach and alerted the others. By the time Three Hands and the stranger had arrived, every occupant of Chip Dip was standing on the porch of the general store to greet them—and to satisfy their curiosity. Their first impression was that Three Hands had found a lost child.

When the trio came close enough for their eyes to focus and present a clear picture of the stranger, their reaction to the walk of the "child" brought a smile to the face and a distant rumble of an impending storm of laughter within each inhabitant as it rushed to be ejected. Before the rumble could complete its catharsis from silent to oral mirth, their eyes moved to those of Three Hands. The intensity of the signal they saw there was received and sent on its way to dissipate the "laughter storm" within, leaving only a smile on each face.

The messin man introduced his companion to those gathered. A short social exchange followed, putting the guest at ease. Three Hands suggested to Seth that he see to the needs of the small one for the night. Out of their guest's hearing, Three Hands filled in the others on his learnings and thoughts about their guest. "Let it nae be said and remembered that the heart of the small one was burdened by any actions on our part. We accept him for who he is," he warned.

Leaving that thought to guide the Chip Dippers, the messin man returned to his people. Short Tree In A Big Wind was the subject of the council fire that night. The Hiup were fascinated by the graphic description woven by their messin man; when he demonstrated the walking position, laughter erupted from his audience. Thoughts quickly sobered when he continued the tale and shared the torment of the small one. It was never the nature of the Hiup to insult or to add to the torment of others, for having had no enemies in the past, they never had learned that technique.

Three Hands had planned to return to Chip Dip at the next sun to wish the small one well when he left on the trail. His plan was put on hold by the sounds of an approaching wagon train, and his role of toll collector was his top priority. The Chip Dippers would have to give the farewell.

Tribal duties (including the emergency needs of several maidens) kept Three Hands from attending to the maidenly needs in Chip Dip until the passing of four suns. As he approached the general store, he saw that two groups of twin small structures had been erected about fifteen paces opposite the store. As he passed the structures on his way to the smithy, he pushed open the door to one and peered inside. The structure contained only a boxed platform, about knee high, with two holes cut into the top. The purpose for such an arrangement was not immediately evident, so he would ask Seth to enlighten him.

Mixed emotions gripped the messin man upon entering the smithy as he found, not only Seth, but Short Tree In A Big Wind! He was pleased to see the small one, yet felt outraged that the law of the trail had been broken. He would seek an explanation before reaching any conclusions and taking action.

The two workers were stripped to the waist and sweating profusely as they labored to complete a wheel rim. Three Hands signaled a greeting, then waited patiently until their task had been completed. He then signaled Seth that he wished to speak with him. It was time for answers!

"I see the small one is still with ye. Who among ye stepped forward ta remind him of the law of the trail and the penalty for breaking it?" he asked.

Seth responded, "There is obviously a misunderstanding between us. It was our understanding that you detailed the trail laws to all who came to the pass. When we saw you personally escort him here, we thought that you had made a special arrangement for him, so we awaited your word on this. He has been so busy since that last train left that the subject was not brought up."

"Busy? You mean helping ye?" asked the messin man, still perplexed.

"Not only me but everyone else. He was so disgusted at the way the train people emptied their 'thunder jugs' on the campground, or in the stream, that he went with Zeke on the trail and brought back a wagon loaded with wood. He dug a trench and built those four outhouses across from the store, two for men and two for women. The place should smell a lot better if we can get the train people to use them instead of going behind trees to do their business. They will be required to empty their 'thunder jugs' in the outhouses. He even plans to build some outhouses at the edge of the glade above so that those who stop for the night will use them instead of the forest. That man may be small, but he is a tireless worker!"

"Outhouse? Thunder Jug? Business? These are words new ta me. Explain if you will," requested the messin man.

"Business, in this instance, is the depositing of the remains of last sun's meal once it has passed through your stomach. An outhouse is the place where one goes to make that deposit, and a thunder jug is a container one uses at night instead of going to the outhouse," chuckled Seth. "Where do the Hiup deposit their shit and piss, or don't they do this?"

It was Three Hands' turn to chuckle. "This is proof that the red man does have something in common with the white man. We dig a hole in the ground and then cover our 'business' ta eliminate the smell."

A thought came to the messin man. "The breaking of the law by the small one was the result of my forgetfulness. Say naething of our council until you hear from me!"

That night, after a long period of meditation, the messin man spoke to his people in council. He shared his error in failing to instruct the small one of the law. He also told of the industrious activities carried out by the small one to improve conditions in Hiup lands around Chip Dip, as well as his plan for the glade. He presented two items for the council's consideration. First, was such an industrious attitude an asset to the Hiup? And, two, the Hiup could show greatness of compassion by offering a place of peace for the tormented mind of the small one. Would they do so, or would they send him back on a trail of agony?

The council responded with a resounding nod to the affirmative to both questions. Short Tree In A Big Wind became the latest (and last) resident of Chip Dip. Three Hands relayed the decision personally.

Within a year, Short Tree In A Big Wind had undergone significant changes. The first change involved his name. His Injun name was perfect in the eyes and ears of the easygoing red men, but the nature of the white was tuned to speed. The name took too long to pronounce when it was used so frequently in daily communication. The name was thus shortened to Short Tree, and eventually to Shortee. The original name was used only in the presence of Three Hands.

Shortee's wit and endless sense of humor made it impossible to dislike him; in time the insults ceased. One would think that this would thus eliminate the need for wearing his guns, but he continued to wear them for some time, as his physical size was still a problem for him. The guns remained a necessity as a counterbalance when wearing his "heels." The guns were worn until the fateful day that was long remembered as O. S. Day in Chip Dip.

Shortee had continued to be a positive asset to Chip Dip since his arrival. He helped Seth in the smithy, Goodson in the store, and Zeke in clearing the trail. Through clearing the trail, he became self-sufficient by setting up a resale shop where he sold items discarded by others along the trail. Women could not resist his bargains. He also put on shows to entertain the weary and bored travelers, in which he displayed the art of the fast draw and trick shooting. Friendly wagers were made on those invited to compete against him. Those who observed his unbeatable speed chose not to offend him with insults of size, which eliminated one of his worst torments.

O. S. Day was named after an incident that took place across the way from the general store. There was nothing out of the ordinary in the daily routine to forewarn of the impending event. The initial stages began innocently enough, then erupted upon the tranquillity of the scene like a dormant volcano exploding to life!

As a matter of daily routine, Shortee strutted from the smithy to the outhouse across from the store. On this particular day, he routinely unbuckled his gun belt and hung it on a peg. He routinely deposited the "last sun's meal" from his seat over one of the holes. He routinely wiped himself with a Ucumfastus leaf, then routinely buttoned his trousers. He routinely lifted his gun belts from the peg to strap them to his leg; at this moment, however, one of the guns, aided by the friction-fighting bear grease, slid unroutinely from its holster and disappeared through the hole just vacated by its owner! Total dismay blanketed Shortee as he stood peering through the hole at his beloved gun lying nearly submerged in the residue below, just beyond his grasp. His brain frantically signaled that some action must be taken for recovery before the weight of the weapon overcame the resistance of the residue and disappeared from sight. He flung open the door and ran outside to locate a retrieval stick. Finding a short broken branch of the proper size and length, he returned to the outhouse to commence the retrieval procedure.

A trial-and-error approach was undertaken. He soon found that the hole in the seat was too small to peer into and maneuver the stick effectively at the same time, for his hand and the stick blocked his vision.

He solved this problem by peering into the hole over his gun and maneuvering the stick through the adjacent hole. Through determined effort, he finally had the stick in position through the trigger guard to begin raising the gun, but good fortune was denied him. The stick came into contact with the hair-trigger, which routinely reacted to this slight pressure by routinely moving the firing pin forward to make contact with the shell rim, causing a routine explosion.

The explosion accomplished two things: it startled the inhabitants of Chip Dip and a nearby train. At the same instant, it caused the face of Shortee, framed in the hole above, to be covered with residue, some of which he had recently deposited! One thought dominated his mind as he dove from the outhouse and into the horse trough in front of the smithy—the humility he would suffer if seen in this condition by his people.

His "people," who poured forth from the buildings and train, thought he had been shot in the face. Before they could rush forward to assist him, he was out of the trough and running back to the outhouse and slamming the door. They did hear the expletive, "Oh, shit!" as he dashed past them. Seeing that their fears were groundless, they returned to their routine activities.

Shortee quickly resumed the process of retrieval, only to learn, once again, success was to be denied him by the inadvertent molestation of the hair trigger by the stick. Explosion number two was produced, followed by the "Trough Trot," the emergence of folks nearby, the expletive, and the slamming of the outhouse door! A third explosion soon followed. The townsfolk and the "trainees" decided to take positions of leisure outside the buildings to see the full scenario, from explosion to Shortee's return to the point of origin.

The stick was rejected by Shortee after the third explosion. After emerging from the trough, he headed into the smithy to secure a piece of wire. His thought was to hook the wire around the trigger guard in such a way as to avoid the mutinous trigger. Seth was standing at the entrance. Shortee quickly explained to him his need for the wire.

Emerging from the smithy with the wire, he saw Lotta streak from the saloon toward the outhouses. His fears were not aroused at the time, for he knew that the outhouses were segregated for men and women.

What he could not know at the time was that Lotta had yielded to temptation the night before. Overindulgence in numerous spicy pastas had severely tested her system's ability to retain it; her system failed. Nature was now in the process of quickly expelling the surplus.

It was Lotta's intention to use the outhouse designated for women, but the intense internal pressure told her that she would not make it. A decision was made, and she disappeared into the nearest facility—the same one Shortee was heading for! His worst fears realized, Shortee ran toward the outhouse screaming for Lotta to hold on, begging her to correct her mistake and depart for the one reserved for women. It was too late, and even his silent prayer that she was not over his gun was not answered. Lotta soon emerged with a look of relief on her face and an apology to the waiting Shortee on her lips. Shortee dashed past her, entered the outhouse with his wire, saw his worst fears realized, then bent to continue his task.

Seth passed among the spectators and shared the problem faced by Shortee. Friends usually rush to the aid of friends in need, but no way were any of them rushing forward in this instance! They decided to give vocal encouragement instead. Another explosion reinforced the wisdom of that decision as they watched their friend heading on the track to the trough. An "Oh, shit!" was again heard as he passed.

Shortee's dilemma proved to be such good entertainment for those in attendance that they did not wish the performance to end prematurely due to dejection on the part of the star. They shouted words of encouragement, such as, "You can do it, Shortee!" "Stand in there!" and "Don't give up, you can lick it!" This last statement was spontaneous, with little thought given to its added meaning, yet, after a moment's thought, it became the favorite of the spectators!

The patience and eyes of Shortee were sorely tested that day, because two more explosions, baths, and expletives took place before the gun was finally retrieved. It wasn't until the next day that his sense of humor had returned, so that he could laugh along with others without offense being taken when the event was retold. He even volunteered some of his thoughts while occupied within the facility. In his honor, the Chip Dippers proclaimed the day to henceforth and forever after to be known as Oh Shit Day!

The event brought about two dramatic changes concerning Shortee. He never again wore his gun belt, except when putting on shows. Since the guns had acted as a counterbalance to his "heels," Shortee removed the heels. For the first time in a long time, he stood erect on his own. True, he was shorter, but those around him had accepted him for who he was, not how he looked. The final link of peace was in place. An atmosphere of tranquillity finally had returned for all of the inhabitants of Hiup lands through an unroutine performance by its smallest adult.

When Three Hands returned to Chip Dip (in response to the smoke signal from the chimney of Fireanda's tipi) and fulfilled his "missionary" duties, Fireanda suggested, with a giggle, that he ask Seth about O. S. Day. His curiosity was aroused, but he did not ask her to inform him, as his concept of a squaw's position was limited to action, not words. He inconspicuously made his way to the smithy to make his inquiry.

Seth, usually a man of few words, complied with his request by unfolding the story in meticulous detail, yet expanding each detail through the imagery techniques of an unbridled mind! The sides of the messin man were severely strained to remain intact as laughter undulated within before exploding orally.

Making his way back to camp, his laughter continued as he mentally recalled every fine detail of the tale. That night at the fire, the great improviser retold the tale to his people, adding his own refinement and embellishment. Laughter exploded continuously when he acted out the scenes as he envisioned them, while carrying on a descriptive commentary. Shortee's predicament had provided entertainment for the Hiup, as well as for the Chip Dippers!

Laughter is good messin, for when used, it eases one's torment. For the Hiup, the laughter was soon to be replaced by a force heretofore unknown to them as a people—pain!

← Chapter Thirteen →

The instincts of the wolf and the eagle are honed by survival. The instincts of man are dulled by complacency.

The passing of years and wagon trains within the parameters of the red man's plan became routine with complacency, wearing the sharp edge of instinct into dullness. The Hiup gradually lost interest in the movements and activities of the white man as he passed uneventfully through their lands. The drum activities that kept uneasiness and doubt foremost in the minds of the trespassers dwindled to silence, except for ceremonial purposes. Cubs grew weary of the "chip" pranks, and their thoughts leaned toward more adventurous pursuits in the west when they became of age. In their mind, the white man posed no immediate threat to them. Their messin man or their allies would alert them in time to avoid confrontation.

Complacency, routine, and boredom are plagues to an active mind. Wakan-Manitou had an active mind, to be sure, and moved to make certain that His activities did not parallel those of the Hiup, within the parameters of His plans. He turned to His favorite option to combat any drift toward boredom with the Hiup. The dilemma bull was prodded into action!

Three Hands, with periodic boosts from Span Ishīly, was weathering the passage of time gracefully; his mind and body were as honed as the finest lance point. True, he was a part of the "routine" diorama, but his was such an interesting and varied routine that boredom or complacency were nonexistent in it. His quick movements, however, caught the eye of the dilemma bull like the waving of a red blanket. Alerted, the bull trotted toward his favorite quarry, with horns primed to impale!

Through observation and experimentation, Three Hands had learned that Span Ishfly was not the potion he thought it to be. This instrument of survival had shown side effects not unlike the ripples produced by a stone cast into a still pond. While the euphoria of the male Snow Hairs lasted some time, the euphoria of their squaws began to be replaced with ripples of discontent. At first they were highly pleased by the new level of performance of their men, but the passage of time saw a change in their feelings.

The consultation schedule of the messin man was, in time, being overbalanced by Snow Hair squaws. Their complaints were as one—the new character of their man was creating problems for them. Routine tasks were becoming more difficult to complete due to fatigue, a shortened work day, and sore joints! Their "milk of pleasure" was beginning to curdle. Since their messin man had been the instrument of introduction to their woes, they expected him to be capable of resolving them.

Their messin man barely felt this prick by the horns of a toying bull, nor did he sense the significance of it. This squaw problem presented no challenge to him, since the solution was so simple and logical. If Span Ishfly could introduce the feelings and spirit of youth in the male Snow Hairs, it could do likewise in their squaws. Any problems of aching joints and routine tasks would be a thing of the past.

If a bull could smile, one of ear-to-ear length would have been created by this simplistic logic!

Squaws, as recipients of a lower rung on the ladder of caste, could not drink from the same gourd as the male Snow Hairs. The ingenious custodian of Span Ishfly created a new instrument of delivery: a hollowed-out length of reed filled with the potion and plugged with a twig. These could be made in large numbers and stored in his medicinal tipi. Whenever a Snow Hair squaw felt the need for rejuvenation, she could merely empty the reed into her elderberry tea (the only cooking done in the privacy of one's tipi).

The logical conclusion assumed by the messin man seemed appropriate. The female Snow Hairs found that their new vitality cured their work/time concern, as well as their stiffness of joints. His mind was put at ease and open to more challenging endeavors. Had he been aware that his "solution" was merely a technique used by the toying bull, his peace of mind would have been replaced by intense concern.

This revitalization of the Snow Hair squaws did not, or could not, go unnoticed by other members of the tribe. For one thing, the loudness, the length, and the frequency of the nightly activities prevented sleep on the part of those in adjacent tipis!

While the spirits, attitude, and demeanor of the Snow Hairs soared, the rest of the tribe was becoming short of patience; their eyelids drooped and their hunting and working skills were dulled. It became increasingly difficult to conduct a council meeting, because only the Snow Hairs and the messin man could stay awake.

The lack of sleep and its effect on daily activities was only another by-product of the playful bull. Those close to the status of Snow Hairs, yet not close enough to qualify for the Span Ishfly program, felt the flames of injustice being fanned by jealousy. Both sexes shared this jealousy of the Snow Hairs' ability to perform so consistently and still exhibit no strain on their vitality. The discontent grew until it was presented to their messin man as a formal complaint by a spokesperson of each gender.

The horns were becoming more forceful in their efforts to capture the undivided attention of the messin man. Upon observing the messin man's indifference to his efforts by adhering to simplistic actions to resolve this complex problem, the grin quickly faded from the face of the bull, to be replaced by a determined locking of the teeth and jaw. Playtime was over. An aroused bull moved into his impaling mode!

Three Hands did not move to decision in a manner consistent with his usual habit of option inclusion. A thorough review of the problem and possible solutions was carried out. To him, his line of logic needed no revision. What had worked with the Snow Hairs should work with the next ripple in the Hiup pond. He, too, was approaching Snow Hair age and had been using the potion for some time with no side effects. He reasoned that a simple expansion of the "user group" should solve the problem. This rationale resulted in his impalement on the horns of the bull, and in the introduction of pain to his people.

Time proved that his action of tossing the Span Ishfly stone into the pond created endless ripples. The Snow Hair ripple had created another ripple, which was soon to create other ripples until the entire pond was in turmoil. The process is as natural among humans as it is with still ponds. In time, the messin man had to dispense the potion to every adult member of the tribe. This was the depth that the messin man had not probed, resulting in a side effect beyond his control.

Three Hands' simplistic solution failed to take the human nature factor into account, and in so doing compromised the honor of perpetual sex for the Hiup. It was the Snow Hairs who were to be the recipients of this honor. They were the ones of greatest need. By applying simplistic logic, the messin man had reduced the effect of this great promise to commonness. Who would need the ritual of the Spring Awakening, when all one had to do was sip from a gourd to be awakened?

In time, this fact was viewed as unnatural by the young adults, who inwardly harbored resentment. It was common knowledge among all tribes that Wakan-Manitou had long ago placed his favor of highest sexual performance on the young adult in order to maintain tribal numbers. Had He withdrawn this favor and placed it first on the Snow Hairs, and now on members of all ages? Seeking to regain their old status and favors, they asked their messin man to communicate with Wakan-Manitou and plead their case.

The depth of his dilemma became more apparent to Three Hands. The more he examined the problem and the options left open, the more he saw himself holding a rattlesnake by the tail and trying to grab the head to neutralize the danger of the fangs. That snake just wouldn't hold still long enough for him to make his move. If he replaced the potion for all with a harmless powder, then he would be right back where he started. If he decreased the potion for the Snow Hairs only in response to the young adults' request, then he would be withdrawing the promise of perpetual sexual activity in Hiup lands only.

It was crucial that this legend continue. If he increased the potion for the young adults, they would once again be the top performers, and therefore content. The Snow Hairs would retain their present level, as well as those near them in age. The survival of his people depended on his choice of options. He chose the latter and not only introduced pain, but at the same time projected to future generations that too much of a good thing can be bad.

The reed container became the common method of dispensing Span Ishfly at all levels of adulthood. It was never done openly, for each gender and age level was kept ignorant of its use by others. Each individual had to request a vial from the messin man. The medicinal tipi was lined with shelves containing reeds classified by age level and calibrated for respective levels. Complaints by the young adults then evaporated until the advent of pain!

Vials of added strength distributed to the young adults did, indeed, quickly restore them to top status. The odds that such a wonderful, fulfilling, challenging, and satisfying activity could be associated with pain seem infinitesimal, but the combination of Span Ishfly and the missionary position tremendously decreased these odds.

If a squaw who favored the missionary position (and most did) felt a "need," she would use her vial and reach the pinnacle of delight with her brave. If the brave was the one to use a vial, he would reach the pinnacle sought. If both used their vial, the result was quite different, for the resulting fervor sent them to unbelievable heights where all earthly concerns were erased by ecstasy.

When the female reached this height, she did two things simultaneously. She vented her joy and pleasure with a loud exclamation like "Wahoo!" She also reached out for something to hold onto that would extend her ecstasy. This object, unfortunately, was the hair of her partner above. Her hands pulled with such force that his hair separated from his scalp, creating excruciating pain. Her partner, who had been equally diligent in his concentration to reach his pinnacle, gave up the quest abruptly when pain broke his concentration, and he vented his frustration and agony with a loud "Eeow!"

When the flames of passion, ardor, and pain had cooled, an examination of the brave's head was made. Balm applied by a contrite squaw did little to smooth the ruffled feathers or to replace the lost hair of the brave. Pain, in time, would be replaced by the reawakening of natural needs, but the problem of hair loss grew. The expected regrowth did not occur, for the roots also had been removed by the squaw's actions. The bald spot was enlarged by each subsequent simultaneous vial use.

Ingenious methods (and some lacking ingenuity) were used to cover the problem to avoid another loss—loss of face! Reweaving of the remaining hair was tried, but soon resulted in braids of unequal length. Some braids became so short they stuck out like the tail of a pig instead of hanging down. Some squaws tried to weave the hair that was pulled out into a form resembling a blanket patch, which was placed over the bald spot and affixed with porcupine quills. This device was subject to the whims of the wind and proved embarrassing during a conversation with one's peers or during ceremonial dancing.

Covering the bald area was not the basic problem for the braves; sobering reflection, at times when the flames of need were dormant, gave them insight into the cause. Whenever they reached the pinnacle first, the loss of hair did not occur; they became determined always to be first there. This technique resolved their problem, only until the squaws took time to reflect on their new problem when their flames had cooled. Being consistently denied the joy of pinnacle conquest, they moved with equal determination to be the first there, the result being (when the odds of both using the potion were high) action of unbelievable intensity matched by equal levels of pain and vented exaltations. The odds were being changed to even, for at the first sign of glowing embers by one, the other reached for his or her vial.

Driven by desperation, the young braves sought other means of avoiding hair loss. The depth of desperation was exemplified by one brave and proved so successful that it was adopted by many others. This brave, after long reflection, decided to try to find a substitute for himself when his squaw showed signs of need and he didn't. He knew that no Hiup male in his right mind would chance further hair loss with another man's squaw when he had his own to please. The brave got his idea while observing the activities of a wagon train in Chip Dip. He saw a distinct pattern and made his plans.

The next time he observed an awakening by his squaw and had noted a wagon train was in Chip Dip, he made his move. Waiting until it was dark, he made his way by a back trail to the saloon. He hid in the shadows until a train member staggered from Lynn Gweeney's and headed for his wagon. After making sure that no one was near, the brave applied a stick to the head of his victim, rendering him unconscious. The victim was shouldered and taken to the brave's tipi. Inside, his squaw lay aroused by her potion and ready for action. The white man, just regaining consciousness, found himself beside an overheated female and made haste to take advantage of his good fortune before it had time to change. He proceeded with true missionary zeal!

When the squaw reached her pinnacle and demonstrated her pleasure through shouts and hair removal, the accompanying scream of pain from the "substitute" had just commenced when the stick was reapplied to his head. While the squaw was still overcome with joy, he was quickly removed and returned to the train at Chip Dip.

The pain in the scalp returned with consciousness, along with an added headache. The "substitute" only could remember past events vaguely, since he had been in command of his senses for only a short time that night. He recalled drinking at the saloon, leaving to return to the wagon, darkness, a delightful session of fornication with a sensuous female, a searing pain in his scalp, darkness again, and finally awakening on the ground outside the saloon.

He was now sober and in need of a plausible story of explanation for his puritanical wife. He was confused, but not to the point that he would confide to his wife that he had bedded another female in her absence. A simple fellow, his story also was simple—he had fallen and hit his head on a rock, causing hair loss and lost consciousness.

The success of this brave was repeated with later trains and would have gone practically unnoticed if the human nature factor had not been injected by the bull. The brave's self esteem grew inflated, so that he had to share his cleverness with someone or he would burst. His sharing did not impact on him for some time, but it did on some members of the next train, for two members surrendered consciousness to the stick. The technique was passed along until every young brave had adopted it.

Whenever a train arrived, the braves were prepared for action, but the men of the train were not. They were puzzled by their experience, and their apprehension of trail dangers was heightened. They could not be certain that the woman each had "pleasured" was Injun, yet they were certain that they had never experienced such heat with a white woman; thus the legendary passion of Injun women was born.

Some—the majority—of those who had experienced this passion harbored the hope that it would be repeated as they moved west among the Injuns. The loss of a little hair was a small price to pay for an exhilarating period of indescribable passion.

The pendulum of fate had begun to swing with the actions of the first brave, cutting the "hair" solution effortlessly and completing its arc before returning to cut the next hair. With the passage of time, the number of hairs became so great that they stopped the movement of the pendulum. A wagon train stopped at Chip Dip and forty-eight of fifty men, including the wagon-master, suffered hair loss. Wives do talk with their counterparts of other wagons when carrying on morning chores; and the common thread of 'falling against a rock' soon bound them together. Nursing their wrath until all husbands had been gathered together, they released it in a demand for a more plausible explanation—now!

No description of the frantic mental activity of the men to meet this demand could be accurate. In any large group of individuals, the chance that one brain would not succumb to the intense pressure and malfunction completely, although small, is still possible. It was the wagon-master who saved the day for the other men. "Ladies," he began, "I was hoping to spare you from being subjected to worry, if it could be avoided. I see now that it is impossible, in light of what happened last night. I swore the men to secrecy and made up the story of falling against a rock. The truth is, we were attacked and scalped by those invisible Injuns!"

The sweat was running down his forehead as he completed his "tale" and awaited the reaction of the women. The other men were also anxious to see the reaction before making a move. The women bought the story lock, stock, and barrel. As one, they demanded to leave this trail of misery and possible death, return to St. Lou E, and warn others of their close encounter with death at the hands of these savages. Though in disagreement at turning back, the men knew the misery they would face if they did not comply, and so prepared for the return trail immediately.

Three Hands, unaware of the activities of the young braves, was alerted by the sounds of a large party moving back up the incline; he made haste to investigate. The speed of the wagons and the hostile looks on the faces of their occupants made him decide not to try to collect toll for return passage. He would make his inquiries at Chip Dip for the reasons behind this movement.

Upon inquiry, he was informed that the Hiup had been accused of atrocities on the whites, who were returning to inform their government of their treatment and of the broken promises of the red man. Even the inhabitants of Chip Dip were uneasy until reassured by Three Hands that he would guarantee their safety.

The potential reactions of the white man for reprisals presented a serious problem. The messin man hastened back to camp and reported his findings to Chief Has It Made, who called for a council. The unseen movement of the bull's horns to insure deeper penetration into his quarry highlighted the messin man's desperate attempt to free himself.

At the council fire, Three Hands told his story of the white man's retreat from Hiup lands and the reason for it. The word of the Hiup had been broken and disgrace brought down upon them by the actions of unknowns. No one came forward to admit responsibility, for, although the results were identical, it was an act carried out without the knowledge of other participants. One man could not come forth and admit that he had committed forty-eight acts of dishonor. Each one, in his own mind, accepted guilt for only his own act, thus silence prevailed.

Three Hands presented his summation. "The mystery remains unsolved. We cannot truthfully say who committed these acts of dishonor, yet we know they were committed in the lands of the Hiup, who will be blamed. The danger lies in the reaction of the whites and their leaders. Will they send the Blue Coats back in greater numbers and overrun us? They will not be deceived, as before.

"We must now learn to act as protectors and prevent such actions from being inflicted upon the whites again. This new rule of the trail will be strictly enforced! We can only wait and see if our plan has been destroyed by these actions of the unknowns, or if time will heal the wounds inflicted upon the whites."

It was two moons before the next train arrived at the pass, and it was a big one. The logic of safety in numbers seemed to be the force behind their movement. A great deal of water had passed over the falls since the ill-fated train had turned back, and it had fallen on red and white alike.

The disgruntled whites had made their plight known to their leaders in Washington, including the army, but were reminded that they had been strongly discouraged from travel in the lands of "those savages" and had reaped the results of ignoring that advice. The memory of Colonel B. U. L. Dozer's experience with the invisible Hiup and the threats of their messin man had not been forgotten. In fact, it had been reinforced by these latest complaints. Posters were placed in every river town, restating the government's position on travel west.

The water falling on the Hiup during those two moons was not without force. Its impact was felt most by the young braves, for now they were denied the "substitute" resolution of their problem. The added weight of dishonor also fell upon their shoulders, as they felt great remorse for their part in the action that had brought dishonor to all red men. They, as individuals, still had difficulty understanding how a basic function of man could result in negative reactions. Their reasoning began to lean in the direction that they had fallen into disfavor with Wakan-Manitou because of their insistence on their right to be the most sexually active, not the Snow Hairs. Their messin man was at fault because he had misinterpreted the signs.

The return of train passage served only to lift the sense of remorse from their shoulders, for the young braves knew that the day of the "substitute" was gone forever. With the return of pain came the desperate attempt to be free of it forever. If they had to live with this pain until they started their trail to the Camp of Many Lodges as Snow Hairs, the reward of remaining in Hiup lands, bereft of all hair, lost its appeal.

The first silent packing of tipi and belongings went unnoticed until the camp awakened the next sun. It was not a mass departure for the young, but a gradual one, as each man reached his limit of pain tolerance. The problem of the young going west was back, but with greater impact. Now they were taking their families with them! Since no forest can survive if new seeds aren't produced, the imminent demise of the Hiup was apparent to all.

The problem was discussed at every council meeting, yet no solution was achieved. Those who harbored the thought of leaving did not wish to jeopardize that option and remained silent. After all, it was their complaint that led to the problem, and to admit error would bring loss of face with their peers. To add to the problem, the increased activity of the Snow Hairs was hastening their departure on their final trail. Only the middle age group remained in numbers, and their own increased activity was rapidly moving them toward Snow Hair status!

The mental and physical actions taken by Three Hands were severely limited by his impalement on the bull's horns. He had tried counseling, poultices, and even varying the strength of Span Ishfly prescriptions—with little recognizable results. The problem was definitely beyond his control and he knew it. It was time to put the "new M.O.M." to the test!

Messin Man

Putting Shortee to work as toll collector, the signal fire was lit and the reply signal received before the messin man took the trail north. Arriving at the lake, he spoke his greetings and heard M.O.M.'s invitation to advance.

Forsaking the challenge of the ledge, he took the direct trail to the summit. Going through the living quarters in the cave, he emerged into the sunlit alcove to find "M.O.M. Jock" reclined, not on the rock seat of his predecessor, but on a bearskin-covered chair facing the sun. Upon hearing Three Hands' greeting, M.O.M. stood and moved (unspiritlike) to greet his old friend. He was dressed only in a loincloth, and the flame of his red hair was somewhat subdued by the snow of age. The formality of greeting was replaced by the formality of nourishment, during which time each brought the other up to date on events that had occurred since their last meeting.

With social amenities and the meal completed, Three Hands presented his problem, his attempted solutions, and the resulting dilemma he faced because his first solution was too successful.

M.O.M. listened intently. He knew that he was facing the reality of having to provide a solution for the problem being described to him. His mindful intensity was not so great that it obliterated recalled visions of the joys of his own youth, sans Span Ishfly, from flashing down the back roads of his mind. Could it be true that one could get too much of such a delightful pastime? Certainly not in his experience!

M.O.M. knew that his time of testing had arrived. His forehead wrinkled in deep thought as he pondered possible solutions, and a short time passed before he spoke. "Your problem is basically due to the position that you and your people have assumed. You, my friend, have been as busy with the potion as the beaver building a dam. The pond formed by the dam gives the fish more room to move about, which is good, but what of the fish below who now cannot swim upstream to lay their eggs?"

"There is less water for them and the dam prevents them from moving upstream, so they must move downstream to find enough water for their requirement of life," replied the messin man.

"Are your Snow Hairs unlike the fish above the dam who enjoy new freedom of movement?" questioned M.O.M.

"No, and the young braves are not unlike the fish below the dam who find it easier to swim downstream to find better conditions for reproduction than trying to leap over the dam," said an enlightened Three Hands.

"And if one wishes to return the stream to its original course, what action must be taken?"

"The dam must be removed," came the messin man's reply.

"Age has not destroyed your ability to see a solution once the eyes are not blinded by the dazzling luminosity of the problem itself," a smiling M.O.M. went on. "Your Span Ishfly dam was strengthened by the missionary position your people adopted from the white man. Go back to the ones that would cause no pain, even if your potion is used in moderation. A squaw's hands, in the position of body support, cannot reach for her brave's head without falling. It may seem like a backward approach, but it worked for your people before."

"Angus, your mind and wisdom have reached the level of the red man. My heart sings with the knowledge that many of my red brothers, who seek your words, will be led to resolution of their problems. I must return at once to put your thoughts into action and to return the stream of the Hiup to the vibrancy it once knew."

"Go in peace and harmony, knowing that my heart will be sorry until I hear that our people once again know happiness in their hearts," said M.O.M.

"Your words and thoughts will speed my moccasins!" replied Three Hands as he turned and departed on the return trail.

Arriving back at camp, the messin man reported to his chief, who called for another council meeting. At the council fire, Three Hands noticed that the number of his people had grown even smaller in his absence. He shared the message of M.O.M. and repeated the importance of returning to their old customs and rejecting the position of the white man. He injected the threat of disharmony with the spirits if they did not comply. "Wakan-Manitou has shown his displeasure that we have replaced an honored tradition with one of the white man's. This leads Him to think the white man's position seems superior to that of the red man in our eyes. We must show him that this is not true!" he intoned.

Those who remained went back to the old positions, but found them less appealing and less sensuously rewarding than the missionary's position. The choice of staying in Hiup lands also grew less appealing to the young braves. What good is having the great favor of lifelong ability if the pleasure is minimized by choice of position? The squaws, in particular, were completely dejected by their loss of attaining the "Wahoo" plateau.

Once again the trickle west began, and the dam began to collapse in a disorderly process, for these young braves were the hunters who brought meat to the luk pots. It was their children who gathered wood for the cooking fires, and it was the strength of the young squaws that tilled the soil and did the harvesting. The status of the Snow Hairs did not change, for their responsibilities were limited to providing wisdom and guidance in tribal decisions.

The solution suggested by M.O.M. was not creating the end result desired. The means were providing a slowing action, but not a cure. Too many Hiup "seeds" were being sown in the west, rather than in Hiup lands where perpetuation was needed. The Hiup customs were eroding, and signs of social decay were becoming prominent. Any sounds of celebration that could be heard were those of age—slow and deliberate. There were too few inheritors of the dance and drum skills to create the excitement for daily living. Life began to have less purpose for the remaining Hiup.

Three Hands spent more and more time pondering and groping for a solution. The signs and sounds of decay did not fall like a tree in an unoccupied forest! They could be seen, as well as heard. He knew that an attraction of greater force must be found to return the young and to restore the feeling of pride in being a Hiup in Hiup lands. The trail had gone full circle and returned to the point where Span Ishfly had been thought to be such an attraction, but had proven to work an opposite effect. It was M.O.M. time again!

The trail, although well-known to the messin man, seemed longer each time he made it, and the complaints of his muscles and joints seemed louder; but the needs of his people muffled those complaints. When once again in the presence of M.O.M., he presented his problem in fine detail, leaving not one item out.

"M.O.M. Jock" pondered the facts, which had rendered the options to minuscule proportions. There was doubt in his mind that an option really existed. Water over a dam could not flow back up and over unless driven by great force. What such force existed for the young Hiup? There was no enemy or danger present to act as a rallying force. The gift of Wakan-Manitou had best be forgotten, for it had become a destructive force.

His mind was blank, but he was not ready to give up! "We must sleep and make our minds open to receive new thoughts. I will send mine on a vision quest at once," he suggested.

In the solitude of night, "M.O.M. Jock" methodically listed all the assets of the Hiup lands. What did they have that was unique to them, that set them apart from their brothers? What did the other tribes have that set them apart from the Hiup in a unique way? Ponies! He remembered the joy and pride when the two ponies were given to the chief and symbolically shared with his people. It was only a flicker of hope, but the wind of hope fanned it until the flame of enlightenment grew so bright that it illuminated an option—money!

The next sun, he continued his council with Three Hands. If his plan had any value, it had to stand the test of value with his red friend. He began, "I sent my spirit brother soaring like the eagle, where freedom of thought soars undisturbed. My spirit returned and told me the solution lies sleeping in my brother's mental tipi, which has been cluttered with false signs and useless actions. Your thoughts must be cleansed and replaced with logical resolutions. If you can answer two questions given me by my spirit brother, your solution may be at hand. Do not rush to answer, for your first reply cannot be altered. Are you ready?"

Three Hands paused to cleanse his mind and recover from the intense impression Jock had made on him with his words. As M.O.M., his words, thoughts, and demeanor were impressive! The red man was in good hands with this M.O.M. "I am," he replied.

"Then tell me, what three possessions would light the fire of pride of ownership in the eyes of a Hiup brave?"

Three Hands closed his eyes to concentrate on a list forming and reforming in his mind. The list not only had to be complete, but in priority order to select the top three. He answered, "A pony, a thunderstick, and the metal knife of the white man."

"Good! Now for the second question. What did you do with the toll money you collected?" asked the sage.

"It is kept in jars too numerous to count, in one of my tipis." came the reply.

"Very good! Your answers have fallen on the ears of my spirit brother, who is pleased with your answers. He has given me the plan that you must follow to bring your people back and return harmony to your lands," continued M.O.M.

"My ears are eager to hear the plan of your spirit brother," a hopeful Three Hands replied.

"You must first send word to your people in the west that Wakan-Manitou's heart is full of sorrow that His favored Hiup have rejected His gift of endless activity. He will withdraw that gift and replace it with one that His children can put to better use. Each Hiup brave who returns to his lands will find a pony, a thunderstick, and a metal knife waiting as gifts. You, Three Hands, are His representative to provide those gifts."

The messin man was astounded! "My people will ridicule me, for I cannot provide those gifts."

"Oh, but you can—and will," chuckled M.O.M.

"How?" asked the incredulous messin man.

"Listen carefully and lose not one of my words! Is Lynn Gweeney still at Chip Dip?"

"Yes."

"Take all of your tolls to her and ask her to keep them for you until you ask for them. She will be pleased with your trust. I told you that the white man's wampum would be of good use some day, and that day is here. Go to Goodson Wares and tell him that you need one hundred thundersticks with ammunition, one hundred knives, and one hundred ponies. When you receive them, you must send a messenger on one of the ponies, with a thunderstick and a knife, to your people in the west.

"Once they hear Wakan-Manitou's offer and see the samples, they will start back to their lands, eager to receive their own gifts!" Jock knowingly declared. "One last question: what three items would light the same fire in the eyes of their squaws?"

The messin man, using the same process of prioritizing that he used for the braves, answered, "Beads, a metal skinning knife, and some bright cloth with sewing items like the white squaws use."

"Good! Then add those items to the list you give Goodson. A happy squaw makes travel easier and faster." said Jock.

"There is but one problem that prevents me from carrying out the wishes of the spirits," stated Three Hands.

"And what is that?" M.O.M. asked.

"Who can I use as a messenger? Those of my people who are still in camp are too old to make such a long trail and would probably forget the message if they did get there."

"Then I will send you my two sons, Ian Coyote and Wee Gordie Light Of Foot. They are out on a squaw-seeking trail now, but I will send them when they return. I will light a signal fire for them to return here for instructions. You should have the items we spoke of by the time they get to you."

"My heart is a mixture of joy and sadness—sad that we must part, yet overflowing with joy at the prospect of my people returning to our lands. The snow on my head gets heavier, and I may not make this trail again. Peace be with you, my friend," the messin man finished, somewhat sadly for the occasion.

"My heart shares your feelings, and my peace will rest with our people finding peace once more," replied M.O.M., Jock MacDaniels.

The soaring anticipation of the messin man to put the plan into action was severely impacted upon when he returned to camp. The camp was empty! It seemed that he was the last Hiup in Hiup lands. As he looked about, he became more puzzled. Tipis were undisturbed, luk pots were hanging to accept ingredients for the next meal, but no Hiup could be found. The only sign of life was Surefoot, who was grazing next to the stream.

The solution to this mystery, although not known to the messin man, was simple. During his absence, Chief Has It Made, at the insistence of the remaining Snow Hairs, had ordered the packing of their travois before leading the group west. It seems that they wished to see the lands that held their children in its grasp, but, more importantly, they missed their grandchildren! They planned a short visit, intending to return before Three Hands returned from his trail to M.O.M. Surefoot was left as a sign that their absence was temporary, in case Three Hands returned before them. The mystery could wait. His top priority was to put his new plan into action and free himself from the horns of the bull.

Seeking out Lynn, he outlined his plan to use the tribe's money to make some purchases from Goodson. He asked her to keep it in a safe place.

"How much money are we talking about?" Lynn asked.

Three Hands could make change in small amounts, but to add coins and bills was beyond his capability. He was not about to admit this to Lynn. He resorted to "double-talk" to disguise this shortcoming. "It is the custom of the white man to count and place barriers on the trail, saying, 'This is the end,' while knowing in his heart that it is not true. There are no ends for the red man, for his trail is a circle and has no end. When we say that the tree has many leaves, we are content with the word 'many.' The white man, however, has to count each leaf to know the meaning of 'many.' Our tolls are like many leaves."

"I see your point, and it is wisely taken. If you are to bargain with the white man, you must use his system of counting," chuckled Lynn, not at all fooled. "Why don't you bring the tolls here and we can count them, then you will know how much bargaining you can do with the whites."

"I accept your words and your offer. The tolls will be brought here."

Three Hands next went to Goodson and requested the use of a wagon. The request granted, he then sought out Shortee and asked for his help. The two made their way up the incline to the Hiup camp. It would be the last time a white man would set foot in the camp.

As they made their way to the tipis of the messin man, Shortee took in the scene and was truly in a state of confusion, since he could see no humans. The only evidence of habitation was the circles on the ground, each with an ash pit in the center, and the few tipis standing in the direction they were headed. "Where are your people?" he asked.

Shortee had not been brought to the camp by Three Hands without his usual preplanning. Shortee's inquiry was expected, and the answer kept in waiting. He put on a look of astonishment and replied, "Why, they are here—all around you!"

The confused mind of Shortee became even more so! "My eyes must be playing tricks on me, for I see no one," he stammered.

"Your eyes are not playing tricks," said the smiling messin man. "Our great spirit, Wakan-Manitou, has made the Hiup invisible to the eyes of the white man. Let me prove this to you." The messin man shouted out greetings to his invisible people and, of course, supplied the responses to the left, to the right, and in the distance. He even threw in the growl of a dog next to the wagon. He stole a glance at his companion and saw acceptance of his presentation. (When you're good, you can't help flaunting it!) "Come," he said, "we are not here to visit. Help me take these jars to the wagon."

When the task was completed and his farewells shouted to his people (and replies received), the two headed back to Chip Dip. Upon arrival, the wagon was unloaded and the counting begun, with the Wares and Brimstones assisting. Shortee was off to find Zeke, whose ears and imagination were subjected to a detailed (and exaggerated) description of his experience with the invisible Hiup.

"Twenty-five thousand, seven hundred and seventy-five dollars!" stated Lynn when the counting task was completed. A veritable fortune lay before them. "What do you wish to do with it now?" she inquired.

"I will take it to a place of safety," Three Hands replied.

"Then I would suggest that you change all of these coins into bills, for that will make it easier to handle," Lynn suggested.

Three Hands had no clear understanding of the meaning of coins and bills, or of their value in the world of the white man. "Your words are wise and I will follow them. Tell me how this can best be done," he requested.

"Let Goodson take the coins back across the big waters and change them for bills. Shortee can go with him and be his guard," came her reply.

"So it shall be, but first I must have words with Goodson." Turning, he instructed Goodson, "Come, let us walk and talk."

Walking to the general store, Three Hands presented his proposal to the storekeeper, with just enough spice to make him conducive to the request. "Take the tolls to the big camp and exchange them for bills. Use part of it to bargain for one hundred thundersticks and the fire for them. Also bargain for an equal number of hunting and skinning knives. I will also need great numbers of beads, needles, and bright cloth for our women. Bargain also for two good ponies. This will be only the beginning of the Hiup exchange of tolls for goods you can supply."

Goodson's eyeballs rolled back into his head in an ecstatic demonstration of delight over the possibility of great wealth in this and future dealings with his neighbors! "Your wishes will be carried out exactly as you have stated," he told his newest customer. "I will prepare for the trail immediately!"

The tolls were returned to the wagon, along with provisions for the journey. Shortee once again had put on his gun belts and, with the addition of a rifle, sat perched on the wagon seat, eager to carry out his role as protector. All the Chip Dippers and Three Hands gathered to see them off.

As the wagon pulled away, Lynn shouted out one last request, "Pick up one strong box with a good lock!"

The messin man was lightheaded at the prospect of a plan now in action that would restore the lands of his people to the glory days of the past. If the truth were known, this lightheadedness was due more to his being tossed into the air once again by the bull than to any action on his part!

His fall would be a hard one!

⇐ Chapter Fourteen ⇒

Man has been given a degree of latitude in creating the trail he will walk on the Circle of Life, yet it is the Everywhere Spirit who determines when the last step is taken.

Although alone in the Hiup camp, boredom was nonexistent for the messin man. There was much planning to be done before Goodson returned with the supplies, and before Ian Coyote and Wee Gordie Light Of Foot arrived to carry the message west. The timing must be precise; not a moment could be lost in carrying out M.O.M.'s plan. Constant planning and thinking can lead to mental exhaustion and loss of sharpness of thought, so Three Hands injected some leisure activities to offset that possibility. The most widely used was "tea" sessions with either Fireanda or Bea. For many summers he had utilized Span Ishfly to make certain their "firepits" were of the same temperature as the poker that stoked them. That they, too, were Snow Hairs was forgotten in the heat of exchange, after sipping tea from a pot laced with the potion.

Upon returning from one of his "teas," he found two men standing at the edge of camp, awaiting permission to enter. The messin man signaled the two to enter and watched their approach. There could be no doubt as to their identity, for they carried the redness of the setting sun in their hair. One wore his hair in braids, while the other had hair that hung to his shoulders. "Welcome, Ian Coyote and Wee Gordie Light Of Foot; I have long looked forward to your return, Ian, and to meeting your brother, who was but an added weight carried in his mother's stomach when you left. Our camp is empty, but that will soon change with your help. You have been on a long trail and need rest and refreshment. I will coax the flame of the fire to warm the pot of chico bean soup. Then we will talk."

The time for talk was a bit long in coming, for Ian and Wee Gordie's taste buds were titillated by the bean soup; thus eating did not end until the luk pot was empty. It was not long afterwards that talk (and "explosions") began.

Three Hands went over his problem and the means to its end in detail and repeated them each day as they waited for Goodson and Shortee to return.

Twenty suns had passed when Goodson's wagon came to the pass and continued on to the store. The thundersticks and the other items were unloaded and placed inside the store. Two of each item were kept out as "samples" to be taken west on the ponies by the two messengers. Three Hands took the strong box containing his change back to camp.

A final council was held with his messengers to make certain that the three thought as one. The messin man showed them the strong box and its key. "Within this box lies the future of our people, once they return. I will keep the opener in my messin pouch around my neck. The box I will place in the sacred cave, to be used when it is needed. Let us begin the return trail of our people to their rightful lands!" The two messengers checked to make sure they had enough of their newest passion, chico beans, for the trail, then the three descended the incline to Chip Dip.

The Chip Dippers stood engrossed with the scene as Ian and Wee Gordie arrived with Three Hands to begin their trail. It was the first time that they had seen any Hiup besides Three Hands, and one common thought ran through their minds as they looked upon the newcomers: the Hiup certainly were an interesting breed. Here were two light-skinned Injuns whose hair was as red as Three Hands' was black. And when they spoke, it was with a Scottish brogue thick enough to slice! What would the rest of the tribe look like if they became visible? That answer would never be forthcoming. The group watched as the two mounted their ponies and became lost to the eye in the distance; they then returned to their own routines.

Three Hands had carefully calculated the time for the trail of the two young ones to and from the land where he thought his people to be, with allowance for unexpected delays. The timing was vital. He not only had to make arrangements for the purchase of one hundred ponies, but he had to have the ponies there when his people returned.

On the precise day, he made his way to the general store. Unknown to the messin man, it was the last item of the plan to occur on schedule;

Wakan-Manitou was about to cross off the next item on His timeline concerning his favorite messin man!

The messin man was in his usual confident and positive frame of mind when he entered the store. He found Goodson unpacking a box and placing its contents on a shelf. To expedite the task, in order to have the storekeeper's undivided attention, Three Hands took each item out of the box and handed it to Goodson. Whether it was an act of curiosity or just idle chatter (or perhaps a design of Wakan-Manitou), the messin man examined a bottle and asked, "For what reason does the white man place water in such containers?"

Goodson laughed and replied, "That's not water; that's hair restorer. If anyone drinks that, he would have hair growing on his tongue!"

"I dinna comprehend the meaning of your words," stated the messin man.

"Hair restorer is used to cause hair to grow where one has lost it," Goodson explained. "You have seen men in the trains who took their hats off and had only skin on the top of their head. If they rub some of this hair restorer on their head, it is supposed to cause new hair to grow, and the man would have a full head of hair again."

The eyes of the messin man grew larger as his mind instantly projected the possibilities of the white man's liquid on the scalp of the "Wahoo" Hiup. He became ecstatic over the possibility that Wakan-Manitou had provided a solution, via the white man, that negated the effects of Span Ishfly! And he wasted no time in taking advantage of this opportunity! "Goodson, I have come to you to bargain once more for my people. We wish one hundred of the white man's ponies and an equal number of such containers as these."

Now it was the storekeeper's turn to experience a widening of the eyes. His mind projected the effect of such an order on his pocketbook. He was eager to hear the details. "I would have to go back over the big waters for such a bargain; I would have to ask Seth, Shortee, and Zeke to go with me to herd the ponies on the trail. I figure I will need two thousand dollars to make the deal," he explained.

"I will bring the box, and you will take what you need. Prepare for the trail as soon as possible," instructed the messin man.

Goodson's feet fairly flew as he went to tell Bea of his great news and to make arrangements with the men for the trail. Three Hands went to the sacred cave and procured the strongbox from its hiding place, then returned to Chip Dip. In two days, preparations were completed and the group headed east.

Once again it was waiting time for the messin man and for the female inhabitants of Chip Dip. Only two small trains passed through to break up the daily routine of the women. Three Hands made his presence known when the train stopped, to make certain the women were in no danger.

The estimated time of arrival grew near for those expected from the west, as well as for those from the east. The adrenaline coursed through the veins of the messin man as the "E. T. A." approached. The sweet smell of success was adding a sugary coating to his hopes of being reunited with his people, and each new sun would find him perched on his favorite ledge that projected from the canyon wall, overlooking the trail west.

He missed messin his people, but he missed the tantalizing scent of a bubbling luk pot filled with a wide variety of delicacies even more. Now his diet was pretty much limited by his culinary skills to chico bean soup. Game was still abundant, yet beyond reach. He had chosen long ago to forego the role of hunter to become a messin man, and it was too late to change or go back. The proof of his solitary diet was definitely in evidence this day as he passed the time reminiscing and indulging in the art of loincloth rippling, a subtle demonstration of superb emission control.

But wait! His concentration was broken when his peripheral vision picked up a belch of black smoke exiting from the chimney of a building to his right in the valley below. It was a signal he could not ignore, for it created a sudden heat in the area of his loins that was unrelated to the chico bean! This heat obliterated all thoughts but one.

Leaping from his perch, he descended the incline to the valley below with such speed that only a trail of dust indicated the direction of his passage toward the source of the smoke from the chimney.

Wakan-Manitou's smile slipped from his face as he reached for his Terrible Swift Tomahawk! The messin man had changed the plan He had provided to remove His favorite from the horns of the bull. The messin man had the effrontery to place personal relief as more important than the needs of His people!

The black puff of smoke had been ejected from the chimney of Bea Ware as her signal to Three Hands that she was desirous of his "tea" service. Although it was not common knowledge, it was the same signal used by Fireanda when she was in need, only her smoke was white.

Formalities of tea sipping completed, the two moved quickly to join in the activity of mutual service. The polite, dulcet sounds of sipping had been replaced by loud, intense sounds of lust, synchronized with the squeaking of a complaining bed. These sounds of communal fornication totally drowned out the sounds of Goodson's horse as he rode from the store to his house to inform Bea that he had returned.

Goodson had left Seth, Shortee, and Zeke to unload the wagon after they had driven the ponies into the corral. Weeks of abstinence on the trail had resurrected a long-dormant itch in his loins, and he was eager to be "scratched." As he dismounted, he heard what appeared to be animal sounds and loud moaning coming from the direction of his bedroom. His first thought was that a marauding raccoon had gotten into the house. Removing his derringer from his shoulder holster, he cautiously approached the window and peered in.

What he saw was a blur of flailing arms and legs and what appeared to be an animal bouncing up and down atop Bea! The blur he saw was due not only to the speed of the flailing parts, but to Goodson's poor vision. He had store-bought spectacles to improve his weak eyesight, but he could not wear them while riding. There had not been time to put them on before taking action. He aimed his derringer at what appeared to be an animal similar to a one-eyed walrus with a single giant tusk that seemed intent on impaling Bea. He fired one shot. The beast paused for just an instant in apparent disbelief, then collapsed and became still.

Rushing into the house, Goodson found Bea standing in shock beside the "animal" and looking down upon it with open mouth. Putting on his spectacles to get a clearer look, he, too, became overwhelmed with shock when he recognized the "animal" to be Three Hands! His state of shock even overpowered the realization that neither his wife nor the messin man had any clothing on.

As the shock wore off, realization did come, and Goodson looked to Bea for an explanation. Fortunately for her, Bea's shock wore off first, and her mind raced to provide the explanation that was certain to be requested. She knew that her explanation had to be simple as well as logical. She resorted to the old standby, "He went berserk! He came in and attacked me for no reason!"

Goodson bought it. He knelt to examine the messin man and found not only that he was deceased, but that his manhood was still standing erect in all the magnificence it had in life. He tried to roll the body over, but the length and rigidity of the digit limited the roll to his side.

There was no trace of blood or wound. It was apparent that his shot had missed. He assumed that the messin man had died of natural causes, perhaps a heart attack. The struggle his wife had put up to defend her honor had put too great a strain on his heart. In truth, the shot had not missed. It actually had succeeded in overcoming staggering odds by striking the cycloptic sphincter muscle "eye" full-center and moved on to terminate in a vital organ—a prime example of a "clean shot!"

The sound of the shot had aroused every Chip Dipper, and they moved to investigate its source. Hearing the sounds of approaching footsteps, Goodson moved quickly to make the corpse a bit more presentable, while Bea hastened to make herself the same. Securing the loincloth around the waist of the messin man, Goodson tried to cover the towering appendage, but only succeeded in draping the end over its head. The loincloth held this position only until the inhabitants were crowded around the prone figure, then accepted the folly of its tenacity and slowly slipped to recline at the base of the appendage.

The face of each of the new arrivals went through four rapid metamorphoses: shock, horror, sympathy—and total admiration! Shortee was the first to recover his composure and ask the inevitable question, "What happened?"

"Three Hands was visiting Bea and apparently had a heart attack. I fired my gun to alert you for help," replied Goodson.

The three women glanced at the lifeless body, then hastened to see to Bea's well-being. They found her crying in the kitchen and muttering, "I can't believe he's dead," over and over. While trying to calm her down, her words struck home to Fireanda and Lynn. The realization caused tears to flow freely from their eyes as each mourned their loss individually. Their "tea" sharer was now just a memory.

Lotta was puzzled. The attack on Bea she could understand, but why the river of tears from the other two? The ignition of understanding came so swiftly that her thought was ejected verbally. "Why, you all screwed him!" Reason returned and she added, "You had better get yourselves in control before one of the men gets the same message!" There was no denying that danger, so each put on a new face.

Meanwhile, the eyes of the men had moved as one from the speaker to the body. The same question resided in the mind of each, but only Zeke mumbled it in a chuckling manner: "I never heard of a heart attack creating a hard-on that big!"

Shortee, after ingesting that thought, gave his rationalization. "Maybe that's the way heart attacks affect Injuns!"

Had they been familiar with Wakan-Manitou, they may have recognized the situation simply as an example of His compassion, delivered with a sense of humor.

Seth, the realist, came forward with his thoughts. "Regardless of the cause and effect, how are we going to break the news to his people? What are we going to do with him in the meantime?"

"I would say that they are going to be very upset over this!" Shortee exclaimed. "Three Hands told us that his people did not want us here anyway and only agreed to let us stay at his request. When they hear that he died here, they might not buy the heart attack theory and decide to kill us all."

This possibility became very real, and a solution was sought. Everyone threw out their thoughts, then concluded that Goodson's was the most logical to buy time for them all.

Goodson went on to outline his plan. "I say we tell no one what happened. We must bury him, not only out of respect for a friend, but also to hide the evidence. If anyone asks, we can tell them that we last saw him heading for the canyon to pray. This will give us time to pack our things and head back to St. Lou E. It is vital that our daily routines be carried out as usual, in case we are under surveillance by the Hiup. Do your packing after dark. Shortee should collect the toll if a train arrives, for he has done this for Three Hands in the past without challenge. Let us not panic, but be ready to leave at the first sign of danger."

Seth nodded in agreement and added, "Zeke and I will take charge of the burial. I'll bring the wagon here and we'll keep him covered until a coffin is made and a hole dug. If there are no other questions, let's get on with it."

Get on with it they did. Seth and Zeke picked up the deceased and proceeded to carry out the activities for burial. It was not a simple task. While Zeke sought out planks for the coffin, Seth measured the messin man. To his chagrin, he saw that rigor mortis had set in while the Injun's manhood was still erect. (The effect of Span Ishfly was limited to time, not events.)

This presented a problem of variance in coffin design and construction, and lumber was scarce. Not only the width and length had to be accommodating, but also the depth. If the depth was maintained the entire length to enclose the body, the coffin would be too bulky, too heavy for transport, and would lack the dignity of a well-fitting final resting place. The decision was to make the lid flat and low to cover the body, with a vertical boxed extension to enclose the towering appendage.

Fearing possible discovery from above, or by an invisible Hiup near them, the burial hole was not as deep as usual; thus, the mound of earth over it looked like someone had left a shovel sticking out of it. A brief service was held and words spoken, but the eyes of each mourner were mesmerized by the "shovel handle" in the mound.

After the service, daily routines were followed according to plan. There was little time to breathe easy, however, for on the third day after the service, Shortee ran to alert the others of an approaching dust cloud on the trail from the west.

The inhabitants gathered in front of the general store to await the arrival of the creators of the dust cloud. It was not a long wait, for soon three riders burst from the head of the dust cloud and into the clearing of Chip Dip. One rider turned and stopped, while the other two, riding low on the backs of their ponies, raced full speed in a circle, emitting loud cries and whoops.

After a proper display of their riding skills, they rode up and stopped before the Chip Dippers. Their ponies, snorting and pawing the ground, seemed disappointed that their display of skills had been cut short. The two front riders were recognized as the two who had left to ride west. The third rider was a rather plump Injun girl. Looking over the group and noting that Three Hands was not among them, the riders wheeled and sent their mounts racing up the incline to the Hiup camp.

Goodson summarized the thoughts of all. "The time may be here for leaving! When they tell their people that Three Hands was not here and learn that he has not been seen for three days, they'll want to know why. They'll be back for answers. Bea and I will move to the store; I would suggest Fireanda should move to the smithy. We don't want to be spread out, in case of attack. Everyone be prepared to move at a moment's notice!"

Questions did arise as soon as the three riders rode into camp and found no sign of Three Hands. Ian finally had found a squaw to his liking, Singing Wind, and now put her to work preparing a meal while he spoke with his brother.

"It is not a good sign that Three Hands was not here to greet us and learn the news he has been seeking," said Ian.

"It is possible that he is in the forest gathering herbs for messin and will return soon," Wee Gordie replied.

"Herbs? For who? There was no one here but him until we came. His people are still visiting the Kansas. I just don't like the signs. We will go to the camp of the whites at the next sun, and speak with them. The ashes of the fire were more than three suns old, and not a sign of one waiting here to hear our news," a concerned Ian stated.

At the following sun, Ian and his brother mounted their ponies and rode down the incline in search of answers. Arriving at the general store, they sat on their mounts, awaiting a sign of welcome, a courtesy strictly enforced by all red men. Goodson had watched their approach. When he saw that they remained mounted at his door, his imagination shoved logic aside and screamed, "Confrontation!" He thought, "They know everything. They know that I killed him. Their invisible brothers saw the whole thing and sent these two to kill me!"

Seth also watched the approach of the two, as everyone was on the alert. He walked from his smithy to where they sat on their ponies. Goodson exited the store, rifle in hand, just as Seth arrived. The change in the expression on the faces of the young men and their movement to finger their own weapons indicated to him that they had been caught off guard. He moved quickly to extinguish any spark of confrontation. "Put your gun aside, Goodson, for there is no need for it among friends. Don't you remember, these are the friends of Three Hands," he said in a quiet, reassuring tone of command. Goodson quickly complied.

In the same quiet tone, Seth continued, "Come, friends, be welcome. Let us sit in council and share our thoughts. We are happy that your trail has brought you back to our camp." Seth had limited experience in dealing with the red man, for he had known only Three Hands. He remembered, however, the messin man's high regard for courtesy and protocol.

The words of Seth were actually the words the two had been expecting, as a matter of courtesy, and so they took Goodson's appearance with a thunderstick as a misread sign. They dismounted and squatted on the steps of the store.

Wee Gordie, master of word and song, sensed that all was not in harmony in Chip Dip. The thunderstick sign, although erased, had still been displayed. He decided that caution should be followed in this council until clearer signs appeared. "Our hearts are in sorrow that our friend, Three Hands, was nocht here ta greet us," he stated. "He has nocht been seen in our camp for four suns and does nocht appear ta be in your camp. We come ta his friends that they might point out his trail ta us sae that we might fin' him and cast out this sorrow."

Seth glanced at Goodson and saw the fear in his eyes and the shaking of his hands. This behavior certainly would not be misread by those skilled in reading signs. Goodson was about to fall apart and could act precipitously. He decided that truth, so respected by the red man, was the best route to follow. It was only a matter of time before the Hiup found out—if they didn't already know. Being "invisible," some could even have been standing with the messin man when he died and left when the whites arrived.

"This could be a test to see if the white man spoke straight or with forked tongue, as Three Hands used to say. It could mean life or death for us all." He made his decision, saying, "It grieves our hearts to tell you this, but Three Hands is dead. He was visiting our camp to see that our squaws were not in any danger while we were away getting your ponies. When we returned, we found him dead and gave him a respectful burial, as we thought his people would want it. Our hearts are also overflowing, for Three Hands was our friend, too."

Again, for just a fleeting moment, the expression on the faces of the young men changed, then reverted back to a stoic mask. They rose as one and mounted their ponies. "We will speak on this again," said Ian. The two wheeled their mounts and rode up the incline.

Goodson ran to inform the others of what had occurred. Preparations were made for an instant departure when the trail was clear.

Ian and Wee Gordie arrived back at camp and sat in stunned silence. Singing Wind, sensing something was wrong, made haste to bring each a bowl of steaming chico bean soup, knowing its delicious smell and taste could distract one's mind from bad thoughts. It worked! The soup acted as a balm to revive them from their state of shock. Ian finally spoke, "I read the signs correctly, but never thought of their meaning as death. May our good news of the returning of his people follow him on his trail to the Camp of Many Lodges so that he can enter with a singing heart."

"Aye, may it be so," Wee Gordie agreed, "but the plan must be carried out completely. The ponies and the other goods must be here when his people return, to make their hearts joyous. Only then will we tell them of their messin man's death. His words still ring in my ears that the survival of his people lies in the box hidden in the sacred cave. Should that box also be here to be given to his people? We are the only ones who know of its location."

"Your words are as true as the straightest arrow, Brother," replied Ian. "One, no, two problems face us. The opener is in Three Hands' messin pouch around his neck, and we do not know the exact location of the box in the cave."

"We must also deal with the whites," added Wee Gordie, "for only they know the location of Three Hands. They must be fearful of something, or they would not have greeted us with a thunderstick. Three Hands convinced them that a Hiup could only be seen by whites when that Hiup chose to be seen. We must take care not to destroy that illusion, as part of the master plan. Our moccasins must caress Mother Earth with a light step."

"If we reassure the whites that they have nothing to fear, we will have an easier time dealing with them to recover the opener and to get the ponies and goods from them. I think only one of us should act as spokesman, so the other is free to read the signs of their eyes," suggested Ian. "You have the greatest ease with words; you be that spokesman."

Wee Gordie accepted the responsibility. At the next sun, they returned to Chip Dip to put their plan into action. They sought Seth to initiate action, for he had proven to be calm in nature and to speak true. Wee Gordie asked Seth to gather all the Chip Dip men for a council. Once gathered, he began his words of reassurance. "The hills and the canyons ring wi' the wailing of the hearts of our people in farewell ta our brother, Three Hands, on his final trail. A part of our hearts sings for the kindness ye hae shown him in life. He considered ye his adopted brothers and held ye in high esteem, or you would nocht hae been allowed ta stay in our lands. He gave his word concerning your safety, and that word will be kept by every red man as lang as ye keep your word ta him."

The Chip Dippers were relieved to hear these words. Wee Gordie continued, "Our brothers are concerned about whether their messin man was properly prepared for his last trail. The white man is nae familiar with our ways, sae we wou'd ask ta see his body ta assure them that our custom has been followed. Can ye tak us ta his death scaffold?"

Death scaffold? That meant something above ground! Seth spoke for the group. "Not being familiar with your customs, we placed our brother in the ground, as is our custom. I will show you the place where he lies and assist you in correcting any violation of your burial custom."

Seth led the way to the grave. Ian and Wee Gordie were a bit confused by the profile of the grave site, but acted to carry out their objective. "He must be removed from the confinement of the earth covering so that his spirit may soar freely on the trail to meet his ancestors," said Wee Gordie. "His body can then be placed in the sacred cave."

Seth and Zeke shoveled the dirt aside and exposed the coffin with its towering "shovel handle." The two young braves, not knowing the state of the messin man's manhood after his demise, took the elevated portion of the box to be a white man's custom, which they did not question. They would carry out the traditional burial rites themselves.

Once the whites had departed, the two opened the lid to free the spirit of their brother. A glance at his lower extremity not only brought a clear understanding of the purpose of the "shovel handle" enclosure, but also a sense of admiration for their brother. Ian took his knife and cut the cord of the messin pouch, then tied it to the sinew of his loincloth. The coffin was then carried into the cave and placed to rest in a small alcove to one side. They wanted to proceed with the search for the box, but the cave was illuminated only near its entrance by outside light. They knew that torches would be needed before they could proceed. Back to camp they went to prepare for the search.

Singing Wind had a steaming pot of chico bean soup ready when they returned, and a rabbit she had snared was cooking on a spit. Once the meal was consumed, a plan of action was formed. Ian brought forth the messin pouch and fingered it lightly. "There is a hard object inside, which must be the opener of the box," he conjectured.

It was taboo for another person's messin pouch to be opened, for it was sacred to that individual. Although it was with mixed emotions, Ian knew that it was the wish of Three Hands that they would do so, if he could not do it himself. Loosening the drawstring, he reached into the pouch and withdrew the hard object. The opener was covered with a fine powder, which Ian wiped off with his fingers before handing it to his brother. "I wonder if this is medicinal powder or sacred powder?" he said as he placed his fingers to his lips to test it.

"It's probably a dried and ground-up toad!" chuckled Wee Gordie. His chuckle terminated abruptly as he observed the change of expression on the face of Ian.

Ian leaped to an erect position, and his loincloth did likewise! Wee Gordie and Singing Wind were frozen into inaction by the sight, but Ian's heat moved him to carry out a natural reaction. He took Singing Wind by the arm and quickly guided her to the nearest bush. A fast and furious mauling of the bush area took place before the two returned, Ian with a look of peaceful exhaustion, and Singing Wind with a look of peaceful contentment!

"If dried and ground-up toad causes that reaction, then we should forget the box and collect all of the toads we can find!" Wee Gordie suggested as he completed his chuckle.

Ian cautioned, "No, as great as the power of this powder may be, we must not lose sight of the needs of our people. We can examine the powder at a time when my strength has returned. We need all of our strength to make torches for locating the box."

The two braves, aided by Singing Wind, spent the remainder of the day constructing torches, while collecting and consuming their favorite delicacy, the chico bean. They would need a great deal of nourishment while carrying out the search for the box. It was decided that Singing Wind would join in the search, in order to cover more area in the shortest amount of time. The box had to be found before their people returned.

At first light, the trio consumed a generous meal of bean soup and spring water, then made their way to the cave entrance before the inhabitants of Chip Dip awoke. Torches were lit, and the search began. As early as it may have been for a mortal, Wakan-Manitou (He Who Never Sleeps) soon made his presence (and sense of humor) known!

The trio found that the sacred cave was but one of many caves connected by passages; their numbers seemed without end. While they were hard at work to find the location of the box, their internal organs were also hard at work converting the bean and spring water to another form of energy—gas!

It may be remembered that the Hiup took this process and its by-product in stride, even developing emission control to a point of pride. Ian had been away from Hiup land so long that the control and pride he once possessed had vanished through disuse. Wee Gordie and Singing

Wind were neophytes in sphincter control, having only recently been introduced to the chico bean. As a consequence, the three let nature take its course; the emissions were frequent—and loud!

It started with small explosions, which aroused humor and a playful attitude among the trio, then Ian proclaimed, "Singing Wind, in honor of your ability to not only produce the greatest soup but to produce the loudest sound, I am changing your name to a more appropriate one. From now on you will be known as 'Passing Wind'!"

The three laughed, and their humor was elevated by an unannounced contest to see who could produce the loudest ejection. Unknown to them, the sound of their contest drowned out the laughter of Wakan-Manitou. He allowed them free rein in their endeavors by allowing the sounds to travel the entire length of the Kie Ro Practic mountain range. Each passage and cavern amplified the sounds it received before passing them on to the next cavern. The reverberations grew in intensity as they moved up and down the range, gaining decibels as they moved. The ground beneath them began to shake and the roofs of caverns began to rain down earth and stones.

The searching trio soon grew apprehensive at the situation that was developing. They were deep inside the cave passages and became aware of the need to abandon the search for the box and remove themselves from the increasing danger. They made haste to return to the cave entrance and the safety beyond.

Wakan-Manitou once again demonstrated that humor and compassion could be in evidence simultaneously. As the three were passing through the second cave from the entrance, Ian's eyes caught a glimpse of a hole in the cave wall and a rock on the cave floor that apparently had been used to close the hole. The shaking activity had dislodged the stone, and a quick examination of the hole produced the box they sought. The instant they burst from the cave, its roof collapsed, sealing it and all of the caves beyond. They returned to the camp in great haste!

The reaction produced by the young searchers impacted on others, near and far. Nearby, the Chip Dippers felt the tremors of the ground beneath their feet and grew concerned, but not alarmed. It was just a natural phenomenon—just a slight quake. Those living along the entire mountain range, including M.O.M., also felt the tremors and thought they would soon cease. Not so, for the collapse of the entrance cave had sealed the explosive sounds below ground, and they continued to reverberate unabated and to build decibels.

By the end of the second day, the tremors had not abated, as hoped by those in the area involved. It was obvious that danger was not only present, but was constantly increasing. The time for decision had arrived, and that decision was unanimous: move out of the danger area!

As the entire mountain range from north to south was affected by the tremors, the choice of direction to flee was limited to east or west. Those on the eastern side of the range moved quickly east to the banks of the Mississippi River. Those just west of the mountains moved farther west until the tremors could not be felt. The exception was the Chip Dippers, who crossed the Hiup Pass and moved east toward lands familiar to them.

Ian and Wee Gordie, knowing that the only trail from the sacred mountain was east, decided that it would be futile to make the long trail back along the ridge to their parents; they, with Passing Wind, also headed east. The Hiup who were on the trail back to their lands were stopped by the undulating ground beneath their feet. They decided to retrace their steps west until the spirits had vented their rage and the trail had returned to normalcy.

The tremors continued to increase in intensity and scope with each passing day. On the twelfth day after they had begun, the tremors reached their peak. The chico bean by-product, so easily, so naturally, and so profusely ejected by the searchers of the caves, had been denied escape into the atmosphere (where it could have disseminated harmlessly) by the sealing of the cave entrance. It traveled the entire range, pushed along by the sound waves it had produced, seeking escape. This movement of the sound waves produced friction through molecular interaction, which in turn caused the gas to expand. This expansion then produced internal pressure on the confining roofs and walls of the caverns, terminating in a cataclysmic explosion that future scientists would refer to as the "Super Flatus"!

The pressure of the gas lifted the entire mountain range high into the air as one piece of earth, allowing the sound and gas to escape. This created a malodorous shock wave extending beyond the banks of the Mississippi River to the east, and to the base of the Rocky Mountains to the west! It was witnessed and recorded in the east that the waters of the mighty Mississippi flowed north instead of south for half an hour!

The entire mountain range, now bereft of the lifting pressure of the gas, acquiesced to the demand of gravity and plunged downward, collapsing in a tower of dust to completely fill the open caverns below. Four suns later, the enormous dust cloud cleared, revealing an almost level terrain where the mountain range once stood. Gone were the snowcapped peaks, the streams, the canyons, the waterfall, the chico bean, the giant Ucumfastus forests, and the passes.

Gone forever were the lands of the Hiup!

Epilogue

Even a good chew of tobacco reaches its limit of pleasure-giving.

To the Indian, the destruction of the Kie Ro Practics was symbolic and gave birth to a legend. The Hiup, due mainly to the skills and actions of Three Hands, had been perceived to be highly favored by Wakan-Manitou. Their messin man, chosen by the spirits to hear and relay their words, held the most respected position a mortal could achieve. His master plan of battle had provided control over the minds and movements of the white man in relation to Indian lands.

In time, the Hiup rejected the favors of Wakan-Manitou. By leaving their choice lands and the vital pass, they had subjected their brothers to certain attack by the whites and their Blue Coats. Wakan-Manitou became enraged by their acts of contempt for His wishes. He performed the Death Dance upon their lands until the entire mountain range had been reduced to a level that matched that of their brothers of the plains.

The western tribes, eager to minimize their responsibility as participants and regain favor in the eyes of the spirits, placed the mantle of disgrace upon the Hiup—with the exception of Three Hands, who had kept his word until death. All Rem A Nissers were forbidden ever to mention the Hiup.

The Hiup, who had been on the return trail to their lands, now found themselves to be outcasts, rejected by their brothers. They wandered aimlessly, hoping to find a place of solace. Finding none, they broke up into family groups and renounced their heritage. By posing as refugees from the western advance of the white man, they gained acceptance into various tribes.

To the whites, the demise of the Kie Ro Practics was simply the result of a tremendous earthquake. The range had been located over a fault in the earth's crust. The pressure responsible for its birth had now returned to reclaim the range in its entirety. When the dust had settled and the profuse watering of the eyes (brought on by the acrid smell of the implosion and the chico bean emissions) had ceased, there was an unrestricted view of sunsets on the western horizon.

The president, an old "Injun" fighter, saw this as a prime opportunity to resolve a problem that had been festering in his mind for years. The Supreme Court's recognition of Indian rights, according to signed treaties, was ignored. He ordered the U.S. Army to round up all Indians east of the Mississippi River and move them to lands west of the big river.

When the leaders of the Cherokee balked, he initiated the rumor that large deposits of gold had been discovered in Georgia, the center of the Cherokee Nation. The rush of the white men for "yellow wealth" pushed aside the Indian and his rights; the Trail of Much Crying followed.

The government promised that the land west of the big river would be Indian land forever. This promise was soon broken. The white man, held in check for so long by fear of the invisible Hiup, was unleashed by a former resident of Chip Dip, Goodson Wares.

Goodson and Bea traveled east to St. Lou E, where Goodson reestablished himself in the hardware and supply business. Business was slow until he made the rounds of the taverns, spreading the rumor of a vast fortune hidden in a sacred cave. As a former resident of the lands described, his word was taken as fact. His business promptly picked up as a stampede of treasure seekers came to him for supplies and for clues to the treasure's location. The floodgate to the west opened, and the wealth-seeking whites poured through!

The U.S. Army, seeking to regain credibility, sent scores of scouting parties across the Mississippi River. There was no Three Hands to stop them this time. The encroachment tactic of the whites was in force once more. Meanwhile, the western tribes had reverted to settling territorial disputes among themselves. Never again did they display unity against the invading white man.

The former residents of Hiup lands who had chosen to flee east, unlike Goodson, had no impact on the western situation per se. Lynn returned to the northeast, taking Lotta and Zeke with her. She spent the remainder of her life managing a tavern and singing in the local opera house. Seth and Fireanda made their way to Pittsburgh, where Seth went into the ironworks business. Shortee joined a traveling show with a wild-west theme and became its star performer with his quick-draw and shooting demonstrations.

Jock and Swift Feet, who had had enough foresight to evacuate before the final explosion, were reunited with their sons and with Ian's wife. Ian divided the contents of the strong box equally among the family, then they all went separate ways. Upon hearing of his long-time persecutor Ian Stewart's demise in a drunken brawl several years before, Jock was finally free to go where he pleased. He and Swift Feet meandered east, until Jock stumbled upon a spring with water so pure that it gave his Blend an unparalleled smoothness of taste. Using his share of the toll money, he went back into the distillery business. He gained wide recognition among "drinkers of distinction" with his Jock MacDaniel's Blend.

Ian moved on to take up residency in North Carolina, where he began a school for bagpipe instruction, catering to Scottish immigrants. He also enjoyed (as did Passing Wind) the benefits of the messin man's magic powder—until it was depleted. He attempted to increase his dwindling supply by having a sample analyzed by a chemist. Every component (yes, there was some ground, dried toad) was identified through chemical analysis except one, thus making duplication impossible. The one unknown substance was the root of the now-extinct Ucumfastus tree.

Wee Gordie Light Of Foot used his share of the tolls to finance his urge to wander, sing, and compose songs. He drew upon his life's experiences and pride of heritage for his material. He became a performer and was in great demand wherever he went. His folk songs were simple and sung with a sweet voice. His three most requested songs then, which remain as classics today, were "There Never Was a Lowdown Hiup," "Kie Ro Practic High," and the unforgettable "Messin Man," whose ending lyrics were so prophetic:

> "The Messin Man did his very best
> Until his unexpected end.
> His dream was crumbled into a cloud of dust
> By the Chico Bean and Passing Wind."